From Him To Eternity

Vampire State Book One

Kevin Dickson

VONSSON PRESS

Cover artwork by André Trindade – @cvspe

Back cover photograph by Steve Gidlow

Contents

From Him To Eternity

Vampire State Book One

Kevin Dickson

VONSSON PRESS

For George Castro,
Miss Tuna, Graciela & OIivia
My Los Angeles Lock

Prologue

The wind whipped Sara's dark hair into her eyes, already stinging with tears from the icy blast, as she searched for the building number. Raindrops, frost-hardened pellets, joined the assault on her face and she raised a shielding hand, her eyes squinting in the winter dusk. There! The street number she sought, in peeling once-gold metallic stick-on numbers, pasted vertically on a rusty door between a bodega and a laundromat on the most depressing block of Lexington that Sara had ever seen. Hurriedly she tugged on the handle, surprised when it opened, ushering her into a dark foyer, its floor strewn with junk mail, food wrappers and leaves that had fallen several months earlier. Peering into the darkness, she was able to discern two staircases, one up, one down. She knew from all their shared hours in therapy that Laura lived in a subterranean apartment. She leapt from the top step to the bottom, her fist rat-a-tatting on the door before she'd even regained her balance.

"Laura, it's Dr Berger, are you there?"

She tilted her head, nervous, not expecting an answer. Shuffling sounds from inside the apartment told her that someone was inside, and if Laura's stories were to be believed, it could only be her.

"Laura." She knocked again, glancing around the landing. It bore once-tan vinyl floor tiles now gray with grime and use, some peeled and some missing, pieces of broken tile showing beneath them. A chain of dust-bunnies rimmed the perimeter, rustling in the breeze from her entrance.

Just as she raised her fist to knock again, she heard the familiar New York greeting of chains and bolts grinding rustily against their cylinders, and the door opened slightly.

"Doctor Berger," came a voice. "I... uh... why are you here?"

"Laura, may I come in please? You missed your appointment, and you didn't answer your phone. I didn't think you'd like a house full of policemen and EMTs, so I thought I'd pay you a house call. Are you okay?"

Instead of answering, Laura let the door swing open. Sara inhaled deeply and set her face to non-reactive, then stepped into the apartment. Ahead of her, Laura, in a tattered nightgown and crocs, turned and walked across the room. Sara took the chance to quickly assess the surroundings, finding them to be exactly as depressing as her patient described in their sessions. The apartment had flooded in a storm in 2021, drowning one of Laura's heroin-addicted parents. Water damage was visible up the warped walls, almost to the ceiling. The carpet beneath her feet felt irregular, ridged like worn rock. New electrical wiring hung, exposed, from walls and ran across the roof beneath duct tape. An overpowering smell of mildew and something darker filled the air, and Sara forced herself to breathe only through her mouth.

"I didn't expect you to come," Laura said, without turning around.

"You know the deal," Sara said. "If you pull a no-show, I'm supposed to notify the authorities, and they'll come and do a wellness check."

A horrible, dry laugh came out of Laura, and she turned slowly. Sara saw that she had been crying.

"Can you imagine a wellness check in this place?" Laura's voice broke as she limply shrugged her arms out. Sara fought to remain neutral.

"I thought you said that they'd agreed to fix the place up?"

The same dry sandpaper laugh.

"They agreed, and then they didn't do it. I pay four hundred and sixty-eight dollars a month for this place. That doesn't really cover what it would cost."

"They could get it from FEMA."

"Dr Berger, they got it from FEMA. They made more money from the flood that killed my mother than they've made from us as tenants in over fifty years. They want me gone."

Glancing at the tattered couch that she knew Laura had dragged in from the street, Sara wished for somewhere clean to sit. The only other furniture in the room was a large, boxy television and a side table covered with books and an overfull ashtray.

"Laura, what if I take you somewhere? I can cover a hotel for you, for a week or two, just so you can get a different vantage point."

A grimace settled onto the woman's face, matching her unkempt gray curls. "What? That's not your job."

"You're right, and it is definitely an unusual offer, but I think that being here is making it harder for you to heal, so, you know, desperate times, desperate measures. And Laura? I'm a New York psychiatrist. I can afford it. Please, let me help you, no strings attached."

Laura's pale blue eyes finally met hers, and Sara's heart broke. She saw nothing but hopeless pain and sadness gazing back at her. "Laura, please, let me help you. I think that a few weeks in a nice hotel, and increased therapy visits, might help us onto a better pathway."

"Oh, you mean so I wouldn't have to look at that?" Laura's voice rose as her hand pointed to an irregular stain on the destroyed carpet.

"I wasn't lying. That's my father's blood. He slashed his wrists right there."

Sara nodded, acknowledging the stain that she'd already looked for. "Yes, among other things, we've talked about how important it is to look outside of this apartment, these walls. There is still a lot of possibility and potential for you, and I want to help."

Laura took a step backward into the darkness of the hallway behind her.

"Yesterday was my birthday," she said feebly.

"Of course it was," Sara said. "Did-"

"No, Dr Berger, nobody remembered, and what of it? I turned fifty-seven. Alone. And you know what? Somehow that was even less disappointing than having my *asshole* father around for it. At least I didn't spend the day hearing what a piece of shit I am."

"I'm sorry, Laura." Sara grappled for the right words. "I truly am. What do you say to getting dressed and at least going out and getting a coffee and something to eat?"

"Dr Berger, please stop. It really fucks with my head because you're only nice to me because it's your job."

"Fire me," Sara said. "Fire me as your therapist right now and I'll take you out as someone who cares about you."

"That's unprofessional."

"Maybe, but I think it's also in your best interest. Laura, I know how you feel. Life is never easy, for anyone, and you've been double served at the shit buffet your whole life. I'm sorry your parents let their addictions rule them, and as a result, they weren't able to give you what you need, but they're both gone now, and you can-"

"I can what? Start over? Get a good job, a new apartment, a boyfriend? Those things won't stop the nightmares, Dr Berger. They won't stop what I see every time I close my eyes."

"You know what *will* help? Time, Laura. Time. It's human nature, pain subsides."

"Not mine." Laura stepped forward into the dim yellow light of the living room, strange shadows moving across her gaunt, tortured face. "My pain snowballs. And every time I think it can't get any worse, somehow, it does. I can feel my heartache in my fingertips, down my legs. My blood feels like tar in my veins. I know the only thing that could help me would be the heroin that made my parents' lives worth living for them, but there... is... no... way I will be like them."

Straightening her back, Sara nodded kindly. "Laura, please, I'm begging you, let me help you. I'll wait while you shower and pack a bag. We can get something to eat and then I'll take you to your hotel. You never have to come back here. I'll find you subsidized housing, in any part of the city that you like."

Laura's shoulders heaved up, then down, slowly.

"Okay, Dr Berger, you win," Laura said quietly. "I'll go clean up and pack. I'll try to be quick."

"Take your time, Laura. I'm here if you need to talk while you pack."

Without a word, Laura nodded, then turned and vanished into the darkness, leaving Sara alone. Now that Laura wasn't watching, Sara surveyed the apartment, surprised that it was even worse than her patient had described it. She couldn't imagine living her entire life here, caring for abusive, addict parents, unable to make or keep friends. Gasping involuntarily, Sara realized that the dark rectangle high on the wall to her right was actually the only window in the room, a grime-streaked sliver of glass revealing the feet of passersby on the street above them. Then she glanced down at the remnant of the very large blood stain on the carpet, the aftermath of a particularly cruel suicide. Laura's father, despondent since the drowning of his wife in this very room, had injected more than enough heroin to finish himself off, but then went to the extreme step of slicing both forearms along the vein, and leaving a note for his daughter that reinforced that he blamed her entirely for what he was doing.

Sara stared at the rusty stain clinically and wondered why the blood didn't bother her. She inhaled, her nostrils filling with the scent of decay and bleach and that acrid sweet smell of the industrial cleaner that bodega owners liked to slosh on the sidewalk, but no blood. A rustling noise from the hallway snapped her out of her reverie.

"Everything okay, Laura?"

"Yes, Dr Berger, I'm just going to run the shower."

Sara gazed down the hallway, shadows in the darkness. A sliver of light lanced along the rippled carpet and then extinguished as Laura closed a door behind her, and soon enough, she heard the metallic whoosh of water through ancient and apparently somewhat blocked pipes. Lacking somewhere to sit was oddly disconcerting, she realized, suddenly antsy. The hotel idea had come rocketing out of nowhere, borne of necessity when she saw Laura's face. She knew that without a drastic move, the woman would not live another week. Her mind rattled through the next steps, realizing that most of this would have to be off the books. The increased visits would draw attention from Laura's case worker, but this was New York; she'd either approve them or not, and then Sara would still treat her as often as she saw fit.

A noise like a muffled gasp or cry ripped Sara back to the dimly lit room. She listened intently, her heartbeat the only sound in her ears.

"Laura?" she called, loudly. No response. The hair stood up on her neck and arms and a surge of worry tickled her nerves as she began to move into the darkness of the hallway. Finding a light switch, she flicked it, and more dim yellow light spilled a few feet into rooms so dark they resisted identification. Her eyes were drawn to a line of light around one doorway at the hallway's end, the same doorway with the sound of splashing water.

Lurching forward, Sara twisted the doorknob and pushed the door open. In the split second before she lost her mind, Sara saw Laura, still in her nightgown, bent and broken backward over the edge of the tub, arms akimbo in the air, blood spurting weakly from her slashed wrists. But that wasn't the worst part. Frustrated by the slowness of her demise, Laura had also slashed her own throat. Jagged, dripping arcs of blood extended from wall to floor and across the ceiling. The stench of blood in the steamy air hit Sara like a punch between the eyes and she staggered backward, gripping the door frame, as a wave of something unfamiliar and metallic grew in her heart. She tried to run, but something else overpowered her, collapsing her knees. Reflexes she hadn't felt or used in lifetimes overtook her and a burning acid growl thrummed out from her heart into all of her veins, every capillary in her body screaming in a way that was beyond her control.

Her knees buckled all the way. Sara felt herself falling toward the floor and briefly prayed that she was fainting. Instead, when she hit the floor, her fingers, like steel hooks, pulled her forward in a fog of increasing blackness that wiped out her consciousness, like a blanket made of ice, or drowning in a frozen sea.

When she finally felt herself surfacing through the darkness, she was disoriented yet wildly alive. Her hands were gripping something tightly, pressing it to her face where it held cold and slimy against her lips. She knew before she opened her eyes that it was Laura's arm, and her lips were pressed deep into the wound.

Gagging violently, she pushed herself back from the body, wiping furiously at her lips with the sleeve of her overcoat. Hauling herself to the filthy toilet, Sara thrust a finger down her throat. To her dismay she was unable to gag. Her body was not going to surrender its feast that easily. The sound of her panting breath was deafening in the wind tunnel sound of the water from the shower hitting wetly on the corpse in the bathtub.

What the fuck was she to do?

Shakily, Sara forced herself to stand upright as waves of intense pleasure rolled through her, her skin coming alive in her clothing. Glancing back at Laura, she knew that the woman was dead and the only thing for her to do now was get out without being seen. Stumbling to the foggy mirror, she wiped it clear with the same sleeve. Her reflection shocked her. Instead of her usual pallor, she looked ruddy and hyper-alert, blood smeared over her face from eyes to chin. As she stared, her eyes glow yellow, like an owl.

She was in trouble.

Stepping around Laura's outstretched arms, careful not to leave footprints in the blood, Sara gently used the side of her hand to angle the shower head so that the spray covered both of the dead woman's arms, as well as the floor where Sara had... fed. Cupping water from the shower in her hands, Sara rinsed her face as well as she could until the water in her palms stayed almost clean. Grateful that she hadn't sat anywhere, she slowly, carefully walked along the hallway, then taking a Kleenex from her purse, she opened the front door and let herself out into the landing. She strode up the stairs and out, into the cleansing, freezing rain.

The feeling of Laura's wound on her lips kept playing over and over in her mind, and she gagged furiously each time.

She had never felt more alive, and she hated herself for it.

Chapter One

The perfect suicide note had been eluding Sara, five hundred years old and feeling it, for the best part of a century. As she saw it, once a suicide note was indeed perfect, then the suicide part would be easy. Life, for the note's author, had been as long as it needed to be, and there was nothing to be gained by living for any additional time.

But it wasn't that simple.

Nothing ever was.

This night, one of those chilly New York May nights that tease a spring that feels like it will never arrive, found her, once again, at her iMac, in the apartment she should have moved out of at least twenty years earlier, a Mazzy Star album spinning lazily on the turntable, the air filled with music so soft it felt deafening.

Habit and a fondness for the brutalist bare bricks and rhomboid room shapes kept her here, in this fifth floor walk-up apartment in a high security Upper West Side compound she herself had designed and supervised the construction of, a century and a half prior.

Tucked into her home office—a small desk in a tight corner, between a spiral staircase and a kitchen wall. She stared at the screensaver – some rocks in an unnamed ocean - and inhaled deeply, comforted by the smells of her home: assorted green cleaning products and a sandalwood candle; beneath that: the leather of her couch, the dust on the brick wall above the fireplace and something else, that uniquely New York scent of subways, ozone and steam, that was always there.

Briefly lost in her memories, Sara was gently jolted back by the sound of the record player clicking the tone arm back into its holder. In the ensuing silence, she glanced at her phone, and grimaced at the scroll of missed calls from Desdemona signaling a conversation she had delayed for too long. As leader of the New York Lock, it was technically her job to talk to her, since Desdemona held the same position, in the Madrid Lock. But once again, it wasn't that simple.

Sara had left her birth family before she turned twenty, but she remembered her biological siblings vividly: bursts of color and movement and emotion that the centuries had failed to temper. She'd known them so briefly. She now remembered the five long-dead children as totems of innocence and simplicity, castmembers of her own origin story, children forever.

Desdemona—a sister of sorts--was the diametric opposite of those kids, with all the rivalry, jealousy and bitterness of modern sisterhood, and none of the love and support. Crina, one of the Great Mothers, made both of them in the murky years around The Purge, Sara in her village outside Bucharest, Desdemona in Constanta. The women didn't meet until many years later, when a large group of sisters, tired of the brutal Romanian winters, began the lengthy pilgrimage that ultimately brought Crina and Sara to New York.

After a stay in Rome, where several elders were busily establishing the approved template of a Lock, a group including Crina and Sara traveled to Barcelona, where Crina reunited with Desdemona. Already, Desdemona was ambitious and aggressive as she jockeyed for position in the nascent Spanish Lock. Though Sara and Desdemona were each aware of the existence of the other, Crina's wish for them to get along like sisters fell apart immediately in a wreckage of envy and ego. As Sara liked to joke to members of her own Lock, Desdemona just wasn't her type of girl. It was that incompatibility that inspired Sara's journey onward. At the time she said she wanted to study in Paris, but that was only a partial truth. She just wanted to get further away from Desdemona and her drama, her jealousy and her slippery, self-serving logic. After moving her Lock inland to Madrid in the nineteenth century, Desdemona refused all efforts to modernize, and to this day, the Madrid lock was infamous for her draconian, unbending rules.

Desdemona was the last person Sara wanted to think about now of all moments. With the silence crowding around her, still at her seat in her apartment, Sara's mind turned back to her planned activity. Writing a suicide note. Writing *the* suicide note. An accurate barometer of whether she was truly ready to let go of this life, simultaneously crowded and exhausted by it. Freed from the natural timeline of life, she was preoccupied by how long her own life would be, and if she was just stuck, running in a hamster wheel, nothing left to engage her. With a sigh, she began to rise, planning to flip the record over, when another call from Desdemona appeared on her screen.

"*La dracu!*" Sara hissed in her mother tongue, her finger sliding the bar to answer the call, her hand swooping the phone up to her ear.

"Sarita," Desdemona cooed in her most sanguine voice. "You didn't send me to your voicemail."

"Desdemona, mi hermana, so lovely to talk to you. Sorry, I was charging the phone in the other room, I just now went to-"

"It's been charging for three weeks?"

"Unlike you, Desdemona, I have a job. I work. Also, I hate talking on the phone. You know this."

"I do, I know that. I also know when you are avoiding me."

"I'm not avoiding *you*, I'm avoiding an argument," Sara said, already too angry to remain seated, now pacing, frustrated that Desdemona was pushing her buttons so easily.

"This conversation is overdue. You are about to oversee the addition of a new sister to your Lock. At a time when the more... responsible... among us are choosing to let our kind die out. Natural attrition. Extinction. I just want you by my side, on the right side of history."

Inhaling deeply and hoping it worked, Sara fought to keep her voice even.

"Desdemona, my position remains as it was. Your points are valid and I imagine that at some point in the future, we may need to move in that direction. However, unlike you, I do not see it as inevitable." Sara paused, listening to Desdemona's deliberate breathing, smiling at the thought that she was getting under the woman's skin. When Desdemona did not speak, Sara continued. "If that's all you called about, I must go. I really need to prepare for my Lock meeting tonight."

"Yes, your selfish plan to create a new Cursed woman." Desdemona's voice rose sharply. "Is it fair to create a long life, at a time when a growing number of us are working on our end game? Also, Sara, as of today, Edinburgh is with me, and they have pledged to follow my Zero Population Growth plan."

Sara was taken aback. Edinburgh was one of the oldest surviving Locks and it, alongside New York, was usually a front runner of progressiveness.

"You're kidding me," Sara said, mainly to buy some time.

"Mija, I never kid," Desdemona cooed. "You know this. So that makes five Locks that have agreed to add no more to their number, and to allow natural attrition to bring about their end."

"Well, it's a personal choice," Sara said, her voice steel. "I'm saddened to hear it, but it is within each Lock's power to make such a decision."

"Don't toy with me, Sarita," Desdemona said tersely. "You know that all of us have stopped the process of admitting new sisters."

"Yes, by the choice of the individual Lock," Sara said. "Respectfully, these decisions do not contradict any of our foundational writings. If all members of a Lock choose surrender, the Lock and its sistren cease to exist."

"You're being glib. Typical Sara." Desdemona's voice got louder. "The facts are clear. It is harder and harder for us to go unnoticed, and if a single person figured out that drinking our blood would afford them almost endless life, it would lead to the end of civilization as we know it. How do you sleep with that kind of weight on your mind? How, Sara? How? Because I can't. I won't stop until I get all of us onto the same page, which is, it's time for us to choose surrender. The risk is too great. I am calling to beg you to join our alliance. As the sole surviving North American Lock, you pose the greatest danger. The mob mentality in that country is terrifying. Dear sister, as we have seen time and time again, men have no problem at all with killing for food."

"I know all of that," Sara said, deliberately, quietly. "Not that you've ever asked, but we have contingencies that will make it very easy for us to vanish, safe and alive, if anyone ever discovers us. You remember how efficiently I dealt with the San Francisco issue.""Crina helped you," Desdemona said snottily. "Like she's helped you for the past century."

Sara shook her head. Here we go again.

"I'm not going to play games with you, Des." Sara fought to keep her voice light. "You have unilaterally decided that you want us all to go extinct, for us to consider some sort of cult-leader suicide bullshit. You do you, girl, but come on, just leave New York alone."

"Have you even discussed this with Crina? I talked to her last week, she said she hasn't talked to you in so long, she can't remember the last time."

"Five hundred years and you still check up on me? You really need to get a life, Des. And what kind of relic are you with phone calls? Crina and I text. We send emojis and memes and gifs. We don't talk on the phone. Nobody does. I can guarantee she doesn't want to talk to you."

"Nobody wants to be ignored, Sara. Nobody. You sit there in your fabulous city and you hang out with Teddie and Heather and you let the others fend for themselves."

Sara froze. This kind of gossip was too specific to be idle. Almost all of the women in her Lock had come from somewhere else, and they all still had relationships with sistren around the world. Because a retort didn't fly to her lips, she laughed, knowing it would drive her adversary crazy.

"I see I scored points with that one."

"Hardly. You just proved that you're still a five-hundred-year-old teenager, and this whole forced extinction thing is just your latest fad and sister, I ain't gonna fall for it."

"Well it's a fad that a number of the women in your Lock support."

"I know now that you're talking to my women, which is certainly undermining. So, if that's it, I'm going to go. Thank you for letting me know about Edinburgh, but please, from this point on, can you just keep your fucking nose out of my business?"

A long inhalation on the other end told Sara she'd pushed Desdemona's buttons too hard. She knew what was coming.

"You spoiled, shallow idiot," Desdemona hissed. "You run your Lock like a daycare for pampered bitches. You let your women go out in the world, you let them fuck, you let them work, you let them do whatever they want. You-"

"I let them live, Desdemona. You should try it some time."

"I've done more living than you ever will, and I know you're about to hang up on me, *coño*, so before you do, let me say this: Keep up this bullshit, and you'll have trouble on your hands."

Sara couldn't resist it.

"Oh boo hoo I'm so scared." The edges of her mouth turned into a smile.

"It's a shame you'll die without ever having grown up. Five hundred years and you're still a spoiled bitch."

Sara held the phone away from her ear, listening to the chatter intensify for several seconds before she ended the call. Dropping her phone onto the couch, Sara pressed a single finger between her temples, trying to defuse the anger that was boiling inside her

Glancing at the time in the top corner of her screen, she saw that she now had less than an hour before the meeting. The thirst of her addiction, awoken by her anger, sunk its talons into the back of her throat, and she felt the heated friction of her blood inside her veins, as if they'd turned to sandpaper. She rose stiffly, cracking her neck left and right, trying to dispel her anger and failing. Reaching for her top cabinet, she opened it, then fossicked behind boxes and jars of spices until she found the bottle she was looking for, hemoglobin pills she had ordered from India so as not to arouse suspicions, hidden inside a rectangular container that previously housed paprika.

Her hands beginning to shake, she emptied six capsules into her palm, tossed them all into her mouth at once, then bent to the faucet at the sink, swallowing them with some difficulty. Once they were down, she relaxed back against the cabinets, her foot tapping anxiously as she waited for them to work. Instead, the clawing in her veins worsened. With a sigh of frustration, she snatched up the paprika box, shook out a capsule and bit into it with her teeth, spilling wretched rust-flavored powder into her mouth, mixing it with her saliva and spreading it around her gums with her tongue. Almost instantly, the symptoms lessened and her breathing steadied.

As the tension drained from her shoulders, Sara inhaled deeply as a new anger rose within her. Ever since the incident with Laura it had been a struggle to get her viral load down and there was nobody she could ask for help. Hence the rapid delivery pills from India, weaker than the ones that the nurses in her Lock obtained. At first it had taken twelve capsules every morning and night, but now she was down to six.

Seven. You just took seven.

Pushing the thought away, she began to walk back to her desk when her phone rang again. Crina. On Signal. She had to take it.

"Mom," she said, happiness in her voice

"My love." Crina's voice, low and raspy, always calmed her. "I'm sorry, it's been so long, I-"

"Let me guess," Sara interrupted. "You had a call from Desdemona?"

A dry laugh echoed down the line. "I wish it was just one call. It's at the point where I have to lie to her, which isn't ideal. So, if she asks, I'm practicing transcendental meditation and going weeks without speaking."

"That's actually pretty close to what I think you do anyway, you woman of mystery."

"Well, far be it for me to burst your bubble," Crina chuckled. "I wish my life was that interesting."

"You're calling to check in?"

"Not exactly, my love. I know better than to get involved in spats between you and Desdemona, and as I just told her, she is overstepping her boundaries with this whole push for extinction thing."

"Oh." Sara was surprised by Crina's bluntness. "I thought you might have been on her side."

"I see her point," Crina said. "And there are many solutions. But does that mean that after nearly six centuries, we have to change the rules? I don't think so. I think that we all have to ramp up our contingency plans in case of detection, but that is something that you and Heather have kept up on."

"Thank you, Mom."

"So, you're taking a vote tonight, on making the new girl?"

"We sure are, but Marguerite doesn't have the votes."

"That's rough. But you think the girl is a good candidate?"

"She is. But some of the women just resent Marguerite so much, they are not voting by the rules, they're just being petty. And we have a few who've been talking to Desdemona and they're in favor of not making any new sisters. Once again, they're not voting along the rules, they're voting with their hearts."

"You don't need their approval, Sara."

"I know, Mom." Sara paused. "But we've been a democracy since you and I founded this Lock. Can you imagine the outcry if I change it all now?"

"Well, to be frank, change is coming, one way or another. Desdemona is right in many ways. It could be said that we are being incredibly selfish, to continue living as we do. It was easy, and simply, now it is not. We are leaving too much evidence, evidence we don't even know is being harvested. But, like I said, these are procedural issues, and you have a meeting to get to."

"Would you like to be on speaker phone?"

"Darling, Heather always has me on speaker phone at the meetings."

Sara paused. She hadn't been aware of that.

"Oh, of course she does," she covered, perturbed. "I'm sorry, we haven't even gotten to talking about you."

"We can do that soon, in person. I will come into the city for the confirmation, if it gets that far."

"It will," Sara said firmly. "Talking to Desdemona has made me even more determined to stick to my guns."

"Good," Crina said. "Now go do whatever it is you do to get ready for your women."

"I love you, Mom."

"I love you too, Sara."

Another wave of anger rolled across Sara's chest. Heather was her confidante. Why wouldn't she tell her that Crina had been present for all the meetings on speakerphone? She cast a blaming eye at the phone in her hand, a miraculous minicomputer that did things she could never have conceived of, even a hundred years ago. She flipped it onto the couch where it bounced a few times before landing face up, its screen a tickertape of incoming texts. It was always this way before the monthly meeting as sisters pushed their agenda.

No one ever asks how I'm doing.

With a knot of frustration growing in her stomach, her jaw clenched, Sara returned to her desk. On top of the usual, reliable demands, her inability to control the virus in her body was wearing on her last nerve. Maybe tonight's suicide letter would be the one to convince her that it was, finally, time to go.

Narrowing her eyes, she clicked her mouse through her finder down into her system files to the stashed folder buried among similarly named files. Slashpub.lib. She clicked it open, her eyes scanning the creation dates of the files. The most recent one was almost a year old. She considered reading them, these files, all attempts at the perfect suicide note, but recognized her procrastination immediately. She didn't need to read them. She knew the contents of each letter perfectly, like lines of Shakespeare, ready to be delivered in theater.

Only not nearly as well written.

She opened a new, blank document, flinching as the bright screen cast its antiseptic white light deep into her gold-flecked brown eyes. A surge of defiance burned like mercury in her veins, Desdemona's smug grin rising in a memory. Her wrists resting on the fake wood of the small Ikea computer desk, her fingers poised over the G and the H, she realized she didn't even know where to start. She only knew she had to.

Who was the audience for this letter, she wondered? Who was any suicide note actually written *for*? Her past attempts showed her that she did not need to fill her note with recriminations; her lust for life was in a dry spell, and that wasn't anyone's fault but her own.

In her current outside-world incarnation, she was Lily Berger, a psychiatrist specializing in suicide counseling. She frequently used the suicide note concept as a tool to investigate her patients' deepest motivation, and in the vast majority of her cases, people just wanted to be heard. Once she figured out their audience, she could transition their treatment, usually successfully.

It was the ones who said they didn't plan to leave a note that fascinated her the most deeply. They were also the hardest to save.

So, who is this damn note for?

Her fingers twitched.

It's for us.

Instinctively, her fingers began to type.

Never may it be written. A simple command, the backbone of my life. Clearly, I can write. What must not be written is the truth of my life. The truth that, in modern parlance, I am a vampire. The intake of human blood grants me extended life. That's the part that can't be written.

She paused, a tremor racing up her spine. In all of her attempts, she'd never put it this simply. What next? Was this a suicide note or an explanation?

It's an attempt at a legacy.

Sitting upright, her elbows tight by her sides, she whistled softly. Was that it? After all this time, was she writing the wrong thing? Didn't really matter, she thought. This letter, these words that existed only as electrons inside a computer, was still a death wish. And this played right into Desdemona's hands. She wanted to write an explanatory letter, to a mythical public.

She didn't want to be forgotten.

The suicide note was a sistren tradition, the final act of a concluded life lived in secrecy. For sistren, it existed as a final, powerful chance to make a final point in a forbidden format, truth told in writing, set on tangible media, an artefact that briefly held both rebellion and explanation, before it too burned alongside the remains of the woman who wrote it . Some women took the opportunity to settle old scores, others simply treated theirs as a list of gratitudes. The letters were read aloud, and then ceremoniously burned, existing thereafter only in the memories of those who read them, or in the oral history that the women shared. With an almost pleasurable acknowledgement, Sara saw that she wanted something for her ego.

In her heart, the defiance intensified, a tasty, metallic sphere, a stranger she hadn't welcomed in so long that it felt like an alien growth inside her. She wanted to harness that power. She consciously decided to get out of the way of the emotion, and let it control her. She resumed writing, honestly, bluntly.

If a nuclear bomb landed in Manhattan, would you try to run, spending your final minutes in panic, or would you turn to face the firestorm, your final seconds spent bravely lost in the beauty of the swirling orange-red-white-cloud hurtling toward you?

I would face the fire, die in beauty.

And that's what I am doing now. I am bored. I am drained by responsibility, and I'm exhausted from parenting. I have devoted my life to the preservation of a lifestyle so outmoded, so dangerous and ultimately, so shallow. I want to be ready to die.

She paused, backspacing over the final seven words angrily, before continuing, her typing picking up speed.

I have lived a tortoise's life in the fastest city in the world. The virus that made me who and what I am has placed countless restrictions upon my life. I accepted them blindly, working with the ancient precepts. Even now, I do not mind. The alternatives are brutal, bleak and at times, unthinkable. The rules that govern all of us, my sisters, in Locks around the world, were agreed on by our foremothers, who singlehandedly fought back against the men cursed with the same virus as us. These men became killers, sadists and monsters. True monsters. Our foremothers won. They eradicated the men, the men who used a need for human blood as an excuse to become murderers, and we became the silent order. We copied the ten commandments, because at the time, forming nunneries was the easiest way to avoid detection. We had ten rules to live by. Solid, broad, guaranteed to keep peace.

The foremothers could never have predicted what life would become, nor that living a long life under such restraint would become a challenge in itself. For normal folks, a life well lived is a race well run. For me, I've felt like my race was run for many years, and I have been limping to the finish line, for so long.

Pausing, Sara went and poured herself a schooner of Guinness. Returning to her task, she sipped the warm beer slowly, the iron in each sip further calming the tension at the back of her throat. Teddie would be bringing fresh blood to the meeting, and the thought soothed her. This letter wasn't too bad. It was basic, but maybe that's what was needed.

The silver defiance inside her chest grew, its light pulsing down her legs, up her throat and out to her fingertips.

What have I done with all of this time? Aside from keeping my Lock--my sisters--safe and housed, I have anonymously supported countless causes. That's a great legacy, and I don't want any recognition. The virus prevents us from having children, but I raised the girl I later blessed with the Curse, Theodora, and she is my life's greatest work. And yet, as I look back, all I can see is that my life does not amount to a hill of beans.

This life, lived in the shadows, was rarely truly full. Out of necessity, our kind regards men as dangerous. Weak and dangerous. Some Locks forbid their sisters from entering relationships with them. I have let my women enjoy men, with a time limit. Four years. That's how long we agreed that love can last. After that, the entanglements are too deep. Men forget quickly. Women do not. I remember the stories of the brutality of Cursed men more vividly than I recall my own mother. Since the purge, not a single cursed woman has committed a murder. It is our belief, and central tenet, that no man could say the same.

A virus shouldn't turn a man into a murderer any more than a common cold should turn a person into a rapist, but that is not the case. Outsider history books still revel in the tales of the Cursed men of Romania, who created fiefdoms based on ritual murder, elevating brutality to an art form that resonates to this day.

What is not reported is what happened to those men. That's the Purge. A group of cursed women slowly convened across Romania in the late fifteenth century, and in a tightly choreographed pogrom, all men with the Curse were slaughtered. Our Original Mother, Stefanya of Walachia, set out the rules that our society has lived by, despite the challenges of the ages and epochs. The rules, watertight and steadfast, govern us. I suppose now would be a good time to share them. They are:

Never Make A Man, Nor Permit A Cursed Man To Live.

Never May It Be Written.

Never May You Kill.

Never Engage With The Faithful.

Never Exceed Your Debt

Never Betray Your Lock

Never Be Remembered.

Never Enslave A Human.

Never Become A Relic.

Never Pick A Mother.

I have practiced five hundred years of obedience. For what? We have established Locks around the world. We manage our hemoglobin requirements medically. Each Lock features nurses, doctors, bureaucrats alongside a floating group of other roles. I've been all of those things many times over. The doctors and nurses help secure blood, safely feeding Lock members. Our bureaucrats perform an equally important function. They resuscitate the legal records of women who depart suddenly, unclaimed and alone, at all ages up to the mid-thirties. Armed with social security numbers, birth certificates and more data, these identities serve us, temporarily, until either the cover is blown in some way, or we simply age out of the identity. Physically, we don't age, so once it becomes impractical to continue pretending to be twenty-eight or forty-eight, we finally kill the identity and we step into some new shoes. The real Lily

Berger died in plane crash in Alaska when she was four, but she would be twenty-eight now, which is around the age I was when I was made. I have been Dr Lilian Berger to the outside world for eight years. It's time for me to kill her off and become someone new. And that's the problem. I don't want to.

Sistren life is a challenge. On top of the stringent rules to maintain a peaceful existence, we face the greatest challenge that a human can know:

How to live an interesting life.

Suicide is now my only option. If I quit ingesting blood, I'll eventually die, but cold turkey is brutal. We shrivel and a burning pain takes up residence in every nerve ending. It's awful but the main danger is that a desperate woman will do anything to survive. Anything. The nightmarish fate we call Ourobouros, where the pain of blood starvation becomes so unbearable that the virus takes control and a Cursed person will begin to feed on themselves, thrashing and screaming, but not stopping until either blood loss or physical damage makes it impossible to continue. It's a death so hideously slow and painful that all Locks keep a large supply of Opioids on hand. Opioids and suffocation are the most humane ways to terminate a Cursed person. Disabling the spinal cord works equally well.

This informative letter to your editor is me knocking that first domino over, knowing that the end result will be my Ceremony of Surrender, where my sistren will help me to die.

Interesting, when it comes to suicide, I have two options. One, the braver one, the one that I hope for, but don't seem strong enough for, is to simply ask my sisters to help me surrender. The other option is that I get convicted of breaking any one of our ten commandments. This letter, believe it or not, is grounds for death. Print it if you wish but know this. Once my Lock know that I have broken a rule, I will be ushered into our surrender room and denied oxygen until I cease to exist. It ain't pretty, but they do say it's painless.

This letter, ironically, is the least of my transgressions. There are ten commandments, but within that framework exist many commonsense adjustments that have evolved over time. We don't change the commandments; we just learn to broaden their scope.

While I won't write what I've done—I don't have the words that I can use that demonstrate the dark corner I've painted myself into—I can say this.

Never have I killed, but I have tasted living blood. And it is good.

Sara hit the final full point with gusto, an angry woodpecker stab with her finger. This letter was just as bad as the last one. Angry word vomit. Formal. Pretentious. So self-conscious. A wash of clammy shame came over her. She glanced at her computer clock and saw that she only had a few minutes before she was due to preside over the monthly meeting in the communal room on the roof deck.

Her eyes drifted back to the page she had just written. If her search for the perfect suicide note was her last procrastination against actual suicide, she'd need to step up her game, or she would have to live another hundred years.

A terse dry laugh escaped her throat. There was no point for someone who didn't believe in life after death to take her secrets to the grave, but so far, she couldn't find an acceptable alternative.

The spirit of defiance is impossible to bottle. As Sara's system moved past the initial thrill of the act of writing, she felt petty, childish and cold.

In the spirit of that unpleasant trio of emotions, she decided to lean in.

Fuck it. She was wearing fur to the meeting.

Chapter Two

Standing upright, careful not to bump her head on the circular staircase that led to her loft, Sara stalked around the apartment, confident of her steps in the near dark.

Why the hell did you write that ten minutes before you have to go to Lock Coven?

Self-sabotage. Der. Her phone dinged and shook like a pinball machine as messages flooded in from the nine other women in her Lock. Even though any of them could take the floor and speak for themselves, it had somehow become standard practice that almost everyone just texted their grievances to her, and she brought them up as neutral discussion points.

Cowards.

A message from Teddie caught her eye and she picked up the phone. Teddie was going to be late to the meeting. Indicating that the delivery of blood that was the central ritual of any Lock meeting was delayed. That meant two things. One, she definitely needed another heem pill or two before she got into that room, and second, she had to get up to the roof house ahead of anyone else, unlock it and set up for the meeting. Usually, Teddie liked to set up the meetings, unlike the other women in the Lock, who just liked to arrive and be waited on.

"Piss," Sara whispered angrily. She only had a few minutes to reach the roof and she was still vibrating with tension.

She grabbed a glass bottle filled with New York's finest from the small refrigerator and moved to her couch, chugging water in between long, deep breaths. She attempted to shake out the heeby jeebies, flicking her hands away from her, dispelling the confusion. She needed the calming ions of a shower. There wasn't enough time for that, and that was her fault. Some of the other sisters would definitely have showered. They were busy right now getting hair and makeup just right. These meetings were one of the few places that the women could be beautiful, and they took it seriously.

After downing the last mouthful of water, she returned to her nook kitchen. This time she took two capsules from a prescription bottle, provided by Yukari, their resident epidemiologist, placed them in her mouth, then bent and drank from the faucet, washing them down. While she waited for these stronger pills to take the last edge off of her cravings, she went into her bedroom, darkening with the dusk, its all white motif – curtains, coverlet, carpet – turning shades of silver.

She pressed her shoulder against the row of clothes hanging in her wardrobe, creating a wedge between bland, sensible work outfits that she could slip her hand through and feel a second row of hanging clothes. This was where she hid the clothing of her true life. Clothing that she loved, some items tailor-made in eras past, others newer but definitely too memorable for outside wear. She ran her fingers along the edges of various fabrics until they suddenly plunged deep into the silky warmth of fur. She raised her hand and gripped the hanger, wresting it forward, through the drab uniforms of her public life.

She laid the floor-length white arctic fox fur onto her bed. An impulse buy at an estate sale some time during the 1920s, the coat was a long-simmering source of tension between her and Teddie. While

Sara did not approve of the fur trade, the coat's immaculate pale blue satin lining and craftsmanship gave her solace and helped her overlook its grisly origins.

It slipped off the hanger smoothly, and in one sweeping motion, Sara slipped one arm, and then the other, into the coat's enveloping warmth. She decided to pair it with her usual, a harp seal fur hat, just as white, the fur impossibly denser. Pausing by the mirror that hung behind her bedroom door, she saw a vision of white marred almost violently by her jet-black hair and dark rimmed eyes. All her life, downplaying her beauty had been essential, and she never wore makeup in public. Over the preceding century, it had become an unwritten rule of Lock life: Women without makeup were more easily forgotten, by men and women alike. As she stared into her reflection, she felt the pills start to work, and the dark bruise-like circles under her eyes lightened.

Satisfied that she was dressed defensively enough to keep these bitches on their toes, she made for the staircase, but stopped dead in her tracks when she saw her computer screen, displaying the last words she had typed.

> I have tasted living blood.
> And it was good.

She lunged at the iMac, uncertain of whether to just shut it down or to delete the heretical writing exercise.

Her fingers hovered over the keyboard momentarily before she hit command S and quickly saved the file. She named it "Plumbing Instructions" and stored it in her fake system folder containing .lib files. Sighing deeply, she went to select shut down; then at the last minute, she went back to her finder, and dragged the new file to her trash. She swept up the tight, spiral stairs, across the small meditation room, and up the two steps that brought her to the door that led out onto the roof garden.

It took her a moment to undo the four heavy deadbolts, then it took her shoulder to push the steel door ajar. Immediately, an evening wind blew in around her, a small tornado of dust and dead leaves. Hurriedly, she pulled the door closed behind her.

She stepped away from the door and spun slowly, taking in the night and the expanse of the roof deck, the size of the city block beneath it, dotted by loft rooms and raised garden and flower beds, bordered by thick hedges on all sides.

Beneath the roof were eight buildings, all owned by the New York Lock. Slowing her spinning when her eyes reached the roof house, which was their central meeting space, Sara gazed into its dark interior behind a wall of floor to ceiling windows. To her relief, nobody was waiting at the door. As if, she chided herself. Nobody ever was. The Governing Mother always arrived first.

She paused, relishing the strange silence of New York City. The pills were definitely working now. She felt relaxed. She walked slowly to the center of the roof, the wind ruffling the fur around her face, and listened intently for sounds of the city that surrounded her, unable to discern so much as a siren over the comforting white noise hum. She resumed spinning, squinting her eyes to see if she could find any stars amid the light pollution. The sky was a troubling gray yellow, like a fading bruise, or the color she saw when she had a migraine. She didn't locate any stars, but she enjoyed the dizzy sensation that was accompanying the rush from her heems.

"Y'all gone full Stevie Nicks there?" came a throaty, husky voice and a laugh that always warmed her heart. "Even in her worst cocaine days,

Miss Stevie would never been caught in head-to-toe dead endangered mammals."

Sara smiled, stopping her spinning when she came face to face with Teddie, the only sister that she had ever made. They'd been together nearly two hundred years. Sometimes it felt like forever, and sometimes, like now, it felt like five minutes. Sara still missed her when they were apart, even for a day.

Teddie, in a nurse's uniform under the Lock's preferred public wear—a floor length North Face—had come directly from work. A knit hat and a bulky rose-pink scarf obscured all but her happy, piercing eyes, which locked on Sara's as she wrapped her in a big hug.

"It's good to see you, stranger," she said into Sara's fur before recoiling in slight disgust. Teddie hated fur and had been in favor of the destruction of Sara's vintage collection for countless years. She would prefer it if Sara began smoking cigars over wearing fur.

"You in reverie?" Sara asked, breaking the hug, referring to a common condition for women of their age, where every moment triggered a tumbling of remembrances of so many other moments. It was all too common for a sister to drift off mid-conversation. Rather than taking offense, it was recognized as reverie, a rabbit hole of thoughts and memories so deep you could drown in it.

"I'm in reverie over how much I hate pressing my face into the skin of a hundred corpses." Teddie tugged her scarf down so she could speak clearly. "You ready for tonight?"

Such a loaded question. Sara grinned, a tight, businesslike smile.

"Well, I was, before back to back phone calls from Desdemona and Crina."

Teddie's mouth opened wide in cartoon shock.

"Oh girl, there's bullshit and then there's that. How's your nerves?"

"Fried, slightly, I guess. Desdemona wants us all dead and Crina wants us all to get along."

"Oh, so nothing has changed then."

Sara laughed and locked arms with her friend, guiding her toward the roof house door.

"If anything, it made me more determined to give Marguerite what she wants."

"A feeling I will never understand."

"I can handle Marguerite," Sara said, scanning the orange-gray sky six stories above West End Avenue. Truthfully, she couldn't really manage Marguerite for much longer. Fifty years ago, when she had welcomed the fiery, self-centered artist to New York at Desdemona's request, she would have relished the negotiation, the thrill of making a new Lock member, a newly Cursed woman, but these days, she only saw hassles, not magic.

"From the look on your face, sister, the opposite is true."

Sara sighed.

"Well, it's not just Marguerite. Des told me that Edinburgh have signed on to her crusade."

Teddie stopped dead and cocked her head, intrigued.

"Get the fuck outta here. Did you call anyone to verify?"

Sara shook her head. "I didn't have time, I literally just got off the phone." She hated lying to Teddie. Even more, she hated how much more frequently she had to of late. "So, now she has Edinburgh, Milan, Warsaw, and Helsinki on board, plus her own Lock in Madrid."

"So what do we have left?" Teddy's eyes were wide.

"I spoke to Lindsey in London last week, they're aligned with us and Paris and Bucharest. But we can't do anything about Desdemona's influence except try to get our own sistren to resist it. It'll be difficult.

She has some of us on her side already, and she has decided that zero population growth is the only way forward, for all of us."

Teddie froze.

"They can't enforce it, can they?"

Sara looked at her and shrugged.

"But…" Teddie stammered. "There's nothing at all in the rules about zero population growth. They can't issue a ban on making new sisters!"

Sara reached out an arm, and Teddie begrudgingly let her wrap it around her.

"Desdemona tries to do a lot of things she can't do," Sara said. "The only way it can happen is if all the Locks decide on it, on their own. Until then, she's just a loud barking dog."

"Okay," Teddie said, relaxing against her slightly. "Fuck knows what's going on over there. I hate it when them bitches start acting like they can add rules. Ten is enough. Ten rules are all we need."

If Teddie knew what I just did… Sara's mind trailed off mid-thought, the taboo of the act of simple writing of forbidden facts still racing her pulse.

They reached the roof house door. Teddie leaned and punched in the thirteen-digit security code and pushed the door ajar, letting Sara enter first. As Sara stepped in, the room illuminated automatically courtesy of Teddie's obsession with smart lighting. Incandescent LED bulbs shined in wall sconces, and glowing pools of blue, pink and orange flooded up from the floor of a room that looked like an Architectural Digest feature on castle makeovers.

Teddie pulled a lighter from her work satchel, then dragged a chair over to the center of the space, where a medieval chandelier hung on heavy black chains. Climbing up onto the chair, she lit the squat melty candles on the chandelier's circumference, then stepped back down. She and Sara took stock of the room.

Only the front wall had windows, which looked out onto the deck. The back wall featured a bar, an upholstered teak fixture that had been "liberated" from a Harlem speakeasy during prohibition. In front of it, a ringed circle of seating centered around a dais, upon which stood Sara's chair, almost as old as she was, burnished wood and thread-bare embroidery that she'd had restuffed more times than she could remember. She was quite liking its current fill, memory foam. Sara walked over and adjusted the chair so that it was directly opposite the chairs that the other sisters would occupy. She liked to face the meetings head on, even though she'd never warmed up to sitting with her back to a wall of windows.

"Is everyone coming tonight?" Teddie asked, moving to the bar and hauling her work satchel up onto its oiled, weathered surface. When Sara didn't answer immediately, Teddie turned to look for her, finding her standing motionless, looking out a window, her shoulders set high and forward, a tell-tale sign that Sara was stressed. "Sara?"

"Oh, what? Yes, wait, no, I'm not sure," Sara said with a curt laugh. "You know how it is, it's kind of hard to plan when nothing can be written." She winced inside. A lame joke borne of a guilty conscience.

"We can text," Teddie said sarcastically, slipping off her coat and hanging it on the rack by the bar. After waiting for Sara to respond and not getting anything, she returned to the bar, one eye on her maker.

Sara circled the room and absently lit candles and fluffed pillows ahead of the evening. When she was done, she pulled out her phone and flicked open the Sonos app, pausing to consider her music choices. A glance back at the chilly spring night sealed the deal, and within seconds the intricate piano of Bill Evans was mirroring the dance of the light reflected on the wall of glass windows.

Teddie smiled at the music choice. She fished in her basic Michael Kors purse, which lay on the ornate marble bar top, and retrieved three bags of donated blood, easily purloined from her work in the epidemiology section of Columbia Hospital.

"Mom, I need a head count," she called over her shoulder. "I need to know how many bags to open and how many to refrigerate."

Sara did some mental arithmetic. The worldwide maximum membership for a Lock was a hard twenty. No Lock could ever grow beyond that. The structure of each Lock was different, decided by its Governing Mother. The New York Lock functioned as a lean machine. Ten working sistren, four scholars, and six vacancies. Over the years, Sara had come to believe that this model caused the least stress and strain. All the sisters had theoretical access to a vacancy, allowing them to entertain the notion of making a new member, if they had the credit to make someone. This meant that a sister who had previously chosen Surrender had willed the credit, her life, to them. Scholars, older sistren who craved solitude and wisdom, resided on the periphery of the Lock, their participation in Lock matters not compulsory. Some Scholars returned to Lock life, but a greater percentage of them eventually chose death, known as the Ceremony of Surrender.

In Sara's calculations, none of the Scholars that they supported were likely to choose anything other than Surrender. Crina, for example, who'd fought in the original war against men and was now a Scholar, was enjoying her time in upstate New York way too much to ever want to be a functioning part of this Lock. When a Scholar announced that they planned to attend a Lock meeting, it usually indicated that a somber decision had been reached. No Scholars were coming tonight, and Sara ransacked her memory, sifting through texts and phone calls. Nobody had told her that they weren't coming, which was mandatory.

"I think all ten of us will be here," she replied.

Teddie opened an ornate wooden cabinet below the bar and removed a set of ten goblets, elegant, pewter. She fell in love with them during a sojourn in Paris in the 1920s, their vinelike stems reminding her of the Metropolitaine signs. Carefully, she pierced the first blood bag with a pocketknife on her key chain and filled goblet after goblet with deliberate precision. Halfway through the second bag, she was done. One by one, she moved the goblets to a small warming oven on a shelf inside the bar. When they were all nestled inside, she set the temperature to one hundred degrees and closed the door.

"Is everyone going to be late?" asked a gruff, accented voice at the door. It was Marguerite. Teddie busied herself at the bar, not answering. Marguerite was in major politicking mode over her new candidate. Teddie was one of the sistren with reservations.

"Hi, Marguerite. It's just gone seven," said Sara, popping up from behind a bookshelf room divider at the rear of the room. "Could be a problem on the subways."

"I took the 1," Marguerite said, shaking her thick black hair. "All the expresses were jammed. I thought I'd be the late one."

Sara eyed Marguerite carefully, wondering which version of herself Marguerite would be tonight. If her outfit – a red and black Valentino pantsuit and chunky black wedges – was a flag, it would be the version best suited for battle. Nothing about Marguerite was subtle. Sara braced herself for hostility at the meeting, her mind searching for solutions that would defuse Marguerite.

A central tenet of all sistren life in Locks around the world was open honesty and peaceful negotiation, which was fine in principal but rarely practical. The discipline to live accordingly was hard to come by for almost everyone, and the burden of peace almost always fell on the shoulders of the Governing Mother.

Marguerite's choice of protégé, a young woman named April Veronica, was ruffling feathers with other Lock members, and it was Sara's job to absorb their concerns and transmit them to Marguerite. Moody, highly intelligent Marguerite.

Still gazing at her with the heems swirling around in her bloodstream, Sara realized that she was in no condition to oversee this highly important job at the moment. She wished that Marguerite could just get the votes and make her damn novitiate.

"Cat got your tongue, Sara?" Marguerite said. Without breaking eye contact, she swept dramatically into the room, her flared pantsuit twirling around her legs as she slowly folded down into her personal chair, a family heirloom from Galicia: immaculate Spanish upholstery with turned walnut arms.

"Me?" Sara snapped out of her reverie. "Sorry, no, I was lost in some work drama, I was letting it occupy me."

"I don't know why you're so drawn to psychiatry," Marguerite said dismissively, her faint Spanish accent playing around the edge of her new, American one. "It's almost impossible to feign interest in normcore anymore. And you do it daily. You must be a good actress."

Sensing that Marguerite was itching for a fight, Sara remained silent, refusing to be drawn into a losing battle.

She could never admit to anyone just why she found psychiatry so rewarding. She saw it as a window into a life she could never have, and she never grew tired of it.

The arrival of a cluster of sistren in a gust of wind and chatter forced her into the present. She stood and opened her arms, palms up, in greeting, as Fran, Liz, Eleanor, and Rosa tumbled in, all of them in evening wear. Sara guessed that they'd been pre-gaming in one of their apartments. She smelled wine on their breath and swatted away a pang of FOMO.

"Ladies, welcome," Sara said warmly, doing a quick mental roll call. Heather, Imani and Yukari were still on their way, and since they were often delayed by work, she jumped right in.

"If we can all take our seats, I will get started and the others can get here when they get here."

"What about first toast?" Marguerite, irritable.

Sara fought to keep her eyes from rolling or crossing. Marguerite knew that first toast could only happen when everyone had arrived, and Teddie had only put the goblets in the warmer a few minutes earlier. They weren't ready yet. Nobody liked cold blood.

"First toast will have to wait, take it up with your sistren if you'd like them to be more punctual. If you're jonesing, pop a heem to carry you over."

Sara ended her sentence with a thin smile and fought off a sudden wish to be back in her apartment, at her computer. Writing. Her smile faltered at the curveball of such an illicit word and she struggled to keep her face calm as she watched Marguerite angrily open her purse and pop a pill. It was frustrating when sistren didn't manage their viral needs, especially a sister as seasoned – and temperamental - as Marguerite.

Sara moved to her space in the center of the room, facing her Lock, and prepared herself for the meeting ahead.

"Greetings be to my sistren members of the Great Lock of New York," she said warmly, her voice filling the room. "I am Nomine Sara, and never have I killed."

"Never have I killed," repeated the women seated around her.

"Welcome to our May Lock meeting," she continued. Noise at the door stopped her, and Yukari, Heather and Imani tumbled in like a mess of kittens, mumbling apologies and offering smiles and hugs. It was hard to be angry at any of these women, and Sara wasn't. She just wished that their naturally happy nature would rub off on Marguerite, whose raised eyebrow and pursed lips made it clear that she didn't appreciate their tardiness.

Sara nodded at Teddie, and her old friend removed the goblets from the warming oven, setting them on an ornate pewter serving tray. She carried the tray from one woman to the next until there were only two goblets left. Teddie presented one to Sara, then took the final one for herself and set the tray back on the marble countertop before returning to her chair.

Sara held her goblet high.

"New York Sistren, I welcome you all to the May Lock meeting. May we drink now, sustenance in our hands provided by health and happiness, not by suffering."

Sara brought her glass to her lips. In the split second before the thick, warm fluid hit her tongue, she watched her sistren following her lead, before the sanguine fluid filled her mouth, and the intoxicating elation rushed through her body. Silence fell over the room as each woman sank into the true peace that accompanied the intake of blood; the virus in their cells—the twisty, codependent illness that could kill them so painfully if they didn't feed it—passed them into a short, dreamlike wash while it assimilated the new fuel.

Sara stood perfectly still, waiting for the little flickers around the darkness of her closed eyes to peter out. As normalcy returned, she fully, finally willed away the guilt and confusion that her earlier transgression laid upon her heart, before she resumed the meeting.

"We thank you, to our anonymous donors, and to our sister Teddie for bringing us our sustenance and keeping us human and whole."

"Thank you, sister Teddie," the seated women said, still bleary from their intake.

"And with that, I bring the meeting to order," Sara said, deliberately only making eye contact with Teddie. "Who would like to talk with us first?"

Marguerite's fist shot up and she began talking without even being invited.

"Nomine Marguerite, and never have I killed," she said, rushing through the formality, steel in her voice. "It is time for us to vote on my decision to make my novitiate into a member of our sistren."

Sara raised a hand, trying to pacify Marguerite without angering her further.

"Marguerite, we will get to you. I promise. But ahead of that, and because it has direct bearing on your wishes, I wanted to let you all know that I just had the ... *delight* ... of speaking with Desdemona from Madrid, and she was happy to inform me that Edinburgh has joined her crusade."

The room erupted in chatter. Instead of trying to hear all that was said, Sara focused on the body language and the groupings that emerged. Predictably, Liz, Rosa and Fran huddled and whispered. She knew they all supported the ZPG movement, and she wondered which one of them was talking to Desdemona. She also paid careful attention to Marguerite, whose time in the Madrid Lock had ended due to friction with Desdemona, but the Spaniard merely sat and seethed.

Imani, Iranian English and reliably stalwart, her eyes glittering beneath a charcoal turban, raised her hand.

"Scuse me, guv, but last I checked, zed pee gee was being adopted on a Lock by Lock policy."

Sara raised an eyebrow and nodded for her to go on.

"I just feel like Europe steps on our toes for the bleedin' sake of it," Imani said, "and I don't appreciate their need to get everyone on board with zed pee gee."

Yukari, seated next to her, raised a hand and set it gently on Imani's arm.

"They do have a point," Yukari said, her voice almost inaudible. "With all the things going on in the world, we do need to at least discuss our own extinction. Are we too dangerous to have around? Are we being selfish by making new sisters when we know the toll that we take? The potential for disaster has grown exponentially as surveillance technology improves."Liz, a whipsmart but snarky California blonde and Sara's least favorite Lock member, turned to Yukari.

"I can never figure you out, Yukari. Every time we've talked about ZPG, you've said you're against it, but now you think it's a good idea?"

Yukari shook her head, her pigtails flicking side to side. When she spoke, it was even more quietly than before. "I'm not in favor of anything except critical thinking," she said. "If Locks around the world are reaching the place where they decide to die out, then I assume they've put a lot of thought into it, and that makes me not want to dismiss it out of hand."

"Pick a side," Liz said, mainly because she loved having the final word. Yukari waited until Liz's head turned back away from her and then flipped her off. Sara grinned.

"Liz," Sara said. "Why must I always remind you that we are dedicated to peaceful negotiation? Yukari is right. This movement is not without merit. No other Lock in the world is making new sisters, but tonight we will vote on such a thing."

"It's bullshit," Liz said, not exactly under her breath.

Before Sara could react, Heather, the Lock's bookkeeper and backbone, leapt to her feet and in two bounds was standing knee to knee with Liz.

"Do you know what's bullshit?" she asked, the lilt of her Scottish accent doing nothing to contain the threat in her voice. Calm Heather was formidable. Angry Heather was terrifying. "It's bullshit that we took your sorry arse in after you were dumb enough to almost blow the cover of the entire San Francisco Lock, and yet for forty years, you've treated this like an Airbnb that has to feed you. You work in clinical trials and you haven't supplied any blood to us in how many months now?"

"Six," called out Teddie. "She just leaves it to me and Eleanor every goddamn month."

"Right. Six months. So please, before you think about some smartarse comeback, maybe just shut your mouth until you give your brain a chance to get into gear."

A million insults visibly piled up behind Liz's pursed lips, but she blinked and remained silent.

"I thought so," Heather said, returning to her seat. "Sara, please go on."

"There's not much to go on about, I'm afraid. It's a movement and it's gaining traction. I'm not recommending that we adopt it as policy, but it would be foolish of us not to acknowledge it ahead of a vote to make the first new sister since you, Fran."

"I'm tired of being the baby," Fran said without looking up. Sara made a note to check in with her. She had been very unlike herself lately. Fran, the only member of their Lock with gray hair, shook her head, then put strands of long, straight hair behind each ear. "But I'm not tired enough of being the baby to vote on making one just because Marguerite can't make any actual friends. There's a lot of responsibility that comes with a neophyte and I personally don't have spare time to jump into the parent trap."

Marguerite shot to her feet, and Sara raised her palm again.

"Marguerite, if we start arguing, we will get no further than we have in past months."

The Spaniard sat back down, her face a tapestry of anger and frustration.

"Fran, am I right in hearing that you will not vote for Marguerite in her quest to make a convert of April Veronica, a woman she has mentored for many years and whom I myself believe would make an excellent addition to our flock?"

Fran nodded once, angrily. "You know how I feel."

Sara cast her eyes about the room. Everyone stared back at her, except Liz, who predictably stared at the floor like a child.

"Liz, have you changed your mind on the conversion of April Veronica?"

The Californian shook her head but remained silent.

Marguerite glowered in her seat, her body fairly writhing with anger. For once, her anger was justified. There was no concrete reason for either of those women to stand in her way. Sara searched her mind for a way to simultaneously transition the meeting away from this topic and maintain peace.

"Marguerite, I want you to know that I stand with you on this matter," Sara said firmly. "It is up to all of us as a Lock to listen to opposing viewpoints with an open mind. Additionally, bringing it to a vote is not mandatory. By the letter of our laws, Marguerite has the credit to make a sister. It is courtesy that we indulge in this vote. At this time, I'll remind you that the New York Lock is not a part of the ZPG movement, and we should not let that influence us. Liz and Fran, I'd like you to both step back and consider your votes within the context of the rules, not your personal feelings. Next time we meet, we will take a final vote on this, but I warn you, if anyone is voting anything other than fairly, I'll step in."

"Oh, so you're saying my vote doesn't matter," Liz said, snottily.

Sara fought to keep her voice calm.

"Liz, please see me privately if you wish to discuss this. Now, before we move on, Fran, I believe you have some security updates for us all?"

Fran stood and approached Sara's dais, perching herself on the arm of Sara's chair, her uniform of blue jeans and a white linen shirt belying her legendary embrace of the sixties.

"I'm tired of telling you all this," she began. "If I find out that one of you has been using any device that's connected to the internet without a motherfucking VPN, I will literally block the internet from your apartment and I'll also cut off your fucking cable. Do you hear me?"

Sara saw Heather roll her eyes and it made her smile. Every other woman in the room grabbed their phones and held them up to Fran, gesturing that they were definitely using the VPN.

"We've had several weird hacking attempts lately, the usual DDOS kind of crap. We are supposed to be a silent order of nuns, not a bunch of bitches obsessed with online shopping. Please only use the phones assigned to your public personae out in public. Not inside these walls."

"Are you done?" said Marguerite angrily. She had clearly expected the vote to go differently and now she just wanted to get the hell out of the room.

"Oh hell no, honey," Fran crowed. "I'm just getting started."

Chapter Three

Exhausted, Sara pulled hard on the door to her upstairs room. It always stuck when the weather changed. Teddie and Heather stepped in behind her and she forced the door closed, noisily pushing the four deadbolts back into place and turning the deadlock.

"Thank god that's over," Heather said in her lilting Scottish burr.

"Marguerite is cruising for a transfer," Teddie said. "And am I the only bitch that comes straight from work? Oh hey, right, I'm a nurse and I'm feeding all of you. Don't worry about me."

"Was there a problem this month?" Heather said. Heather was the Lock's great peacekeeper, methodical, kind and honest.

"Not quite but almost," Teddie said. "I was held back waiting for the blood to be cleaned, due to a scheduling issue in the lab. I'm just being a baby. All y'all turned up in furs and finery and here I am in scrubs and a puffer."

"And still so naturally beautiful," Heather said with a genuine smile. Ever since Heather had transferred from the Hamburg Lock when it was dissolved during the Second World War, she had made Sara's job – and life – infinitely better with her matter-of-fact common sense and huge heart. As much as Sara was pining to be alone on this cold night, she could never refuse a post-meeting post-mortem with these women.

"I fancy a wine," Heather said, stealing ahead of them and down the narrow spiral stairs. "Do you have any more of that Spanish tempranillo?"

"Yes," Sara called down after her.

"Are you okay, Mom?" Teddie asked, her hand grasping Sara's elbow. Sara smiled at the use of their private nickname, for she was indeed the one who had made a bright, intelligent orphan named Theodora into her first and only Cursed charge, centuries earlier.

"I am, I'm fine. That was rough. Marguerite is technically right, she *can* make someone if she wants. I guess it's partially my fault. I threw it open to votes and now we have death by committee. The whole process sucks."

"If she thinks this sucks, wait until she deals with a poor choice."

"Oy vey," Sara said with a laugh. "Let's not even go there. But that's the thing. I don't think April Veronica is a poor candidate for our life. I should have handled this better."

Teddie paused on the spiral stairs and looked back at Sara with concern, and love.

"Bitch, you're in a tight spot. I don't envy you. And we all know this wouldn't be a problem if Marguerite was a team player, but come on. How many years are you going to let her be a failed artist? It's time she got a nursing degree and went to work."

Teddie was entirely right. Lost for words, Sara shrugged and motioned for them to continue their descent to the living room.

By the time they got to the bottom of the stairs, Heather was seated on the oversized leather couch with three glasses of wine on the glass coffee table in front of her. Sara tossed the fur coat and hat onto her bed, then collapsed at one end of the couch, exhaling loudly.

"I thought you said you was fine, girl?" Teddie waved a hand in front of Sara's zoned-out eyes. She smiled and batted it away. "That meeting was rotten meat."

"It really was!" Sara reached for her wine, holding it beneath her nose, inhaling the fruity, earthy tangle of notes. "Heather, how do you do it? How do you stay so enthused and engaged? I really need to know."

"It's my OCD," Heather said with a laugh, looking at the floor. "Everything has a place, and I like to keep things in their place."

"Nobody can manage four hundred years of OCD," Sara said, her friend's modesty making her smile warmly.

"You need a vacation," Teddie said.

"Wait. Me? A vacation? I wouldn't know what to do with myself," Sara said, hearing herself and hating the apathy in her voice.

Heather and Teddie exchanged brief, worried looks.

"Girl, how long since you got laid?" Teddie kicked her legs into the air comically before setting her feet on the coffee table.

"As if you don't know the answer to that one," Sara said, finally taking a sip of her wine.

"Getting laid is important," Heather said piously.

"It's a hassle," Sara said.

"Yes, because keeping a secret society of vampire women alive and safe for a century in New York is smooth sailing," Teddie said.

"What the hell could I get out of it at this point?" Sara said, already defensive.

"Forgetting," Heather said. "I do it for the forgetting."

"Fuck that," Teddie cackled. "I do it because it's fun."

"I'd like some forgetting," Sara said. "I don't have the energy to go through all that small talk and bullshit for a predictable outcome."

"Gamble on a one-night stand," Teddie said. "You have nothing to lose."

"What about my sanity? I'm tired of being told I'm crazy just because I've heard it all before. Whether I stand up, surrender, insult or placate, I've played all the responses to every possible thing that comes out of a man's mouth. Why keep on sticking my finger in the electrical socket?"

"Do it for the D," Teddie whispered.

Sara groaned. She'd considered finding a casual affair, on and off over the last decade, but nothing alluring had presented itself. As things stood, the thought of a one-night stand was not enough to motivate her through the whole production of dressing up and leaving the house.

"I found a great new bar," Teddie said. "It's in Bushwick, and the men are eager, fit and usually high enough that they're never going to remember my face."

"Sounds nasty," Heather said, finishing her wine and heading for the second bottle on the kitchen counter.

"Kinda, maybe," Teddie said.

"I don't need nasty." Sara made a face. "And as we've discovered, even in the diviest of bars, I'll find a psycho who wants a relationship."

"It's easy to avoid relationships these days," Teddie said. "Just act like you want one desperately and you'll be single for a decade."

"Can we drop it? I'd like your help with Marguerite."

"I'll drop it if you promise to come to Bushwick with me." Teddie nodded thanks as Heather refilled her glass. "Because I'm also not convinced on this April Veronica girl."

"Okay, fine, whatever, if you promise to get off my back, I'll come with you. And while we are there, we can work on your issues with April Veronica."

Teddie raised a fist in victory.

"I mean," she said, laughing, "how do we even prepare to deal with a millennial?"

"I dunno," Sara said with a grin. "Binge watch The Office and some SpongeBob? That should do it."

Heather laughed harder than Teddie.

"That's not what worries me," Teddie said. "Young people worry me, but they always have. Young people start bands and take drugs and skydive and obsess obsess obsess. I'm voting for her confirmation, but I really don't want to have much to do with her for forty or fifty years if that's okay. It's just exhausting."

"I think that's actually Marguerite's plan. I doubt anyone will be seeing that girl for quite a while," Sara said. "That's another reason I'm in favor of it. We also won't see Marguerite too much."

"Sara, that's such a plus," Heather said enthusiastically. "What do you need us to do to make the Marguerite thing easier on you?"

"It's gonna happen," Sara said. "Marguerite's heart has been in this for so long. But she's never been good or close to Liz or Fran, and that's hurting her now. They're using old resentments to block this and that isn't fair. Can you see where they're at and gently nudge them? I need to be able to begin the process before the next meeting. If we don't have consensus by then, Marguerite is going to become... problematic."

"I'll take Liz," Heather said. "She'll come around."

"I get Fran? Awesome," Teddie deadpanned. "Nah, seriously, really? Fran? She hasn't changed her mind since the sixties."

"If anyone can do it, you can," Sara replied.

"Are you working tomorrow?" Heather asked, and Sara nodded.

"I don't know how you do that," Heather said kindly. "Counseling navel-gazing manic depressives day after day."

"It's my death fetish," Sara said drily. "The thing we can't have, and these people want it too, and it's truly fascinating to hear them justify why they want to die, usually in tandem with a deeper desire to just be loved."

"And this is all for a thesis?"

"Of course not, it's for me," Sara said gently. "You know this."

"Do you think you're headed for your Scholar phase?" Teddie pushed.

"Jesus, Teddie!" Heather raised a hand. "You can't just say things like that."

"She can here," Sara admonished. "This is the vault. We can discuss anything, because we are safe and contained, and I have held your confidences alongside my own, for many a year."

"Nice deflection, Mom." Teddie rolled her lithe form into a tight ball, her legs pulled against her chest, her head relaxed on the couch. Her hazel-flecked brown eyes locked on Sara's.

"The whole Scholar thing just doesn't resonate with me," she said. "I'm looking for the next bridge, the next obsession, something to light my fire."

Teddie went to speak, but Sara cut her off.

"It will not be a man," she said, kindness in her voice. "It might be a dog, but right now, I don't want the responsibility. My work is good; it's gripping. I have some fascinating patients and their sessions are insanely riveting, just a brutal, honest look at whether or not life can ever be worth living, or worthwhile."

"You aren't sharing their dilemma, are you?" Heather said, pointedly. It was almost impossible to get anything past her.

Sara looked Heather in the eye. "Their dilemma is the crux of all of our lives. Just because we live so much longer, it doesn't free us of the question of why we live, what we're supposed to do on this planet. I like to listen to them talk."

"Do you like them?" Heather asked.

"For the most part I do. They're all intelligent and compelling. The majority of them have pretty standard parental issues. And then some of them are too smart and sensitive for this world."

An image of Laura, standing in a filthy hallway, filled Sara's mind, and she stumbled to change the subject. "There's one last thing that we need to decide before approving Marguerite's request."

Teddie sat up, alert, and Heather raised a telltale eyebrow.

"Which one of you bitches wants to sign on as monitor?"

Heather shook her head.

"It's not out of cowardice," she said. "I've done it before, in Scotland."

"I know," Sara said.

"I'm swamped with admin," she continued. "Two sisters will be re-birthing this year, so I'm building the new identities, and if Marguerite is really gonna make someone, then that's a third identity. We have spares, of course, but I'll need to build the past history to match April Veronica's appearance."

"I know you're slammed," Sara said. "I've been meaning to ask you, do you need help? I can assign April Veronica to assist you once she's in the Lock."

Heather shook her head no. Sara wasn't surprised. Heather liked things done a certain way, hers. She'd rather work an extra day a week than take on an assistant.

"So it's me then," Teddie stated. "So, on top of not really wanting to let her make a new sister, I have to agree to..." she paused and gulped down the rest of her wine, "...kill someone. You guys know I'm a gold star girl. I ain't never killed anyone. I'm proud of that fact."

"Teddie, I know. And it's such a low likelihood thing. If I thought that was likely, I wouldn't be in favor of approving her. It's a formality. It's procedural. And, Theodora?"

"Yes?"

"If it gets to that point, I will be by your side. You won't have to do it alone."

Teddie closed her eyes and pondered for a moment, before nodding.

"Fine, okay, sure. I'll happily break my peaceful record because Marguerite needs a new pet."

"Thank you, Teddie," Sara said, slipping back into Mother mode. "I know the score, and if Marguerite doesn't settle down after she makes April Veronica, I'll be talking to her about changing Locks."

"Nobody wanna touch that bitch," Teddie said with a laugh. "I told you we should have left her in Madrid."

"Sometimes, you have to help a Lock that's at breaking point. It hasn't been that difficult."

"Easy for you to say," Teddie said. "You ain't been charged with killing a crazy bitch's new BFF."

Chapter Four

New York's spring showers were more like chilly monsoons, and Sara, vaulting over flooded gutters, wondered if snow was out of the question. Equipped with an invincible golf umbrella, knee high galoshes and a long, ugly waxed grey raincoat, Sara's walk to work was unpleasant and saturated. Wading across a small lake at 110th, she'd had to leap out of the way of a rat looking for anything to grab onto before it washed down to the filthy waterfall at Riverside Park.

When she arrived at her storm-darkened office on the outskirts of the Columbia campus, her socks somehow soaked through the rubber boots, she wasn't surprised by the messages already on her machine. Three of her four morning appointments were canceling. Exhaling at the end of the messages, only then realizing she'd been holding her breath in dread that her most fascinating patient was canceling too. He hadn't. She shook her head in anger at herself; she was too invested and too eager.

It was unprofessional.

After washing down two heems with a fresh cup of black coffee, Sara faced her unexpectedly empty two hours before the only remaining appointment. She fired off a series of texts dealing with the Marguerite problem, somehow not surprised when Heather replied immediately that she'd already had breakfast with Liz and "the issue has become a non-issue." Heather never let grass grow under her feet.

A rattling on her desk startled her. It was a Signal call coming in. Crina. She answered it immediately.

"My child, how are you?"

"Fine, for the most part, Mom. What's up?"

"I am calling to see how you felt after last night."

"It wasn't as bad as I expected so I feel good. Why?"

"There has been something else on my mind. I... well, I think it's time you considered stepping down."

Sara froze, mild paranoia flooding her mind. Crina continued before Sara could formulate a response.

"You are still doing a magnificent job, my love, please don't be offended. I think that it's merely time for you to have some me time."

"And what would I do with this me time?"

"You could come spend a few years with me. I'd love nothing more."

"That does sound lovely, Crina. But I'm not ready to go Scholar yet, and I haven't groomed anyone to take over."

"Everyone presumes the next mother will be Teddie."

Sara gritted her teeth. She hated gossip and nostalgia with a passion, because she saw them as toxic snowballs that interfered with the Lock life.

"I'm glad you're all talking about my replacement. What about Desdemona? She's been the mother of Madrid for twice as long as I've overseen New York."

"Right," Crina said, her voice suddenly bright. "Madrid is basically Miss Havisham's bedroom, a museum piece, nothing changes, nothing evolves. You've overseen the most progressive, integrated Lock in the world for one hundred and twelve years. You've weathered cultural shifts that Desdemona never even heard of. The work you've done has been backbreaking and also amazing. I'm so proud of you. But it would be remiss of me not to suspect that you are tired, that you need a break from this routine."

Sighing heavily, Sara glanced at the clock. She still had an hour.

Crina is right, she thought. And she's coming from a place of care.

"You know what? Thank you for being brave enough to say this to my face," Sara said, her voice wobbly. "The simple fact is, I don't know who I am outside of my job. Let me think on it, because you might be right."

"It ain't no big thing." Crina laughed. "Just come home with me after the confirmation hearing. We can hunt and fish like the old days, and we can talk for hours. I've missed you, Sara."

"I uh.. thank you, Mom, I've missed you too. That might be too soon, but I guess it's best to just rip off the band-aid."

"I'll prepare the spare room," Crina said. "Just in case."

"You know I hate to let you down."

"You never have," Crina said, her voice low. "I"ll let you get back to work, I just wanted to hear your voice, suddenly. I'm a sentimental old fool."

"And I'm luckier for it. I love you, Crina."

"Awww, you make an old woman blush." She paused. "Before I go, Sara, do not let Desdemona get away with shit. Promise?"

"I promise."

"Excellent. Thanks and I hope I'll see you in a couple of weeks. Get your bags packed."

Setting the phone back on her desk, Sara rocked back in her chair, her eyes gazing at the ceiling and the spiderwebs she never cleared. The tides of her Lock always pushed and pulled her, powerlessly, from one crisis to the next. She couldn't be annoyed at Heather, or Crina, for pointing out something that she could also see clearly but had not acknowledged.

She drank a second cup of coffee, absently looking at dogs on the North Shore Animal League Rescue website. Then she pulled the file for her remaining morning client, Silas, a gloomy, handsome oddball who just didn't fit into life, took every setback personally, and felt no joy in the day to day. He was unique in that, of all the people she'd treated in her current guise of Dr Lillian Berger, he was not a cry for help, or affection, or attention. He really did not connect with the world in any way that rewarded him. She had talked about him so much with Teddie that Teddie had given him a nickname: the ghost. It was apt. He was like a ghost, passing through his life in a transparent gauze, never catching on branches, never getting tangled in something that could brighten his outlook. Silas fully captured her attention, and she found his situation compellingly similar to her own.

She squeezed her eyes shut and pressed the heels of her hands against them. She was tired, but not in a way that sleep could help. She had loved and lost, she had fought, and she had enforced peace. Again and again. She felt like she had exhausted the spectrum of human existence after living through every iteration, every possible outcome of everything from a conversation to a fling to a relationship. She moved her browser from adoptable dogs to Spotify, and played her anthem of the moment, I've Seen It All by Björk. The lyrics sliced her to the core, a woman making excuses for losing interest in life, in a future.

Don't you ever get tired of being so negative?

I'm not negative, I'm honest, she argued with herself. Maybe life wasn't meant to be eternal. The thrill of science, of discovery, electricity, surgery, physics, philosophy, universal exploration, women's equality, all magical times to be alive, watching and hoping for the best.

The cynical malaise that gripped society at the start of the twenty first century bled into her bones slowly, before she even noticed, and by the time she realized that she had become jaded, humorless and flat, it was too late to turn the ship around.

Without warning, her mind returned to that night in Laura's dank apartment, a rapid jumble of slides in all senses – the sad visual squalor, the heart-crushing emotional wasteland, the dank aroma of mildew – culminating in what happened after. Sara knew what came next. This wasn't the first time her mind had done this to her. The final, unshakeable memory was of regaining consciousness with wet, cold flesh pressed against her hungry lips, simultaneous waves of repulsion and ecstasy rolling through her, uncontrolled. This time, her mind skipped back to her last moment with Laura when she was alive, saying she needed a shower, her eyes flat, absorbing and not reflecting light. The last moment Sara could have intervened and saved them both.

And then the tears started, heaving her chest, the first few sobs catching in her throat, then escaping in gasps, so raw they sounded almost animal. Pushing herself back in her chair, Sara tried to breathe deeply, every attempt thwarted by another convulsion of pain and sadness, choking her bitterly. Unable to stop the flow, she let herself bend forward, her head almost to her desk, frozen in the moment, so unable to cry herself out.

Eventually, the sobbing subsided and Sara was able to push herself upright, dragging the back of a wrist across both eyes until she could see to find the box of tissues on her desk. As she blew her nose, she still couldn't shake that last moment of eye contact with a doomed woman, her last chance to avoid whatever it was that the virus had done to her shortly after. Pushing the thought out of her mind from fear that she'd start crying again, Sara tapped her phone to see the time, gasping when she saw that she only had a few minutes before Silas was due to arrive.

You need to get your shit under control.

Yanking open her drawer, she dug around until she found a makeup compact. Flipping it open, she checked her reflection in the small mirror: her eyes were puffy and rimmed red, her cheeks wet. Angrily, she snatched two more tissues from the box and pressed them against her skin, grateful that she didn't wear makeup.

Her doorbell buzzed. Silas.

She hurried to reach for the buzzer on the desk, knocking her coffee --not enough to spill it but enough to slosh some onto his notes. Buzzing him in without speaking, she stood, breathing deeply to dispel the panic that was rolling around inside her, and straightened out her top. Then she pulled her hair behind her ears and put on the glasses she wore for his sessions even though she didn't need them. She was still tidying up her desk when Silas knocked on the inner door, and let himself in.

"Doctor Berger, hi!" he said affably, turning as he removed his long black coat and curiously dated bowler hat. Sara took stock of his outfit while his back was turned. He was dressed in a snug black cashmere sweater and black jeans that were darker from the knees down, soaked in rain. On his feet, weird waterproof boots. Almost instantly, the air filled with his mild cologne, notes of amber and leather and tobacco.

"Silas, I'm glad you could make it.," she said, her voice throaty and congested. "I...uh just spilled some coffee on your folder. If you'll just give me a minute, I'll fix that."

"You've been crying."

She stopped wiping the coffee from the paper, but didn't look up.

"Yes, I'm sorry, I... had some bad news. It's fine, it's just, I didn't have time to call and reschedule you. Especially not on a day like today." She gestured to the rain beating on the window.

"Well, please, take all the time you need. I can answer some emails if you need a minute."

Without another word, he settled into the client chair, whipped his phone out of his pocket and began tapping away. Sara tidied the top of her desk, glancing at his notes as if she hadn't memorized all of it anyway and sipping her coffee. Every now and then she stole a glance at him, noticing that his bowler hat hadn't done a great job of keeping his hair dry. His jet-black hair, normally swept back from his face, was plastered wetly to his scalp with little curls behind each ear. His handsome face, also wet, was smooth and freshly shaved. He looked almost peaceful. As if he sensed her staring, he looked up.

"Are we ready?" he asked. He seemed lighter today. "If you like, I can still reschedule."

"Sorry, yes, I apologize and also, today, we can talk as long as you like or need. I know boundaries are important, but, full disclosure, you're my last patient for the day."

"That's a lot of pressure to put on someone in my shoes, to come up with enough anguish to fill the rest of your rainy day."

"Of course," Sara said, visibly flustered. "The standard therapy hour it is."

"Dr Berger, I'm just messing with you," Silas said, his gaze softening. "I appreciate it, but I do have somewhere to be after this. So we can just play by the rules."

"So, how have you been this week?"

Silas shrugged, his eyes searching the corners of the ceiling. "Same old same old," he said eventually. "Lots of walking and thinking, lots of being yelled at by hipsters on bikes, hipsters in running shoes and hipsters walking dogs."

"Why were they yelling at you?"

"Guess I was in the way," he said, as if it was obvious.

"What else have you been doing since we last spoke? Have your moods improved?"

"My moods don't really improve," he said, clasping his hands together. "I'm pretty even-keeled, it's just that my keel is below the water. It's comfortable down here."

"Sometimes, I don't know if you're joking, or playing games with me,"

"I'm not. I'm being as honest as I can be. I know it's your mission to put me onto a path where life is sparkly and effervescent but that's not who I am, I suppose."

"Life is neither sparkly nor effervescent, all the time," Sara said, strangely on guard. "I'm sorry if I ever gave you that impression. I'm treating you for depression, but the alternative to depression is not a fairy tale life."

"Goshdarnit," Silas said, standing as if to leave. When he saw the flash of panic on Sara's face, he softened. "I'm sorry, Doctor Berger. All my jokes are falling flat today."

"To be honest, I feel like you're trying to entertain me, and that's not your job. Why don't you tell me what's been going on with you this week?"

"Okay." Silas settled back into his chair. "But I have a question. I have been to so many therapists, but you're the first one that I've wanted to know this about."

"Yes?"

"Does this line of work ever upset you?" His dark eyes fixed upon hers. "I feel like I know the answer but, honestly, I wanted to ask you before I got here today."

"Well, uh, yes, of course. I'm human. No matter how clinical my approach is, I never lose sight of the fact that I'm working with a fellow human being who is hurting."

"That's what I was thinking. I can sense that things people tell you can really get under your skin."

"Well," Sara said brusquely. "That means that I am failing professionally. I would like to reset this meeting. We aren't here to discuss me. I... uh, once again, let's get this meeting back on track. This isn't helping you."

"I disagree," Silas said, leaning forward in his chair. "This is the most interested I've been in a conversation in quite a while."

Sara sat quietly, unsure of what to say.

"Isn't this what you've wanted from me? For me to engage in things, to not pass things by without regard?"

Sara nodded. "Yes, but just not me. It's not supposed to be me."

"You are the only person I speak to regularly. I'm connecting to you. Is this not what we are working toward?"

"I'm sorry, Silas, this is outside the therapeutic bubble," Sara said, her voice flat. "Either we turn the conversation back on to you, or I am unable to continue this session."

"Okay, okay, Doctor Berger. Sorry, I was just messing with you again. Let's get to business. This week, I did nothing. I felt nothing. Was there anything exceptional that happened? No. Did I have thoughts surrounding the end of my life? Not in any real way. I guess you could say I've been keeping myself busy."

Swallowing loudly, not realizing how dry her throat had gotten, Sara slipped back into her psychiatrist mode, picking up her notepad from her desk.

"And what do you think changed in the past week?" Outside, the rain got heavier. Finally, Sara was able to slip into her work.

Chapter Five

After Silas left, Sara gave herself over to reverie, her only time-keeper the beat of raindrops on the window. Silas's session had been torture for her. She was distracted, messy and overly personal. She wondered what he had thought of her, and chastised herself all over again. For longer than an hour, Sara watched the rain trickle down her windowpanes, wondering if she, like Silas, was deeply depressed, and whether her grinding ennui could be healed with Xanax. She'd tried it a couple of times, but it made her less vigilant, and that, to her, was too much risk.

When the rain slowed to an annoying mist, she closed up her office and walked home, grabbing herself a bagel with lox from Absolute Bagel and a venti Americano from Starbucks. While she waited for her coffee, she texted Marguerite, who responded immediately.

They made an appointment to meet at 3 at Marguerite's apartment. The rain picked up again, and Sara barely made it to her door before the heavens reopened anew.

Freshly showered, her thick black hair tucked up inside a knit cap, Sara looked at herself in the mirror. Her wardrobe choices – yoga wear, an old shapeless sweater, leggings and memory foam slippers she bought for five bucks in Chinatown, never wanting to subject her feet to heels ever again – were deliberately disastrous. In her experience as Lock leader, the less officious the wardrobe, the less pushback she encountered at difficult meetings. Marguerite was tricky, and she'd definitely see through the gambit, though she'd also likely appreciate it as a peace gesture.

She was still freaked out by the breakdown in her office, finding herself using all of her professional training on herself to analyze whether it was just related to Laura's demise, or if it was stress-based, or something deeper. All of the above, she decided, making a mental note to have talk to Heather, the only New York Lock member who advised her, to see if she had any tips. Sara had studied Buddhism seriously, a long time ago, attracted by its peacefulness, but she had arrived at the decision that mindfulness was for the young, and their relatively empty minds. Staying in the moment wasn't going to dig her out of this particular hole.

Sighing, Sara moved to the brick wall in the back corner of her living room. Flicking two latches built into the brick wall, she leaned against it and it slid open with a groan. She stepped through into the dimly lit secret hallway that ran behind and connected all of the apartments in the complex. Waiting while her eyes adjusted to the dim yellow bulbs in the ceiling, she pushed the wall back into place, realizing as the latches clicked closed that she'd left her keys on the counter in the kitchen. She'd have to get someone to let her back into her own apartment, and that someone could not be Marguerite.

When the block of land on West End Avenue became available, over a century earlier, Sara built her masterwork: What appeared to be separate apartment buildings on all four sides of the block was actually a single edifice, connected in the back by a labyrinth of tunnels and hallways. This enabled the women to come and go from different buildings whenever they rebirthed as a new identity. Rent from other buildings scattered around Manhattan and Brooklyn provided sizeable income, the overages of which were donated to scholarships and support networks for women.

April Veronica, Marguerite's potential new Lock member, had come up through this program, an orphan bouncing around the foster system. Marguerite took April Veronica under her wing when she was working on her PhD, on a scholarship from their order. Since then, Sara had often gone on observation missions to oversee her progress, and the young woman did seem to have the strength and intelligence required of all sistren, as well as the interest in philosophy and existential study.

As she walked along the dimly lit, airless hallway, she wondered if she would have made April Veronica if she'd encountered her first. The truth was, since she made Teddie, Sara had never entertained the thought of making another sister.

She passed the door to the storage room, which Heather had taken to calling the Room Of Requirement. Sara smiled, envisioning all the weird old things that were stored in there. Looms, medieval weapons, strange, outdated tools that were kept mainly for sentimental reasons. She decided to ask Heather to meet her there later, so they could talk openly, surrounded by things from their pasts that made them happy.

After living here for well over a century, she didn't need to count the doors. Arriving at the door to Marguerite's apartment, Sara rapped her knuckles on the bare brick, and within seconds, she heard the latch clear its teeth. The door swung open, nearly hitting her, revealing Marguerite in a geometric hot pink and black robe, her raven hair bouncing in new curls, her makeup heavy and bold.

"You're dressed up to stay in," Sara said, leaning forward and kissing the other woman on both cheeks.

"Sometimes I just like to be fabulous," Marguerite said with a neutral smile. "Please, come in, I've made coffee. You look a bit green, do you need a heem?"

Sara fought to maintain her poker face. She had taken more than anyone knew, but she still needed more.

"You know what? That would be great," Sara said. "I got caught up at work and the rain has got me like..."

Without another word, Marguerite reached into a pocket in her robe, handing Sara a full bottle of capsules. She then turned and walked down the short corridor to her living room, following the scent of a complex, robust coffee brew. While she was gone, Sara opened the bottle and poured five pills into her palm. She put two into her mouth and pocketed the rest, resealing the jar as Marguerite returned with a tray with a pot of coffee, some cups and a plate of shortbreads.

"You seem tense," Sara said. "There's no need for that, Marguerite. I think that we are moving in the right direction for April Veronica's confirmation."Marguerite paused, turning slowly, one eyebrow raised.

"Seems like you and I are getting very different stories, mija," she said, her voice flat as she poured two mugs of coffee, holding one aloft for Sara.

"I don't know, Marguerite," Sara said, taking the coffee and sitting in the loveseat across from her. "It's always a process, and we—"

"Madre mio, for once, spare me the party line bullshit, Sara," Marguerite interrupted. "Can we please speak plainly?"

"I'm happy to speak plainly, but I fear you won't like what you hear," Sara said, taking a quick sip of the too-hot coffee to mask her sigh.

"I'm a big girl. Hit me." Marguerite fixed her chocolate eyes on Sara's.

"Okay, here we go. There is some understandable resistance considering the failure of your previous convert."

"I assumed so."

"Well, it's also something you've been... reluctant to discuss."

"It was a youthful error. The Spanish Flu forced my hand."

"You attempted to convert a Christian, which is against the tenets."

"I did not realize the depth of her faith, and like I said, she contracted the flu, it was then or never. And I cleaned up my mess. I. Nobody else. I. And it was a nightmare, it replays in my mind over and over. Do the sistren not realize that it haunts me still? No. Nobody walks in my shoes. Nobody knows my pain. They just think that somehow, I was born a bitch."

Sara looked into the oily depths of her coffee, realizing that she hadn't given too much thought to the formative events in Marguerite's life. She knew about the failed convert, but if she'd ever heard the details, her mind had filed them as unimportant, and then written over them.

"April Veronica is not like her," Marguerite continued. "She is without faith, if anything, a little too much. Like many of her generation, she is almost a blank slate when it comes to spirituality."

"She is also a millennial," Sara said. "Locks around the world have reported issues with attempts to convert members from her generation. You do realize that no other Lock has brought a millennial so close to confirmation? Millennials 'do not like to follow rules,' they are all about the 'life hack' and the 'instant grat' and also, they've been raised without consequences. Padded playgrounds, helicopter parents, these kids never get hit hard by their mistakes, never suffer consequences. Marguerite, you know how grave *our* consequences are. This life is not for everyone."

"Broad strokes are never terribly accurate," Marguerite said, frustration in her voice. "Yes, she is of an age, yes, she is technically a millennial, but she has been under my tutelage for eight years. I will be aging out of this identity within the next year, and I will not be able to contact her again if I'm not able to help her convert before that time."

"I understand the time crunch," Sara said. "I've asked Teddie to step in, if things go wrong."

"What for? I never asked for her help."

"And she doesn't want to offer it," Sara said. "But that's exactly what I'm talking about. You've never been pleasant to Teddie, but she agreed to step up and do something she's never done before. And instead of being appreciative, you get thorny."

Marguerite blinked very slowly, inhaling deeply.

"I'm sorry. That is a very fair point, and I apologize. I'm caught unawares, and a little humbled that she agreed to do it. That surprises me."

"I think a lot of the women would surprise you, if you'd just..."
"Yes?"

"Be nicer," Sara blurted out, before sipping her coffee again and scalding her tongue.

"I'm nicer than Liz. To everyone. And it's just—"

"Let's not get sidetracked, Marguerite. We can work on your internal relationships after the confirmation. I just wanted to make you see that you'll be asking a lot from the Lock, and it's really up to you to foster relationships so that people don't begrudge the extra work."

"I said I would do extra work. I will go without blood if we run short."

"It's not about that. It's about asking Teddie to kill a human being if your instinct proves to be flawed."

Marguerite nodded slowly.

"Yes, but I'm certain it will not come to that."

"And that's your problem," Sara said, bluntly. She didn't have the energy to be political. "You're not certain. None of us can be about these things. Making a new sister is fraught with peril, and so much of it is unpredictable. As much as I endorse April Veronica, you and I both know that many things can go wrong."

"Please take this the right way." Marguerite held her steaming coffee in front of her face, as if warding off a blow. "This Lock is functioning for everyone except me. I am unpopular, and my work is not appreciated."

Sara nodded.

"You're thorny. It's your nature to be thorny. We knew that when we accepted your transfer from Madrid. And I accept that we are all free to be our true selves, but seriously, Marguerite..."

"Yes?"

Sara took a big sip of her coffee, then fixed her gaze on the combative woman.

"Would it fucking kill you to be easygoing? Would it be impossible for you to get along with, and maybe even be friends with, any of us?"

Marguerite's eyes widened and rolled.

"Si, si, it's all my fault. Do you even see how political this Lock is? I'm just not into playing games."

"This Lock is no different from any other Lock in the world. We are not politicians, we are human beings. We have a set of rules, we obey the set of rules, which is a small price to pay for our life."

"The rules are nothing but surface. The real instruction is in our hearts, in our souls, and that is where I'm coming up short here. I have been open to relationships with my sisters, but none have felt the same."

"You and I both know that is not the truth," Sara said. "You attack, you belittle, and you criticize. You swan around, shit talking this and laughing at that. You hurt people's feelings. You've been our artist in residence for how long? And pity the sister who asks you for help." Sara paused, catching her breath, starting again before Marguerite could interrupt. "

Imagine if Teddie asked you to help her with something? You'd blow her off without a second thought."

"You've guarded that woman like a wolf, since before I got here. She has had a charmed life. Her hands are clean."

"My point," Sara said firmly, "is that I am asking a woman who owes you nothing, a woman who supplies the blood that you drink, a woman who has never broken a rule in her life, to agree to potentially murder someone, for the first time in her life."

"Take this the right way, but boo fucking hoo." Marguerite made a crying face, actually wringing her fists in front of her eyes. "I mean, congratulations, Theodora, on being able to keep the blood off your hands for so long, but you and I both know that the foundation of Lock life is violence. Our Orders came into being on the back of bloody slaughter, and we can pretend as much as we like, but we are still feudal, and we shed blood when required."

"This is exactly what I'm talking about," Sara said, her voice steel. "Instead of accepting that someone is about to do you a favor that costs them more than it costs you, you fly off the handle and give me an ethics lecture. I'm talking about mutual effort."

"I worked as a nurse through three identities back to back. I worked in the Bronx, Queens and Staten fucking Island, for almost thirty years. Did any of those women thank me when I fed them?"

"Is that why you don't thank Teddie? No, wait, don't answer that. *I* thanked you, Marguerite. And you always shrugged me off. And that's what I'm talking about. What is stopping you from being friends with these women? They're all so different. There must be someone that you enjoy, someone you can engage with?"

Marguerite shook her head angrily and Sara was shocked to see tears forming in her lower lashes.

"There are two cliques, and you know it. And neither of them has room for me. It's fine. I know it's weird to make a sister just so I have company, but that's the way it's unfolding."

"What I know is, things change. Constantly. Today's cliques are short lived. In ten years, who knows who will be hanging out with whom? All I'm asking is, why the hell can't you make it a little easier to get close to you?"

"Please don't tell me I need to become some Little Women fantasy, an opinion-free autodidact who only speaks the party line."

Funny, Sara thought, that's exactly how I live, but whatever.

"Look, I didn't come here to criticize you, and I also didn't come here to pep talk you into making friends with your Lock. It's your eternity to manage, and if you want to do it alone, then fine."

"That's why I believe now is the time for me to make April Veronica," Marguerite said, the flame in her eyes dwindling. "She and I have very complementary personal interactions. She is blunt like me, she suffers fools with the same iron tongue."

"Well, that's the damn problem right there. Nobody in any Lock anywhere wants to multiply a problem, and Marguerite, it's time for me to be very honest with you. If this doesn't work out, I will have to talk to other Locks about your potential transfer."

Marguerite froze mid-sip.

"I've tried to guide you as best I can in a way that will make peace for all of us, but you continue to be incredibly incendiary."

"You can go," Marguerite said. "Just go."

"I can't go. I need to reach accord with you on this, and I need to do it today. You have some very valid points. You've done all of the work that you need to do, and there is no reason we haven't given you the permission. Well, there *are* reasons and that is what I'm hoping to iron out, but you're already dismissing me."

A tear plopped out of Marguerite's eye, trailing mascara along her coffee-colored cheek.

"Do you think that was fun for me?" she said, her voice thickening. "To learn that your sisters all view you so poorly that you get sent off like a rescue dog? To arrive in a city where my reputation preceded me to the point where I could not get treated fairly by any of you, and I—"

"It wasn't your reputation, old friend," Sara said. "I'm not here to dredge up past events, but you arrived in this town with both guns blazing and a take-no-prisoner attitude."

"Oh, sorry, I should have come in like a grateful abused dog, licking your asses and begging to be liked?"

"Why do you have to be like this?" Sara said, a reed of anger in her voice. "We were excited to meet you and to welcome you. You blew into town, after so much careful planning on our part for your travel and your new life, and you hated everything, told us that you hated this awful old building, and then you hid out in that apartment for several years, contributing nothing, but consuming your share of sustenance. It's unfair for you to cling to this notion that you weren't welcome. You were. I was there."

Marguerite exhaled loudly.

"Sara, I appreciate your candor, I really do. The answer is simple. I probably should never have been made. I'm abrasive. I have never felt like I was part of this secret society. That said, I love my life and I love what the Curse has given me. My life of artistic exploration and philosophy has been the greatest reward. I'm just not a warm and fuzzy person. I'm kind of just an old bitch." She laughed, drily, and reached for her coffee.

Sara watched intently, suddenly wondering if Marguerite had ever drawn a thrill from breaking a tenet, wishing she could ask, knowing she'd never get an honest answer. She knew from her therapy work that women still spanked their kids, and then kept it as a dark secret from other mothers.

"We're all old bitches." Sara smiled. "I actually came here to tell you that you finally have the votes to move to the next phase of April Veronica's process. I'll tell the Lock to break out the nun costumes."

"Wait, what?" A surprised smile spread across Marguerite's face. "I'm not sure I follow."

"Like I said, you've fulfilled your side of the bargain. Honestly, you shouldn't have had to work this hard. And Marguerite?" Sara paused and the Spaniard cocked her head. "You need to thank Heather and Teddie, because they worked on the holdouts. They helped you."

Marguerite placed her coffee mug on the table and clasped her hands in front of her heart. "Why did you toy with me like this?"

"I wasn't toying. I just didn't want this to be something minor. It was a big, difficult decision, and it's only fair that you know that a lot of work happened behind the scenes to make it happen."

"I understand." Marguerite bowed her head. "Thank you, Sara. I will go to see those women tonight, I will thank them like they've never been thanked. And April Veronica. You'll see. She is very good, and I think she will make a very beneficial addition to our little group."

Sara nodded. "I hope so."

"So, how are you?" Marguerite fixed her with a stare. "I've been getting a very strange vibe from you, over the past years. Maybe you need a man."

"My man days are behind me," Sara said. "I am considering getting a dog."

"Save that for your Scholar days." Marguerite waved a dismissive arm in the air. It was well known that on top of everything else, she hated pets. "Just drop your expectations and go date for a while, it's good distraction."

"You sound like Teddie."

"That girl does it right," Marguerite said, laughing. "I wish I had her chutzpah."

"She sure is something," Sara said. "I'm going out with her, tonight, to a bar, and she's gunning to get me laid."

Marguerite nodded, then theatrically performed the benediction at her. "I hope that you have sex with a skilled gentleman, and I also hope that it takes some of that tension out of your shoulders."

"I'm afraid that would take more than sex. It would take a sledge-hammer and a boatload of valium. And now I really need to get back to my apartment. I'll timetable the confirmation process and I'll let you know as soon as it's locked down. Is that it?" She drained her coffee and stood to leave.

Marguerite smiled. "You surprised me, Sara. And you've made me see that just maybe, I can fit in. That means more than you can know. I have some work ahead of me. But thank you."

"I'm glad," Sara said. "Don't get up. I'll let myself out."

"Have a good night, girl," Marguerite said, her attention already on her iPhone. "I hope he curls your toes."

Chapter Six

"There are titties everywhere!" Sara laughed, glancing around the bar that Teddie had pushed her into after a sudden downpour curtailed their search for a new bar when Teddie's first choice didn't pan out.

"Yes, Mom. It's called BOOBIES. Is this okay or do we need to keep searching?"

The first stop of the evening, a pitch-black hipster blur called Mood Ring, had raised Sara's hackles almost instantly. Swarmed by handsy fake-id urban beekeeper types, the air thick with dry ice fog and techno, Sara instantly shut down. Before they even made it up to the bar, Teddie, who recognized the signs all too well, snatched Sara by the wrist, hauling her out onto busy Myrtle Avenue.

"This seems fine," Sara said, struggling to sound positive about a gimmick bar based on childish calculator smut code 800813. At earlier times in their shared life, Sara had loved nightlife, and she and Teddie became mainstays on various scenes as long as they could without becoming memorable. Prohibition bars, Coltrane at Birdland, Studio 54 and CBGBs had all in turn occupied their hearts and given them a brief period of belonging to something exciting. The twenty-first century, though, with its fragmented scenes and the emerging generation's reluctance to waste money on liquor, added up to a big snooze for Sara. She felt a reverie start, her mind hearkening back to the last time she went bar hopping with Teddie.

"I mean, I like it so far, I can hear myself think, there's some light, and nobody has grabbed my ass. But I don't know why we couldn't just go to that great bar we went to last time."

"Honeygirl," Teddie said as she bellied up to the bar. "That was Matchless. That closed years ago."

Sara gave her friend a disbelieving look as she cast her mind back to that night. It was definitely not in the past year, but she just couldn't believe that multiple years passed since then.

"Teddie, have I become that person?"

A nonbinary bartender with smiling eyes and tasteful face tattoos rocked up to Teddie, recognizing her.

"I'll have the usual, Juniper," Teddie said. "And my friend will have a double Patron soda with two limes."

When you've been drinking with someone for two hundred years, their choice of cocktail became a secret code. By ordering a double of a drink that Sara loved and would down quickly, she was saying that tonight was a fun night, no business talk, no Lock shit. A friend night, she called it. Sara shrugged and smiled at the bartender as they handed her her drink. "Thanks."

"Hey, there's a table." Teddie moved so swiftly that Sara made a mental note to remind her friend, for the one billionth time, to watch herself in public. In the blink of an eye, Teddie, her drink and her pink and orange velour jumpsuit appeared at a newly vacated table, the wreckage of a Jenga game and two empty glasses on its surface.

Sara plopped herself down at the table.

"Hey, Captain Marvel, you need to can it with the speedy moves."

"That's Okoye to you," Teddie said, refusing to be chastened. "Get your superheroes race-right. Cheers."

Sara raised her drink, touching it to her lips, still unable to relax.

"Hey, can we swap seats? I don't like having my back to the room."

Teddie did a dramatic sigh and shook her head.

"Nope. I gotchu girl. Anyone starts shit, I'll move you out the way."

Sara slumped into her chair and began to fiddle with the Jenga pieces, needing to either put them neatly back into their box or start another game.

"Wanna play?" she asked meekly.

"Sure," Teddie said, surprising her. "But I'll build the tower while you focus on your drink."

Sara gave a weak smile. She was certain that Teddie had a pretty good idea that she was burning out, but the fact that they were here, in a breast-themed young people bar in Brooklyn instead of in front of a tribunal, told Sara that Teddie did not suspect just how dark she had gotten.

Obediently draining her drink, Sara sat back and watched as her best friend dexterously rebuilt the tower of wooden rods. Teddie was her delightful rock. Strong, smart and very wise, she hid her true self under a very believable, carefree exterior. "I ain't getting wrinkles over nobody's shit" was her favorite response, made funnier by the fact that nobody who got made got any additional wrinkles after that point in their life.

"You're going first," Teddie said. "Make your strategy move while I'm getting us refills."

"This time, just a single please," Sara said, as winningly as she could muster, and still failing.

"I'm sorry, I don't speak boring." Teddie laughed, moving with cartoon slowness in the direction of the bar. "This okay for you?" she called over her shoulder.

Sara turned her attention to the Jenga, her eyes scanning up and down its sides, looking for an easy pull. How many games of Jenga were in her past? She banished the thought. Could someone's thousandth game of Jenga be as fun as their first? Sistren were taught that the answer "has to be yes" and that it was up to them to find their own way to find joy in things. Sara's answer was always that it depended on the company, nothing more, and for that she knew that she was lucky to have Teddie, and her unpredictable, huge heart.

If anything, her love for Teddie was what kept her on track for so long, and now, considering an end for her life, it was leaving Teddie that held her back. In the past she had given herself a panic attack just imagining that conversation, telling Teddie she planned to surrender. There was no scenario in which Teddie would actually let her go through with it.

A raucous cheering from the bar area interrupted her introspection. Glancing up, Sara could see that Juniper was now dancing on the bar top, waving a rusty old pair of dressmaking scissors above their head. The crowd parted slightly, and Sara saw a young guy in torn shorts and a stripy woman's blouse dancing in time with the bartender. As the crowd's cheering grew unbearably loud, Juniper swooped down and chopped off the patron's man-bun, holding the fashion offense aloft as the crowd roared.

A chant began. "Burn it! Burn It!" Juniper shook their head, before theatrically impaling the knot of hair onto a spike sticking out of the wall above the cluttered bar. Squinting in the darkness, Sara realized that the odd things on the wall were indeed other doomed man-buns, all severed and impaled the way Cursed men used to do to humans. She shuddered at the memory, then joined in the cheering, her mood suddenly buoyed by the tequila in her bloodstream, and the good, simple humor of a happy crowd.

Stirring the ice in her glass and watching Teddie at the bar Sara got a sudden feeling that someone was behind her. A gentle hand on her shoulder confirmed it.

"Lillian? I mean, Doctor Berger?"

Sara recognized the voice immediately, and then the cologne confirmed it. It was Silas. She composed herself and turned very slowly, seeing Silas's wide, friendly face, his dark brown eyes absorbing the dim bar light like two tiny black holes.

"Silas, how are you?"

"I'm good!"

Sara stood and leaned in close to his ear.

"I'm required by law to tell you that I am willing to leave the premises immediately. I'm sorry that this has happened, I didn't expect our paths to cross out here in Bushwick."

Silas's face fell.

"Oh, Doctor Berger, no, I'll go. I'm sorry, I got caught in the storm and just came in here for a quick drink on my way home. I don't want to spoil your night. I'll take off."

Silas turned back to the doorway. Outside the storm had intensified, with visible walls of rain slashing to the ground.

"Well, you can't leave in *that*," Sara said. "Look, I guess we can make small talk until the rain eases. If it doesn't, I'll call us both a water taxi."

Silas laughed. "Well, what can I get you from the bar?"

Sara looked at Silas. His face was happier than she could remember seeing, his dark eyes now sparkling with something approaching mischief. Her first response was to decline the drink, but something in her just couldn't knock him down. He looked happy adjacent, and she knew that was a fragile state. She glanced over at Teddie, who was doing shots with the newly shorn hipster and joking with Juniper.

"No, sit, please. My friend is at the bar. I'll text her your order."

"I'll take a tequila soda please," Silas said, pulling up a threadbare footstool and easing himself down to the table.

"How many limes?"

"Two, of course," he replied, his attention on the Jenga pile.

Whipping out her phone, Sara fired off a text to Teddie.

Hi it's Lillian, can you get my patient Silas The Ghost the same drink you're getting me? Thx.

Keeping her phone raised as if she was texting, Sara stole a glance at Silas, and, after making sure he was focused on the table, allowed herself a longer look. His hair, again bedraggled from the rain, hung in near-curls, droplets of water bouncing with each movement. Brown kind eyes, long lashes, and stubble around his full lips.

Snap out of it, sister!

"So," she began, unsure of what she'd planned to say next.

"So?" Silas said, a broad grin making his eyes dance.

"Huh?"

"Usually, so is the gateway word to a sentence," he said, his eyes never leaving hers.

"Sorry." Sara laughed, hating how nervous it sounded. "It's just that fraternization with patients outside of the therapy bucket is danger-ous. I'm just not sure how to get around it but I do not want to watch you drown on Myrtle Avenue."

"What if I fire you as my therapist?"

"What if you what?" Teddie said loudly as she tried to figure out where to put the three cocktails she was juggling. "Somebody help a sister out?"

Sara deftly wrapped her fingers around two of the glasses, passing one to Silas.

"Nakeah," she said, using Teddie's current outside-world name, "this is my friend Silas." Teddie did her worst poker face as they shook hands, her eyes darting from Silas's to Sara's and back again.

"So did anyone make a move while I was gone?" Teddie smiled knowingly until a sharp kick at her shin changed it.

Silas glanced from one to the other.

"Is everything okay?" he asked.

"Sorry, Silas, apparently I'm interrupting. I'll leave you two to the scandalous pastime that is Jenga."

A little too quickly once again, Teddie was back at the bar, joking with the haircut hipster.

"You didn't have to make her leave," Silas said. "Now I feel like I've wrecked your night."

"Not at all," Sara said. "She did that whole thing just so she had an excuse to go hit on that dude."

"She would have left you alone?"

"No. That's my point. Your turning up has given her a hall pass, she doesn't have to babysit boring old me all night."

"Self-pity, thy name is Doctor Berger."

"Look, for tonight, please just call me Lily," she said. "The doctor stuff just seems weird in a bar devoted to mammary glands."

"It really is. I gather this is your first time here?"

"Silas, in the interest of your treatment, the best thing for us to do here is sip our drinks and play a few rounds of Jenga and then we can go our separate ways."

"Didn't you hear me? I fired you as my therapist, like all of two minutes ago. So drop that shrink crap and let me thrash you at Jenga."

Sara did not know what to do, and the sensation was enjoyable. Every instinct she had was telling her to get up and leave, but at the same time, another voice told her that the damage was done. She had breached the therapeutic barrier with a patient, a depressed one at that. Professionally, she was bound to hand him to another therapist, but personally, she doubted that his low commitment to counseling would weather a change in therapists.

"My professional advice would be that you don't fire me, and that we finish this game, and we never speak of this again. But," she paused, trying to avoid his eyes glinting above his raised drink, "the decision is yours to make. If you feel that this encounter has compromised my ability to treat you, then I am indeed fired."

Silas pushed himself away from the table dramatically, causing the pile of wooden rods to waver. Rising to his feet, a smirk playing at the corners of his mouth, he locked eyes with Sara, who was cursing her decision to accompany Teddie out on a weeknight.

"I'm sorry, Silas," she began.

"Sorry? I'm heading to the bar. You just got fired. We need to celebrate!"

With that, he turned and sidled in between Teddie and a group of patrons who definitely looked too young to be drinking. A wave of panic ran through Sara like a chill and she decided to ghost. She loved ghosting and had been doing it for centuries before it was given such a cute name.

Yes, that's it. One more drink and then I'm out. No callbacks, self.

Sara shook her head at her own ridiculousness. Arguing with one's self was what she imagined Scholars did for years at a time.

"A penny for your thoughts?"

Silas was back in his seat, handing a drink to her. That was bad. He'd crept up on her. She needed to be more vigilant. Alcohol affected her slowly, and she wasn't even feeling tipsy from the first two drinks. Maybe this third one was a bad idea.

Lately, you haven't met a bad idea that you haven't liked.

She took the drink and raised it.

"Thanks, Silas. So tell me, what brings you out on a night like this?"

"Well, the forecast was for scattered showers, and I like walking when it's raining. Gently. Instead, we got this... what is it? Biblical flood? End times?"

"You got me there." Sara laughed, relaxing slightly. "Let's go with flood."

"So, yeah. I like the peace of walking at night. Just sampling other people's lives, peering in windows, watching to see what normal people do in their homes."

"That's w—"

"I know it's weird."

"I wasn't going to say weird."

"Yes, you were, and you caught yourself because it's a judgement word."

"Uh, ok, Silas. It is weird. It is weird to walk around on a rainy night and spy on strangers."

"I may have oversimplified. The snooping is a tiny part, it's not a stop and stare thing, it's a briefly acknowledge and keep walking kind of thing. I love that about New York. It's countless, literally countless apartments, all of them containing a full life. It's a universe of different people, all doing a unique life. It's just kind of reassuring that all of this happens independently. Whether I'm here or not."

Sara winced.

"Am I really fired as your therapist?"

Silas nodded.

"Well, then I have to ask, would you talk existentially with any other woman on a date?"

"Is this a date?"

Sara felt her cheeks burn. She'd nearly choked on the word, knowing it was wrong as it passed her teeth.

"Of course it's not a date," she said, hurriedly finishing her drink. "It's a casual encounter. And mental health is not an appropriate subject for one of those either."

"Sorry, my bad," Silas said. "I just get in my head too much, trying to explain things. I've never been good at separating what should stay in my brain and what should come out my mouth."

"Welcome to my world," Sara said. Her third drink was finished. She knew she should leave. She fixed her cutest smile on Silas. "Want another?"

To her dismay she realized she was flirting. And she was rusty, so rusty at it. She felt awkward, like she was wearing clown shoes. Something in Silas's face changed, but Sara wasn't paranoid to think it was about her. After decades in mental health, she knew the face. He was listening to his inner voice. She wasn't surprised when he shook his head.

"No, Lily, thank you. I... uh... this has been a sweet surprise, but I should get back to my walking."

As Silas stood and reached to shake her hand, she tripped on her imaginary clown shoes and half-fell back to her seat.

"Weird flex but okay," he said with a gentle smile. "I'll call you tomorrow." He paused and gazed out into the street where the rain had stopped completely. "Looks like I've timed it perfectly. Good night. Tell your friend I said goodbye."

She watched him weave deftly through the bar patrons, disappointed that he did not look back before vanishing from sight as he walked up the sidewalk.

"You're ridiculous," she hissed at herself. A quick glance at the bar showed Teddie and the former man-bun owner locked in a tight kiss.

When Teddie opened one eye and looked at her, Sara hitched her thumb in the direction of the door, then made a call me motion with her hand. Teddie managed a quick thumbs-up before returning to her prey. Sara pulled her coat on and called an Uber.

Safely back in her bed, Sara battled wave after wave of confused, anxious thoughts. Her cavalier response to seeing Silas outside of her practice was unconscionable. Forced to admit that she was either attracted to or fascinated by Silas, she was also forced to confront the selfish, unforgivable position she had taken, flirtatious levity with a depressed patient.

Former patient.

And now was not the time that Silas should be without a counselor. She rolled the situation around in her head for hours as sleep eluded her; a heady brew of regret and self-recrimination kept her tossing and turning as the hours clicked by. When dreamy tendrils finally clouded her thoughts just before dawn, Sara relaxed at last, knowing that sleep was finally coming to take her.

Ding.

Sighing, she considered silencing her phone but of course, she grabbed it and tilted it so she could read. Teddie, already up for work, with details of last night's sexual escapades. Sara would read the whole thing later, marveling at Teddie's stamina. When she was Teddie's age, Sara had certainly kept a similar pace, with both socializing and men. These days, just the thought of chasing men exhausted her, much less actually catching them. She was happy to live vicariously through Teddie, and frequently devoted whole evenings to listening to her friend's post-date analyses.

Morning check-in texts began to pour in. It was standard practice to text back to the main building any time a sister changed locations, and somehow, Sara had become the recipient for everyone's updates.

The first set were from Heather, Yukari and Eleanor, all working out in their apartments before work. "You're only as old as your hips," Heather was fond of saying, and she was right. All sisters the world over practiced yoga daily. Sara tried to remember the last time she'd done her daily practice, and couldn't. She wished she could join a gym or go to a yoga studio, or at least, she wished she'd known about such things when she'd created the plans for this compound, using eight different architects, none of whom suspected the scope of their work.

Arriving to set up the New York Lock in 1706, Sara purchased plots of land and existing buildings around New Amsterdam, with monies provided by the Great Locks of Europe, under the aegis of the Sisters of Holy Silence, the ancient Catholic order that all Locks operated under. Pretending to be nuns afforded them a lot of freedom, and anonymity, but it was still important to always remain prudent.

A reverie is not sleep, Sara reprimanded herself angrily, grimacing at the thought of a day at the office on no sleep.

Ding.

> Sorry I ghosted. Hope you got home safely.

Silas. Forcing her hand. Now she had to reply, and a reply would mean that she had a choice: To attempt to simply resign as his therapist and never see him again, or to take the other route, a route she'd never taken before, and transition a patient to what? A friend?

Ridiculous.

She texted back.

> I did, thank you. Hope your walk was

She paused. What? Fun? A walk through saturated Bushwick on a weeknight could not be fun. Or any other adjective she could think of.

> Therapeutic.

She hit send. He replied immediately.

> It was interesting. Bit chilly. I was wondering if you'd like to maybe have dinner with me at some point?

Sara tossed her phone from one hand to the other, back and forth, like worry beads. Finally she replied.

> If I say yes to dinner, it means we can never have a professional relationship again. I'm not sure that is the right decision for you at this stage in your treatment. Sorry.

Standing upright, she shook her head to untangle the cobwebs. A text came in and she looked at her phone.

> I need a date more than I need a shrink. How's tonight? Dinner and a night walk? I want to show you what I get up to, so you don't think I'm weird.

> I think you're weirder now than I did before. OK. I'll say yes. Tell me where to be and when.

She shook her head, shucked her pajamas and headed to the shower. In her stomach, a lightness fluttered. As she waited for the water in the shower to heat up, the lightness reached her chest. She was excited.

She'd never expected flaming out to feel so good.

Chapter Seven

The jumble of clothes piled on top of her bed, rejected candidates for her evening's outfit, infuriated Sara. She clenched her fists, then angrily rifled through the pile, again discarding everything as unsuitable. This wasn't a date. This "meeting" with Silas in just over an hour from right now was not a date. It was a meal. Just a meal. And even if it was just a meal, she didn't have anything to wear. Of course it made perfect sense that sistren members dressed in drab fashions: it was key to not being memorable. It just didn't help on nights when one might want to be... ugh. Memorable.

This is not a date.

She briefly considered calling Teddie, for either fashion advice or loaner clothes, but that would mean admitting that she was seeing Silas and then the ribbing would be relentless.

Lingerie was the one thing that sistren could indulge in, but Sara hadn't bought anything new in longer than she could remember. Heather had gifted her some fancy English lingerie several Christmases ago, when was that? So long ago that moths had probably feasted on it. Where was it? Dropping to her knees, Sara crawled to the back of her closet, over shoes and random boxes of mystery contents. She could remember the box, sleek and black with embossed gold leaf lettering. She just couldn't find it. Angrily, she backed out of the closet and stood up, breathing heavily. Her wet towel suddenly felt clammy against her skin and she undid it and let it fall to the floor. Catching sight of herself in the mirror, she paused.

"You need to calm down," she said to the mirror. "There's no chance that anyone is seeing your underwear."

Agreeing with herself, she stepped into the least voluminous undies she could find, then pulled a plain white sports bra over her head. Looking in the mirror, she really did not like the way her breasts flattened.

"It's cold out, Sara," she scolded her reflection. "This will all be buried under layers."

A burst of inspiration struck, and she darted to her closet, shoving aside the row of boring day wear, flipping past her arctic fox fur until she came to a zippered-up black silk garment bag, its rich fabric deliciously smooth to her fingertips. Snatching it, she yanked it out of the closet and laid it on her bed. Unzipping it slowly, slightly afraid to see a moth fly out, she uncovered a wonderfully simple black Chanel dress that she had acquired back in the forties or fifties. Fifties, she decided after a quick mental cataloging. This dress, plus black tights and a cashmere cardigan.

"And then bury the whole thing under a puffer," she muttered as she pulled the tights from their package. A brief impulse to cancel crossed her mind and she paused, considering.

"Nope." She clicked her fingers, banishing the potentially derailing thought process. "Suck it up. It's an early dinner. He will probably either ghost you or leave suddenly during dinner."

She continued dressing, her reverie-prone mind trying to catch her on any number of unrelated thoughts. Earlier that afternoon she had sent a blanket email to the entire Lock, Scholars and all, advising that it was time to begin the indoctrination of a new novitiate, and she'd set a meeting time for the following Saturday "in chambers" which was code for either of two meeting rooms housed in the central basement of their complex. As soon as the email hit, the phone calls started, and the rest of her day was spent in a chain of discussions. Liz and Eleanor, as always, saw a bargaining opportunity, though what they ultimately wanted wasn't yet fully clear. They finally agreed that the process could begin, and Sara sensed Heather's behind the scenes intervention. That woman could bring peace to any situation. Sara envied her patience.

Slipping the highest button on the Chanel dress through its buttonhole by her throat, Sara stepped back to admire her outfit. She looked like she was headed out for a spot of shopping. In Paris. Fifty years ago. The plans to wear her hair in a ponytail felt cliched, so she shook her hair out of the knot it was in, letting it tumble down past her shoulders. She begrudgingly admitted she looked okay.

Moving to the bathroom, she chose a subtle burgundy lip and a very mild smoky eye. She finished with a light powder, having never been fond of foundation; its thickness made her feel suffocated.

Glancing out the windows, she saw that the all-day gray was finally cracking as sunset approached, sending slivers of weak blue across the heavens, razor wisps of sunlight slashing the air above the buildings across the street and out over the Hudson. She sighed, her shoulders slumping. She had occupied this apartment for two decades, and she knew it was time for her to move to another apartment in the complex but this view, with its sliver of river and wall-to-wall views of the sky, lifted her heart on a daily basis. None of the other apartments had a view like it.

I'll move, I promise, she thought. Next year.

She had to leave now if she wanted to walk, and after today's inactivity, she needed the exercise. She had told Silas to meet at Patsy's

Pizza, which was dear to her heart, a buffer against all the change in New York City. Though nostalgia was something all sisters struggled to avoid, she held a deep love for the place. She'd first eaten there in the early 1930s, and even though she got delivery from Patsy's at least once a month, actually going into the historic building did something good for her soul, whatever that was.

With a grunt she hauled the ugly navy blue puffer off the hook by the door, refusing to put it on until she was about to step out on the street, grateful she didn't encounter any of her sisters on the way down the steps.

She walked across town and at 117th St, she spied Silas, barely discernible in the failing light. He was bundled from head to toe in a black wool coat and a hat that was surprisingly hip, a fedora that she'd been seeing a lot of on trips through SoHo. He wasn't looking at a phone, which surprised her since that was what everyone did these days while they waited. Instead, he was gazing north up First Avenue, the red lights from Patsy's sign illuminating his face. She paused, taking him in anew. Regarded outside of his previous status as a depressed cynic, he was handsome, in a way that made her wonder why she had not truly appreciated it before. When he first came to her practice, over a year earlier, the urgency of his depression and his unfailing lack of lust for life had overshadowed any appreciation of his facial features. It wasn't until he crashed her night out with Teddie just a day earlier that she had noticed his full lower lip, his long dark eyelashes and his brown-orange eyes, cat-like in their color and their relentless curiosity.

As she crossed the street toward him, he turned, and a smile spread across his face.

"You came!" he said, genuine surprise in his voice. Sara's pace slowed.

"So you think I'm a flake?" she said, drawing closer to him.

"I bailed on you last night, I don't really deserve anything better."

"You were out on a walk and got rained out, it wasn't like it was a…" she paused.

"No, it wasn't a date." Silas laughed. At this point, she was close enough to him that some sort of greeting had to happen. She extended a hand, and Silas moved as if he was going to copy her, but then his arms wrapped around her, and he clasped her gently, twice, before letting go.

"Thank you for coming, Lily," he said, pushing the door open, then waiting for her to enter before he went to the maître d'.

"Table for two, Oppenheimer," he said, notes of confidence in his voice. Sara hadn't heard them before. It made her suspicious, in a low-grade way. She batted it away. Suspicion was second nature to Lock members. *You've come this far. Try to enjoy something for once.*

After handing their coats to their waitress, they settled into a corner table at the rear of the room. The golden glow of the bare LED filament bulbs came close to recapturing the hazy ambience of the place as it had been in the forties. She looked around. The number of photos on the wall had increased since her last in-person visit twenty-something years back. She tucked her napkin across her lap and looked up to find Silas staring at her, a crooked half smile on his lips.

"Yes?"

"Just watching you settle in," Silas said. "I don't actually know if you like wine. Do you?"

"We are in a vintage New York Italian restaurant, Silas. We are bound by duty to order at least one bottle of the house chianti."

Silas's half-smile blossomed into one so full it almost pressed his eyes closed. He motioned to the waitress, and before long, they were nursing glasses of wine.

"What should we cheers to?" Silas asked, almost playfully.

"We're cheersing? Okay, let's send a salud to... hmmmm." Sara paused. "To different paths."

Their glasses clinked as they both repeated the words.

"You seem quite...I'm not sure if I should say it, Silas."

"Go ahead."

"You seem happier than I've ever seen you."

"Good," he said, taking the comment in his stride. "I do feel quite happy, I was able to walk the whole way here. I love walking the Park from top to bottom, even when it's muddy and stinky."

"Ah, so the park made you happy," Sara said, hating it as soon as it left her lips. Why was she fishing?

"Always does," Silas said, taking a sip. "I also anticipate a night of good conversation, and if I had to name one thing as a favorite of mine, that would be it."

"Oh, I better bring my A-game banter then."

"Yes, you'd better." Silas set his glass on the table. "I wanted to address the elephant in the room; in fact, I spent most of the walk up the park running through just how to address said elephant. But now that we are here, I don't sense the elephant and I'm not sure if bringing it up will make it better or worse."

"You're talking about how we met," Sara said. "Well, I'm not treating you anymore, but I can't pretend that we didn't have that relationship, or that I didn't hear the things that you said. I did. I know that side of you, but right now that side of you is curiously absent."

"Curious must be the word of the night," Silas said with a polite laugh.

"Whatever," Sara said, the wine emboldening her. "I literally should not be here. It's pretty much the most unprofessional turn that our relationship could have taken."

"And yet, here you are."

"And take this the right way, but you do not seem to be troubled at all."

"Is that why you came? Out of worry?"

"I honestly don't know why I came," she replied, finishing her wine and pouring a new glass for herself, consciously setting the bottle back down without filling Silas's glass. "I've been asking myself that all day."

"And did you arrive at an answer?"

"Let's go with no," Sara said. "I'm not trying to be evasive or elliptical. I guess it's not often you're faced with an entirely new situation, which this is. So here I am, in uncharted waters."

"Are you nervous?"

"Why would I be?"

Silas shrugged and refilled his own wine glass.

The off-center feeling that was darting around her heart came to a head suddenly and she blurted. "I'm actually starting to feel a little bit played, Silas. I don't think masquerading as a depressed patient is a good way to get someone to go out with you."

"You think I was faking that?"

"That's harsh. No, not that. There's a lightness to you that you didn't bring into my office. You seem genuinely happy."

"I can be happy now, happy is just another emotion. People put too much store in emotions. They're not real, they're chemical responses, and they're temporary. Don't you think that any of your other patients experience happiness?"

An image of Laura's face popped into Sara's mind.

"I know that some of them don't."

"Fair point then."

"Silas, are you like that woman in *Fight Club* who just goes to self-help groups so that she can feel?"

"No, Sara. I feel. I feel too much, most likely. And I'm not here because I think you're going to be more effective at my salvation now than you were as my doctor. I'm human. I still enjoy interactions, occasionally. I still find delight in some things. I'm not existing solely in a black box of nihilism. The black box is just where I like to hang out, it's my comfort zone."

"And now you're untreated and in free fall."

"I thought we agreed to terminate the patient doctor dynamic."

Sara nodded, and silently lifted her menu, even though she knew she was going to be ordering the bistecca, rare.

"I'm sorry that got so heated," Silas said. "I swear I was not manipulating you. Are we good?"

Sara met his eyes and, after a beat, nodded.

"What will you be eating?"

Sara laid her menu down. "I always get the bistecca," she said. "And yes, I'm sorry too. It's not just the way we met. It's... I haven't ah, I haven't..."

"Are you about to volunteer some personal information?" Silas sat forward like an eager student, a boyish smirk on his face.

"I was only about to tell you that it's been quite some time since I agreed to a date."

She expected him to laugh or express some doubt or something. Instead he sat patiently, waiting for her to continue.

"What? That's it. I don't date."

"May I ask why?"

"Sure, but I won't make you. It's not a big deal, I've just seen it all. I've heard every excuse, every lie, every coverup. Since social media took off, people – not just men – have embraced a new level of self-absorption and it seems to enable truly crappy treatment of other humans."

"So we'll never be Facebook official?"

"Afraid not, Oppenheimer."

"Do you even have social media?"

"You already looked."

"I did." He nodded. "Due diligence and all that."

"Sorry to disappoint," she said, waving the waiter over. After they placed their orders, she continued. "A lot of therapists don't have any social media," she lied, reverting to an old cover. "It, like this dinner, can be inappropriate."

"I actually don't have any socials either," Silas said. "May I ask how old you are? Where you're from? Your family situation? Clearly, you know a lot about me, and I'd like to address the imbalance."

"Not much to tell," Sara said, mentally running through the Lily Berger file that Heather had created for her. "Born in Alaska thirty-three years ago, parents died in a seaplane accident when I was two, no other siblings, raised by grandparents in Wyoming. Hated Wyoming, came here after high school on a church trip, and made it my mission to move here."

"Ah, so you're religious?"

"Not at all," she countered. "However, I did benefit from the kindness of some local churches when I was younger. There are good people everywhere. I moved to the city around a decade ago, and I've been in this practice six years."

"Married? Divorced? Children?"

"I would have mentioned any of those things," she said, before giving an entirely involuntary coquettish smile that was too close to flirtatious for her comfort. What the hell was she doing?

The waitress arrived with some calamari and some eggplant rollups, pausing the conversation. They ate in silence. The real Lily Berger had perished alongside her parents in the plane; the rest was all Heather manipulating public records. Sara was grateful that Silas seemed satisfied with her story and did not present additional questions. She glanced up and watched him slowly chewing his food. His positive demeanor tonight made him more attractive. During their sessions, he had always seemed pale and pained, but tonight, his skin was a faint olive, and his eyes danced with light, like he was always about to share a joke.

"Have you got any ex-wives hidden away?" she asked suddenly. Still chewing, he shook his head. After swallowing, he locked eyes with her.

"You're not the only one who's heard it all, Lily," he said quietly, and she thought that this would send him back down his rabbit hole. It didn't. He set his fork down.

"I'm honored you came here tonight," he said, his voice naked. "I really didn't expect you to, and I've been considering doing this for quite a while."

"This?" She really didn't know what he meant.

"Switching you from therapist to... something else."

Sara was still uncertain about his veracity. The change in his bearing was not just dramatic, it was opposite. Gone was the forlorn, existential sad sack, and in his place was a vibrant, seemingly content man. It wasn't right.

"What kind of something else?" she asked..

"That remains to be seen," he said. "Bit early yet, I'd say. But I will also say this. I'm enjoying tonight, so far."

"I am too."

"That dress, it's beautiful."

"Thanks, it's just some vintage I picked up down at St Mark's a long time ago."

"The dress isn't the only beautiful thing I can see."

"Heavy handed, Silas. Heavy handed."

He laughed out loud, a full, hearty belly laugh that even a day ago she would never have believed him capable of.

"Take a compliment, Lily."

She felt a blush burn her cheeks.

"You don't look too bad yourself."

"It's amazing what you can do with fifty bucks at Century 21, if you find a supportive sales lady."

"You bought all this today?"

He nodded. "Guilty as charged."

"Okay, full transparency, an hour ago, I was wishing I had gone shopping today too."

He smiled, and before she knew it, both of his hands had enveloped one of hers.

"That settles it," he said with a triumphant smile. "This is a date."

Sara quickly batted her adrenal system down, and forced her hand to stay where it was, pressed between Silas's surprisingly callused hands. She couldn't remember the last time she'd encountered callused hands in New York City.

"Lily," Silas said, interrupting her mental assessment of his hands. "Is this okay?"

She softened and gave him a warm smile and let her hand relax inside his.

"You do realize that formally labelling this as a date makes my professional transgression even worse, right?"

"It's not like I'm going to file a complaint."

"People who suddenly terminate therapy don't tend to file complaints. It's their families that do that. After, you know."

Silas gave her a wan smile. "I think that my mother would prefer this trajectory for our relationship. She worries that I've been alone for too long."

"See? I already know that, because you told me in session."

"I saw you wince when I said it too."

"Well, it's not easy to hear things like that. Declaring yourself a professional therapist doesn't mean you can seal your heart."

"You play poker?"

She shook her head.

"Damn, I really could have cleaned up. Your face is an open book."

Sara briefly wondered if that could be true, given the fact that she had spent five centuries perfecting her inscrutable air.

"See? I got you again!" Silas laughed. "I was just—"

He was interrupted by the arrival of an older man at the side of the table. He wore a stained white apron over trousers and a blue check shirt.

"I'm sorry to interrupt," he began, addressing Sara. "Miss, you're the very image of a customer of mine, I used to see her come in here from time to time. I was working out in the kitchen just now and I saw you, and stupidly, I forgot about all the time that has passed. It of course can't be you. Maybe your mother came in here when she was younger?"

Sara was grateful for her poker face now, as she visualized a much younger version of the man and recalled him as a flirty buck of a chef from thirty years earlier.

"I'm sorry to disappoint you," she began. "I'm an orphan, though, and I don't believe my parents ever came to New York, though I'm sure my mother would have loved this place as much as I do."

"Everybody got a twin, they say," the man said, pressing his hands together and bowing. "I'm very sorry I interrupted your dinner, I'm just an excitable old fool."

"Please," Sara said, placing her free hand on his arm. "Never apologize for yourself, it's lovely that you remembered her that well."

"She really could be your twin, even the voice." The man shook his head in wonder. "Order some dessert, on me. Enjoy your night."

Sara thanked him, and he was gone. When she returned her attention to the table, there was an expression on Silas's face that she couldn't place. He was annoyed? Amused? Both?

"A penny for your thoughts?" Sara repeated his phrase from the bar the night before.

"I'm just glad I didn't have to challenge an old man to a duel over the hand of a fair maiden."

"Ugh," Sara said, laughing. "I hate it when a dinner ends in a duel."

After they finished their complimentary cannoli, Silas insisted on paying for their dinner, then helped Sara back into her overcoat.

"Seems a shame to cover up such a beautiful dress," he said, helping her arms along the sleeves.

Outside, night had closed in, a crisp breeze blowing north up First Avenue.

"Still up for that walk?" Sara asked.

"You really want to do this?"

She nodded. Silas put his fingers to his chin in concentration.

"Okay," he began. "If you are up for a short walk, I find that in this neck of the woods, a stroll around Mount Morris Park should show you what I'm talking about."

"I love it up there," Sara blurted, instantly wishing she'd shut her mouth. The most dangerous time for her was newly dating, when information is shared carelessly in the mix of excitement and anonymity. Sure, she'd been in that area of the city. She remembered going to a party up there, with Heather, after they saw the Stones at Madison Square Garden in the early seventies. Those were the things she wasn't equipped to cover up, so she dug into her lie. "Sometimes, when a patient cancels, I'll walk around."

Silas didn't notice her subterfuge. He turned to face north, then crooked his arm. She slipped her arm through his, and they began to walk in silence.

Turning left on 120th, Sara began to wonder how long the silence would last. As if he read her mind, Silas spoke.

"I'm not giving you the silent treatment, but I should have explained myself. The best part of this thing that I do isn't the watching, it's the listening."

"Okaaaay," Sara said, not getting it.

Before Silas could answer, voices emanated from a window in a brownstone to their left, from an open window on the second floor. A mother talking to a child, explaining why it was wrong to spit on kids at school. They kept on walking, and a few buildings later, they overheard two voices that sounded older, arguing over a credit card bill. Sara gave Silas a quizzical look, and he held a finger to his lips, his eyes widening encouragingly. They kept going.

Another brownstone along the block had street level windows that they could see into. A young Black couple was fixing dinner, she setting the table, he cooking at the stove. He said something funny, and the woman laughed, looking at him with love. Sara watched as a smile broke over Silas's face. They crossed 120th, to the corner of Mount Morris Park, the streetlights sending little bowls of yellow light down to the sidewalk.

"See?" Silas said, coming to a stop. "I don't stop. I don't stare. I just watch and listen."

"And?"

"And nothing, it's just that even on that one block, those things, those conversations, snippets, they're all humans, just like us, focused on each other, and then you step back and look at this city, this dense, overwhelming city, and every room, every street, every park, is filled with that same level of human interaction. It's like each of them is a tiny strand in an incredibly rich tapestry, one that is woven anew with each day. Every strand is a life, or a love, or an intense depression. And each thread is incredibly important to the person it represents, but we know they all end the same way."

"Silas…" Sara began, unsure of what to say next.

"I like it," he said, meeting her eyes. "Instead of overwhelming me, it makes me see things from a perspective that works for me. I can see that everything is temporary, but human nature just makes us search for permanence in other people. It's comforting. It makes me feel less stupid."

Sara tilted her head. "Stupid?"

"For caring, for being such a self-indulgent, navel-gazing fool," Silas said, laughing at himself. "We're all in the same boat, headed for the same rapids, the same waterfall, and we all think we're in it alone."

"So do these walks cheer you up or mess your head up?"

"They calm me down," Silas said, turning to face her. "I feel like I get a good view of the river we are all in. It's humbling and it's inspiring and it's reassuring."

"But…" Sara cut herself off.

"But what?"

She shook her head. "No, sorry, I was almost very blunt."

"You can be blunt."

Swallowing hard, Sara continued.

"Aren't you just emotional window-shopping? You're just sliding past all this humanity in order to feel like you're part of something, without really digging in and feeling it yourself?"

Silas pursed his lips and knit his brows in thought.

"Maybe?" he said eventually. "I was half expecting you to say that, I mean, it's not like that didn't already occur to me. But I don't do it to avoid feeling, Lily. I do it to try to find a reason to enjoy my own tiny thread."

"I shouldn't have said anything," Sara said, cursing her words.

"No, I'm glad you did. I'm glad you felt like you could. Speak freely, I mean."

Sara scuffed her shoe on the sidewalk, staying silent while an old man walked by with an elderly Pomeranian on a leash, waiting for him to pass.

"Evening," Silas said to the man, and the man smiled, doffing an imaginary hat.

"Same to you, son," the man said, still smiling as he walked on.

"I've made it awkward, haven't I?" Sara looked into Silas's eyes.

"Are you kidding? This whole thing is awkward," Silas said with a gentle laugh. "I don't hate it. Do you?"

Sara shrugged. "I still feel irresponsible."

"When does irresponsible become such a bad thing? When you're a kid, it's everything. When you're an adult, it's frowned upon."

"Someone could get hurt here, Silas..."

"Me? Lily, I was engaged in this discussion in therapy, but it was... stifling, because I could sense things about you, things that I'm see-ing."

"Misery loves company," Sara said, dropping her eyes.

"Indeed it does," Silas said. "How about we call it a night, and you and I can go unpack it all. I'm not going to play games. I'd like to see you again."

Sara looked up to find him staring right at her in a way that wasn't startling. There was a gentleness to him that she hadn't perceived when he was in treatment, and she was annoyed that she had missed it. It wasn't just her Lock she was being half-assed with, it was her patients, and she didn't know who needed her more.

"I had a very…" she paused. Nice wasn't the right word. "I loved tonight, thank you. And thank you for dinner. I would not say no to another night like this."

Silas smiled broadly.

"Good news, good news," he said. "I have some business to attend to outside the city, but I'm back either Saturday or Sunday. How's your next week looking?"

Sara's mind flashed to April Veronica's confirmation, which meant Crina coming to town. She almost groaned out loud.

"Work is shit next week, and I'm not being avoidant, it's just the truth. I have some fundraisers and whatnot. You know what? Let's talk early in the week and we can get something on the books."

Silas nodded sagely, then, without speaking, he leapt into the street, arm aloft, flagging a taxi. At first Sara thought he was panicking and leaving, but when the cab stopped, he held the door open for her.

"For you, m'dear. I'm not done walking."

He didn't attempt to kiss Sara or touch her at all as she slid into the cab's back seat. He pressed the door closed and watched as the cab lurched out into the street. Sara waited until he was out of earshot and then told the driver to take her to 105th and Riverside, her head swimming the whole way.

Chapter Eight

On most Saturday mornings, Sara liked to sleep late, then take a long walk through a different part of the city, coming home with her arms full of fresh bread and fruit. This Saturday, however, was different. After much juggling of schedules, it had been arrived at for the date of the final vote on Marguerite's candidate, including an in-person audience with April Veronica.

She'd stayed up late, texting and talking, which resulted in restless sleep. She'd awoken to even more texting and talking, and was now in full nun robes, on her fourth coffee of the day, sitting in silence on her couch, looking out of the windows onto the sunny street below, happy to see so many green leaves appearing on the trees.

She was adjusting her wimple and smoothing out her habit when a knock at the door startled her. Blinking the cobwebs away, she pulled the door open without checking the peep hole, entirely unsurprised to see Heather standing there, slightly comical in her habit, her expression all business.

"We need a quick chat before the meeting," she said, brushing past Sara.

"Good morning to you too, Heather. Top of the morning, in fact."

"Don't try to butter me up, mum," Heather said, chuckling as she took a seat on the couch.

"Oh, shit, we're sitting? I need to get up to the roof house."

"You don't need to be first to every meeting."

"It sets a good example."

"Is it in the handbook?" The existence of a handbook, which was clearly forbidden, was Heather's favorite running joke whenever Sara faced a Lock problem. Sara found Heather's amusement more amusing than the joke itself, since a handbook would be pretty fucking useful most days.

"Fine, we won't be first. What's your problem?"

"I just have a bad feeling about this, something in me waters. I was up all night creating her identity, and I know this is unfair, unfounded, but she's a millennial, and I've spoken to other Lock admins and they've all had such issues that they've derailed the confirmations. Completely. Even before this whole ZPG thing, any candidates that they had bombed out early on. These kids don't like strict rules and in their early days they are obviously potentially very dangerous."

"I can see that," Sara said, wishing she could just abdicate all responsibility to Heather, knowing that Heather had enough responsibility already. "But nobody's made a new convert in how long? And how long has it been since someone had to actually hit the switch?"

The switch was Lock shorthand for the preferred method of sisterly dispatch, a vacuum chamber disguised as just another sitting room, with a fireplace and a mantel. Once a sister was locked inside and the doorway sealed, the Monitor was tasked with pressing the button that ignited the gas fireplace. The flames consumed the oxygen in the room. Unconsciousness occurred long before death, and the thrashing of the lifeless corpse as their bloodborne virus fought to retain life was definitely not pretty. Cleaning up the room afterward was a dirty job shared by the entire Lock, a job so repugnant that it actively limited the desire to make new members.

"And Teddie hasn't backed out of the Monitor gig here, has she?"

"Well, she wants to get out of it but—"

"She's avoided it for two hundred years. Sorry Ted."

"She knows. It's just been so long since anyone got made here, and this one does seem a bit—"

"Fraught?" Heather raised a lone eyebrow.

"I was going to say iffy," Sara said with a diplomatic smile.

"Do you really think it could end badly?"

"Have you met me? I wake up every morning certain that the day will end badly. I spend eight to ten hours a day putting out bureaucratic fires. When I finish for the day, if our world is safe and still standing, I call it a good day and pour myself a wine."

"But this transition in particular?"

"Maybe I'm overreacting," Heather said, ironing the pleats of her habit over her thighs with both hands. "If I'm honest, I think that we barely have balance at all in the Lock. Marguerite has been divisive since she arrived. She's dismissive of Eleanor's art, she thinks Fran is too promiscuous and for some reason she thinks Imani doesn't like her."

"That's what everybody thinks at first," Sara said of their Iranian-British member, haughty and icy raised to an art form. "I'm sure if you asked her, Imani would say she's very fond of Marguerite."

"I did ask her and that's *not* what she said."

Sara groaned.

"Anyway, we are a bit late, so it's time to head to the roof. I just wanted to air the old grievances. Feels a bit unfair now. I'm sure we can manage it."

After stealing a quick glance in the mirror, Sara bounded up the spiral stairs to the loft.

"Come on, Trainspotting. We have a minefield to dance across. And don't forget you need to get Crina on loudspeaker."

The gobsmacked look on Heather's face made Sara's day.

"Is there a problem?" Marguerite, pacing nervously, greeted Heather and Sara as they entered the larger meeting room in the basement of the complex. Glancing around at the group of expectant nuns, Sara saw that they were in fact the last two to arrive.

"We had a few last-minute details to discuss regarding April Veronica's new identity," Sara said, fighting to keep her voice light. Without a word, Heather slipped around behind her and headed for her own seat, a boxy, carved wooden throne she'd brought from the Shetland Islands. Sara watched as she laid her iPhone on one of the chair's arms and pressed a few buttons.

"Let's begin," Sara said. "Welcome to the first phase of conversion for Sister Marguerite and her novitiate April Veronica. The New York City Lock is now in session, we will consider in open conference for a time, and then, all going well, we will meet with April Veronica. My name is Sara, and never have I killed. I welcome you, and with that I declare the meeting open."

"Are we getting some blood or not, coz I dragged myself out of bed early for this." Imani, an exquisite turban of rose and gold crowning her habit, spoke from her throne. She sounded like she was still half asleep.

Sara shrugged. "If you need a pick me up, help yourself to the fridge in back. Just keep it light, and make sure you wipe your mouth clean. We have an outsider coming in."

"What a bloody liberty," Imani said theatrically before winking at Sara.

"Sorry not sorry." Sara grinned. "Better to pop a heem. We shouldn't be too long here."

Without another word, Imani rose, wraithlike, and moved to the fridge by the heating oven in the room's rear corner. She deftly opened a bloodbag, squeezing quite a serving into a glass, then downed it cold with a shudder. After she rinsed the glass in the sink, she wiped her mouth with a wet hand, then helped herself to a pill from a bottle on a small shelf, washing it down with some water cupped in a hand.

With a dramatic eye roll, she returned to her seat.

"Like I said, bitches. Rough morning."

"I am now going to hand over the floor to Sister Marguerite." Sara nodded at the Spaniard, who had remained standing. With a perfunctory smile that revealed her nervousness, Marguerite stepped beside Sara.

"Nomine Sister Marguerite, never have I killed. Thank you all for coming here today. Before we meet my novitiate- "

"Potential novitiate," corrected Eleanor, arms folded tight across her chest, her brown curly hair pulled back into a severe ponytail. Beside her, Rosa gave her a thumbs up, so Eleanor continued. "Didn't you kill your first convert?"

A round of gasps, then silence, filled the room. Sara made to reply, but Marguerite raised a staying hand.

"A matter of... housekeeping... such as that is forgiven under the writings, Eleanor. Additionally, I don't feel that it's fair for you to bring up something you know nothing about. Now, if nobody has any further objections, I'll continue."

Marguerite pursed her lips and visibly counted to five before beginning what was clearly a well-rehearsed speech. "April Veronica is a rarity among women, and this is why I believe she has the potential to become a vital contributing member of this Lock.

"I first noticed April Veronica when she was one of our order's beneficiaries, bouncing through the welfare system. After I secured the girl's safe haven with the city, she was a recipient of our scholarship program for many years. She recently completed her second PhD in epidemiology, she claims atheism, she is boundlessly curious, and she satisfies all the selection criteria. I have prepared a white paper for you all about it, it's on the table at the back. Please read it before we bring her in. She is waiting down the hall in the other meeting room. She thinks she is joining an order of nuns devoted to silent study."

"That's great about the epidemiology PhD," Yukari said. "My workload ever since COVID has been increasing dramatically. We need to be ahead of the curve next time."

The entire Lock nodded in agreement. While COVID wasn't fatal to the cursed, their own blood-based virus fought it so virulently that it caused almost untold suffering to the few Scholars who'd become infected, mainly in the Bucharest Lock. One surviving Scholar likened it to "strings of chainsaws slipping along your veins."

"I'm just worried you're trying to make a friend the old-fashioned way, since you haven't really tried with any of us." Eleanor could be withering when she wanted to be.

Sara pressed her eyes closed, ready for a trademark Marguerite meltdown. It didn't come.

"Contrary to popular belief, I love each and every one of you," Marguerite said, raw honesty in her voice. "I'm not warm and fuzzy. I don't care for hugs. Those things were true before my conversion. I have little time for small talk, and I abhor the banal. I don't care for gossip. I respect and honor my Lock, but I seek my stimulation elsewhere, and that is not illegal. Additionally, I have been here for sixty years, and I hope to be here for at least that again, and I feel that in that time, I will cycle through periods of closeness with all of you."

"Does anyone have any questions for Marguerite before we summon April Veronica?" Sara spread her palms wide, inviting the room to join in.

Almost everyone raised a hand.

"Who will be the Monitor?" asked Yukari.

Teddie stood up and hitched a thumb at her chest.

"This bitch here gonna be on the new girl like a ton of bricks."

"Are you sure you can do what must be done if it's required?"

Teddie shrugged. "I've never done it before, and I hoped to never do it, but if the scene calls for it, I'm down."

Yukari nodded, satisfied.

"What makes you think that she will want to spend any more time with you than we do?" demanded Fran. "I think that's the fundamental concern here."

"I have maintained a direct relationship with April Veronica for the last eight years. We have a solid foundation for friendship and mentoring. And Fran, may I say that friendship is a two-way street and if you weren't so desperate to always—"

"And thank you Fran," Sara cut Marguerite off. "Imani, did you have a question?"

"My question is for the nurses, actually," said the very taciturn Brit. "Will the added mouth to feed create any tension for you at work? You were late to the last meeting for some supply-related reason."

Teddie stood back up. "Thanks, girl. Yeah, we good, I'll know in advance so I can create lab orders. The lab has just been unreliable since the pandemic, if there's a flareup my shit gets bumped. That's what happened before the last meeting. The heem pills are easy, and it's not a hassle to get an extra pint every week. Don't y'all worry about me. I got you."

"I'm moving back to active lab work, and I'll be back on the supply train in a week or so," said Liz without making eye contact. Sara fought to control her retort. Liz had used that line so many times, but she still wasn't providing.

"Is that it?" Sara looked around the room. Only Teddie matched her gaze; all the others preoccupied with lint on habit skirts and sleeves. "Marguerite, would you please go and get April Veronica?"

Without a word, Marguerite spun and left, her habit flapping out around her. Predictably, as soon as the door closed, the chatter started as everyone moved to the back table to get a copy of the white paper.

"Nope," Sara yelled out, shushing them all. "The time for talking was while Marguerite was in the room. Please obey the ceremony rules. Nothing may be shared unless Marguerite is present, we already have enough of a problem with dissension in this Lock. Fran, Rosa, Eleanor, Liz, I'm mainly talking to you. No more behind-the-back chit-chat."

The four women glanced at each other and rolled their eyes.

"Yes, you lot. I hate saying shit like that too," Sara said, her voice rising. "But it's true. You don't have to get along. You don't have to do anything except treat each other with honesty and respect. No trolling, no hating."

"And you're in favor of this April Veronica?" Eleanor spat, her golden-brown eyes glinting angrily, her crazy curls bobbing emphatically in their ponytail.

"I am," Sara said in her calmest voice. "I've sensed that Marguerite was nurturing her for many years, and I've been monitoring her and the situation. I do think Marguerite might have found the only obedient Millennial in the five boroughs, and also, her work alongside Yukari will be invaluable."

"Have you observed her in true crisis?" Fran's eyes bored into Sara's as she spoke. "Have you?"

"Several. She was assaulted several years back, and she did not seek violent retribution. She has weathered the usual crises of her twenties with dignity and aplomb."

"And she is currently how old?" Rosa was running a finger along the lines of text on Marguerite's paper. "Ah, here it is. She's thirty-two."

"Yes," said Sara. "And Marguerite has been tending to her for eight years. She will need to abandon her by the end of the year, when she ends this current incarnation of herself."

"Doesn't mean I need to jump to attention, is all," Rosa said.

"Sulking is not good on you," Sara said.

"Oh, *desculpe*, Sara. You offer help to Teddie, to Yukari, but everybody forgets me, the one who manages all the buildings and investments. I'm the money honey, and it's not exactly fun to work as hard as I do, and then have to agree to raise a new baby."

"Amen sister." Eleanor high-fived her. In her seat in the back row, Liz raised her hands in devil horns, laughing. Sara inhaled deeply, refusing to rise to the bait.

"I'm not helping out!" Fran leaned forward defiantly in her chair. "If I vote for this, that's the extent of my help and involvement."

"Same here," said Rosa, the quietest sister. "It's not even sour grapes. I'm busy as hell managing our businesses. Do you know how many times I've asked Marguerite if she can help me? And she doesn't just say no, she tells you for half an hour how much she would hate to do what I have to do daily. So, I'm not letting her add to my workload."

"Well, I'm sure she's not asking you," Sara said, her voice as placating as possible. "For better or worse, Marguerite is very self-aware. She knows that she can't ask for your help, Rosa. Marguerite is happy to do all the heavy lifting. I really think you're all going to be pleasantly surprised."

"I fuckin' hope so," said Teddie. "I ain't ready to pull a switch on no bitch."

"Damn straight," drawled Liz, her California drawl twanging incongruously. "I was talking to Heather and she's like, yeah, why are we upsetting the apple cart?"

"That's what I say when someone gets a bloody cat," Heather squawked. "Don't quote me out of context."

"I didn't," Liz countered. "But it's a fact. We exist in a very fragile peace. What about if someone uncovers us? Do you think it was easy to rehouse fourteen women in other Locks? To give up our entire San Francisco situation? The monastery, the private school for women? I never got over it. As soon as I can get back to California, I'm out."

"Wait, you think you're going back soon?" Yukari perked up. "I was eyeing a move to the San Francisco Lock before it all went south."

"Won't be San Fran," Rosa interjected. "We are looking at options in Southern California. Most likely San Diego, with financial interest in Tijuana and surrounds. The women there need us, and the city is sprawling and distracted. We should be acquiring lands soon."

A burble of chatter broke out as the sisters absorbed the news. The hubbub ended suddenly at the sound of two very solid knocks at the door. Once silence settled, the door swung open and nine sets of eyes alighted on the slight, wide-eyed girl with mousy brown hair in a tumbling, loose hipster cut who stood beside their sister.

"Sisters of Holy Silence, please welcome April Veronica Copper," Marguerite said, her voice understated for once. "April Veronica, please come inside."

As the young woman moved into the room, Heather bustled up with a chair, one with a heavy wooden frame, intricately carved and topped with a red velvet seat. Sara noticed that the chair would be much too heavy for a normal woman to carry so effortlessly, hoped that April Veronica wouldn't notice, then wondered if Heather, who would never make a mistake like this, was more confident of Copper's future with the Lock than she let on.

"Th-thanks you guys," April Veronica said. "Wait, what do I call you? Sisters? That seems strange."

Sara stepped forward and took her hand in hers. "April Veronica, welcome. Today is an informal meeting, but yes, please call me Mother, and everyone else will answer to Sister. Please, take a seat. Don't be nervous. This is as much for you to decide about us as it is for us to get to know you."

"I'm not nervous," April Veronica said with a weak smile as she took her seat. But a look of surprise crossed her face as Marguerite moved to take her regular seat among the other women.

"Just you and me up front," Sara said, patting April Veronica's leg. April Veronica moved her leg slightly away, and Sara felt a small burst of doubt. Nobody would greenlight another difficult, moody sister. This young woman was going to need to turn on the charm if she wanted to get to the next stage. Sara pondered whether to try to nudge her in the right direction, then realized that from here on out, it was beyond her control. Either it worked or it didn't. Sure, Teddie would be scarred by pulling the switch, and they'd all be despondent after cleaning the surrender room, but it would pass. Everything always did.

"So, Karla has told me a little about your order, and I think that the work you do is phenomenal," April Veronica said, using Marguerite's present real-world name, and clearly reciting a memorized essay. "My name is April Veronica Copper, I'm thirty-two and I believe that I am a perfect candidate for joining your order. I am the product of the good that your order does, and I feel blessed that I have made it this far.

I am insanely grateful for the changes you've brought to my life, the academic opportunities as well as the support you gave me through the welfare system. Since meeting Sister Karla when I was in my twenties, she has shown me tireless devotion to helping the needy, as well as a refreshing reliance upon science."

Sara watched as the young woman's eyes moved from woman to woman in the audience, and she was grateful that the Lock were treating her with respect. As she spoke, April Veronica's voice became fuller, more confident, and her eyes began to sparkle. She glanced at Marguerite, and Sara watched as the Spaniard nodded and smiled, and the speech continued.

"I never dreamed as a little girl with an interest in biology that I would encounter a monastic order of nuns who prefer science over myth, and silence over chatter. Karla has told me of lives spent in pursuit of scientific breakthroughs, social support, repairing injustice and helping the have-nots of the city. To be honest, I would have struggled if this was a religious order, because I do not believe in serving a flying spaghetti monster, or any notion of worship. If my life ends and there's a god waiting there, I'd rather say I spent my time doing good and learning and growing than being a wretched beast who sat on her phone posting selfies and acting like some huge thirst trap. Amirite?"

Sara laughed. Even though she hadn't heard a novitiate's entry speech in a long time, April Veronica's irreverently earnest take was a gust of fresh air. She liked the girl already.

"Indeed, you are right," Sara said. "Sorry, I'm not hip enough to know the correct positive response to 'amirite.'"

"All good," April Veronica said. "So, have we come to the question-and-answer portion of the show?"

Eight hands shot up.

"Uh, Mother, I might need your help here."

Chapter Nine

As soon as the door closed behind Marguerite and her young charge, hoods were whipped off and the room erupted into chatter. Sara remained still, and silent. The divisions in her Lock were immediately visible to her: Liz, Rosa, Fran and Eleanor stood and walked to the back, speaking quietly together. Yukari moved over to where Teddie was sitting, engaging her in conversation. Heather and Imani spoke briefly before inviting Sara for coffee in Imani's flat. Politely declining the invitation, Sara sat, pretending to be in reverie when in fact all she wanted to do was power up her phone and see if she'd heard from Silas. Nobody paid any attention to her.

Standing slowly, Sara walked to the bathroom in the opposite corner of the room, closing the door behind her. Before she sat down, she fished her phone from the pocket in front of her habit. Since almost everyone she knew had just been in a room with her, her home screen was relatively clear. A Signal message from Crina – "well done on the meeting, excited to meet the new girl" – but nothing from Silas.

Once she was done peeing and washing her hands, she stood there, trying to ignore the weird dejected feeling that was orbiting her heart. She focused on the ancient, worn tile on the floor and walls. She'd purchased it herself, from a stonemason who worked for the Rose Brick company, the pattern now worn so bare that there was more bare cement than tile. This room was just one of many in the complex that she loved, that she had been instrumental in the design of. She batted the reverie away. Silas hadn't called. She had other things she could do with her day instead of pine.

Exiting the bathroom, she saw that Teddie and Yukari had left, and there were just the four women standing around the counter. A silence filled the air, the kind of silence that happens when people stop talking suddenly, because they were interrupted when they had thought they were alone.

"Hey, you guys." Sara smiled. "Mind if I join you?"

Enjoying the awkward nods from the quartet, Sara bellied up to the small kitchen counter.

"So, I wanted to thank you all for being so, I dunno, professional isn't the right word but you know what I mean. Thanks for that meeting. I know it might not have been the easiest thing, but you all did the right thing."

Nobody answered, and Sara watched as the four women exchanged glances and shifted their weight from one leg to the other.

"Okay, I get it, sorry I'm interrupting, I'll leave you to it." Sara couldn't keep the bitterness out of her voice as she turned to leave.

"Wait," said Rosa. "Please stay. Sara, thank you for what you just said. I think you took us all by surprise, saying that."

"By surprise, huh?"

"Well yeah," Fran said, and Sara steeled herself. When Fran uncorked, it was usually blunt. "I mean, you knew our reservations but you didn't even reach out to us personally. You let Heather and Teddie do your dirty work."

"If any of you wanted to talk to me, you know where to find me," Sara said, trying not to sound defensive. "I'll admit it, this negotiation wore me out. I work, I run the Lock and I talk to each of you, daily.

Sometimes, I'd like to be less involved. This time around, there was nothing in the rule book to block Marguerite's choice."

"We are on the wrong side of history if we make that woman," Eleanor said, surliness in her voice.

"If?" snared Liz. "If? We just voted on yes. It's happening."

"I'm confused," Sara said carefully. "Did you all not like April Veronica?"

More silence and shuffling followed, with Sara determined to wait it out.

"I liked her a lot," Fran said, finally. "But it's not like we are buying a new puppy here."

"I liked her too," said Rosa, and Liz and Eleanor nodded in agreement.

"I have a question," Sara said, and all four heads snapped to attention. "Honestly. Is the issue Marguerite or ZPG?"

"Marguerite, hands down," said Fran.

"The other one," Rosa said quietly, and Liz and Eleanor murmured their agreement. "The more I think about it, the more I feel that we are being selfish and thinking we are above everything, when we pose a risk to the entire world."

Sara took a deep breath, knowing she should have had this conversation a long time ago and deciding that now was as good a time as any.

"How about we open a bottle of New York's finest and have a good old-fashioned discussion?" she said.

"Can we?" asked Eleanor.

"Nothing in the rules says we can't," Sara brushed past her to get behind the bar. She opened the fridge, pleased to see four unopened bags of blood plus the remnants of the one that Imani had helped herself to. She lifted that one, plus a full one, onto the bar top, selected five glass tumblers from the cupboard below the sink, spiked the bag, then filled them, slowly. Without a word, she put them all in the warming oven, set it to 100 and returned to face them.

"This is unusual," said Eleanor. "I feel weird."

"You guys, I'm trying to be spontaneous. Let's have it out. You can bitch about me after I leave."

Liz let out a shocked laugh, her hand rushing to cover her mouth too late to stop it.

"Being a Lock mother doesn't make me any different from you guys," Sara said, looking around. "I'd bet that none of you would rush into a conversation that you'd find unpleasant, or an argument that you would lose. That's my day-to-day. So, I'm gonna admit to you, here and now, that yes, I knew the conversations had to happen, and I knew they'd be hard, and I'm just gonna say that I frankly just couldn't be fucked."

Four sets of widening eyes made Sara very happy.

"No offense," Sara said. The timer on the warming oven dinged and she moved back behind the bar, opening the oven door and handing a glass to each of them. Turning and holding hers aloft, she made eye contact with Fran.

"Are we chugging or sipping?"

Fran laughed. "Let's be civilized and sip."

To her left, Liz raised her goblet to her lips, tipping the warm blood into her mouth and swallowing.

"Sorry, too late," she said, a trickle of blood at the corner of her mouth. Shrugging, Rosa and Eleanor did the same.

"Fuck it," Sara said, downing hers, watching as Fran followed suit. Instantly, Sara's body came alive as her body responded to the fresh blood, light coursing through her veins and black veils clouding her vision. For a second, she wondered if her knees might buckle, but they didn't.

"That hit the spot," Eleanor said, her eyes still closed.

"Might we have some more, Sara?" Rosa held her empty glass up. "This time we will sip."

Sara knew she should say no, but her addiction started to pull at her, and she didn't want them to see any signs of it. "Sure," she said, quickly gathering the glasses and refilling them. Once they were in the oven, she turned.

"So, which one of you bitches has been talking to Desdemona?"

This time it was three sets of shocked wide eyes, and one sister looking at the floor. Rosa.

"Well, that was easy," Sara said, putting a hand on Rosa's shoulder. "It's not a crime, you're not breaking any rules."

"I know that." Rosa didn't look up.

"What you are doing, however, is making my job really difficult."

"That wasn't my intention."

Wasn't it? Sara thought, then said, "I understand, but Rosa, my goal for all of us is a fully transparent Lock. I realize that's idealistic and almost impossible, but if we all strive for it, we can get as close as possible. I have five hundred years of history with that woman, and she will use anything she can against me."

"So she's supposed to report to you any time she has a conversation?" Liz was being antagonistic.

Sara shook her head. "Not at all, but I'd imagine that if you're talking to another Lock about ZPG and airing your grievances with them, and then not telling your Lock Mother, you're setting that Lock Mother up for failure."

Fran inhaled sharply and Sara shot her a glance. "What?"

"I told her to tell you."

"It doesn't matter," Sara said. "This isn't kindergarten. The point is, this Lock offers the most freedom to its sisters. With that freedom comes additional responsibility. For all of us."

The oven dinged and she continued speaking as she retrieved the newly warmed blood. "It may surprise you to know that I see the benefits of ZPG. I obviously see the risks of our discovery, particularly in a country as increasingly lawless as the United States."

Eleanor went to speak and Sara cut her off.

"However, and please, just let me finish Elle, amending the constitution of our lives is unprecedented and it would take a unanimous agreement by all the Locks. My purview is that, for now, the Locks will arrive at their position independently. And in time, this may become the position of this Lock, but right now, I am excited to welcome April Veronica, and see that she is made in full accordance with our governing principles. Eleanor, what were you about to say?"

"I don't think you do see the risks," she said plainly. "Fran and I talk about it often, that we basically need all of us to sequester. The surveillance in the outside world is too great. This is what keeps me awake at night. Is there someone following us? Collecting images, filming us? We do not know."

"And to that, Eleanor, there are several options. You have worked at the hospital for what now? Six years. You have two years to go. If you would like to retire your persona early and spend a decade or two within these walls, that option is available to you."

"I like my job," Eleanor said. "Working in the hospice heals me. And the people who might remember me all die. It's a good setup."

"All of us like our jobs, Sara," Fran said, sipping at her blood.

"Then I'm not sure what you're asking for?"

Liz rolled her eyes. Sara was growing increasingly tired of her. "We want to be ZPG."

"An hour ago you were boasting about setting up a new Lock on the West Coast," Sara said, unable to hide her frustration. "Is that your idea of attrition? A satellite Lock three thousand miles away? Sister, you're talking about expansion, not extinction."

"I'm not," Liz said. "No new sisters. I've been talking to my former sisters from the San Francisco Lock. Some of them want to come back."

"That would be a massive undertaking," Sara said, realizing that this would be the next project, once April Veronica was made.

"Not really," Rosa chimed in. "I've been looking into properties and doing feasibility studies."

"And were you planning on telling me?"

Rosa shrugged. "I didn't know I had to. There's nothing in the rules about it."

"Fair," Sara said, downing the rest of her blood, waiting for the rush to pass. "But that brings us to my point. There are five Locks who embrace ZPG. All four of you are welcome to go and join them."

In the silence that followed, Sara glanced from woman to woman, almost daring them to speak.

Rosa began to speak then cut herself off.

"Yes, Rosa?"

"Desdemona said you'd say that."

"So fucking what?" Sara bit her head off. "What other option do you have, Rosa? Either you convince this Lock to go ZPG or you move to a lock that has already embraced it."

"This is going well," Fran said and Liz chuckled.

"Guys," Eleanor raised her palms. "Slow it down, this isn't going anywhere."

"Oh, it's going somewhere," Sara said, her voice shaking. "This is precisely why I avoided this conversation. You four have decided that you're outcasts, and there's nothing I can do to change your minds. My job is, above all, to unify the Lock, and when I can't, I reorganize. It's that simple. Here. Rosa. You can go to Madrid. I'll have Imani take over your tasks. Liz, you're heading back to California. You can ZPG all you want in between burritos and margaritas. Eleanor, do whatever will make you happy. If you can be happy. And Fran, honestly, I'm not sure why you're even in this group."

Fran chugged her blood. "Because they're the only ones who will have me. But I'm a New Yorker. I ain't leaving."

Before Sara could reply, Liz and Rosa stood up.

"We actually had plans for the afternoon," Rosa said. "Thanks for the... drink." She turned and left. Liz followed without a word. Eleanor waited until they'd closed the door behind them.

"I'm sorry, Sara. I wish that had gone better."

"Me too." Sara was seething.

"Fuck," Fran said, glaring at her phone. "The wifi is out. Sorry, Sara, I need to get upstairs."

"Unplug it and count to ten," Eleanor said. Fran flipped her off, holding her finger above her head as she exited the room.

"Well, this is awkward," Sara said.

"Not really." Eleanor surprised her by wrapping her arms around her. "I'm leaving too. You good to wash up?"

Sara nodded against the woman's neck.

"Thank you for trying, just now," Eleanor said, breaking the hug and walking out of the room.

Unsettled, Sara gathered up the glasses and set them in the sink, running them under warm water, using her fingers to remove the bloody residue from the rims. Once the glasses were cleaned and dried, she set them back in the cupboard.

Angrily, she noted that once again, she'd been left to attend to the cleanup.

All that was left to do was to seal the bloodbag and put it back in the fridge.

Or drink it.

Carefully, she slipped it into the pocket of her habit, and stepped out, locking the door behind her.

Back in her apartment, Sara hid the bloodbag in her fridge behind a bag of spinach that had gone to liquid. It needed to be thrown away but for now it was an excellent shield. Enervated by the discussion with her rebel alliance, she switched her habit for yogawear and did two hours of Peloton power yoga. One of the downsides of Cursed life was that tendons shortened over time, and stretching daily was a necessity. Today, after the meeting, Sara's hamstrings and shoulders were supertight. She liked to joke with Heather that after four centuries of ballet, tai chi, yoga and Pilates she should be able to kiss her own ass. She blamed today's tightness entirely on Liz and her smug, childish antics. The sooner she went back to California the better.

No sooner had that thought entered her mind than she began running through the logistics of setting up a new Lock. She knew that the groundwork would fall into her lap.

It was a small price to pay for getting rid of the irritating woman, but once again, so much for savasana. The tension was returning to her body before she'd even left her yoga mat. Pushing herself up to standing, she picked up her phone, scanning the tickertape of notifications. Seeing that a lot of them were from Teddie, she pushed through to a phone call without reading them. Teddie picked up before Sara heard a ring tone.

"Mom, there you are!"

"Here I am. What's up?"

"From the sound of you, I should be asking you. Sup?"

"Four power yoga classes with my boy Denis, but right at the end, Liz popped into my mind and now I'm as stressed as I was before."

"Well, at least you've done your stretches for today," Teddie sang. "But what the hell did that witch do now?"

"It wasn't just her." Sara sighed. "The four of them stayed behind after the meeting, so I tried to engage them in, you know, a regular conversation. Hell, I even popped open a bag like it was happy hour up in that bitch."

"Great," Teddie groaned. "More work for me. Let's not forget we are christening a new girl next week. You want the blood to flow or nah?"

"Ted, I'm sorry. I thought it would help the discussion."

"I gather it didn't."

"Not one bit. The four of them are just determined to be sour."

"So what did you tell them?"

"That they're welcome to move to any of the Locks that believe the same things they do."

"Ouch," Teddie snickered. "I bet they loved that."

"Well, Liz is all gung ho to set up her California dream Lock."

"Who doesn't want their extinction to come with an ocean view?" Sara laughed out loud.

"So, wanna come out again? I've heard 8008135 is even more fun on a Saturday."

"I don't think I could handle any more 'fun' than I've already had, thanks. I am leaning to either a long walk, or a Katharine Hepburn marathon."

"You can do those things any time."

"Yes, my love. But the time I choose is tonight. Have fun with the young people. This old bitch needs a break."

Teddie laughed, blew her a kiss and hung up.

Darkness had fallen during her yoga classes, and the only light in the apartment was whatever was bouncing up from the street. Sara leaned a hip against the armrest of her couch, taking in the stillness, feeling the smooth yet jittery warmth still coursing through her veins from the blood she'd drunk earlier, pondering what to do with her night.

The blood in the fridge called out to her, forcing her eyes to scrunch shut in frustration. This was the exact opposite of what she should be doing to bring her levels down after... after what happened. She still couldn't think back to that night without focusing on the feeling of dead flesh pressed against her lips, but as time passed, another sensation affixed itself to that memory. Now, she also remembered the way her body thrummed with power, like a sports car getting a tank full of high-octane fuel.

That night, after she left Laura's grim apartment, her power had been almost impossible to control. Her muscles moved against each other like butter as she flitted from shadow to shadow along the chilly, empty streets. Entering the park she was finally able to open up to full throttle, racing along a bike path, waves of nausea fading as a feeling of deep wellness ran through her. Pausing for a breath beside the great lake, her waking image of Laura's wrist in her hungry mouth flashed before her eyes, and she buckled to her knees, trying to make herself vomit unsuccessfully, her body again refusing to surrender the blood it had consumed.

That's what she wanted. That was all she wanted. To run in the park, to be one with the night, forgetting New York and its burdens, embracing the life she'd known as a girl, nights when Crina taught her to hunt alongside wolves.

Irresponsible, she teased herself, but the heart wants what it wants.

Several hours, a long shower and some chronic wardrobe indecision later, Sara stepped through the gate on Central Park West into the fecund darkness of the North Woods. Wearing a full black leotard and a long black sweater beneath a puffer coat she planned to hide under a bench while she ran, she merged with the shadows. Her trail runner shoes left crisp footfalls with each step, so she paused every now and then, one ear raised, but she couldn't hear any other humans. She loved the way the city melted away as soon as you stepped into the North Woods, the ancient trees absorbing the sounds and lights of the city beyond the walls. After so many visits, she didn't need a map; her feet led her without guidance, deeper in until she found herself by a small lake, moonlight rippling across its black surface.

After several covert glances to make sure she wasn't being watched at all, she reached inside her leotard, where the bloodbag had been warming against her chest, and pulled it out. With no ceremony at all, she slipped the tube into her mouth, and drew deeply on the blood within. The bag had been about half full, and she was done in seconds, her throat swallowing the blood convulsively.

The uncontrollable drinking was new, a troubling sign that her addiction was not lessening. Her knees weakened, sending her staggering in the direction of a bench by the lake, stuffing the now-empty bag into a pocket in her coat. Breathing deeply and fighting to keep her eyes open, she felt the surge in her body that seemed to start everywhere at the same time, a light breeze across her face feeling like a caress, distant sounds taking on shapes in the darkness. She scoured her surroundings for a place in the shrubbery where she could safely stow her coat.

As her eyes fixed upon a low tangle several steps from a path, her phone vibrated in her pocket. She pulled it out. It was Silas calling.

"Hello?"

"Hey, Lily, it's me. I got back into town early and I was just wondering if you might like to maybe grab a bite?"

At the sound of his voice, the swirling exhilaration shifted down from her stomach and she was overcome by a wave of horniness that she hadn't felt in a very long time.

In for a penny, in for a pound.

"Hey Silas, that would be lovely. I'm out for a walk, where should I go?"

"Where are you walking?"

"I... uh... I was out running but now I'm in the North Woods."

"Drop a pin and send it to me. I'll be there as fast as I can."

Chapter Ten

While she waited for Silas, Sara meditated, sort of. Relaxing on the stone bench, she enjoyed the bite of cold against her ass, and closed her eyes, listening to the sounds of Central Park at night. She could now hear the omnipresent ebb and flow of sirens in all directions, as well as closer, stranger sounds that she delighted in identifying, as if she was a contestant on a radio call in.

The most constant sound was the gurgling of the stream, down the embankment to her left. Even though she couldn't see the water, it sounded as smooth and round as the pebbles it shaped. Above her, restless birds refused to settle in for the evening, and Sara delighted in visualizing their puffball feathers ruffled against the cold spring night, then squinted her eyes, happily able to see them.

The last time she was this intoxicated, she hadn't been in a mindset to enjoy these new sensations. Her pupils felt like they were drinking in light from unknown sources; she could see details deep between the foliage that wouldn't even be clear in sunlight, with its sharply contrasted lights and darks. The wind carried scents, with the fetid pond by her feet the dominant aroma, but also, she could differentiate the smog from nearby car exhaust. She felt light glowing in her chest, and annoyingly, in the pit of her stomach. She went deep into an open-eyed reverie, scanning her body, relishing the weightless wellness she felt within.

Somewhere in the bracken behind her something was scratching. Bigger than a rat. She listened to the weighty paw-falls and bet on raccoon. Sure enough, the rolling lumbering trail sounds manifested themselves a short way down the path as not one, but two, burly raccoons on a mission. Sara watched them sense her but not see her, their noses twitching in unison. She held her breath until, bored, they waddled away.

The thrumming in her veins would not quit, no matter how carefully she regulated her breathing and she needed to get it under control before Silas arrived. First off, she scolded herself, why the hell did you let him come to you? She hadn't controlled that conversation, and now she was waiting in the darkest part of a park with waves of lust surging through her.

Okay, she negotiated with herself, when he gets here, we will go for a walk until we decide on where to eat dinner. Anything else would be unfair. From memory, Silas lived in the West Village, but with some luck and an empty A train, he could be arriving at any second. At the thought of seeing him, the blood rush surged again, curling outward, warmth down her legs, up past her heart, down to her fingers and then shivering up the back of her neck, circling her in a pattern. She wondered if this was what doing molly was like. She'd never know, because the virus went into shock over any amphetamines, activating fight or flight tension across all muscles, the renal system flushing it out rapidly, leaving the sister aching and cold. Opiates worked, but blood was the only drug a sister ever craved.

A tug at her foot snapped her back into the present and she glanced down to see one of the raccoons holding the lace of her ugly trail runners. Staying perfectly still, she watched its problem-solving skills as it tugged on the various loops and strands of her shoelace. Suddenly it sat upright, its ears tilting and swiveling like a radio dish before laying flat against its skull as its nose pointed in the direction of the sounds that Sara heard too. Sara followed its gaze and smiled when she saw Silas materialize in the dark.

"Over here," she called, scaring the shit out of the raccoon which fixed her a baleful stare before ditching her shoelace and rolling into the underbrush.

Do not sleep with him. Sara. Do not.

"Over here," she yelled again, waving an arm in the dark.

"I can't see you."

"Follow my voice."

"Or, if you can see me, you might walk here." Silas stopped in his tracks, unable to see his way as the path dipped into shaded moonlight. Der, he couldn't open his pupils as wide as she could after so many years of practice.

"On my way," Sara called, her voice not as loud in her ears as the blood buzz. Standing slowly, she dusted the front of her puffer, took two deep breaths and began wending her way with exaggerated slowness, pretending the dark was a barrier.

"There you are," he said, his voice definitely happy-adjacent, a new timbre Sara was not yet used to. When she reached him, he extended his arms for a hug, and without thinking, she leaned in, suddenly engulfed in an overwhelming barrage of scents. His soap, his shaving cream, hair gel, laundry detergent and most distressing of all, his skin and the blood beneath it. With an electric jolt, she pulled away from him.

"I'm sorry," she said, too hastily. "I... uh.. we aren't at the hugging stage."

"We hugged last time," he said, giving her a quizzical look. "Doesn't that usually place two people at the hugging stage?"

"Oh, right, I…"

"Forgot?"

She slugged him gently on the arm.

"No, I didn't forget, I'm just really rusty and…"

"And?"

"Are you enjoying this? The torturing of me?"

Silas smiled, gently curling a finger beneath her chin and raising her face toward his. He's going to kiss you, her mind panicked, just before he did. Leaning down slowly, he let his lips, cold and full, press against hers. She could feel every soft crease in his bottom lip as she slowly took it between hers. His hand vanished from beneath her chin and reappeared behind her lower back, pulling her to him. Waves of warmth flooded over her, and she clenched her fists at her side to prevent them from grabbing him as she wanted to. Sensing her hesitation, Silas broke the kiss, pulling back slightly.

"Is this okay?"

She loved the tear in his voice, the sotto voce rasp that belied just how much he wanted this. Sara gazed into his deep brown eyes and nodded.

"Good, because I've wanted to do it for quite a long time."

"Then do it again." Sara barely got the words out before his lips were upon hers again, and she finally released her fists, wrapping her arms around his broad back, her palms flat against his jacket, pulling him closer. He kissed her deeply, their faces blurring, Sara struggling to hold herself back, shocked by the power of her desire, worried she'd break him.

As another surge flowed through her, she hurriedly unzipped her down coat, pulling his arms inside, needing contact with skin. She felt his fingers pull her sweater out of her pants, and gently trail along her side. *Get a grip* ran like a mantra through her head but she was losing the battle, and her fingers were acting independently, suddenly at the button on his jeans and the kissing stopped and she was standing there, eyes closed, aware that he had stepped back.

"Steady," he said, his voice rough with passion. "What are we doing, Lily? I'm thinking that we just went straight to Go, without collecting the two hundred dollars."

"You're making a Monopoly analogy at a time like this?"

Silas nodded as he made sure his jeans were still buttoned.

"It's a terrible analogy but I needed to derail the train before we both end up on obscenity charges. The last thing I need at this stage in my life is to be put on the Miranda register."

Sara waited for her breathing to return to normal, but her heart wouldn't obey. Adrenaline rushes were heightened and intense for sistren, and she couldn't remember the last time her pulse was this staccato.

"You're right," she said, her voice giving away her struggle. "I don't know what came over me. That was intense.'"

She was looking down, or sideways, or anywhere but at Silas.

"Lily?"

Turning her face toward his feet, she began to raise her eyes, pausing at the tent in his pants. Following her gaze, Silas laughed.

"It still is intense, for one of us," he said. "We should decide where to eat."

"Doesn't look like we'll have to hurry that decision." Sara laughed, resting her forehead on his chest. "You're not going to be able to walk anywhere until that goes down."

"Fair point," he said. "But why don't we just get something simple like Shake Shack and then we can maybe come for another walk in the woods?"

"I can do Shake Shack," Sara said, wrapping an arm around his back.

"Nice, my treat," Silas said. "I'll even get you a concrete.""Just the thing on a sixty-degree night," she said, taking his hand and leading him along the dark path.

"You got night vision?"

Damn it. Sara shook her head. "No, I just know the North Woods like the back of my hand. I walk here whenever I don't want to be around people."

Up and down they traipsed along serpentine, narrow pathways between patches of blue-gray moonlight.

"You're in a good mood tonight," Silas said after some time had passed.

"I guess," Sara ventured, because she certainly hadn't been until she saw Silas. "You too."

"I don't do good mood," he said with a chuckle. "Or at least I didn't. I dunno. Maybe this is a good mood. I was looking forward to some good existential conversation, maybe some wine. Instead I got some outdoor hanky panky and now I'm getting a mushroom burger. Life really is a confusing game."

"We kissed. Briefly. That's hardly hanky panky."

"You sound disappointed."

"That's what I get for trying to be spontaneous." Sara laughed.

"I like spontaneous," Silas said. "Don't get me wrong, that was definitely something I wanted, but I kind of expected to have to work harder to get it."

"What are you saying?" Her voice was slightly arch.

"Oh nothing dramatic, nothing stereotypical, just that I had no inkling as to whether you'd entertained the same thoughts that I had."

Sara winced in the darkness, grateful for its cover. She'd been so distracted by Silas's existential dilemma that she hadn't paid too much attention to his appearance. Something shapeless tweaked her suspicions again, because the Silas she was seeing outside of her office was nothing like the man she'd met in treatment, and she wondered if he was maybe schizophrenic, undiagnosed, on an upswing.

"Did I lose you there??"

"Oh, no, I was just thinking, and I'm just going to say what I'm thinking, but you seem very different from the person I was treating."

"Yeah, sorry about that," he said. "I'll be blunt. I was attracted to you. I continued seeing you because I liked you, and couldn't figure out how to, you know, transition in that direction."

Sara slowed on the path, still holding his hand and turned to face him.

"That's a lot to process," Sara said. "And against the rules."

"In a world of rules, sure, that's the outcome, but this isn't a world of rules, is it?"

Sara skipped a beat before answering. "Isn't society founded upon rules?"

"Yeah, sure, but do you follow all the rules? Do I follow all the rules? Nobody does. And maybe that's why society is in the pickle that it's in today. Today, everyone is chasing the short cut around the rules. And they erode the good pillars of society, leaving the shitty pillars to hold the roof up for everyone. And those pillars are wonky."

"There you are!" Sara clapped her hands together. "There's the Silas that I know and..."

Her words trailed off and they stood in silence for several moments, eerie quiet hovering around them.

"I told you. I am who I am. My existential issues are my own and they're very real. I never lied to you. I do wonder if you may have jumped to a conclusion about how dark my mindset might be."

"Oh, so you're only a nihilist," she said. "That's a relief."

"Why's that?"

"Statistically, your prognosis is good."

"Don't go thinking you can change me or save me. That's not what this is about."

"It must be, at least slightly," Sara said, tentatively. "I mean, if you fell in love and it was everything love is supposed to be, wouldn't that be sign of a fundamental shift, that you'd be happier to move through each day?"

"You know, maybe? I guess. But no relationship could survive that kind of pressure."

"You said 'relationship.'"

"I'm not too worried about the future, as you well know. I'm presently much more preoccupied with hoping that there'll be more kissing in my future."

Sara absently rubbed at the side of her lower lip, where his stubble had grazed her, the area now smarting in the frigid air.

"There could be more kissing," she said, beginning to walk again. "But I have patients on Monday and I can't go in there with red all around my mouth."

"Hey, I was being gentle."

"Why do men always say that after basically rubbing your face with sandpaper?"

Silas stopped walking and pulled her back to him. Placing a hand on each shoulder, he steadied her, before leaning in and grazing his lips across hers, back and forth, back and forth very carefully, no stubble grating across her skin. The buzz in her veins gained volume and intensity, sounding like a distant rustling of dry leaves, whirring around her brain and making her dizzy. Every time she inhaled him, she felt herself weaken. Damn pheromones.

Pressing her palms against his chest, she broke the kiss.

"If you actually want to eat dinner, we need to get to it. Otherwise, my desire to eat is very happy to take a back seat to whatever is going to happen next if you keep on kissing me."

Sara was shocked at her level of disappointment when Silas nodded in agreement and pointed to the Natural History Museum, a collection of white dots of light visible through the trees.

"I'm starving," he said. "Let's eat."

After catching a glimpse of herself in the bathroom mirror at Shake Shack, eyes slightly wild, her normal pallor suffused with a blood-glow, Sara quickly suggested getting their food to go. As a result, she found herself sharing a rapidly cooling mushroom burger on a stone bench in front of the Natural History Museum.

Eating in silence, she feigned hunger, quietly stifling nausea as she ate. The virus liked to absorb blood on its own schedule. Even after a heem, it was best to avoid solid food for an hour or two. Still, she'd been acting a fool since Silas showed up, struggling to appear a bit more normal, so she chewed, her mind darting around, the words suddenly out of her mouth without warning.

"Silas, this thing between us, it's nice."

He paused mid bite and raised his face to her level, the blue white of the overhead LED streetlight catching him perfectly.

He locked eyes with Sara, his expression kind, yet searching as if he needed to say the right words.

"Yes?" Sara said when he hadn't spoken in almost a minute.

"If I say the wrong thing, you're going to raise your walls even higher."

"That's always a risk with me, buddy." Sara laughed. "I'm a therapist, I know all the tricks."

"Precisely." Silas paused, taking a deep breath. "Okay, here goes. I feel something strange, like a commonality. Between us." He flicked his eyes from the bench up to hers, held her gaze for a second, then, to Sara's chagrin, dropped it.

"Go on," she said quietly. "I haven't run away yet."

"Lily, I felt like I met someone who had the same lack of engagement in life as I do. You weren't just saying therapy speak. You began speaking deeply, and you never called out my more... let's say nihilistic statements."

"So, my lack of lust for life was what lured you in?"

Silas chuckled and took her hand.

"I'll take common ground anywhere I can find it."

"Fair enough. So what are you expecting from our new..." Sara paused. She'd almost said relationship. "...arrangement? An award for gloomiest couple ever?"

"I never said you're gloomy. I don't think that a healthy cynicism is gloomy. The world is fucking grim. It's like we have front row seats to the end of the world and they let Michael Bay direct it."

"And what's our role in the movie?"

"Sadly, our characters always die in that movie," he said, with an incongruous smile. "We're the rebel alliance who ultimately sacrifice themselves so that the world can live."

"To hell with that," Sara said, giving his hand a squeeze. "Like I said in session, if they dropped a bomb on the city, I'd rather stand still, breathing deeply and watching the fireball rush toward me. No point screaming and scrambling in your last seconds."

"And that was the exact thing that you said that made me see something in you."

"Hmmmmmmm," Sara said, mainly because she didn't know what else to say. "

"So you gambled pretty big on this?"

"I had nothing to lose."

"You had this to lose."

"It was worth the gamble."

"Your burger is going to be frozen solid." Sara cocked her chin at his half-eaten burger on the bench between them.

Silas lifted it to his lips, almost like he was going to kiss it.

"Too late," he said, wrapping it up in its wrapper. "I'll give it to those raccoons on my way home."

Sara's heart sank, even though she'd spent the past hour convincing herself that she wasn't going to sleep with him. At least he could have tried.

"You're going to walk back across the park?"

"Yeah, I need to get my steps in." He chuckled. "

"Fair enough." Sara's voice came out way too perkily. "I'm sorry this wasn't my finest hour, luring a handsome man into a dark forest then ravishing him with cold burgers and clumsy conversation."

"I didn't hate it." Silas smiled. "Wait, you think I'm handsome?"

"Oh come on, you're an adult, stop fishing."

"I love it when you're thorny."

"Be careful what you wish for."

Silas reached his hands out and clasped her face, the freezing cold of his fingers startling her. Before she could protest, he pulled her in and kissed her again, perfectly, softly. Since he hadn't been too receptive to her roaming hands she kept her palms pressed against her thighs, returning his kisses by copying his moves. It felt weird to be so passive, but it also felt nice, very nice. The humming in her ears picked up again and her hands needed to touch him, so she moved them from her thighs to his. He didn't seem to mind, so she stepped up the kissing.

"Get a room, you two!"

They pulled apart, startled. An old lady with an fuzzy dog on a leash waved at them. "Just fucking with you. Don't mind me, lovers."

As they watched her totter along Central Park West, Sara couldn't help but steal glances at Silas. Something about him comforted her. His face was broad and pale, his eyes darker than chocolate but not black. Crazy long eyelashes that looked like they blocked his vision. Very full lips. His dark hair was tousled, partly by the wind, partly by her hands.

"It's rude to stare," he said, his mouth extending into his crooked smile. "Didn't your mother ever teach you that?"

As he spoke, she was struck by a wave of familiarity, as if they'd met before. She wracked her brain but found nothing but a bare whisper of familiarity.

"You zone out a lot, don't you?"

She blinked away the cobwebs to find him staring into her eyes.

"Sorry, yeah, I tend to be pretty internal. Silas, I do need to tell you, I'm generally not fit for human consumption."

He pulled her closer and kissed her again.

"I strongly disagree," he said into her mouth, in between kisses.

"But," he said, breaking their kiss, "I do think it's time for me to go. I know we have a choice to make right now, and the smart choice and the right choice are probably the same, but I... uh... I'm not good with fast-paced change, so I'm going to go home. I'm going to regret my decision the whole way home, but I think right now, it's the best decision."

"Who are you trying to convince, buddy?"

"Myself, der," he said, kissing her forehead. "I'd like to see you again."

"I'd like that too."

He kissed her one last time, languid, warm, all lips, she wanted it to go longer but he broke it off, stood, and saluted her.

"Good night, Lily. I'll be in touch about your follow-up visit."

She was still smiling as he crossed the wide, empty avenue and vanished into the darkness of the park.

She pulled out her phone and texted him.

> Say hi to the raccoons. I hope they like the burger.

Chapter Eleven

The walk up Broadway, a walk that Sara usually performed perfunctorily, barely noticing the changing storefronts from year to year, tonight felt different, sharper, like someone had turned the contrast way up. Definition existed between letters and backgrounds, sidewalk and bitumen, treetop and the curious humming gray of the New York night. Everything felt separate and heightened. And it felt good.

Twenty blocks is a mile, she mused to herself, looking around as if seeing this particular mile with new eyes, a febrile happiness inside her heart.

Do. Not. Be. So. Stupid.

She felt like a girl she had never been. A modern, young woman wrapped in the shivers of a new relationship.

Pausing at the bottom of the valley of 96th Street, she gazed down to the river, catching some wavy stars flickering in slivers between the tree branches of Riverside Park. You're acting like you're in a movie musical, she chided herself, before crossing and beginning the uphill part of her walk home. The street was almost deserted. In the distance she could see the homeless, schizophrenic prophet Bobby leaning against a trash can, so she pulled a twenty from her wallet and slipped it into her coat pocket. Every night, Bobby and a group of unhoused folk waited for the Dunkin Donuts to toss out their stale food. It wasn't yet midnight, he still had hours to wait. On the other side of Broadway, she watched a young couple gather so tightly together that she couldn't make out which limb belonged to which person.

Sistren remained alert, at all times, and the party line was that walking at night alone was frowned upon. But she knew they all did it. Sometimes their rabbit-warren edifice felt too much like a crucible, and not enough like a sanctuary. Still, a mugging or an attack would be a disaster. It had been one in the past, many times. The virus, when threatened, did that adrenaline dump, and the results were never pretty, nor easily explained.

"Thanks, lady, stay warm," Bobby said with a genuine smile when she palmed him the bill.

"You too, bud," she said, not pausing. Some nights, she sought him out, conversing for hours, his mental state offering her unpredictable answers. When you've heard it all, sometimes you just needed to not know what someone was going to say. But if she gave him too much money, he would overdose. Twenty seemed safest.

Turning onto 104th, deep in reverie, she shoulder-bumped Marguerite, head down, in a hurry.

"*Pinche cabrona*, watch it!" Marguerite, clearly a full New Yorker now, didn't even look up.

"Karla," Sara called, using the woman's current public name, and Marguerite spun around. In normal people, a smile would demonstrate recognition. Marguerite's scornful contempt remained unchanged.

"Oh. Sa... Lillian."

"You seem busy, I'll let you go."

Before Sara could turn, Marguerite's face softened and she stepped back, taking one of Sara's bare hands in her gloved ones.

"*Desculpe*," Marguerite said with uncommon humility. "I've been doing as you say. Being nice. Sara, it's exhausting."

Sara set her face to frozen, not wanting an unplanned eyeroll to set the Spaniard off. Why hadn't she taken 103rd? This is what happens when you want to end a nice night by checking out the flowers in their buckets outside the bodega on the corner.

"Well, it gets easier with practice," she said evenly. "Anything in particular I should know?"

Surprisingly, Marguerite softened. "No, senorita, no. I just had to be nice to Rosa and Eleanor. It's the price I pay for their votes. Being nice is harder for me than for most people."

Sara met the woman's eyes and smiled. "It's just acting, Marguerite. It might not be easy. It's just necessary."

"Such resolve, I have always admired how you conduct this Lock."

Sara glanced up and down 104th. Discussion of their facts was forbidden outside of their home. The street was deserted.

"I checked before I spoke."

"It's still a rule for a reason." Sara hated being the narc all the time. "How is everything coming along with April Veronica?"

Marguerite nodded.

"She is the easy part. It's the rest of the Lock that is robbing me of pleasure right now. Still, I just had, I hope, my last argument with Rosa about this."

"Wait – you argued? Let's walk and talk, if you don't mind the company."

Marguerite paused a moment while she considered the offer, irritatingly.

"Sure, but let's head down to the river." Marguerite spun so quickly on her heels that Sara missed the movement completely.

"That's against the rules too."

"Like I said before, I looked first."

"Marguerite, look around us. There's probably a thousand windows. We are never alone, there's never nobody watching."

"Or…" Marguerite slowed her pace. "We could race…"

Sara raised an eyebrow, tempted. She couldn't remember the last time she'd run with a sister.

"Wait until we are in the park," she started, but Marguerite wasn't by her side any more. Hurriedly glancing up and down the block and seeing it empty, Sara crouched, then let fly, her legs pistoning effortlessly, her arms jacknifing back and forth, her feet, grateful for the running shoes, barely touching the ground. Leaping down the steps into Riverside Park, she caught sight of Marguerite's red coat flicking between the trees, and like a bull she focused on it, feeling nothing but the wind against her face and the thrill of the chase in her heart.

Closing the gap between them, then overtaking Marguerite easily, Sara whistled down to the edge of the river, catching sight of some late night dog walkers in the distance and slowing herself in the darkness before stepping out into the moonlight at the river's edge.

"You're fast for an old girl," Marguerite said, appearing suddenly at her side.

"I'm in a good mood." Sara spun around to face her, leaning back against the stone wall. "I took your advice. I had a date tonight."

A genuine smile spread across Marguerite's face. Sara had never seen her smile like that.

"That's wonderful, but … Sara?"

"Yes?"

"How come you're here?"

"He's a gentleman?" Sara said with a wan smile.

"You're disappointed."

Sara turned, resting her elbows on the stone wall, gazing out over the river at the lights of New Jersey, remembering a time when she had stood in the same place at night, with only darkness on the other shore. She felt Marguerite's shoulder rest against her own and they stayed silent, listening to the river waves slap against the sea wall.

"You'll see him again?" Marguerite said eventually, and Sara nodded.

"Yeah, hopefully this weekend."

"But you already have plans."

"Oh, right." Sara smiled. "Yes, but I was hoping we could do the ceremony on Sunday."

"Too late," Marguerite said gently. "It was Heather who broke up my argument with Rosa, and she informed us that it has to be Saturday. Even Crina is coming in. I feel so special," she added, in a voice that indicated that was not how she felt.

"You don't like Crina?" Sara kept her voice light.

"Oh, don't get me wrong, I love her. I just don't understand how she is responsible for both you and Desdemona."

Sara chuckled. She'd heard that line before. "It's like any family. Same parents, two kids. One becomes a stable professional with a family, the other pushes away responsibility and becomes homeless. It's not that uncommon."

"No, but also, in that comparison, both of you think you're the former."

"Ouch," Sara said, turning sharply.

"Quit being so sensitive," Marguerite said brusquely. "I'm just pointing out that Desdemona considers herself the responsible one."

"Desdemona has always run to the spotlight. Her current interests are usually just the latest trend to offer her the most power, or visibility. I don't honestly know what she wants."

"I disagree," Marguerite said. "I've been talking to people in my old Lock. They say she's acting like she's on a crusade."

"Well, as long as she keeps her crusade to herself, I don't care."

"Sara, please, listen to me. Do not dismiss her. Not this time. She's dangerous."

"What have you heard?" Sara was curious, and chilled.

"Her crusade is real. She's become a fanatic."

"She can do whatever she wants, in her own Lock."

"That isn't the game she's playing."

Sara went silent, trying to tamp down centuries of a relationship fraught with tension, to see the situation clearly.

"Thank you for your honesty," she said finally.

"And thank you for having the conviction to permit me to convert April Veronica. She will be my life's finest work."

Without warning, Marguerite leaned in and engulfed Sara in a hug. Shocked, it took several seconds for Sara to register that Marguerite expected reciprocation, so she forced her arms up and around the woman's back. Tonight was proving to be one for the books.

Gently, Marguerite broke the hug and stepped back. "Thank you for this, Sara," she said. "I know how much work you put into this, for me. I appreciate it more than you know, right now.

Sara nodded. Before she could say anything, Marguerite switched back to her old curt self.

"Thank you for listening," she said, her eyes boring into Sara's. "Now I would like to be alone and put my thoughts into order. I find inspiration in the darkness."

Without another word, the woman turned away and began striding purposefully away, heading north along the river.

She's so extra.

Sara made herself smile. Keeping up with modern slang was exhausting, but it always felt like a small victory when it organically became a temporary part of her brain. Hey, maybe April Veronica would be proud. Sara made her way out of the park and back to the building. She had to walk past the main nunnery doors and take a left to get to the door that she was using in her Lily Berger life. As she walked, a memory of Silas, and his full lips, smiling under the clinical white of an LED streetlight, came to her, and the warm feeling in her heart and stomach returned. Smiling, she reached the door to the complex, using her key fob at the first security door, checked her mailbox, then opened the second door with a second fob plus a fingerprint scan. Once inside, she let the door close a little too loudly, wincing as she pictured Eleanor, in her apartment behind this wall, checking her security camera to see who made the noise. "I'm sorry!" she mouthed at the security dome on the ceiling.

With a long-absent spring in her steps, she bounded up the five stories to her door, envisioning a glass of pinot noir and a long warm shower. Her face fell when she got to her apartment, 5A. A violet post-it was affixed just below her peephole. The writing was Heather's.

Swing by when you get home, love. I'll open a bottle.

Groaning, Sara let herself into her apartment. Stepping into the bathroom for a quick pee, she caught her reflection in the small mirror above the sink, grateful Marguerite hadn't seen her in bright light. Her skin was radiant, a rosy blush across her cheeks, and her eyes, brown with gold flecks, bordered by some very tell-tale red rings. There was no way she could face Heather like this. She pulled out her phone, then sat on the toilet while she texted.

Rain check old love. Today got me like zzzzz

Then, as she was undressing, her phone dinged on the bathroom counter. Certain it was Heather, she focused on peeling the leotard from her legs. When she stood upright, she smiled to see that it was in fact Silas who texted her.

> Dinner Saturday?

Thinking quickly, she replied.

> I have a boring fundraiser on Saturday. Does Friday work?

Almost immediately, Silas replied with a string of emojis: Thumbs up, smiley face, raccoon.

Chapter Twelve

"I feel like Sleeping Beauty getting ready for her date with the prince," Sara said, laughing. She stood on the bottom rung of the spiral staircase in her apartment. Before her, Heather and Teddie cast approving top-to-toe stares over her final outfit.

"Sara." Teddie waved a circling finger in her direction. "If I asked how long it's been since your last date, and you counted on your fingers, how many times would you have to close your hands and start counting again?"

"Stop it!" Sara smiled. "I've basically been a single mom with nine needy babies for a century."

"What does that make me?" Heather laughed. "The cat's mother?"

Sara slugged her in the arm.

"Oh dayum," Teddie said, her fingers snapping dramatically in the air. "She getting feisty. And if we don't get Miss Thing out the door, her date gonna ghost his ass before she get there, he's gonna think she standing him UP."

"Yes, Teddie. Being extra right now is definitely going to calm my nerves."

"Sorry momma," Teddie said. "Ima just say it. You look beautiful. I'm sorry I made a funny about your boyfriend's fragile state."

"A funny has to make someone laugh, technically."

"Jesus, okay." Teddie bent down and straightened the laces on Sara's black leather boots that a long-dead cobbler in Williamsburg made for her a lifetime ago. "They really don't make 'em like this anymore."

"I must admit I'm a bit jealous," mused Heather, eyeing the boots lovingly. "And disappointed that you're a full size too small for me to borrow them.."

"You are not having sex in my favorite boots," Sara joked, stepping onto the floor where Teddie smoothed her freshly straightened raven hair against her burgundy Dior sweater which was tucked into black Givenchy wool trousers.

"You've really kept your vintage in top shape," Teddie said. "You're lucky. Your fashion cycle is twenty years. Black girls take longer to get sentimental. Just the other day I saw a sister rocking this gorgeous dashiki that I had back in the late sixties. That thing was like a fabric acid trip, and I didn't realize I missed it 'til I saw it on someone else."

"You should have asked her where she got it," Sara said.

"Nah, I'm good. I'ma live in BLM jerseys 'til the work is done."

"Me too," said Heather, hooking a thumb at the yellow fist on her black hoodie. "Now you go and have a good night, don't rush home. We have tomorrow under control."

"Damn straight!" Teddie brushed her knuckles on her chest. "Don't be texting us every five minutes. Everything is ready to roll. The fridge is stocked, the weapons are shiny and nothing can go wrong. Nothing."

Sara paused midway to the door. "Are you sure? I can come home straight after we eat if anything comes up."

"The only room for error at this point, pet," Heather said with a smile, "is Marguerite, and we all know there's nothing can be done there." Sara made to speak and Heather held up a shushing finger.

"Quit procrastinating and get out the door."

Teddie yanked the navy puffer from its hook by the door and handed it to Sara, who bowed as she took it.

"Thank you both," she said, smiling. "I'm a lucky girl."

"A girl who hasn't called her Lyft yet."

"Oh, I'm walking, it's not far, and I'm not late.""Someone is nervous," Heather said to Teddie.

"Lil bit," Sara said, opening the door so they could all leave her apartment. "Just a lil bit." She smiled to herself. Being nervous felt nice.

Dusk fell as she walked up Broadway, at last a promise of spring in the breeze. She enjoyed the way it flipped her hair back with each step.

Am I expecting too much?

She shook her head, annoyed at her self-doubt. After crossing the double expanse of Adam Clayton Powell and nearly colliding with one skateboarder and two Uber Eats delivery bikes, she spied Silas in the distance with her heightened eyesight. He was leaning against a light post, checking something on his phone, his profile bathed in a weak white light, his small, straight nose a perfect foil for his full lips.

When she was still half a block from him, he sensed her approach, slipped his phone into a pocket in his floor length wool duster, and spread his arms wide.

"You came!" he said as she drew near.

Teddie's voice echoed in Sara's head: *Do not kill him with cynicism, girl.*

Sara fought every instinct to be a smartass. Instead, she nodded, then smiled.

"I wouldn't have missed it for the world, Mr. Oppenheimer."

Without hesitation, she stepped up to him, resting her face against his chest as his arms encircled her.

"Me either," he said into her hair. "Lily, it's wonderful to see you. You look so beautiful tonight."

Sara inhaled deeply, biting down every comeback that floated to the top of her mind.

"Thank you, Silas. I'm terrible with accepting compliments, so that thank you was about the only graceful thing I can say. Anyway, is this where we are eating?"

She glanced to her right, to the staircase leading up to a sign that said Seasoned Vegan.

Silas nodded, releasing her slightly.

"I've wanted to try this place for a long time," he said. "It's soul food, and I didn't think vegan would be a problem."

"I actually love it here," Sara said. "You've inadvertently picked one of my favorite places in the city." Her mind quickly scrambled for the last time she had dined in. Maybe some time around 2010, but the risk was acceptable. She'd been with Teddie that night, straight from work. Unrecognizable. Teddie would be jealous she'd gone back in person.

"Ugh, I was trying to find something new for you." Silas was crestfallen.

"Anything in the order delivery radius of my office has been tried. But I never get to go."

"Wait, where do you live?"

Sara smiled, the lie already at her lips because bringing anyone into the compound was obviously forbidden. If a sister wanted a relationship, she had to set up an apartment in one of the buildings that the Lock owned. "Down in Murray Hill," she said. "You know, the OG no man's land."

"Oh, I'm sorry," Silas said. "I presumed you lived up here."

"Psychiatrists tend to give their patients a smokescreen," Sara said. "You're not a patient anymore, so now you know." She tilted her chin in the direction of the restaurant steps. "Shall we? I'm starving!"

Inside, the restaurant was rustic and charming, warm and gently claustrophobic. The air was filled with delicious scents, oil and spices and the sweet brown sugar vinegar scent of barbecue. Standing behind Sara, Silas helped her coat from her shoulders and hung it on a peg by the door, then did the same with his own.

"Uh wow," he said when he turned back to her. "I should have reserved my compliments for later in the evening, apparently." To her utter shock, Sara felt a blush come raging across her chest and up her throat. She took a deep breath to stop it from reaching her cheeks and was only partially successful.

She took in Silas, in simple dark denim jeans, Frye boots and a black cable knit sweater, looking whole and human for the first time ever. Gone was the broken soul who came to her office in khakis and threadbare sweaters, and again she was briefly tormented by the weight of irresponsibility in what she was doing.

"You also look very, very handsome tonight, Silas," she said, her eyes down.

A bubbly young Black woman, her hair a delight of cornrows ending in colorful puffs, directed them to their table. Silas stepped ahead of Sara and pulled her chair out, and Sara nodded demurely as she slid into it, pulling it forward herself, rapidly running through her set of reminders for the life she was currently in. Thirty-three, lived in New York a decade, no siblings, parents dead. She knew she was thin on things that she'd done in the past decade because running the Lock was more than a full-time job and she had honestly not done very much outside of the building's walls.

Silas's hand around hers snapped her back to the here and now and she smiled. "Sorry, I'm a daydreamer," she said.

"I know," he said. "I know the signs. You blink slowly and then your eyes slowly gaze to the left."

"That sounds a bit stalkery," Sara said nervously.

"Think of it as the Yelp therapist review I didn't leave for you."

"It's that obvious during a session?" Sara was aghast.

"It's not as bad as you're making it sound, or I'm making it sound. I tried to trap you a few times but you somehow manage to pay attention and drift off at the same time."

"And here I am thinking I have a poker face."

Silas rubbed a thumb across the back of her hand. "And there I was thinking you're just a woman with a lot on her mind."

A smile creased her eyes and she stared at this strange, interesting man.

"I think that's true of both of us." She paused, glancing left and right, the neighboring tables close enough to make any further private discussion not really possible. As if he read her mind, Silas leaned across the table.

"We can continue that conversation at our second stop for the evening," he said, a half-smile playing across his lips, candlelight sparkling in his eyes. Sara groaned inwardly as she felt the first glacial shift of herself falling for him.

"We should order," she said, lifting the menu so that it covered her face and blocked Silas's probing, deep eyes.

"There are so many things on there that I want to try. Can you recommend anything that you've had before?"

"I usually just grab one of the po'boys," Sara said truthfully. "There are things that sounded a bit decadent for a quick lunch at my desk, like the raw lasagna and the basil garlic crawfish."

"Would you be into sharing? Because both of those things were on my wishlist, alongside the smothered chicken."

"We could share for sure," she said, lowering her menu. "It's so affordable, we could get all three things and just pick at them."

Silas nodded. "And let me see if I remember, you're a tempranillo girl, right?"

"Well, sure." She smiled. "I'm many girls when it comes to wine, but anything dry and sunny and aromatic gets my vote."

"Would you care to choose?"

She nodded, flipping open the wine list, quickly seeing a favorite.

"Before I decide on bottle versus glass, though, Silas, can you tell me what the second part of the evening involves?"

Chuckling, Silas cocked his head and stared directly into her eyes.

"Can you ice skate?"

"Like a fucking champ," Sara said.

"Well then, cocky you and I have a date with some skates at Harlem Meer. My treat. They're open 'til eleven."

Sara's eyes widened. She hadn't skated on ice in forever, but it was like riding a bike, right? *Right??*

"Let's just get our wine by the glass. Okay?"

Hours later, double knotting her last skate lace, Sara looked up to see Silas tottering toward her on his skates, a bronze key flashing in his palm.

"Madam, your favorite boots are now safely under lock and key."

"Thank you so much. I don't think I'd survive their loss."

"They're damn nice."

"They're more than nice. The thought of some millennial treating them badly sends shivers down my spine."

"Aren't you a millennial?"

Fuck. Shit. Piss.

"You know what I mean."

"No," Silas was toying with her, that half smile never far away. "Please tell me how you're different from your generation."

"Those boots are like my children, Silas. I oil them, I treat them better than I treat myself. And the man who made them has passed away, so they're literally irreplaceable. They're also accustomed to a certain lifestyle. They're not ready to be dragged to some party in Bushwick, by you know, someone who will let them *crack*."

After making a dramatic show of zipping the locker key inside his wallet, Silas extended a hand.

"I'd hate to think that you'd use your beloved boots as a diversion to cover up an earlier claim of skating prowess."

Sara gripped his hand, hoping that muscle memory wouldn't make a liar of her, making sure to not crush his hand. In a flash she was on her feet, walking steadily to the gap in the fencing. On the ice, groups of kids played, several sets of older couples made leisurely laps, their arms around each other's waist, and a posse of gay bears ran speed sets, stopping to chug beers when they won a race.

Sliding her skates onto the slippery surface, she dug the blade teeth in the ice and turned to face Silas.

"Is the first lap a race?"

"The first lap is anything you want it to be, Lily," he said. He winked and launched onto the ice from the sodden carpet at the rink edge, his arms behind his back. Crouching, she channeled her energy into her left hip, then shot off after him, her legs pumping the skates until she was level with Silas, the wind whipping her hair back.

"It's on, Oppenheimer," she called before leaning into the corner, feeling the g-forces building in her thighs as she held them steady until it was time to release into the straight, remembering the times she and Crina had skated on various rinks around the city, all long gone now.

Silas was yards behind her, and even weaving around the slowpokes, she had no trouble maintaining a lead. The cold wind against her face and the warmth of her blood pounding in her veins pushed the frigid night air away from her. A space opened up ahead and she threw her feet wide, spinning in a circle and switching to backward skating.

"Forward skating only" boomed a tinny voice over the PA, and in a flash she spun again, dancing around one of the bears.

"Girl, who you racin'?" he called as she passed. "Glad it ain't me!"

She blew him a kiss and decided that she was going to try to lap Silas. She couldn't remember the last time she felt so alive, or so irresponsible. Motion in her periphery startled her. It was Silas, flying up on the inside.

"You snooze, you lose," he yelled as he flew past, and she dug in, trying to catch up to him, surprised to see him slow and move to the rail at the side.

"Why you slowing down?' she called as she glided up to him.

"I think it might be better like this," he said, extending an arm and pulling her against him. She reached her left arm behind her and took his hand and he pushed away from the wall.

"This is a date, not a skate meet," he said, pulling her tight against him. "Let's act like those old couples. You can just tell they've been coming here forever, this is their jam."

"That would be something lovely," she said, lifting a skate to avoid a small girl who fell in front of them without skipping a beat.

"If we make things work, it could become our first tradition."

"Make things work." Sara faltered slightly on her skates."I'm having a good time."

"We are having a great time, tonight. Yes."

"Uh oh. Have I earned a but?"

Sara nodded. "But this is what? Our second date?"

"Third but who's counting." Silas smiled.

"Either way, we should be talking about school and the dog you had when you were six and which sports you like."

"We had a lot of that in your office."

"A lot of that talk told me that you were a very different person than the one I've seen recently."

"I don't even know if I was depressed, or if I was literally, stupidly, over it all, like a moody teenager. Looking back, the things that I said seem almost cartoonish. I was a jerk."

Sara raised her eyes to his, tears welling along her bottom lashes like mercury.

"I can't keep you engaged in life, Silas," she whispered. She was surprised to find herself in the throes of strong emotion.

"That's not your job, it's mine," he said softly. "If I never see you again, you've shown me a possibility. I know it's not love, at least not yet and maybe never, but I haven't felt hope in a very long time. I'd forgotten how addictive it can be."

"That's truly something I never thought I'd heard you say." She managed a laugh. "This is also one hell of a deep second date."

"Third." He kissed the tip of her nose.

"The raccoons got more of that burger than I did," she whispered, "but there was some kissing, so I'll let it count."

"Are you always so technical?"

"Details matter, Silas."

"Yes." He pulled her close and began to kiss her. "They do. "

As soon as their lips touched, Sara cursed not having Rosa prepare an apartment for her at the Murray Hill building. It had been on her to-do list all week, but it seemed somehow presumptuous, so it had gotten lost in the shuffle of preparations for tomorrow. The now-familiar wave of lust and hunger for Silas contact coursed through her tummy, up across her chest, then down. It was just as strong as the other night, but this time, she had not fed beforehand. She was reacting to him naturally. That was infinitely more terrifying.

Sara inhaled him, his palms pressed flat against her lower back, her tummy against his, suddenly aware that there was nothing on her mind except this moment. She banished the thought like a pesky bird, surrendering to the present. When they finally parted, the crew of gay bears cheered, making Silas blush. Sara turned to face them and bowed.

"I'll have what she's having," called one of the men, and the group erupted in laughter.

Silas took Sara's hand, pulling her back onto the ice.

"Come on, it's time for us to couples skate."

This time, Sara found it easy to calm her inner voice as they wordlessly navigated lap after lap around the sparkling, frozen pond.

Chapter Thirteen

"The car service is pulling off the West Side Highway!"

Heather sprang up from the couch and moved to Sara's twin sliver windows, gazing down at the street below.

"I'll go down and wait," Sara said, straightening the bulk of her nun's habit.

"Are you nervous?" Teddie called out from the kitchen.

"Nervous? Why would I be?" Sara tugged on her ugly coat from the closet.

"Coz y'all been pacing around and doing that huffing and puffing breathing thing you do when you can't even get your ass into a good reverie." Teddie stepped to Sara and brushed her cheek with the back of a finger. "She loves you."

Sara took a deep breath. All of that was true, and yet. Crina had been off in a scholarly reverie outside Ithaca for a long time, and Sara's visits to her various homes had tapered off over the last decade, as had Crina's trips into the City. Sara only had good memories of Crina, and was bolstered somewhat by their recent phone conversations, but was currently sidelined by the doubt of living up to a parent's expectations, the same as anyone.

"I know, I know," Sara said with a mix of frustration and resignation. "But it's like when someone comes to clean your place, they find dirt you missed. I know there's something going on here that she'll find, and I'll look bad."

"She forgives," Heather said from the window. "Her thing is forgiveness. And like Teddie said, you'll always be her favorite."

"I'm five hundred, not five," Sara said, removing her bulky key ring from the hook on the wall and pulling the door open. "I'll ask her if she wants to come here or go directly to the quarters belowdecks."

"If we don't see you in five minutes, we'll come down," Heather said. "Whatever you do, do not pull out your phone in her presence."

"Never did, never would," Sara said, pulling the door closed and beginning her descent. Her breathing was a little ragged, so she counted her steps. One breath in, two steps down. One breath out, two steps down. This wasn't going to help.

Sara had spent the first four hundred years of her life in Locks headed by Crina, first in Romania, then Rome, Barcelona, Paris and London, before arriving in the brutal expanse of New Amsterdam. Crina's decision to go Scholar, in 1887, surprised her then, but made perfect sense now. As a very young sistren, Crina fought alongside her maker, Stefanya of Wallachia, in the pogrom against the vile brethren after their bloodlust reached torturous, disgusting heights. She and the original sistren operated a secret assassination squad for nearly fifty years, until all the cursed males were dead. Now, from Sara's current vantage point, the real surprise was that Crina hadn't flamed out sooner. She had immense power, and her insight was flawless. Sara stopped between the third and second floors. If for one second Crina guessed Sara's increased addiction, she'd start asking questions about its cause, and feeding on Laura, by accident or not, was a definite transgression.

"Do the crime, do the time," Sara muttered before finishing her descent.

By the time she reached the sidewalk, Crina's car was pulling up in front of the ornate doorway beneath the small sign that read Sisterhood Of Holy Silence. The smile that spread across Sara's face was genuine, as was her love for the woman who'd been her true mother. She blinked sudden tears away nervously.

A uniformed driver stepped out, tipping his chauffeur's cap at Sara, who smiled politely at him, wishing she could see Crina through the blackened windows, certain she was being surveyed. The old school chauffeur was a nice touch. Heather thought of everything. Before the chauffeur reached the passenger door, it clicked open and Crina effortlessly unfolded onto the street. Her thick black hair was a tumble of curls, and she wore a floor length black leopard coat and midnight black sunglasses. Her full lips were painted a deep burgundy. Definitely *not* in nun drag, Sara noticed with a smirk. A gloved hand waved the chauffeur away, and he busied himself with her luggage. Sara's heart began to thud.

She's not smiling.

Crina's face was so still she looked artificial, like a high fashion eighties goth store mannequin.

Sara stepped closer and Crina opened her arms, her face still frozen. Nervously, Sara stepped forward and was immediately consumed in a powerful hug, her face pulled into the tumble of curls.

"My child, I have missed you with my entire heart," Crina said in her deep, throaty voice. "It is deeply wonderful to hold you again."

"Oh..." Sara exhaled, relief in her voice. "I thought you were mad at me."

She felt Crina's cheek expand against hers in a smile as the woman raised her hands to Sara's shoulders and pushed her slightly away.

"My child," Crina began, and Sara felt tears well along her eyelashes, wishing she could see through the impermeable black shield of Crina's sunglasses. "I could never be angry at you. I'm in awe of your strength, your resilience. If anything, the apology is mine to make. I've spent so long in reverie, I forget to tell my face to move with my mouth. Also..." Crina paused, raising her other hand, which held a Nintendo Switch. "...I was lost in Super Mario Odyssey. I just needed to defeat a cartoon cow turtle."

Sara started giggling and the two pulled apart. The chauffeur was waiting patiently on the sidewalk. Sara approached him, pressed a roll of cash into his palm and bid him adieu. She consciously made an effort to pretend the suitcase was heavy as she began carrying it up the steps to the front door, Crina stepping slowly behind her. Only when they were past the second door did she stop the charade. She could have balanced the heavy thing on a finger.

"Do you want to go upstairs to my apartment, or go directly to yours? Teddie and Heather are in mine. Do you need to decompress?"

Crina paused, apparently thinking. Sara waited patiently, perplexed by Crina's flamboyant appearance. The Crina of old rarely ventured out of the compound in anything but her nun's habit.

"Which apartment am I staying in?" her maker finally said.

"I thought you'd like my old apartment, the one that looks into the sunwell. It's so quiet."

"Yes, that would be lovely. I need to spend some time in front of a mirror. I don't want to look like a wax dummy when I see everyone. I thought I was ready, but honey, it's been a minute."

They moved to the fourth-floor landing where Sara unlocked the door. They entered her old apartment, still furnished with a lot of the old things she had brought with her when she traveled to the United States. Heather had been through recently. Fresh tulips filled vases, and there wasn't a speck of dust to be found.

"I have always loved this space," Crina said, turning slowly, taking in the tapestries on the wall. "Heather doesn't miss a thing, does she?"

"No, and I'm grateful for that," Sara said. She watched Crina walk slowly to the dim window that faced into the shaft in the center of their building, one finger trailing along the ridge of the couch that Sara remembered buying from the Knoll store in 1949.

"Actually..." Crina paused. "Could you send Heather down? I do want to see her; I want to thank her for everything she does for me."

Sara nodded. "Of course." She began to back away. "The initial ceremony begins at four. I'd like to walk in with you, if that's fine?"

Crina nodded and smiled. "Darling, I'd like nothing more."

She paused and removed her sunglasses. Her deep chocolate eyes were rimmed in gray, and her skin, olive and so smooth, didn't wrinkle at all as a smile spread. She gave Sara's outfit a full up and down.

"And we are really doing the whole nun thing?"

Sara chuckled and nodded.

"I fucking hate those dresses." Crina laughed, suddenly walking like a penguin, arms at her sides, fingernails pointing out. "Go. I'll see you at 3:55."

After Heather was dispatched to see Crina, Teddie and Sara sat quietly together on Sara's couch. It wasn't uncommon for sistren to spend long periods of time together, in silence. The right company was calming even without words. But Sara watched Teddie for signs of nervousness, and saw them in a twitch of a finger, the restless shuffling of feet.

"You doing okay, Ted?" she asked finally.

"I've never killed anyone," Teddie replied.

"Experience does not make it any simpler."

"But I like being able to say that," Teddie said. "I'm a gold star girl."

"You sure are. If today ends badly, I will have to begin the process of transferring Marguerite out of New York. She loves living here more than she will ever admit, and she's way too self-centered to risk it."

Teddie exhaled slowly.

"Girl, I hope you hunned."

Sara smiled. As a black sister, Teddie had always had to walk a tightrope of blending in that was more textured than it was for the others, and she always made sure to speak in contemporary fashion. It was a lot of extra work for her, one more thing to be conscious of. Sara's heart welled with love.

"Do I say in response that yaaaaas quaaan I'm hunned?"

Teddie laughed. "You sound like RuPaul."

"I'll take that as a compliment. And Ted? I'll be with you, the whole time. If it needs to be done, I will help. If you falter, I'll step in."

"Are you bringing a Slicer?" Teddie's eyes narrowed as she said the name of the tempered steel bladed weapon that could slice through the spinal column in the blink of an eye, mitigating the damage done when a dying sistren's adrenaline turned her into a wrecking blur of fists and feet and teeth.

"I'm not expecting to have to kill one of us," Sara answered slowly. "Why would I bring a Slicer? If something goes wrong, we will just ask April Veronica to wait in the sealed room, and then you'll light the fire. She'll fall asleep in that armchair and never wake up."

"I've had nightmares that she refuses to wait in there, that Marguerite goes off script. Tons of shit can go bad, tons of shit."

"Well, if you want more nightmares, the presence of a Slicer is a good bet. It's not something you forget. Ever." Sara shuddered at the memory of the time she'd seen a sister be dispatched by the razor sharp knuckleduster in Paris. She hated the fact that the impossibly sharp and strong blade was still a fixture in Lock life around the world. It was a holdover from a violent past, a gothic weapon forged to defeat men, one that she believed should be retired from use. The European Locks disagreed.

Teddie stood and paced slowly around the couch.

"I have a good feeling about today," Sara said finally. "It's understandable to be nervous, but if at any point it seems that April Veronica is ... not going to work out, I will terminate the meeting. We have time to jump out of the speeding car before it hits the wall. Also," she paused and Teddie stopped pacing. "If you had spent some time in friendly conference with Marguerite, I think you'd be a lot less worried."

Teddie rolled her eyes. "I think I'd rather be nervous."

"She's not that bad, I'm finding. Her bark is so much worse than her bite."

"Fine, fine. After this I will make an effort. Pinky swear."

Teddie made a fist then uncurled her little finger, holding it out. Sara gave her the pinky swear.

"I'm going to go get ready," Teddie said. "If we're doing full robe, I need to take this weave out. It gets fucking hot in that room."

Finally alone, Sara silenced her phone and went into her bedroom. She needed to be still, to gather her wits and focus on the upcoming evening. As Lock mother, she was mistress of ceremonies, her script a recitation committed to memory so long ago, she barely recalled the lessons that Crina gave her, in a mountain cabin outside Bucharest. Like a song you sang along to without even realizing it, the words were all still there, in many languages. Running through recitations in her head, thoughts of Silas derailed them, moving her lips into a smile.

Plonking onto her bed, she mentally ran through the previous evening, a smile lifting the left corner of her mouth.

Should she text him? Were they at that stage? No. She couldn't afford the distraction while Crina was here. Daily texting felt weird. But she wanted to hear from him. Was this infatuation or procrastination? Both, she decided, forcing herself to practice her words for the evening. After several successful rehearsals, she rose, moving back to the kitchen and popping a handful of heems. Then she lifted her phone. There were two texts from Silas, and the other side of her mouth lifted into a full smile.

> Good luck today. I'm still smiling from last night.

And

> What's your Venmo? I still think I should have paid for dinner.

The grin on her face was obliterated by an incoming text from Marguerite.

> Traditionally, newcomers have an audience with the mother. How's 3?

It was already past two. Sara had been hoping that nobody remembered that whole audience thing, but of course, Marguerite would be pedantic about tradition. Sara would have to do it. That meant getting ready in less than fifteen minutes. She knew all the other sisters would be deep into hair and makeup already. It was tradition that for confirmation ceremonies, sisters would dress fabulously beneath their habits in anticipation of the party that could follow. A glance in the mirror told her that she needed more makeup than she could manage in fifteen minutes, and the planned chignon beneath her veil was now out of the question. The ponytail that her hair was currently in would have to do.

I will meet you in the basement conference room at 3.

Resigning herself to attending the meeting mostly bare-faced, Sara spent her fifteen minutes pulling a black satin vintage Herrera jumpsuit up over her body. She covered it with her nun robes, hastily fitting her wimple to her head and jamming her ponytail inside it. She slid her feet into patent leather Gucci mules, glancing at the clock on the stove the whole time. A couple quick strokes with a mascara brush, light gray eyeshadow at the outside of her eyes and with a sigh, she set off through the corridor behind her flat.

When she pressed open the door to the conference room, Sara was startled to see that Marguerite and April Veronica were already seated at the heavy oak table on the dais, nervous smiles on their faces. She regarded the newcomer warmly. April Veronica was simply, naturally beautiful in a way that few young woman were these days. Her open, elfin face showed no signs of the tampering so many indulged, no fillers, no Botox, no stupidly plump lips. Just wide green eyes, even skin, barely tamed natural curls in light brown hair.

"Ladies, you're early," Sara said as she approached them.

"Better than late," Marguerite said, her voice tight.

"I suppose so," Sara said, hoping that Marguerite could keep herself in check for the rest of the evening. "April Veronica, it's lovely to see you again."

The young woman stood. She wore a simple black dress, with long sleeves and buttons running down the front from neck to hem.

"Mother," she said, beginning a clearly rehearsed speech. "I am honored that you have considered me for inclusion in your order. The pleasure is all mine."

Sara took a seat directly across the ancient oak table from the women.

"I believe that Sister Karla has filled you in on the nature of our order, and our commitment to social justice, scientific research, and the humanities."

April Veronica nodded eagerly.

"Mother..." She was still standing. Sara wanted to motion for her to sit, but experience had taught her that it was best to wait first, to let the novitiates behave however they wanted, as it was more telling. "I am honored to be so close to confirmation in The Order Of Holy Silence. I am eager to bring this generosity, this spirit, to other women."

Sara smiled warmly.

"Please be seated, April Veronica." April Veronica took her seat beside Marguerite.

"As much as I understand Sister Karla has discussed these things with you," Sara continued, "it is part of the formal induction that for one final time, I ask you these questions."

April Veronica nodded.

"Have you known both love and heartbreak?"

"Yes, Mother."

"Do you wish to bear children?"

April Veronica shook her head. "No, Mother. While I love children, the world is overpopulated, and I believe my life will be better satisfied by continuing my studies of new viruses emerging from the ice melt. I do not wish to bear children."

"Have you ever born a child?"

"No. But I had an abortion when I was seventeen."

Sara gave a brief neutral nod.

"Do you have any affinity for religion?"

April Veronica shook her head. "Science is my religion."

Sara kept her poker face straight. That was a coached answer for sure.

"Do you have any family?"

April Veronica glanced at Marguerite. Sara cut her off before she could speak.

"I mean biologically."

"Oh." The young woman smiled, chastened. "No. After my mother died, I was abandoned on the steps of a cop shop in Washington Heights before I was two. I don't remember any of it."

Another commiserating glance.

"Do you have anyone that you'd die for?"

April Veronica turned to Marguerite. "This one. In a fucking heartbeat. Ooops, I'm sorry."

"No need. That is an acceptable answer."

A patina of sweat rose on April Veronica's forehead. She was nervous.

"Do you feel that long periods of silence will be difficult?"

April Veronica shook her head.

"Nope, I don't speak much anyway."

"Do you have any questions for me?"

A quizzical expression transferred from April Veronica's face to Marguerite's. Sara was pleased to see April Veronica think deeply.

"Have you had any regrets since you joined the order?"

The question took her by surprise, and Sara smiled, mainly to buy herself time.

"Regrets, no. Challenges, yes. Sometimes, this life is lonely. Also, you can't save everyone, so in that sense, every failure becomes a regret of sorts ."

Sara and Marguerite exchanged glances.

April Veronica bit her bottom lip, the wanting in her eyes so clear, so focused.

"Are you doing okay, April Veronica?"

April Veronica nodded.

"May I speak?"

Sara nodded.

"I have learned so much from Sister Karla. At first I was worried that my atheism would be a barrier, but I'm into what you are doing here, you're subverting the religious paradigm in the name of science. This is genius. In my truest heart I know that I am ready and capable of becoming a novitiate in your order."

Sara hated the formality of this part of the process. She wanted to hear April Veronica speak in her own voice, her own vernacular. Marguerite's coaching was robbing the young woman of the chance to show herself, but Sara sensed that Marguerite, against all odds, had made a good choice.

Would you make her yourself?

Sara froze. She would never make anyone, ever again, but the question surprised her. She had almost offered it to Laura, in the form of salvation. She forced herself to return to the present.

"Thank you, April Veronica, Sister Karla. This conversation has eased my mind. As you know, there will be one last formality, at four pm. Once you pass that, we will initiate you. During that formal meeting with the entire order, you will have your final chance to reverse your decision. If you choose to change your mind, you will be free to go. You will receive a generous endowment, and you will be able to continue your studies as a free woman, on the condition that you never reveal what you have learned of us. But also, in that event, once you leave this building, you will never be able to return, and Sister Karla will be forbidden from communicating with you. Do you understand?"

April Veronica stood, her breathing speeding up.

"Mother, this is my destiny. There is no price too high for me. The work you do is the work I wish to commit my life to."

Sara stood, too, and bowed. "Still, we adhere to our rituals, as outdated as they may seem. I will see you again at four."

Chapter Fourteen

Leaving Marguerite and April Veronica deep in conversation in the conference room, Sara glanced at her Apple watch. It was 3:36. Elsewhere in the labyrinthine building, the other sistren would still be hard at work on their makeup and outfits. She leaned back against the wall, feeling its chill seep through her habit and jumpsuit and considered changing it into something better. But being late for the ceremony wasn't an option, not today.

Who am I trying to impress?

Still, the jumpsuit suddenly felt dated and uncomfortable beneath her robes, so she hurried up the staircases and along the hallways until she was back in her own apartment ,where she clumsily threw her habit up over her head and fumbled with the jumpsuit until it loosened and slid to the floor.

Her mind was a mess, scattered and racing when it needed focus. In a perfect world she could have spent today in bed, with a book and some Guinness and the memories of last night, of Silas's lips on hers, his hands pressing against her back, even the sparks she felt when his eyes met hers. These were moments that deserved contemplation, like a bath of something magical that improved the mood and made her eyes close involuntarily. Stupid? Girlish? Yes, but a welcome return to something she'd forgotten.

With a dramatic sigh that made her laugh at herself, she kicked off her mules and went to her wardrobe. Rifling through the rear rack of hanging clothes, she lighted upon a raspberry wool Pucci mini-dress that she had mail-ordered from Paris in the sixties. The mere sight of it made her smile. Pulling her arms inside her habit, she slid the dress up, then wrestled with reaching the zip. It was like getting dressed inside a tent. She took a pair of white sheer tights from her underwear drawer, still in the packet. More wrestling. Once they were smooth against her legs, she stepped into a pair of low black Courreges boots of a similar vintage as her dress. She wished she could see the whole outfit in the mirror, without the robes, smelling as they did of cardboard and time, but time, right now, had run out. She needed to get downstairs. The woman in her mirror looked like any nun, anywhere, forgettable, uniform, which was precisely the point.

Slipping her phone and Apple watch into a pocket in her habit, she did a comically stylish turn before her full-length mirror and set off for the basement. It was time.

She was relieved to be the first to arrive. The "big room" as they all called it was part bunker, part museum piece located beneath the cobblestone floor of the sunlight shaft. It had one door and no windows. On a raised dais across from the door sat four chairs, hand carved mahogany with burgundy upholstery, their legs inlaid with anthracite, their arms bare, pointed wood—a throwback to the days when they could be used as weapons. Another outdated relic, kept around needlessly, thoughtlessly. She decided to bring up replacing them at the next regular meeting.

On the burgundy-carpeted floor, a semi-circle of eight chairs—similar, but lacking arm rests—faced the stage. Always the exact number of chairs matched to attendees. Heather was meticulous as ever. Sara glanced to her left. To the door that led to the antechamber to the surrender room. She hoped fervently that the door would not be opened today.

She glided onto the dais, taking the seat second from left. She would seat Crina beside her, and then Marguerite and April Veronica on the other side. As she fussed with her robe, making sure her boots were duly covered, the door opened and Heather came in, a smiling face in a whirl of black and white.

"You ready for the shindig?" she said, taking a seat dead center.

"As ready as I'll ever be." Sara laughed drily.

"You're not worried?"

"No." Sara shook her head.

"No what?" Marguerite entered, with April Veronica at her side. April Veronica was still in her black dress. Marguerite, like all of them, was in nun drag, yet she somehow still managed to look commanding, and slightly scary.

"I was saying I have no concerns about today," Sara said, deciding on honesty. "Welcome, April Veronica. Both of you, please come sit by me."

As they moved to the stage, the door opened again, and the remainder of the sistren filed in.

Six nuns spread out to take the chairs around Heather. Sara noticed that Teddie, her face frozen somewhere between stoic and panicked, took the seat closest to the door to the antechamber. They locked eyes for a second before Teddie turned her gaze to the floor. Poor angel, Sara thought. We've really asked her to step outside her comfort zone. As the rustling of robes subsided and silence rang out, it was clear that only Crina's seat was vacant.

She'd forgotten to pick up Crina!

"Heather," Sara whispered. "Could you please go and collect Crina?"

"No need," came a voice from the doorway. Heads turned.

Nodding to each woman as she passed, Crina sailed to the dais and took her seat beside Sara. "Mother Superior has arrived.

"Hello, my sisters. I have missed you all terribly."

By now, Sara knew that April Veronica would be noticing that everyone in the room, including Crina, appeared young, possibly close to her age. This was always a risky moment, but Marguerite would have implanted to her that older sisters usually sat out indoctrinations for whatever reason, trusting the young to guide the sisterhood.

Sara rose.

"My beloved sisters, I welcome you today as we greet a potential novitiate." Sara turned and faced April Veronica.

"You've all met April Veronica Copper. She has been guided by our Sister Karla for several years and has benefited for much of her life from our order's benevolence. April Veronica has applied herself to the study of virology, technology, and climate change and wishes to devote her life to the steps we can take to help the planet heal."

Polite applause filled the air.

"Per our traditions, I have explained to April Veronica that we operate in absolute secrecy, out of step with the world. It is at this point that I give her the opportunity to turn back, facing no penalty. April Veronica, you may leave now, with our love and blessing. If you do not, you pledge to spend the remainder of your life as a sister of the Order of Holy Silence. Have you made your decision?"

"I have." April Veronica nodded. "I wish to stay. I fully accept the terms of this Order."

Sara continued facing her. "Do you also accept terms that you may not know yet?"

Fully briefed to expect this question, April Veronica did not hesitate. "Yes. I acknowledge that I am accepting the conditions of the

Order, and that said conditions are necessary for the survival and well-being of the order. It is my stated wish to be governed by the rules of this order such as they may be."

"In perpetuity," added Marguerite.

"Oh yes." April Veronica smiled and blushed. "Sorry. In perpetuity."

Sara cast her eyes around the faces in the room. "Is there anyone who has reason that might preclude the addition of the young woman before us?"

Pausing her gaze on Rosa, Fran, Liz and Eleanor, all noticeably seated in the back row, Sara counted to ten in her head.

"Then we may now begin the Ceremony of Ordination."

Sara returned to her seat.

"Nakeah," Sara said, using Teddie's current real-world name. "Would you please lock the door?" With a nod, Teddie rose and methodically clicked the series of deadbolts into place before returning to her seat.

"It is with great honor that I now ask our Mother Superior Patricia to bring the meeting to order."

Crina rose, a warm smile on her face. She turned to April Veronica, extending both hands. April Veronica took them, allowing Crina to pull her to her feet. They stepped down to the floor, and Crina turned April Veronica to face her.

"April Veronica Copper, today you accept the blessing of belonging to the Order Of Holy Silence. After this ceremony, you will be changed forever."

Sara held her breath. Now came the truth. Crina went on.

"You are going to be gifted with a virus, and that virus will grant you an extension of life. You will need discipline such as you've never imagined; in return, you will receive opportunities beyond your wildest dreams."

Confusion played across April Veronica's bright eyes. She made a face and went to speak, glancing at Marguerite, who held a finger to her lips, shushing her.

"We are a sisterhood which dates back to the late fifteenth century. April Veronica, my name is not Patricia. My original name, my nomine as we call it, is Crina. I am round about five hundred and seventy five years old."

April Veronica's eyes widened. Heather, seated nearest her, steadied herself in case the young woman fainted. It had happened before.

Everything had happened before.

Crina was still speaking. "I have survived by following our rules. They are rules that you must memorize, and more importantly they are rules that you may never break. Am I clear?"

April Veronica gulped as she nodded.

"Are you okay, my love?" Marguerite called from her seat.

April Veronica nodded again, more slowly. "Am I permitted to speak?"

"Not yet," said Crina. "At this point, I must ask Sara to speak our invocation, for I am never able to."

"I got you," Sara said, chuckling, her levity clearly confusing April Veronica. "'I am nomine Sara, and never have I killed.'"

"Thank you, Sara," said Crina, turning back to April Veronica. "I am unable to give invocation, for I *have* killed. I did not kill for my own survival; I killed for the survival of the world, and indirectly for the sake of my sisters. I see that you, a scientist, are filling with questions, and I promise that soon enough, the answers will be yours."

"I need to sit down," April Veronica interrupted.

With surprising tenderness, Crina wrapped an arm around the clearly freaking-out young girl and led her back to her seat beside Marguerite.

"My dear, I have only a few more things to say, and then, we will take your questions. Once you are satisfied, we will transform you, and your new life will begin."

April Veronica gazed up at her, her head clearly swimming.

"These women, the women of the New York Order Of Holy Silence, are not nuns. We are not a holy order. That is a smokescreen, a disguise that serves us well. What our sisterhood is called is a Lock. There are other Locks around the world. We all abide by a fixed code of ethics. The virus that strengthens us and prolongs our time on Earth requires various elements of human blood or else it will consume its host. That means us. It's a painful, nightmarish way to die, as proven by the men who had the virus and allowed it to drive them to incredible cruelty. A virus does not make a person into a murderer. That is a conscious decision. Many years ago, my sisters and I, appalled by the torture that, like us, visited upon innocent people for their sustenance, we formed a small army, and we methodically killed the men. All of them. And we vowed that never again would we allow a man to become infected, for men see strength as power, and they are unable to resist its allure."

April Veronica made a small sound, of panic, fear or confusion. Marguerite wrapped an arm around her shoulders and Sara was relieved to see the young woman relax against her mentor.

"Do not worry, young lady. We have created a global network, a system of obtaining our sustenance without harming a soul. Additionally, scientific advances, on our part and also by the medical community at large, have developed drugs that we can take instead of blood, and survive upon. I may have made this all sound too gruesome.

It isn't. But what we are doing now is offering you the chance to study, and travel, and learn, and love and live, almost as long as you wish."

All eyes turned from Crina to April Veronica, knowing what words Crina would utter next.

"April Veronica Copper of New York City, do you still wish to become the newest member of this Lock?" Sara held her breath.

Without hesitation, April Veronica nodded, her brown curls bobbing.

"Yes, Crina, Karla, all of you. I ... I had suspicions. I mean, I grew up with *Twilight*." She laughed nervously. "So, some of my ridiculous theories aren't so outlandish. Yes. I accept this eternal life."

As if on cue, all eyes switched to Sara.

"April Veronica," she began slowly. "No life is eternal. No life is free of existential questions, and no life is free of exhaustion, both physical and emotional. Crina is one of our oldest sisters. Many before her have chosen to end their time, and we have a painless method of doing so. Such decisions take years, we've learned. Death is not something to be feared," Sara paused, the words catching in her throat. Swallowing, she resumed. "It's just another option."

Sara smiled and April Veronica smiled back at her.

"My scientist's curiosity is about to implode my brain," she said, her cadence chopped by excitement. "How do you do it?"

Sara looked to Heather, who stood up. "My cue. Hi, April Veronica, I'm nomine Heather and never have I killed. Pleased to meet ya. To begin your transition, you'll be injected with blood from Marguerite, or Karla, your sponsor. Only a small amount. This enables the virus to spread slowly, in tandem with your training. You'll need to learn your hunger, to see it when it rises, and to control it when it does. Before I proceed, we will tell you the rules that govern this and all locks. Please, sisters, rise."

All occupants of the room rose, and as one, they spoke, their cadence prayer-like, their voices strong.

"Never Make A Man, Nor Permit A Cursed Man To Live.

Never May It Be Written.

Never May You Kill.

Never Engage With The Faithful.

Never Exceed Your Debt

Never Betray Your Lock.

Never Be Remembered.

Never Enslave A Human.

Never Become A Relic.

Never Pick A Mother."

"Do you accept these terms?" Marguerite said from her place beside April Veronica. The young woman bit her lower lip, then nodded.

Heather reached inside her robe, producing a small, black rectangular leather box. Opening it with a small creak, she withdrew a silver hypodermic needle, the old-fashioned kind with the curled metal finger holes.

"Please extend your right arm, and rest it on the arm of your chair," she said solemnly. "Marguerite, would you please tie her off?"

The Spaniard pulled a length of rubber cord from within her robe and stood to bind April Veronica's outstretched arm.

"You guys keep a lot of shit in those robes," April Veronica joked feebly.

"I know you're scared," Marguerite said, before kissing the woman on both cheeks and sitting back down. "You don't need to be."

Sara scanned the room, the faces of women she'd known forever, all of them fixed entirely on April Veronica's arm and the silver needle glinting yellow sparks from the dull bulbs in the ceiling.

With her left hand, Heather flicked the inside of April Veronica's elbow, smiling in approval at the vein that bulged.

"Would ye prefer to close your eyes, lassie?" she asked kindly.

"No, thank you, Heather. I'd like to watch."

Heather deftly pricked the vein and pressed the plunger down. It only took a second, and she whipped the needle out, pressed a small cotton ball from her pocket onto the injection site, then folded April Veronica's arm closed.

"There you go, love. Welcome to the Lock."

Marguerite wrapped April Veronica in a hug. "My friend, I am so happy to welcome you."

"I don't feel any different," April Veronica said, her eyes jumping from woman to woman. Rosa met her gaze angrily, Fran shook her head, and Liz, not looking at all, occupied herself by inspecting her fingernails.

"You will, lass, you will," Heather said, placing the needle back into its case.

"Wait," April Veronica said, "is it time for me to ask questions?"

"Soon," Sara said, a relieved smile spreading across her face. All had gone more smoothly than she dared to hope. "First, it's time to take off these stupid, awful robes, show you who we really are, and let you get to know us. Ladies, it's time to party."

At once, in a flurry of black and white fabric, eleven women pulled robes over their heads, unbuttoned wimples and whipped off veils, revealing an array of fashions in bright colors and lush fabrics.

Sara put her arm over April Veronica's shoulders.

"Sorry, love, the nun drag is necessary in the outside world, but this is us. Let's adjourn this to the roof. We will answer all your questions, and no, you won't get to them all tonight, but that's fine. We have time. All the time in the world."

"We have time," April Veronica said, still clutching her arm closed. "Are you fucking kidding me? This feels like the best dream I've ever had. What the hell is this?"

"This is your sistren," Crina said. "We are your new family, and we welcome you."

Chapter Fifteen

Sara was overwhelmed by a sudden need to be alone. She begged off from accompanying everyone directly to the roof deck. The weight of the indoctrination hit her suddenly, unexpectedly, and her heart and head were in knots that even her psychiatric training couldn't unravel. She burst into her apartment through the secret wall by the spiral staircase, a surge of panic tearing at her throat.

What the fuck did I just do?

Marguerite didn't have the emotional capability to take care of a kitten, much less a new convert.

That's her problem, she argued with herself, and her breath froze, as if hooked on her vocal cords. With Locks around the world opting for zero growth and the buzz around a global surrender, ending the virus entirely, and consequently shutting down Lock culture forever growing louder every year, she'd just approved and overseen the making of a new sister.

What she needed, with sudden clarity, was a glass of wine, a handful of heems and a valium. She lurched to her small kitchen, emptied eight heems into her palm and poured the last half-glass of the bottle from earlier into someone's wine glass, probably Teddie's judging by the pale beige lipstick marks. A quick swish around her teeth, and then all of it gulped down. The valium would have to wait for later.

It was customary for the Lock leader to accompany the new convert, to stay be her side, for at least the first eight or so hours of conversion. Sara was already out of line.

What are they going to do? Fire me?

No, worse, they're going to notice, that's what they're going to do. They're going to notice that you're not doing your job.

Her breathing began to cycle up, panic blurring the edges of her vision. She hadn't felt this splintered in many years, not since the wave of existential fear and paranoia after the San Francisco Lock collapsed. She walked stiffly to her couch, falling backward into its embrace, forcing herself into a fast meditation, letting go with every breath out, her jangling nerves becoming quieter. Slowly, breath by breath, she calmed herself, finally feeling guilty for indulging her dramatic side. She knew that guilt itself was childish, so she drove down, introspectively examining her motivations. She rolled her eyes.

She resented not being able to see Silas.

What a fucking child she was.

"Okay, you teenage girl," she said into the quietness of her apartment. "Here's the deal. You can call Silas after the party. Go do your job, and then he's yours."

With a sigh and a shrug, she rose from the couch and headed for the party.

The sun was falling as she crossed the roof, the last shards of pink-orange light sneaking between the wall of hedges that bordered the rooftop. She gazed up at the crisp stars pinpointed across the sapphire sky, flickering briefly before light pollution wiped them out at dark. Ahead the roof house loomed, a pitch-black edifice, its darkened windows inscrutable from the outside, no sound audible from within. That changed as she unlocked the door and pulled it open. A gust of modern staccato dance music blared out over an equally loud wall of chatter. Eleven women could make a lot of noise. Predictably, Marguerite and April Veronica were waiting just inside the doorway. Marguerite made an accusatory face. Sara smiled thinly and embraced the new convert.

"Welcome to the truth," she said.

"I can handle the truth," April Veronica said into her hair. "It's not like it's a total surprise, let's face it. With all the conspiracy theories going around in my brain, this was almost a relief. I'm sorry, everything I say sounds better before it leaves my mouth. I need to shut up."

April Veronica gave herself a mock face-palm. She really was self-deprecating and adorable. Sara turned to Marguerite.

"Who has our new member had the pleasure of meeting?"

"Nobody as yet," the Spaniard replied tersely. "Traditions dictate that we were to await you."

"Thank you." Sara forced a chipper smile and placed a hand on the small of April Veronica's back. "So! Are you ready to meet the girls?"

"Yes," April Veronica said, her voice strained.

"Don't be nervous," Sara said. "It's not a test, you don't have to remember names. Trust me, you'll learn them all in time."

"Mother...uh, Sara...I'm sorry," April Veronica paused. "Um, what do I call you?"

"You call me Sara, but within these walls only. Anywhere outside of this building, you call me by my contemporary identity, which is Lily. That's why we won't be testing you. It's a hell of a lot to remember. Outside of these walls, it's easiest to just never interact, but if you need to address me, out there, I'm Doctor Lilian Berger, clinical psychiatrist."

"My head is going to explode."

"Yes, mija," Marguerite interrupted. "Tonight, maybe focus on the broad strokes. We will have audiences with all of the Lock members individually over the coming weeks and months."

April Veronica gazed at Marguerite with a mix of gratitude and love. Sara hated to interrupt, but she had to. She leaned in and whispered, "It's time to get this party started."

Turning, she stepped up to her throne, scouring the crowd for Teddie, who, two steps ahead of her, was already at the bar warming the blood for the toast, Crina by her side. Teddie gave her a thumbs up, and Sara clapped her hands twice, loudly. The chatter stopped, and the music went quiet.

"Okay, sistren," she said. "Today, the New York Lock has welcomed a new member. Please join me in a hearty welcome to nomine April Veronica!"

Applause rang out and Imani let out a deafening whistle. Teddie and Crina circulated, each carrying a tray of goblets, one for each sister, except April Veronica. Crina approached Sara, who took hers then raised the goblet high overhead.

"To April Veronica," she said, and the sisters echoed it, before they raised their goblets to their lips, and silence fell as the customary wave of euphoria washed over them. Sara noticed that Marguerite hadn't drunk from hers. She was whispering to the new girl, most likely explaining why it wasn't possible for her to join in the toast, not yet.

Stepping down from the dais, Sara made her way to the bar at the back of the room, pretending the blood had intoxicated her more than it had, needing more to feel the bliss the sisters around her were sharing.

"Can I get a top-up?" she asked Teddie, who raised an eyebrow. Then she winked and retrieved a fresh, full goblet from the warming oven.

"Don't go getting crazy, Mom," she said. "Actually, I think I'll join you." She took out another goblet from the oven and cheers'ed Sara. "Here's to a bullet dodged."

"I'm sorry I had to put you through it," Sara said, stepping behind the bar and hugging Teddie. Crina appeared beside them.

"Look at those women," she interjected, her toothy smile hiding the edge in her voice. She nodded to the far corner where Liz, Fran, Rosa and Eleanor were deep in conversation. "I had no idea they'd become so... deliberately separate."

Sara shrugged. "They're planning to secede, back to California. Maybe not Fran, I think she still needs New York. But the rest are itching to go."

"Well, they should be kissing your ass," Crina said. "They can't do that without our support."

"Oh, I don't care if they go," Sara said. "The sooner, the better."

"Amen," said Teddie.

Across the room, Marguerite made a frustrated face to Sara.

"If you'll excuse me," Sara said. "Marguerite wants the full dog-and-pony show and it's my job to circulate the new girl."

Slipping between the chairs, Sara made her way back to April Veronica and Marguerite, who were still by the door where she left them.

"Sorry to drink in front of you," Sara said.

"Don't be," April Veronica said, reaching out and grabbing Sara's upper arm. "I don't think I'd be able to..."

"No, not today." Sara smiled. "But it's quick. The revulsion fades overnight. By tomorrow evening, a nice cup of warm blood will start to sound pretty tasty to you."

"That does sound weird" April Veronica screwed up her button nose.

"Think of it like sushi or oysters," Marguerite said.

"Gross," April Veronica laughed. "I don't like either of those things."

"Not to worry," Sara said. "First off, you'll simply enjoy the taste on your palate. Then, if you don't partake, you'll start to feel the hunger."

"How quickly will that happen?"

"Also quickly," Marguerite interjected. "We won't let that happen to you. I'll give you your first blood tomorrow, before you feel the thirst."

"Good, Marguerite, good," Sara smiled, glancing around the room. "My final duty for today is to introduce April Veronica to everyone."

The young woman's eyes widened and she gulped.

"Let's get started with my right-hand woman." Sara snagged Heather's sleeve as she passed by. "This is Heather, you've already met. But she's the one who makes our magic possible. She's our one-woman birth, deaths, and marriages department."

Heather did a small curtsy, then wrapped April Veronica in a hug.

"Welcome aboard," she said, stepping back and giving the overwhelmed young woman some space. "I've brought you a wine. Rosé work for you?"

April Veronica nodded gratefully and took the rather full glass as Heather continued.

"Do you have any questions for me?"

Heather smirked as April Veronica downed the entire glass in one gulp.

"Whew. At least my hands have stopped shaking," April Veronica finally said with a wan smile. "Okay. You do what now?"

"I harvest social security numbers and identities of female babies who pass in infancy. Bit o' this, bit o' that, and thirty years later, we have identities for all of us. Ye get to keep your identity for around a decade, give or take, barring... you know, complications. Being recognized, or broadcast. Then it can be shorter, if need be. But it's not a big deal."

"Apart from having to change every pattern in your life," Marguerite said under her breath.

"Let's not panic the wee bairn, then," Heather said, silencing Marguerite with her trademark death stare. "Let's just say that if anything goes wrong, come to me and I'll fix it."

The wine was flushing April Veronica's face. "You folks have really thought of it all."

"It runs like clockwork," Sara said. She turned April Veronica to meet Teddie, who was approaching from the bar.

"And this is Theodora."

"Jesus, Sara, do you have to be so goddamn formal." Teddie extended a hand. "Call me Teddie. I'm one of our hunter gatherers, I work as a nurse up at Columbia. I get us plasma and pills."

"Teddie is also the only sister that I've ever made," Sara said, wrapping her arm around Teddie's shoulders. "And what a great decision it was."

"Is it rude to ask how old you all are?" April Veronica was studying Teddie's face in wonder.

"No, girl, it ain't. How old you think I am?"

"Visually you're twenty-five."

"I'm two hundred and twelve. I seen some shit." Teddie doubled over guffawing. "Listen sister, the easiest way to get into this shit is to laugh. Don't try to get used to it today. Hell, don't try to get used to it this decade. Shit takes time."

"You're all so nice," April Veronica said incredulously. "I am trying so hard to forget my expectations and roll with this but the one thing that I'm sticking on is, how the hell do people all get along for hundreds of years? How the fuck has this not turned into fucking Huis Clos?"

Imani stood a step behind Teddie, waiting for her moment.

"Philosophy, mate," the tall, ebony-black woman said in a crisp London accent, extending a hand. "My name is Imani. I'm in my second century of the study of human philosophy. That's how I roll with this... circus." She smiled widely.

April Veronica grasped Imani's hand in both of hers. She closed her eyes and inhaled deeply. "Imani, it's my pleasure to meet you. You guys, all of you, you're saying things that my brain doesn't know how to unpack. I think...I think I need to sit down."

Sara took April Veronica's arm and led her to her own wooden throne seat. "Imani, come with us," she said over her shoulder.

Heather, as if reading a silent cue from Sara, took Marguerite by the arm. "How about you and I talk about some new mom details?"

"Of...of course," Marguerite said, allowing Heather to lead her back to the bar area.

"I am sorry if this party is too much for you," Sara said, fanning air onto April Veronica's face.

"I never know if the party is for us or the new girl," Imani said, kneeling beside her.

"I'm fine," April Veronica said, flashing her bravest smile. "Really, I am. Let's keep this train moving." She stood.

"Like a shark!" Imani laughed. "Good survival instincts. Sink or swim and all that."

Sara glanced at the far corner of the room, where Fran, Rosa, Eleanor and Liz were cloistered, deep in conversation. She thought about pre-warning April Veronica but decided against it, not wanting to color her impression, or stress her out.

"Let's go over here," she said lightly, taking April Veronica by the wrist. When Imani saw their destination, she widened her eyes but followed, a few steps behind them.

When they reached the group, none of the women acknowledged them until Sara coughed. Twice.

"Hi ladies," Sara said, and Rosa, Fran and Liz finally stood up, turning to face them. Eleanor scowled and remained in her throne. "I'd like to do a quick meet and greet with April Veronica."

The three standing women went through the motions, saying their name and shaking hands. Eleanor pulled out her phone, ignoring them. Unfazed, April Veronica extended a hand to her and leaned in.

"I'm April Veronica," she said. "It's so nice to meet you."

Only Eleanor's eyes moved, shifting up from her phone to the girl's face.

"I wish I could say the same," Eleanor said, her voice low, her Iranian accent thick. "I think it's only fair to let you know that not all of us were in favor of your creation--"

"This is Eleanor," Sara interrupted. "She's not normally so manners-challenged."

With a bored sigh, Eleanor stood. "Why sugarcoat it?" She faced April Veronica. "It's time you knew. There is an internal movement afoot that will end with all of us choosing suicide, because our existence is too much of a threat to the outside world. Nothing personal, but that's why some of us weren't on board with..." she waved her fingers dismissively in April Veronica's face, "...you."

Imani stepped in between the two women, her face dangerously close to Eleanor's.

"This is her first fuckin' day, guv," Imani hissed. "Press the flesh, slap the back, you know, be friendly."

Fran put a hand on Eleanor's shoulder. "She's right, El," she said, her voice soft. "Discussing our political differences can wait."

"Oh man," Liz said in her California twang. "Don't call our existential crisis a 'political difference.' It's common sense."

"Feels like I've walked into a minefield," April Veronica said. "Listen, I'm very interested in talking with you all about this, and it sounds like a discussion I need to have sooner than later." Bowing to each of them, she continued. "Thank you for your honesty, and I'm sorry that my creation caused so much tension."

The four were clearly taken aback. Sara watched as the three standing women visibly relaxed, and then, to her surprise, Eleanor set her phone down and raised her arm to April Veronica.

"I'm Eleanor," she purred. "I apologize for getting us off on the wrong foot."

April Veronica shook her hand with a wobbly smile.

"I think it's time to keep moving," Sara said, leading April Veronica back into the center of the room.

"That went badly," April Veronica said, her voice thick as if she might cry.

"Wasn't ever gonna go well," Imani said. "Probably a good time to say, you don't have to get along with everyone, of course. None of us do."

April Veronica paused. "Wait. Really? That was something that was really stressing me out. I thought everyone had to like me."

"Fuck to the no," Imani said with a laugh. "Though, the funny thing is, in time and at various times, you'll have periods of closeness or camaraderie with each of us. It's surprising. For years, Eleanor was my bestie. Now she's exhausting. In fifty years, we'll be something different again."

"Yes," Sara said. "Best to put it out of your mind for now. There's always turmoil. Eleanor shouldn't have burdened you with all of that, not today."

"You handled it well," Imani said. "For what it's worth."

"Thanks, but now I think I just need to sit and watch for a while."

Ushering April Veronica to a vacant throne in the room's center, Sara exchanged a concerned glance with Imani, who winked and hunkered down beside the young woman.

"What can I get you, love?" she asked. Sara's heart broke a little at the lost, pleading look in April Veronica's eyes as she shook her head and shrugged, clearly overwhelmed. Sara knelt and leaned in close.

"As long as I am in charge of this Lock, we will never vote for extinction," she whispered. "There are many more solutions."

April Veronica considered Sara's words. When she spoke, her voice was barely audible. "That's good to know, because for a minute there, it really felt like I'd jumped onto a sinking ship. And it was already hard to navigate today, and for a while it looked like a functioning group of adults and now it feels like I've signed onto Mean Girls."

Imani laughed and tucked a lock of curly hair behind April Veronica's ear. "If that was your hazing, at least it's over. You see, love, they all need you. We're a democracy. Fran there, she has her eye on you. She's our cybersecurity expert. She wants you to help her, if you're good at hacking."

"I have more than a passing interest," April Veronica said, brightening.

"Eleanor is a nurse, but she's also in a dark phase, so the extinction thing is her identity for now. It will pass," Sara said, more confidently than she felt. "Liz wants to pioneer a new Lock in California, she will need all of us on board to make that happen. Rosa, she's overworked. She manages our real estate portfolio, and she also needs an assistant.

You'll need her if you ever want to date, because you can't bring an outsider here. She'll arrange a cover apartment for you, in one of our buildings."

"I can still date?"

Imani let out a belly laugh. "Honey, when we said we weren't nuns, we meant it, okay?" Her tone darkened. "But seriously though, it's not advised for new recruits like you. In a few years, if you wish, it will be possible. Right now, you're in training."

April Veronica nodded agreeably. "Makes sense."

"My point," Imani said softly, "is that, in time, you'll get to see that all of those women are good people and eventually, you'll see their fun sides, and you'll like them."

"I think I'm going to like all of you," April Veronica said.

"You're sweet. I like all of us too. You're nearly done. Are you overloaded or shall I continue?"

"Please go on, I like the way you're delivering information. Bite-sized packets. I do have a question. Did all of you form this Lock at once?"

Sara squeezed April Veronica's shoulder and shook her head.

"No, child. The network of Locks around the world is very changeable. Members can apply to transfer in and out of other Locks for a number of reasons. The most common reason is that a sister gets recognized. Eleanor was in the Helsinki Lock when she got recognized, when was it? Back in the fifties. It's impossible to control. You encounter a person from your past, and they have aged and you have not. At that point, a rapid transfer is the best solution. And Liz, she got recognized in a way that indicated that her entire Lock was under surveillance. They voted to close down, and then Locks around the world absorbed their members."

"And all of this is voted on democratically? That's troubling," April Veronica said. "So, we have four members voting for extinction, and seven against? And people can transfer in and out?"

"Exactly," Sara said, her voice calm. "And as Lock mother, I would not accept a transfer member who did not share my vision. The movement is called ZPG, and in most Locks, that just means a freeze on making new sisters."

"Who gets to make a sister?"

"Anyone with a credit," Imani said. "You just have to have a credit for another life. Once a sister chooses surrender, she usually bequeaths her life to another sister. Not always, but usually."

"I have credits for four lives," Sara added, "but I have no desire to make any new sisters at this time. I made Teddie, and Fran was made by a Scholar in this Lock who then chose surrender. Everyone else came from somewhere else."

"This is so fucking fascinating," April Veronica said, the curiosity returning to her eyes and the color to her face. She looked around. "Okay. I still haven't met that woman over there, talking to Crina."

"That's Yukari, our shyest member," explained Sara. "She's Tokyo born, stolen from a slave temple by her maker during a liberation movement by a sister from the old Hamburg Lock. She's been in New York now for about a century, I think? She keeps to herself, but she's a fabulous genius. She's currently studying extinction biophysics alongside epidemiology. And she's devoted to her pet rabbit."

"Oooohhh," April Veronica sighed. "This is like Disneyland for smart girls!"

"Yeah, I figure you'll get along with her, you're science brained, right?"

"You know," April Veronica leaned in conspiratorially, "the one thing that keeps racing through my mind is, I thought I had to specialize in one thing, but now, hearing your stories, I realize I can just cycle through study after study."

"That's exactly what we call it, kid." Sara smiled. "Cycling through. That's what we do with identities, lifestyles, hobbies, studies- "

"And men," Imani whispered. "Or women."

"Eventually, yes." Sara laughed. She thought of Silas with a pang.

"The last thing I want to do right now is date," April Veronica said. "I feel like I could spend a year or two just learning about all of this."

"Your expertise in global warming will also come very handily for us all," Imani said. "That is definitely going to be a challenge for all of us, life in a changing world, especially here in a city that won't survive a four-inch ocean rise."

"It really won't," April Veronica agreed. "Whoa. I used to think about events in the future, events I was able to forecast but never think I'd live long enough to see? For better or worse, I just got a front row seat."

"And it bloody excites ya," Imani said with a smile. "Scares the crap out of me, it does."

"I know you are strugs to func," Sara said, "but Crina is only in the city for a short time, so I do ask that you come and meet her properly. And don't worry, she doesn't bite."

Sara led April Veronica across the darkening room to Yukari and Crina, who were deep in conversation about some contemporary pop musician they both loved. Crina, sensing their approach, turned to face them. Her beautiful face remained motionless, but her eyes blazed with a happy intensity that Sara remembered so well, only now it caused a nervous twinge in her stomach.

"Crina, I wanted to bring our newest sister over before you had to leave." Crina waved a hand dismissively at Sara.

"I plan to stay late! This is the first party I have attended in, oh, it would be rude to say. Let's leave it at, you would have been a mere girl, young lady. How are you coping?"

Exhaling deeply, April Veronica relaxed. "I still think I'm dreaming."

"At my age, it becomes increasingly hard to tell the difference," Crina said, motioning across the room to Heather for another glass of blood. "A curious mind like your own becomes a fertile, magical place to get lost in. I've been alone a long time, so please forgive me if I forget to animate, and also please, be assured that I am thrilled to welcome you aboard. I believe that new energy is essential to the health of a Lock, and I say this with honesty and pride, you've been welcomed into my favorite Lock in the whole world."

"My head is spinning," April Veronica said.

"Oh honey, get used to that! Until you find your rhythm and your callings start to prioritize themselves. After you sleep on it, Marguerite will outline your first year. I'm afraid you'll be spending most of it within these walls, apart from appearances that will be necessitated by your imminent departure from your current life. I'm sure you're already thinking back on the steps that Marguerite has helped you make. You currently have no roommates, no pets, and no job, correct? That's standard. You'll switch your degree to online for now, and then..." Crina paused, taking a goblet of blood from Heather, who also handed another wine to April Veronica. "The old you will die. Cheers!" Crina clinked her goblet against the young woman's. "And then the world is your oyster, very literally. Would you get a load of me, doing all the talking. This is what happens when one disappears up one's own arsehole." Crina paused to titter. "Wait. That would have been funny and inappropriate fifty years ago. I'm not good with contemporary. I really do need to come back to the Lock and get my shit together. I've been watching too much TV."

April Veronica laughed, surprised to find the elder so endearing and friendly.

"It's better for me to let you all do the talking tonight," she said. "I feel like anything I say will just be… I don't know.. laughable?"

"None of the above, kid. You're doing great." Imani patted her shoulder before moving to join Yukari and Heather by the bar, leaving Sara and Crina with the new recruit.

"April Veronica, I plan to stay here in the city for another day or two, and so I am available for any questions you may have."

"Thank you, Crina."

"I will be guiding her in the next days!" Sara jumped as Marguerite appeared beside her charge.

"I have no doubt," Crina said, shooting a glance at Sara. "But I can learn from her, too, you know. It's not just a one-way street." Crina turned to the young woman.

"It seems that your patron would like some time with you, but before we part for now, do you have any pressing questions?"

"I do, I have so many," April Veronica said immediately. "But for now, I think the one that will help me sleep tonight is this. What is the one thing that you miss from life before you changed?"

Crina closed her eyes, tilting her head back in thought, the plains of her cheeks catching candlelight, then changing as a smile spread across her face. She turned her face down to April Veronica's.

"Children," she said softly. "I love the laughter of children, the energy, the enthusiasm, the honesty. So much."

"And you choose to not be around them anymore?"

"No, my child," Crina said gravely. "Children are off limits for us. We can't work with them, interact with them, nothing. Children remember. They remember the faces of the kind, and they will remember that face until they die, many years later. We can't afford to risk our security in that way." She smiled again. "That's why we only deal with adults. Adults are self-absorbed and they only remember faces that make them jealous. Which is why, in our lives outside these walls, we strive to be as plain as possible, so that we are forgotten as soon as we exit the lives we interact with."

"That was a wonderful answer," April Veronica said. "And strangely, you put me at ease. I'm good when I'm of use, when I have a purpose. I was worried about so much, but I'm starting to see that you, the foremothers of this movement, have already done the hard thinking. I'm lucky to come along into a fully functioning environment."

Crina began to say something, then bit her tongue, causing Marguerite to glance sharply at Sara, who shrugged nonchalantly. She wasn't sure what Crina was up to, nor why she was choosing to stay in the city for more time than they'd planned, but she would always back Crina up.

"It's been my pleasure to speak with you, my dear," Crina said, bowing her head slightly, dismissing April Veronica and Marguerite. "Like I said, while I'm in town, come up and see me sometime."

The two moved out of earshot. Sara leaned in.

"You do know that saying went out of fashion seventy years ago."

"Not if you spend your days watching The Criterion Channel," Crina said cheekily. "So, are you going to tell me about this new beau of yours?"

"Did you come all the way into the city to gossip?"

"Yes, der," Crina said, waving her empty glass in Sara's face. "Being serious all the time is such a bore. Spill the tea, Sara."

"This is going to require more blood, or a Guinness."

"Get three glasses," Crina said with a grin. "I'll go get Rosa, it sounds like she will be needing to set up an apartment for you."

"Can you at least wait?" Sara said, as Rosa popped up beside her, a cheeky glint in her almond eyes.

"Did I hear my name?"

"Yes, child," Crina said. "Pull up a throne, Sara's going to get us some fine plasma and tell us all about her new gentleman friend."

"I've been expecting an apartment request," Rosa said as she settled her petite frame into the throne beside Crina.

"How do you all know?" Sara said with mock anger. "Who has been talking?"

Slowly, Rosa pointed an immaculate blood red nail at most of the women in the room. "It would be quicker to say who hasn't been talking." She pointed quickly at Marguerite's back. "But, in her defense, she's been preoccupied."

"I'd pretend to be offended," Sara said, turning to the bar and pouring three glasses of blood, "but the real question is, how quickly can you have it set up for me?"

Hours later, Sara took her leave of the party. The night was fresh, and she'd imbibed so much blood that her veins were humming very nicely. She wanted to go running but leaving the compound the very night a new sister was made would be out of line. Even so, the entire Lock, so eager to get her laid, had agreed they'd all help set up an apartment for her the following day, and she was granted permission to spend Sunday night away from the Lock.

The door to the roof deck room opened, and she watched Teddie move silently across the roof to the stairwell that led down to her side of the building. She looked tired and Sara considered following her. She sent a text instead; Teddie replied immediately that she was fine and needed nothing but "a looooong sleep."

Sara inhaled the smell of New York at midnight, the sweet carbon chill tingling inside her nostrils. She walked to one of the roof parapets, the walls that screened out the neighboring buildings, and extended her bare arms to the sky, feeling the pinpricks of chill wind caressing them. Cold made her feel so alive.

The rarest feeling for Sara, since she moved to New York so long ago, was to feel truly alone. Slowly, she began to roll her head around on her shoulders, dizzying herself, and that singular feeling spread through her heart.

The roof of the building was bounded by ancient hedges, with raised vegetable beds filling one corner and a small water tower beside it. The roof house and a shielded seating area with tables and potted fruit trees filled out the other corners.

She began to meander around the roof, stopping to smell the herbs that had already sprouted in the garden boxes. By the water tower, she looked for the familiar rattan couches, surprised to find they had been replaced by chic metal ones upholstered in smooth gray fabric. She sat on the longest one, then hauled her feet up, laying back and looking up at the sky.

She heard the mutter of female voices each time the door to the roof house opened, then footsteps, another door and then silence. The party was winding down, but Sara knew that Imani loved to socialize, and she would be the last to leave. She paid it no mind, secretly hoping that nobody would see her.

As if she was to be immediately punished for that thought, she heard footsteps crunching toward her, more than one set of feet. She hated that her first thought was that she hoped it wasn't Marguerite.

"Mind if we join you?"

It was Yukari's voice. Slowly sitting upright, Sara turned, slightly surprised to see April Veronica standing between Yukari and Imani.

"Hey you guys," Sara said, as lightly as she could. "Please, pull up a couch?"

The look of relief on April Veronica's face made Sara feel guilty for leaving the party early. She knew that the first few days as the virus took hold were a confusing mix of energy, nausea, and a million questions. At least these days, the answers were concrete and scientific. The night that Crina made Sara, she'd felt like a wolf; she wanted to run and run. The memory, now existing as facts more than images, made her smile. It felt innocent and guileless. She wished she could help the new girl transition as lightly.

"Nobody remembers how to party, boss," said Imani as she settled into a lounge across from Sara.

"Where's Marguerite?" Sara asked, trying to not sound judgmental. Why had Marguerite left April Veronica on her own?

"Oh, she was exhausted," April Veronica said. "She wanted me to go with her, to call it a night, but I couldn't, I can't, I just feel so..."

"Electric?" Yukari took a seat at the end of Sara's couch, and gestured to the new girl to sit between them.

"That'll do, I guess," April Veronica said. Imani caught Sara's eyes and made an I Told You So face, no doubt referring to Marguerite abdicating her responsibilities so quickly. Sara refused to be drawn in.

"We're not interrupting, are we?" asked Yukari. Sara shook her head, doing her duty.

"No," she lied. "I love it up here, but somehow I forget it's up here."

"You should come up and garden with me some time," Yukari said. "Clears the head."

"Can I garden with you?" April Veronica just seemed so innocent that Sara's heart softened a little. Smiling, she sat up and took the girl's hand in hers.

"April Veronica, you're a part of this Lock now," Sara said. "You're new but you're equal. Don't feel like you need permission. If you want to pitch in on anything, go ahead. We're all very friendly. We don't bite."

Imani and Yukari burst out laughing, while April Veronica glanced nervously from one to the other.

"Sorry, that was lame vampire humor," Sara said.

"Oh, finally, someone has said the V-word," April Veronica said breathlessly. "I've been too scared to even think it all night. It kind of felt off-limits."

"Nothing is off limits, mate." Imani chuckled. "You have questions?"

April Veronica nodded. "So many."

"Go on," Sara said, still holding her hand. "Ask away."

"Do you guys really believe that all men will become evil? That it's that black and white on the gender spectrum?"

Sara whistled through her teeth. "Opening with the big guns."

Imani sat back against the couch. "It's not so much that, but maybe our thinking is old fashioned. Short answer is, we don't know but we can't risk it."

"We don't have the bandwidth to deal with that much change," Yukari said, clearly lost in private thought.

"It's a huge issue for Lock mothers," Sara said. "As it stands, the rules aren't changeable, and we've known five centuries of relative peace, so there's been no real rush to do something so risky."

Sara watched as the young woman's head tilted from side to side, clearly filing the information away, and also, at the same time, biting her tongue. Then a smile flittered across April Veronica's face as another thought took hold.

"Are any of the, you know, like the legends and shit, are they true?"

Sara glanced at Yukari and Imani. "Any takers?"

"Most legends have their basis in fact," Yukari said, like the scientist she was. "Ours are no different. The basic stories are true. Men who were cursed became increasingly violent, increasingly disrespectful of other humans. The best person to talk to about this is Crina, since she lived through it. Maybe while she's here you can get her to elaborate."

"She doesn't like to talk about it much, though, does she?" Imani whispered conspiratorially.

"Can't really blame her," Yukari replied. "So, one of the things that the men did was have a smith forge them a set of metal fangs, sharper than a wolf's. They used them to open the wrists... and later, the throats... of the villagers they would capture. From what we know, there were several sets, disgusting, brutal. From what Crina has told me, that was one of the final straws for the women who were trying to navigate their way through the virus."

"What were they made of, these teeth?" April Veronica's eyes were wide.

"Silver," Sara said coldly. "Razor sharp silver. Most of them were melted down to make our crosses once we settled on the illusion that we would be nuns. Crina kept one pair. I have it now."

"What about the other stories?" April Veronica said excitedly. "Garlic, stakes through the heart, mirrors?"

"Mirrors are just plain toxic to all humans, love," Imani said, leaning forward. "You've seen it in your own lifetime. The advent of smart telephones, with cameras and filters and tools to make your reflection look better than you really do. It has enslaved the world, and for what? And now, imagine your face never changing. At first it's a blessing, but as we've seen, a reflection is a hard thing to stare at for millennia. They're best avoided. Quick squizz at the makeup, that's it for the day. Otherwise, you'll go mad."

"The stakes are obvious," Yukari said. "Whispers spread through the villages and people armed themselves as best they could. As the virus becomes stronger in you, you'll need to learn discipline. Your adrenal system strengthens alongside your muscles. Sudden panic, or even worse, frights or threats, turn you into..."

"The Hulk?" April Veronica offered, smiling when the three elders burst into laughter.

"Kinda sorta," Imani said, still laughing. "Except not funny."

"They had to come up with ways to stop us, so they tried anything they could," Yukari continued. "You can't blame them. The men had become monsters, they deserved to die. And a stake *will* work, ineffectively. Because the person pounding the stake won't survive either."

"That's enough," April Veronica said, grimacing. "The visuals, it's just too much."

"I agree," Sara said. "Let's not scare the new girl."

"What about sunlight?"

"Be grateful for sunblock," Yukari said. "As the virus gets hold of us, we lose some pigment and burn easily."

"When I was young," Sara volunteered, "the red of a sunburn was enough to make the locals suspicious. Another benefit of the nun habit is full coverage. A good wimple is nothing more than an excellent visor!"

"I won't even notice, then." April Veronica laughed. "I'm so pale, I put on SPF fifty to go out at night."

"Speaking of going out at night," Imani whispered, "word on the street is that someone is setting up an offsite love nest."

Sara deflected, looking April Veronica in the eye. "One of the greatest challenges of a long healthy life is avoiding gossip."

"You need to date," Yukari said.

"I need a vacation," Sara countered.

"You have a boyfriend?" April Veronica leapt in. "Sorry, or a girl-friend?"

"It's a guy, and he's not my boyfriend, but yes, tomorrow I'm gonna, um, set up in a new apartment in midtown."

"Rosa was asking for volunteers in decorating it in the morning," Yukari said enthusiastically. "I'm so there."

"Thanks, love," Sara said with a warm smile. "But speaking of morning, I know you, Imani, you're gonna want to party all night, and that is not going to happen for me." She stood. "I now bid you all a good evening, and April Veronica? Welcome to the family."

"Thank you, Mother... I mean Sara... god, I'm already so terrible at this."

"Patience, grasshopper," Sara said as she walked away. As she neared the door that led down to her wing, she heard April Veronica ask the others what that meant.

"She's old, she uses outdated references," Imani said, definitely loud enough for Sara to hear. As she entered the door, she held a hand aloft, flipping the bird, and laughter echoed across the roof.

Back in her apartment, Sara rushed to her phone, smiling at four separate texts from Silas, the most recent of which, sent only thirteen minutes earlier, simply read.

Can't sleep you up?

She typed two characters of a text reply, then decided to call. He answered on the first ring.

"There you are," he said, his voice chipper.

"Here I am," Sara said. "Just got done with the stupid fundraiser."

"Did it raise funds?""

Yes, it did," she lied, firing up familiar feelings of guilt, another thing she hated about dating and the lies it necessitated.

"Well, then, it wasn't a waste of time."

"You're right. Why are you still awake and so perky? It's after midnight?"

"Don't worry, I just had some green tea after dinner, felt lethargic, but whoo was it too much. It's wearing off. To be honest, I just wanted to hear your voice before I drifted off. Or tried to."

"That green tea'll kill ya," Sara said with a soft chuckle. "Hey, listen, it's okay to say no, but would you maybe like to come over to my place sometime this week?"

Several seconds of silence greeted Sara.

Shit. I went too far too fast.

"I was hoping you'd say something like that." Silas said eventually ."Really?"

"Yeah, really. I would love to. When?"

"What's your schedule like?" She held her breath. "Does tomorrow work?"

"Tomorrow would be good," Silas said. "A nice Sunday dinner. From Postmates. My treat. At your place."

"How's eight? And it's my turn to treat."

"Lily, I'm not going to play games. You say the time, and that time works for me."

"Okay, Silas. Eight it is. And with that, I need to get myself to sleep, because I have a lot of cleaning to do. I'll text you my address. Thirty-fifth and Lex, basically."

"Got it. Sleep tight, Lily. See you tomorrow."

Her heart pounding, a happy tension she hadn't realized was missing, Sara stood and walked to her bedroom, a little swing in her step.

Chapter Sixteen

Stepping out of the overly bright white and glass shower of "Lily's" apartment, Sara wrapped her long black hair in a sumptuous gray towel, purchased just that morning at Century 21 by Imani on a mission of mercy when she realized that Sara hadn't bought new towels since the nineties. Pressing her face into the spun gray softness, she wished she'd bought towels like this earlier. Just another area of her life she neglected.

Flicking at the screen of her phone by the sink, the time illuminated. 7:41. Silas was due in just under twenty minutes, and considering his lack of social skills, an early arrival was not off the cards.

"Piss." She scowled at the foggy reflection in the mirror before gripping the door handles and swinging the door open and closed in an attempt to dispel the steam. The steam stayed but she got sweaty.

Irritable now, Sara moved into the living space of her apartment, which had most recently been "lived in" by Yukari during a romance the preceding autumn. Clad in just a towel, Sara stood in the middle of the sparse living room, forcing herself to see it as a place she had lived in for years. Heather, Imani and Yukari spent the afternoon with her, running errands and freshening up the place right up to the last minute, having only left a short while before. Teddie had begged off from helping, saying that as Monitor she needed to stay and watch over April Veronica.

Heather, who loved mementoes and full bookshelves, declared Yukari's style as "minimal, bookish, bland," but Sara felt at home in the one-bedroom, top-floor apartment overlooking 35th Street. A dark leather mid-century couch, an enormous Mapplethorpe black-and-white of a lily, and a simple glass coffee table were the only décor in the living room. There was now a stack of philosophy books atop the fireplace mantel, supplied by Imani. Yukari wasted a long time showing Sara how to work the television and the small army of streaming devices connected to it. Angrily, Sara stared at the row of remotes lined up in front of the TV on its low wooden stand. If Silas wanted to watch TV, she'd be in trouble.

Just kiss him! He'll either like it or freak out and leave.

At least she wouldn't have to operate the television.

Sara moved to her new bedroom, which was substantially larger than her bedroom up on West End. During Imani's dash to Century 21 she'd also taken it upon herself to buy Sara's outfit for the evening: simple gray leggings and a black silk wrap top, with ballet flats and two small shell clips for her hair. Sara still thought it was too low key, but Imani and Yukari had insisted that with a bolter like Silas, it was much better to err on the side of caution.

"If you look like a sex wolf, you'll scare him off," Yukari warned, laughing, before reinforcing that changes to the outfit were not negotiable.

Dropping her towel and dressing quickly, Sara sat down at the small vanity, grateful that Imani and Yukari had also donated a lot of makeup and other schmatta that made the vanity look like it got used regularly. She shook her hair out, feeling its wet heaviness between her shoulder blades. She wanted it to dry as much as possible before she used the hair dryer, to let the natural curls form a little. Her olive skin, the palest of browns, was clear as always, but dark circles were forming under her eyes, indicating that she needed more blood despite the amount she consumed the previous night. Interrupting her beauty process, she darted to the kitchen and took six heems. Back in the bathroom, she brushed a light dusting of pressed powder, curled her lashes and brushed mascara on the tips, then dabbed on lipstick just one shade darker than her own lips. Gazing in the mirror, she fought the urge to go heavier. She looked like she was going to a yoga class, not having a date. She definitely did not look like a sex wolf.

With a quick shrug, she inserted the two hair clips, one above each ear. Her hair would have to dry like that. It was now 7:55. It was what it was. A ball of nervous energy was bouncing around inside her, forcing her to pace in circles around the couch. The sudden realization that she hadn't thought about April Veronica much all day drove her to grab her phone and fire off texts to Marguerite and Teddie to check in. In a split second, Teddie responded that she'd had a lovely afternoon with her, and that Crina, after spending the day with her, declared that the young woman posed no threat, so some protocols were being loosened. Marguerite was thrilled to have April Veronica all to herself. Crina had volunteered to run interference, so Teddie was already in her own love nest, literally across the street, for a stress-relieving date of her own.

She glanced out the window to the other 35th St building owned by the Lock. Teddie, Heather and Imani kept stand-by apartments in that building, with the rest of it rented out for income. She located Teddie's apartment, one floor below the top. The curtains were drawn, but a suavely handsome Asian man was leaning out the window, smoking a joint. Suddenly, an arm snaked out from the darkness and hauled the guy back inside. Sara thought of the gossip session she'd have with

Teddie tomorrow, excited to be able to spill some tea of her own for once.

A discordant buzzer filled the room, startling her. Glancing at the door, she saw movement on the small screen beside it..

What? Wait. How was she even supposed to let someone in? Sara dashed to the small color screen. Silas's handsome, broad face was staring right at her. Three buttons, one white, one gray, one red, poked out below the speaker. With no symbols on them. Guessing, she pressed the white one. Silas's crackly voice filled the room.

"Lily, hi it's me..." He paused and looked around. "... Silas."

She took a stab at the red one in the center and as the door clicked open, but the sound dropped out. Silas held it open, talking inaudibly. She pressed the white button again.

"Which apartment you're in?"

She pressed the gray button and spoke. "Apartment four. Top floor."

Silas's lips moved, words then a smile, and he shouldered his way through the door and the screen went black.

"Well, that went well," she muttered to herself, moving to the door, drying her newly sweaty palms against the front of her pants and top. Tilting her head, she was able to hear his footsteps clearly as they made their way upward. When she heard him reach her landing, she pulled the door open to the sight of Silas. He wore gray jeans and a dark blue wool coat, a plaid shirt peeking out at the top; his arms were loaded down with two takeout bags from Wagamama, and a smile was spreading across his face.

"Hey Lily," he said warmly, his smile catching his dark brown eyes.

"Silas. Hi," she said from the doorway, not moving. How was this supposed to go again?

"I... uh..."

"Yes?"

"You're blocking the doorway," he said with a chuckle, and Sara darted back into the apartment, the heavy door swinging shut until he stopped it with the toe of his worn black boot. Pushing the door in with his shoulder, he stepped inside, set the bags of food onto the wood floor, and held his arms open to her.

"I'm so nervous," Sara blurted.

"I can see," Silas said, his eyes softening. "Are you okay?"

Sara nodded briefly, then scooped up the bags and moved them to the coffee table before returning slowly to where Silas stood, still holding the door open.

"Do you want to come inside?"

"I do," Silas said. "But in the version of this that I've rehearsed since Friday, I greet you with a kiss. You know, because the quality of the kissing on Friday was... let's just say it stayed with me."

"That, yes, that would be nice, that kiss was...?"

"Nice?" Silas feigned being crestfallen.

"That kiss was something else." Sara snapped out of her slo-mo. She stepped up to Silas, her chin barely reaching his throat, cursing the ballet flats, distracted suddenly by his knuckles beneath her chin, lifting her face to his. She felt his full, warm lips against hers, and she relaxed as the kiss got better and better. His other hand pulled her against him, and she felt foolish when one of her feet involuntarily rose onto its toes. The kiss was that good.

Her hands, hanging limply at her sides, came to life, gripping his hips. Inhaling him deeply, her knees went soft and she relaxed back into the arm around her. Unexpectedly, Silas broke the kiss, standing her upright.

"Phew, my eyes were crossing, I'm dizzy," Silas said, not releasing his grip. "But we should close the door, and maybe..."

"Maybe?" Sara asked as she slipped out of his embrace and they moved out of the way of the door, letting it fall closed with a loud bang.

Silas stood motionless, his hands clasped in front of his crotch, a blush working its way up his neck.

"Maybe, uh, not let the food get cold," Silas said sheepishly, side-stepping her quickly, his hands still covering his crotch. "Can you get some plates and I'll put the food out?"

"We could go straight to my room," Sara said, wanting his hands on her more than she was worried about scaring him off.

"We could," he said, glancing over his shoulder with a cheeky grin. "But we could also wait a little while. This food is really good."

Confused and a little disappointed, Sara moved into her small kitchen, opening the cupboard where she hoped plates would be, only to find glasses there. She removed two wine glasses and two water glasses to make the move look intentional, and then opened the cupboard to the left of it, relieved to see a tasteful gray dinnerware set neatly stacked on the shelves. She lifted a bottle of tempranillo down from the top of the fridge and wedged it beneath one arm, set the glasses on the stack of plates and carried it all into the living room, where Silas was arranging plastic containers of food on the glass coffee table. The complex aromas of pork, soy, lemongrass and garlic reached her nose, and her stomach growled. She realized she hadn't eaten since last night.

"It's refreshing," Silas began talking while she arranged the plates and opened the wine. "You seem every bit as flustered as I feel."

She paused. "I am. I told you. I'm so out of practice.""Me too. But we can practice together," Silas said gently. "It's not a race, I'm as rusty as you are."

Sara bit her tongue against a log jam of responses flying through her mind, desperate to ask if it was a broken heart, what that woman had been like, what she had done to him.

You need a Xanax, not a heem.

Still standing, she poured the wine. She held a glass out to Silas, who was sitting in the middle of the couch. He took the glass and smiled, his eyes burning into hers.

"Don't make me stand to cheers you," he said with a chuckle. "I'm still not out of the clear on that one."

His guileless honesty gave her butterflies, and she slid onto the couch beside him, so close that they were touching. Without making eye contact, she waved her glass sideways into his.

"This date is awkward already," Sara said sheepishly. "Cheers."

"I'm thrilled that it's not all because of me." Silas took a sip of his wine. "I was pretty confident that I would be the one who messed it up."

"It's not messed up though." Sara straightened and moved a few inches away from Silas, so she could face him. "It's not a disaster. We've kissed, we've set a table, and we have wine."

"I let you down, a few minutes ago." Silas set his wine glass on the table between two plastic containers of food. "And Lily, I want you to know. I want that. I want to go into your room, and I want us to be together, but there's this thing I don't want to ruin."

Sara's eyes narrowed, and Silas's eyes widened.

"No, Lily, I'm not a virgin." His broad smile returned. "But this hunger, this intensity, I love it. This is the discovery phase, and I don't want to rush it. I want to ask you a million questions, and I want to touch you, in a million first ways. I want to brush the hair from your neck and kiss your shoulder. Every glimpse of your skin drives me crazy." He paused and did that thing where he put a curled knuckle under her chin, raising her face to his. "I'm thrilled by this weird ephemeral magic that's going on and I don't want to toss it away just because we are horny like two dumb kids. I don't think this thing, us, is going away any time soon."

"I'd like it to stick around," Sara said, surprising herself, her voice low.

"Me too, me too," Silas said. "I'd like a chance to expand your view of me beyond unstable loner with a challenged future."

"Who says I'm any different?"

"Ha. That's our glue." The smile on Silas's face shrank, giving way to an adorable pout. He leaned in and kissed her.

"Wait." Sara pulled away. 'What do you mean?"

"I'm just trying to give you a door to walk through, or talk through, I guess." He paused for a smile. "We have a vulnerability imbalance."

Sara tensed, worried that Silas was about to bolt, like he'd done at the bar that first night, but he did not move. He sipped his wine in silence, then reached across the table for the bottle, topping up her glass. She nodded thanks, and took another sip, mainly to buy herself time.

She could never meet his raw honesty with her own. This phase, the one Silas was relishing, drove her crazy. It was the most difficult phase for her. The heady excitement of liking someone, always tempered by the fictional narrative she had to sell to them. It was exhausting, and, entirely unfair to someone as open as Silas. She quickly bounced several scenarios around, various answers she could give. She chose the one closest to her truth.

"What do you want to know about me?" Her voice sounded thin.

"Whatever you're ready to tell me," Silas said gently. "It's not a competition. We don't have to be equally fucked up. But we can't go on with me being the disaster and you being the lifeline."

"You're right," she said, wishing she had solid ground to stand on, making a mental note to have a meeting with Crina before she left. Tell her everything.

Almost everything.

"I share your... nihilism," she said at last. "To a degree, at least. But that's common among those who specialize in psychiatry. We hear a lot of very reasonable arguments for solitude. It's impossible to ignore the logic."

"But surely you have a therapist of your own right, to help you sort this out."

Sara nodded. She had several, unofficially. Teddie. Heather.

"Yes, and you're an intelligent, reasonable man. It's not like you came in talking about conspiracy theories and alien invasions. You are in a philosophical pit, and I happen to have one just like it..."

"Matching baggage." Silas smiled. "I like it. You know what's surprising? I've spent a lot of energy not being vulnerable, and here I am, comfortable, even with the... like you know more about me than I know about you, the deep, personal stuff."

"I'll admit one thing to you." Sara spoke slowly. "It's something I've never told anyone. I went into this line of work selfishly. I wanted to save people, but I also wanted to learn from those that I can't. I needed to hear the logic of people with no hope of survival. And I'm sorry, because you came to me for help, and now I'm telling you I had an ulterior motive."

"That's entirely acceptable," Silas said, his eyes on hers again. "Why wouldn't someone want to learn from their vocation? You were always professional with me. But I think this," he moved his hand from his chest to hers, and back again, "connection, that's what I sensed, and why I had to leave."

"Thank you for saying all of that," Sara said, draining her wine again, shaken by the sudden urge for honesty. "I know I haven't done anything to address our imbalance, and so I feel like a fraud, in a way."

"I want to say something improper," Silas said.

Sara raised her eyes to his face, where a smirk was forming.

"This odd conversation, possibly the worst first home-date conversation ever, has done nothing to change my desire to jump your bones."

Sara uttered a short, shocked laugh. "Mine either," she blurted. "If anything, it's made you hotter. I feel weird. I feel like we should eat."

"And..." Silas placed a large, warm hand on her thigh. "I'd like to put it out there now, to avoid further disappointment: I'd like to eat, and then I'd like us to kiss a while, then maybe watch TV. I'd like to raincheck the bone jumping. Just a little longer."

"I get it," Sara said, surprised to be telling the truth, and even more surprised that as horny as she was, this felt right. "I like this too. I like this... what do lawyers call it? Discovery phase."

Silas raised his hand from her thigh. "Pinky swear?"

She wrapped her little finger around his and pressed her lips against his.

"It's a deal."

After Silas left, Sara collapsed onto the gray couch, leaving the takeout containers on the coffee table. Her chest heaving, her mind in knots, she sailed over waves of emotional confusion. Was Silas toying with her, leading her on and then pulling back? Or should she commend his commitment to moving at a pace that he was comfortable with? She wondered if she'd ever been this frustrating to someone she was dating.

Probably. Highly likely.

With a frustrated sigh, she pulled her knees to her chest and rocked herself up to sitting, glaring at the wreckage on the coffee table. She toyed with just leaving it there and taking a taxi back to West End, but the thought of running into anyone from the Lock and the awkward questions that would ensue sealed her decision to stay overnight. As she tidied the table, she glanced out the window. Teddie's windows were dark. She most likely had gone back to West End, obeying the Monitor's rules even though Crina had given her a hall pass.

After dumping the trash into the chute outside her apartment, Sara moved to her phone on the kitchen counter.

If it's a screen full of texts, I'll go home.

Nothing.

She walked to the center of the austere living room, its almost bare walls and alien furniture free of any associations, nothing to trigger her memory. She decided that if she went Scholar, she'd live here. She'd do yoga and read and maybe she could give Silas the next four years of her life, the maximum permitted under Lock rules.

And then what? Dump him?

She winced. She wouldn't have to dump him, she knew from experience. It was depressingly easy to sow the seeds of dissatisfaction that led to a mutual breakup. She felt that he was too perceptive to dupe like that. At least, easily. And then there was the whole added weight of just how hard he'd take the breakup given his background.

She groaned aloud. Why couldn't she be like Teddie, good at no-strings-attached physical contact? Why had she dug herself into this pit?

Suddenly angry, she stalked into the bathroom and helped herself to two heems, swallowing them with palmfuls of tap water, proud of herself for keeping it to only two.

She wished she had a joint. Or sleeping pills.

She focused on trying to feel truly alone, with nothing to encumber her, liberated in this trigger-free apartment.

It didn't work.

Chapter Seventeen

Sara emerged aboveground at 96th Street and inhaled deeply, smelling sweet spring flowers mingling with the dank breath of the subway beneath her. The late morning sunshine bounced off grimy windows along Broadway, which was strangely empty, a few people walking on either side.

Having slept off the previous night's bout of crushing self-doubt, there was definitely a spring in her step. Impulsively, she stepped into a bodega on the next corner and bought herself a bunch of mixed gerbera daisies, a riot of scarlet, magenta, orange and deep yellow, resisting an urge to clutch them to her chest and skip along the block. She felt like a girl.

She felt stupid.

Both were right.

Crossing 101st, her phone buzzed. Heather. She hit the red button to send it to voicemail, but a text popped up immediately, also from Heather.

PICK UP. EMERGENCY.

She stepped up her pace, hit redial and put the phone to her ear.

"Sara, where the hell are you?" Heather's voice was strident with panic, and icy fingers gripped Sara's guts.

"A block away, walking fast. What's wrong?"

"Code red," Heather said. "Something horrible has happened. There's screaming coming from Marguerite's apartment, but the door is barricaded. Hurry."

"Heather!" Sara barked, but the phone was dead. Heather had hung up. Glancing left and right, making sure there was nobody nearby, Sara began to run as fast as she could without drawing attention, dancing around people and dog shit on the sidewalk until she turned sharply into 104th, her mind racing for which of the secret trash-can entrances would take her to Marguerite's apartment fastest. The small alleyway she was looking for appeared and she darted into it, dropping the bunch of flowers in the alley as she punched in the sixteen-digit security code at the metal grille door, then the ten-digit one at the metal blast door beyond it. She entered a dimly lit corridor, three stories below where she needed to be. She stabbed angrily at the elevator button, watching as the illuminated numeral remained on 4, Marguerite's floor. Had April Veronica murdered her maker?

The lit number wasn't budging. She lurched to the fire stairs and hurled herself up eight zig zagging flights. When she reached the door to the fourth floor, she paused, gulping down oxygen, steeling herself for whatever was next. Turning the doorknob, she leaned her shoulder into the heavy door and pushed, her ears instantly filling with the sounds of women burbling beneath the unmistakable, wolf-like howls of a sistren in unimaginable agony.

Heather, Eleanor, Rosa and Fran were clustered by the door to Marguerite's apartment. Fran was hyperventilating and suffering from a headwound, Sara saw at a glance. Blood poured from a visible gash in her scalp; her gray hair was matted almost black around the wound.

"Oh, Sara, thank heavens you're here," Heather said, her eyes wide. "We have a bit of a problem."

Falling against the wall, Fran started to shake, her eyes wide. Stammering, she spastically tried to speak, but Heather raised a palm, silencing her.

"We will take it from here, Fran. Eleanor, can you take her to her yours and get her cleaned up? Then can you rally everyone, this is all hands."

Eleanor, both shaken and shaking, wrapped an arm around Fran and led her to the opposite end of the hallway, where they disappeared behind a fire door.

"Heather, what the fuck?"

"Fran was in her apartment next door and heard quite the commotion. She knocked, no answer. She got her skeleton key, and the door slammed shut on her, so hard it almost knocked her out. It did that to her head."

"Has anyone heard from Marguerite?"

Heather shook her head, then pushed her hair behind her ears with shaking hands.

"Afraid not. But we need to get in there."

Where the hell was Marguerite?

The door at the other end of the hallway creaked open, revealing Teddie and Crina, their faces set like stone. Teddie had a leather satchel slung over her shoulder and a taser in each hand. Crina carefully held two medicine beakers.

"I'm so sorry, Sara." Crina had tears in her eyes. "Everything seemed completely fine yesterday."

"We can talk about that later," Sara said. "We need to get inside and see what's going on."

"When was the last time you talked to Marguerite?" Teddie asked angrily.

"I haven't heard from her since yesterday," Sara said honestly. "I texted her last night and she didn't reply."

Teddie let out an exasperated sigh, and Crina put a hand on her shoulder.

"Not now, Theodora," she said. "We have to get in there."

"Teddie." Heather's voice was serious. "Did you bring the Slicer?"

Teddie nodded solemnly and tapped the satchel. "In its holster."

"Wait – we're killing her?" Sara said. Poor April Veronica.

Crina stepped forward.

"My child. We need to be prepared. For anything."

Another wrenching howl filled the air. Teddie winced.

"That's April Veronica," Crina said, looking around to each of them. "We need to get inside. Heather will open the door. Sara, you and I will go in, with tasers. If we can manage a peaceful outcome, she will drink this-" she raised the two beakers full of almost black liquid, "-morphine and blood. If we can't... manage that... then it will be a matter of overpowering and..."

"Me," Teddie's voice was dead. "I step in."

"Slicer is the last resort." Heather put a hand on Teddie's shoulder. "I doubt it'll come to that."

"Teddie..." Sara began.

"Don't." Teddie's gaze stayed on the ground as another howl rent the air. "We can talk later. Get it sorted. Get it sorted so that I don't have to do this." She finally met Sara's gaze. "*Please.*"

Heather slipped her phone out of her jeans pocket, punching at the screen. "I'm about to unlock the door. As soon as it unlocks, I'll kick it open."

Teddie handed one taser to Sara, the other to Heather.

"If she gets past us, you'll need this."

Heather nodded silently as she took the taser. She slipped it into the front pocket of her hoodie, then raised her phone. She pressed a button on the screen and slipped the phone into her back pocket as the door's pole lock retracted. Then she stepped back, raised one booted foot, and sent it crashing into the door which exploded inward, splintering the bookcase behind it.

As the door flew open, the wailing became almost unbearably loud, and all four women gasped at the gory wreckage of Marguerite's hallway.

There were smears of blood along the floor, red handprints and drag marks disrupting the once-white walls. In a split second, the iron scent reached their nostrils and their thirst bloomed sickeningly in their throats.

"Be strong, lasses," Heather said, crouching, taser extended. Sara nodded at Teddie, who unclipped the cover from the Slicer, dropping the leather sheath to the ground and inserting her fingers through the grip at the bottom. The razor-sharp metal glinted menacingly in the hall's yellow light.

Sara gripped her own taser and took the first step into the bloody hallway, swallowing heavily against the clawing in her throat. Her eyes were fixed on the open space at the end of the hall where the wailing was coming from. She raised the taser and spoke.

"April Veronica?" Her voice cracked. "Honey?"

The howling stopped, leaving a vacuum of silence that was somehow worse.

Crina tapped Sara on the back. "Move up," she whispered, and the pair of them began to advance slowly down the hallway as the sound of heavy, wet sobs filled the air. They had performed this dance together before.

The trail of blood in which they were stepping became wetter and thicker with every advance until, with no option other than to walk right in it, they emerged slowly out of the hallway and into the living room. Sara gasped, and Crina faltered behind her.

The entire floor was a viscous pool of blood, in the center of which lay the body of Marguerite, shattered and clearly dead, mercifully face down. An incision extended from the center of her skull to midway down her back, a clean strike from a Slicer. She had died suddenly. Behind her, pressed against the wall like a cornered animal, crouched a blood-smeared April Veronica, her once-blue jeans and t-shirt so drenched in blood that they were interchangeable, her grief-stricken face also splattered with blood, tears coursing two clear channels down her cheeks.

April Veronica jerked spasmodically as sobs wracked her. The virus that she had ingested with Marguerite's blood pounded her system like jolts of electricity. This could go either way, Sara thought. *Either way.*

"Sara," April Veronica sobbed. "I guess you're here to kill me."

Sara shook her head.

"I'm here to help you," she spoke evenly. "So are Crina and Teddie and Heather. Your sisters. Will you let us help you? I promise you will be all right."

"What the fuck *Game Of Thrones* bullshit is this?" April Veronica yelled, retching and sobbing at the same time. "She just answered the fucking door and she killed her."

To Sara's surprise, Crina, now unarmed, stepped across the living room, and knelt between Marguerite's bloody corpse and the crying, unpredictable young woman. Crina set the two beakers down and displayed her open, empty palms to April Veronica. Slowly, she reached for her, watching for signs of panic. Sara held her breath as Crina was able to place one palm against the young girl's cheek.

"My child," she said, her voice low. "This happened to me when I was very young. I truly know how you feel. And for that I am sorry, for I wish no child to ever feel the agony you are experiencing right now. These two beakers contain blood mixed with morphine, which will help the pressure in your veins. If you would please drink them, we can get you to safety."

April Veronica flinched away from Crina's palm, her eyes rolling.

"She let her in," she sobbed. "She let her in and she... she..."

"You're safe now," Sara spoke softly, knowing that Heather would hear those code words and seal the compound. "Let us help you."

Crina placed her hand back on the girl's face, wiping at a falling tear with her thumb.

"I give you my word, child. Drink of this beaker, and we can take care of you and clean..." she glanced around the wreckage of Marguerite's apartment "...this up. Please."

"If you think I'm going to willingly drink poison, you're out of your fucking mind."

"It's heroin, lass," Heather called from the hallway, her voice dry. "It is a small amount of heroin in some fresh blood. It'll just calm you down. That awful pressure will be gone."

"Yeah, a fucking overdose. Crafty, nah, I ain't gonna fall for it. "

"We can't overdose," Heather said, her voice getting closer as she walked down the hallway. "The virus triggers our adrenal system and counters any shutdowns."

"You drink it then." April Veronica's wild eyes danced from Crina to Sara.

"I could use a break," Crina said gently, lifting the beaker to her lips and drinking a sip. "My child. I swear on us, we are not going to hurt you. We are saving you, while we still can."

Crina's eyes closed briefly and her shoulders slumped.

"How strong is that shit?" April Veronica's wild eyes glanced at Crina, now barely conscious beside her.

"It has to be strong, lass." Heather came into the living room and lifted the beaker from Crina's hands. "The virus is stronger than your body. You're going to have to sleep this off."

"And if I don't take it?"

Heather shrugged. "You might live, you might not. You've ingested so much virus, you're a danger to yourself. Your body isn't as strong as the virus thinks it is." Heather glanced around the room. "We've seen it before, when people didn't understand viral load and all that. It's a slow, painful way to die. We need to keep your adrenalin down or you'll smash yourself up. Or your hunger will flare up and you'll do anything to feed. *Anything.* I'm afraid there's really only one way out of this, and I swear to you, and I don't lie. If you do as I ask, you'll make it through."

Shakily, April Veronica lifted her face to meet Heather's gaze. A quick glance at Marguerite's body wrenched another sob from her, and she recoiled. Crina, returning to consciousness and the moment, raised the beaker to the girl's lips.

"How much am I supposed to drink?"

"Just a wee bit at a time, so you don't get sick," Heather said. Crina tilted the beaker, and they all watched April Veronica's throat to make sure she swallowed.

"That's enough for right now," Heather said. "Give it a sec to work, you'll feel the pressure subside."

April Veronica nodded. She collapsed back against the wall with her eyes closed. Heather bent and gripped her wrist to check her pulse, eyes widening at what she felt, shooting nervous glances at her friends. "Keep feeding it to her," she said calmly to Crina.

"Teddie," Sara called out gently. "April is taking the sedative."

No reply was forthcoming, but Sara heard the gentle sound of metal sliding in leather as the Slicer was placed back into its sheath.

Sara watched intently, sip by sip, until April Veronica finished the first beaker and her eyes rolled back in her head. She passed out, flopping forward suddenly, only Heather's quick reflexes grabbing her arm and preventing her from landing face-down in the viscous red puddle on the floor.

Heather knelt and pushed April Veronica until she was upright, then gripped the girl's jaw with one hand, forcing her lips apart with the other. "Give her a bit more," she said to Crina, who brought the other beaker to her mouth, tipping the remaining blood down her throat, which bobbed as she swallowed. Even in near-unconsciousness, the virus never refused fresh blood. Once the beaker was empty, Crina stood and silently walked back out along the hallway.

"Crina, you're leaving?" Sara asked, But her mother didn't answer.

Heather shrugged. Sara stepped forward. Together, they lifted April Veronica easily, one arm each.

"Maybe take her feet," Heather said, always practical. Sara bent and wrapped her arms around the girl's blood-soaked ankles.

"Take her down to the surrender room," Teddie said tersely, her eyes widening as she caught sight of April Veronica for the first time. "Fuck me, she's soaked in it."

"It's bad, Ted," Sara said. "Honestly, wait here 'til we get back."

"We'll take her." Crina reappeared beside Sara, grabbing at April's legs.

Surrendering her cargo to her maker, Sara stood beside Teddie and watched as the two women carried the unconscious girl into the stairwell.

"Be back in two shakes," Heather said as the door closed.

"That went surprisingly well," Teddie said.

"I guess that was the easy part then," Sara said, glancing down the hallway. "Teddie. It's bad in here."

"I figured," Teddie said. "She's definitely dead?"

Sara nodded and walked back into the living room, Teddie close behind her, their feet making wet sucking sounds with every step.

"Don't touch anything, Ted," Sara whispered, her heart breaking when she saw the look of shock spread across Teddie's face, tears welling at the bottom of her brown eyes.

"Oh no, no, no," Teddie said, her voice thick. "This...this is ritual."

"I think you're right." Sara squatted beside Marguerite's still body, gazing at the deep cut that ran along her spine, vertebrae blindingly white through the gore, and the spinal cord, its dull yellowy softness oozing from the incision, following gravity over the bumps in her spine till it mixed with the blood soaked into the back of Marguerite's top.

"It's perfectly done, at least," Teddie said soberly, analyzing. "She didn't feel a thing. They did it right in the doorway, then April dragged her over here to feed."

"Has anyone looked at the building's camera footage?"

"Fran said she was going to, but she took a fucking whack to the face. She's gonna have matching shiners."

"It has to be Desdemona," Sara said, a dull certainty settling in her stomach. "I should have known."

"You checked Marguerite's credit, right?" Teddie said, the tension in her voice belying the importance of the question.

Sara took a deep breath before she shook her head. This was going to be the worst moment of her life.

"I did not," Sara said, and Teddie flinched. "I mean, I discussed it with Marguerite, of course, but when I talked to Desdemona, we got sidetracked."

"Sara." Teddie's voice was steely. "There are rules for a reason. That's... I mean, that's Lock 101. You check. You verify."

"Heather could have also done that," Sara said, knowing in her heart it was no excuse.

"Heather is not the mother of this Lock, and lately, neither are you."

Sara froze and stared at her friend. Teddie's eyes were narrowed.

"Girl, I've tried. I've tried to talk to you. You're tuned out. I get it, it's a shit job and you've done it for a really long time. But for fuck's sake, this is what happens when you take your eyes off the target for just one second."

"Oh, nice, Teddie." Sara was suddenly angry. She stepped around Marguerite's body.

"Who, precisely, can I give the job to? You? You've been shitting your pants for two fucking days because I gave you the responsibility to kill someone. You've fallen apart completely. I have spent one hundred and something fucking years living in that exact situation. Every decision is life and death. Every day. And literally, the weekend I go on my first dates in fifty years, this happens and it's my fault. Okay. Got it. But right now, we have to focus. Whoever did this could still be here, maybe still in the building."

"I'm sorry, Mom," Teddie blurted. "This is freaking me out and I didn't take my heem and the blood is starting to get to me."

"Go home, shower, don't bother with heems, get some real blood in you, then come back if you can. I need to be here."

Wordlessly, Teddie turned and let herself out of the apartment. A blanket of silence fell, and Sara stared at the gory remains of her sister, grateful that her face was turned down.

In her pocket, her phone rang and vibrated, startling her.

She pulled her phone out and froze when she saw the number. After a pause, she answered.

"Sara, mi amiga vieja," said a deep voice. "It is Desdemona. I am sorry to bring this tidings to you. I have dispatched our sister, Marguerite according to Lock law. She created without the credit, and in violation of our pact, and it required my attention. It was done in accordance with tradition. I am sorry I wasn't able to dispose of her."

"Desdemona," Sara said, her voice harsh. "You could have fucking warned me. Did you know her new sister was in the apartment?"

Sara heard Desdemona's breath catch in her throat. "What?"

"You have created a dangerous, cruel situation for my entire Lock."

"For that I apologize," the Spaniard said. "I am willing to meet you, for parlay, for explanation."

"Meet? If you're so certain you did the right thing, why didn't you fucking wait? Why run off? Come back right fucking now, Desdemona. Let's face each other."

"No, amiga, that is what I will not. You are hostile, and you have more sisters with you than I do. We will meet in public. A bar or restaurant of your choice."

Sara winced. Desdemona anticipated violence.

"I will meet your request," Sara spoke formally. "How many of your Lock will be at the meeting?"

"I will have three. You may bring an equal number. No more."

"When?"

"Now is good."

"Now is *not* good for me, Desdemona," Sara snapped. "The new girl feasted on Marguerite." Another sharp intake of breath down the line. "So, as you can imagine, I have several messes to clean up."

"I do not wish to remain in this wretched city for any longer than necessary. Our meeting will be over breakfast tomorrow morning. Do not speak to any other Locks before our meeting. This is between us."

"You are in no position to ask for my obedience, Desdemona."

"Sara. Marguerite broke the rules, and that means either she or the new girl had to die. I suspected you would not take care of it, and now I am certain."

Sara struggled to keep her calm, not wanting to seem weak to this ancient, formidable woman.

"I have to go, Desdemona. I have... housekeeping... to take care of."

"Then for now, Sara, I must go. But before I do..."

"Yes?"

"We acted in complete accordance. The work is done. You have nothing to fear. I do not want to damage our relationship."

"We have no relationship, Desdemona," Sara said. "Bring every scrap of proof that you have, and Desdemona?"

"Si?"

"You better fucking hope that it satisfies me, or you'll never see Madrid again."

Sara ended the call without waiting for a response, staring at her phone, her mind racing.

A text landed, as if had she willed it into existence. Heather.

> She's secure. Heading back up.

Sara pondered her response.

> Can you reset all access codes to the one only you and I know?

Already did.

We need an all hands in ritual room.

How long do you need?

I need to shower, and we need to clean this up. Shall we do it now or tonight?

Delegate. Let's hold the meeting and then we'll pick the clean-up crew.

Thanks Heather. Everyone in the big room at 1pm.

Got it.

Sara slid her phone into her pocket, surprised when it scraped against the taser that she'd stuffed in there. Sara glanced out through the dirty windows of Marguerite's apartment at the sunny, blue sky that a short while ago had held the promise of a full new heart, and now looked clinical and cold. Like the woman at her feet.

An image of herself kneeling and tasting the potent blood of one of her own flashed across her mind, followed by a gust of nausea so strong it bent her double. For that she was grateful. With a sigh, she let herself out, kicked off her blood soaked shoes, picked them up and began the walk through the hallways and staircases that led back to her apartment.

Once inside, she shucked off all of her clothes directly into a trash bag, knowing that they would have to be burned in the furnace, along with Marguerite's body. She showered and swallowed six heems with a glass of ice water that sat like snow around her heart. She needed to sit and think. She needed clarity before the meeting.

On the coffee table her phone buzzed with an incoming text. Silas.

Thanks for last night. I'm still smiling.

Chapter Eighteen

G lancing at her watch and seeing 12:50, Sara steeled herself for the all hands meeting. The early stages would be chaos, and she anticipated an onslaught of raw emotion that she was incapable of dealing with in her current panic. She decided to meditate, snatching a clean towel from the closet by the front door. She folded it down to a square and sat cross legged upon it. She inhaled, counting to twelve, feeling the strain on her lungs, then held her breath. As she counted another measure of twelve, she focused on the fractured disaster of her mind, unrelated thoughts skittering around, bouncing off each other like electrons. With each exhale, she felt them slowing. After repeating the practice until she felt calm enough to tackle the matter at hand, she directed her thoughts to Marguerite, needing to find clarity around the thorny woman's fate.

Eventually, she was able to divide her confusion neatly into halves – Marguerite, and her demise, and April Veronica, and her future.

If Desdemona was telling the truth, Marguerite's death was a justified but ugly holdover from their governing constitution. But Sara would have no answers until tomorrow.

More pressing was the issue of April Veronica, the sweet, innocent woman currently zonked out on heroin on a velvet couch in a room that could become her tomb with the flick of a switch.

Sara suspected that some of the Lock would want the easy option – to flick the switch while April Veronica slept, let her pass painlessly; while others, Teddie among them for sure, would fight for her to remain alive, accepting the responsibilities of her teaching and governance.

Inside the stillness of her mind, Sara confronted a third option: April Veronica, a newborn, had ingested a massive amount of blood from Marguerite. The virus might kill her outright.

Sara breathed deeply, recognizing fear in her own heart. She was afraid of failing April Veronica, afraid of failing her Lock.

She was afraid of letting Teddie down.

This final realization jolted her from her meditation. She had to own it that her downward spiral, begun so many years ago, almost subconsciously, was tearing her away from her soul mate, her truest companion, Teddie, in ways that they'd never been separated before. Pushing up to stand, Sara decided that if the Lock voted to terminate April, she wouldn't force Teddie to press the button. She would do it herself.

She tapped the screen of her phone. 1:03 and a text from Crina.

> I'm waiting outside your door. I'll walk down with you.

Sara made a face. Crina's text made her feel more like she was being monitored than supported. Sighing, she snapped a black shawl from over a hanger in the hall cupboard, gathered her keyring, and opened the door. Crina was leaning against the far wall, looking down into the stairwell. At the noise from the door, she turned to face Sara.

"How are you holding up?"

"Been better." Sara stepped forward and wrapped her arms around her maker's waist, oddly relieved when Crina hugged back. The held each other tightly, each hearing only the other's breath.

"Take as long as you need, child."

"I can't. We have a room full of freaked-out women downstairs. Can I get a rain check on the hug?"

"I'm going to stay," Crina said. "I want to be here for you, for this. We can hug as much as you like."Sara pulled away. "Thank you, and sorry, I didn't realize how much I needed it."

"It never gets easy, what we do," Crina said, her eyes downcast..

"Come on," Sara said, ushering her down the corridor. "If we're any later, we'll be walking into a mob scene."

The hallway leading to the meeting room was too quiet, their footfalls the only sounds echoing along the brickwork. Hairs rose on the back of Sara's neck and she slowed down briefly. Of course Crina noticed.

"Maybe nobody is here yet," she said, stepping ahead of Sara and twisting the heavy iron doorknob, opening the heavy door with the lightest push of her hand. As it glided open, Sara saw that all eight of the women of her lock *were* seated in the room, scattered among the rows of chairs. Only Liz and Yukari were seated beside each other, holding hands and crying. Everyone else appeared to be in private reverie, their heads bowed. Nobody looked up as Sara and Crina walked down the short aisle and stepped up onto the dais, taking their seats. Sara waited a full minute before speaking, using the silence before the storm to get her thoughts in order.

"The good news, my sisters, is that we are safe," she said firmly, her voice loud. "I have spoken to Desdemona. She takes responsibility for Marguerite's death. Tomorrow, I will meet her to verify her claims that she acted in accordance with Lock rule."

As the words left her lips and echoed in the still room, Sara watched as Teddie's head rose, until her brown-orange eyes were staring directly into her own.

"You granted the permission to Marguerite," Teddie said, her throaty voice breaking. "You were supposed to have validated her credit."

Sara gulped before deciding on brutal honesty.

"I fucked up," she said, holding her hands palm up. "I spoke with Marguerite, of course, at great length. She explained to me the genealogy of her credit, the tale of the Spanish elder, an artist, who chose surrender and bequeathed her credit to a fellow artist so that their vision could continue."

"Cool story, Sara." Teddie's eyes narrowed. "But you didn't bother to contact Madrid to confirm?"

"I did speak with Desdemona." Sara said, only partially truthfully. "She did not say that Marguerite did not have the credit, she only said that she was in favor of no more sisters being made. I may not have asked the right questions, that's true. But at no time did Desdemona dispute the credit issue."

"Well, Marguerite is dead now," Liz said. "Because you didn't do your homework."

"She's dead, yes." Sara inhaled, squaring her shoulders. "I will be better able to answer your questions after I meet with Desdemona."

"So that's it then," Liz said tearfully. "Marguerite lied, you fucked up, so now she's dead and everything's fine?"

"Quite the opposite," Crina said, raising her hand to block Sara from speaking. "We are in very delicate, extremely dangerous territory at the moment. There is a delegation from another Lock in our city. We will meet with them tomorrow morning."

"And?" said Yukari, her eyes challenging.

"We will listen," Sara began. "As is the custom. Then we will ask questions."

"Desdemona doesn't mess around," Heather said, not raising her face. "If she came here to do this, without telling us, she is right."

"She killed one of our members," Teddie said angrily. "Being right or wrong doesn't change the fact that somehow, she gained access to our crib and she murdered Marguerite."

"I left Europe to escape the violent feudalism," Crina said. "This Lock is something that I am so proud of. We are peaceful. We are kind. That is still not the practice across Europe. However, the old ways are still the governing ways. Once a newborn is created, if the credit does not permit it, there can only be two solutions: Either the maker or the made must die. This is our balance."

"That is death penalty bullshit." Teddie's hands were gripping the top of the seat in front of her.

"It is," Sara said, wishing she could be talking to Teddie alone. "This is not how I would have handled it."

"Oh, so now you are handling it?" Teddie spat.

"Ouch, but fair. Yes, I'm handling it. Blame me all you want, but if Desdemona is telling the truth, Marguerite knew she was lying. She knew the consequences. What we don't know is why she pushed ahead."

"She was so full of shit," snapped Fran angrily, black bruises like dark puddles around her piercing yellow-green eyes. "And even in death she's putting us through the wringer. I hate to say I told you so, but now we have a fucking monster in the surrender room, and she's not Marguerite's problem any more. She's ours. And old school super bitch Desdemona is here? That's fun. Crina, why don't you tell us one good thing about Desdemona, because all I've heard is scary bullshit."

"She's honest," Crina said without hesitation. "She's wrapped in the old customs, in ways that I am not. She sees only right and wrong, night and day. She views our rules as fixed and immutable, as they are and must be. But *we* are a progressive Lock. We discuss. We talk. We grant space to our sisters when they need peace or privacy. Madrid does not. Even Scholars must live within walking distance of the central building, and they must attend every meeting."

"Her commitment to her Lock is unwavering," Sara admitted. "I have enjoyed the times I have counted on her guidance."

"How about now?" Teddie said. "Still enjoying it?"

"Teddie, how about you and I talk tonight? We have a lot to get through."

"Nah, I'm good," Teddie said, looking away. "Either say it to me here, or don't. I don't want to talk privately. I want us all to hear everything. I want us all on the same page.""As you wish," Sara said, stung. "But—"

"They came in from the north utility entrance," interrupted Fran. "They used the code provided to all Locks. I've voided all outside access codes, but Sara, we could have changed the code if we suspected danger."

"All Lock mothers have a complete set of access codes to all other Locks. That isn't a secret." Sara looked away. She knew that when Fran got angry, she stayed angry.

"They don't have to tell us they're coming?" Eleanor said angrily, feeding off Fran's energy. "I start work in less than three hours, I can't call out sick if we're going to have enough fresh blood to get April Veronica through this."

Fran, still standing, her chin out defiantly, pounced.

"So, sisters, are we going to get April Veronica through this?" she said, the words flat in the dead air of the room. "Or not?"

"Is there dissension on the matter?" Sara asked, glancing from woman to woman. Only Fran and Eleanor met her eyes.

"Well," Teddie said, speaking slowly. "If there is anyone here who is thinking 'or not,' then we have dissension. We've been through enough death today. Nothing you've said makes it feel right, nothing justifies Marguerite's... murder. And if I hear a single one of you bitches say that you are down with killing an innocent woman, then yes, we have a motherfucking dissension on our hands."

Imani, who'd been sitting at the back, stood and made her way two rows forward, standing beside Teddie. "I'm with her," she said, placing a hand on Teddie's shoulder.

"What's done is done," she said gravely. "Murder needs to be something we don't do."

"Am I going to need to bring this to a vote?" Sara said, rolling into the comfortable ceremony of Lock politics.

"I'd like to at least speak my mind," Fran said.

"Do you wish to come up here?"

"No, I can say what I want to say from here." Fran turned slowly from left to right, waiting until each woman raised their face to hers. "Yes, April Veronica seems like a nice woman, a good solid addition to the Lock. But, and this but is actually really scaring me, let's be honest: We don't know what we will be facing when she wakes up."

"I have some thoughts on the matter," Yukari said, not letting go of Liz's hand as she stood. "I have been running virology experiments, as you all know. Obviously, all of my research is theoretical. And without trying to sound too scientisty, what happened today is very valuable research for me."

Teddie and Eleanor began to mutter, and Yukari raised a palm to them.

"Hear me out, my sisters," Yukari said. "This is an opportunity for us to learn much, without any attendant risk. What's done is done. April Veronica is in a bad position. Her blood is stronger than her body, and viral drain will kill her if I am not able to replace a large amount of her blood with clean blood, blood free of the disease. I will need all three of our nursing sisters to work this evening. And," Yukari turned to Fran. "I accept full responsibility for the newborn. I understand that that means I am responsible for her life, and if necessary, her... termination. But for now, if I have the blessing of the Lock, she is of immeasurable value to me, and also, to us all."

"She's a young woman, Yukari. Not a fucking guinea pig." Teddie's knuckles tightened on the chair back.

"I know that, dear Theodora. Without my help, her future is far from secure, in the short term. We need to get this meeting over and done so that those of us who will help, can help."

Sara stood and opened her palms to the room.

"Do we still have dissension?" she asked.

"I have spoken for a path that we permit the child to survive, and that I will assume responsibility for her," Yukari said.

"Our sister has presented a viable option to our pressing emergency," Sara said. "Are we in agreement?"

"Yes, Imani said. "We are the Lock who preserves life. It is our duty, it makes us unique."

Glaring around the room, Fran took a deep breath.

"This is bullshit and you all know it," she said, her voice low. "Crina, I'm sorry you have to hear this, but we are not doing well. This Lock has splintered and fallen apart. We have secrets. We have lives outside of this room and they are, for some of us, a priority." Crina smiled and stood, wrapping an arm around Sara.

"All Locks have secrets," she said, her voice soothing. "All humans have secrets. Don't mistake my absence for ignorance, my child. I watch you all from afar, I talk to you all. I hear when I listen, and I see when I look. This Lock isn't splintering, it's adapting to modern life. Our lives have a ticker tape running alongside what we see and hear. We are drowning in information and we do not have time to reflect. When was the last time any of you had the time to devote a weekend to a good reverie?" She paused, looking around. "Exactly. And silly old me, I believe that a weekend spent in reflection is key to surviving the week ahead, or the week before."

"Fran?" Sara spoke directly to her. "April Veronica has expressed interest in working with you in security..."

"Quit trying to buy me off," Fran said with a dry laugh. "I don't want to kill the kid either. There's just something attractive about letting this whole thing wrap itself up naturally."

"Fran, shut up, please," Teddie said just above a whisper. "Standing by and letting someone die is not an option, it's not the way this Lock formed, it's not the way we live."

"Frankly, I'm just tired of dealing with Marguerite's shit," Fran said. Fran never backed down.

"Frannie, we all are," Imani said, her voice gentle "Come on, love. We can't go killing a poor girl just coz it's the easy option."

"It's not the easy option," Fran insisted. "I'm just saying that we are all in the middle of a huge fucking charade here and none of us has the time to devote to a newborn."

"And Yukari said she will take that job."

"And I'm down to help," Teddie said. "This is what we do. This is the essence of this Lock. Sure, Fran, you're right. But right now, in the middle of all the shit in the world, we need to lean into kindness, and also, each one of us approved her induction. We are all responsible."

"I'm in," Rosa said begrudgingly. "The April Veronica coaching team is in effect."

"In," said Liz with a wan smile.

"Always happy to help," said Heather.

"I am both in, for helping, and in a hurry, if we need blood," Eleanor said, tossing her ropy curls back. "It's not like we just go to a supermarket and buy all the blood. Emergencies like this require a little..." she shot a knowing glance at Teddie, ...finessing, amirite girls?"

The mood in the room noticeably lightened and Sara exhaled after not realizing she was holding her breath. Crina took her hand and clenched it.

"There are two remaining items to discuss," Sara said. "One is the public meeting tomorrow, with Desdemona. She has three sisters with her, so that is the limit of sisters I can take. A violent response is out of the question."

"Are you worried?" Imani asked. "I'm always happy to run interference."

"Thanks, Imani," Sara said. "I can bring two more."

"I want to go," Teddie said, her voice loud. "I want to talk to her."

"To what end?" Sara wished that Teddie would do this in private.

"I want to see if she has remorse."

"She won't," Crina interrupted. "She is acting in accordance with our rules, rules she helped write. These rules are her backbone. She simply acted in accordance with law." Crina paused, then stepped down from the dais and walked to Teddie's side, taking one of her hands. "I will come with you, Theodora. You deserve the answers you seek, and I know how to handle Desdemona."

Jesus Christ, Sara thought. Has the whole Lock decided that I'm useless? She realized she didn't blame them.

"Okay, well that's that then," she said. "I will inform you of the logistics later tonight. And the final matter for today is..."

"Cleanup crew," Heather said, way too spritely, standing and clapping her hands together like a school marm. "The nurses are out, the ambassador crew is out. Yukari, you're going to go monitor April. That leaves you two, Fran and Rosa. I'll gather the equipment and meet you outside Marguerite's apartment. Please go home and take a double dose of heem. It's going to be... well," she shrugged. "You know exactly how it's going to be in there. It won't be fun, but if we are focused, it will be fast."

"Thank you, Heather," Sara tried a light smile, but it felt weird on her face, so she let it fade. "And thank you, all of you. A lot has happened today, and a lot was said this afternoon. I have listened and I am ready for us to talk, and heal, together in the coming days and weeks and years."

"And centuries," said Crina with a smile. "We have centuries to heal this."

As the meeting began to break up, Sara moved to the door ahead of her sisters. She wanted to be alone, and she hated to admit, she wanted to see if Silas had texted her.

"Sara!" Crina's voice stopped her in her tracks. "I think that those of us meeting with Desdemona should stay behind to discuss protocol."

Sara fought to keep her shoulders from slumping in disappointment.

"Of course, Crina," she said, her back to the room. "That's a great idea."

Chapter Nineteen

An almost-warm spring breeze whipped a curl of Sara's auburn wig into her eye, and she blinked it away angrily. Walking briskly through Central Park on one of those perfect spring days that hint at the summer ahead, she wanted to wish the day away. She loved spring in the city, and the irony of wasting this fine day on a formality with Desdemona was gnawing at her. A feeling uncomfortably close to self-pity was clouding her mind, resentful that just as she began to enjoy a life outside the Lock, Desdemona had swooped in and locked her down. Again.

Around her, somewhere, Crina, Imani and Teddie were making their way to the appointed meeting place, the Loeb Boathouse. As was Lock custom, they were all walking independently, along pre-arranged separate routes, and all of them were in "tourist-lite drag."

The location was just another case of Desdemona following lock law to the letter. It was discouraged for more than two sistren to be seen together outside the Lock walls unless the circumstances were dire, which they currently were. In that case, the venue for the meeting was to be "highly transient" and "resistant to habitual patronage." When Desdemona sent the location that morning, Imani had a field day, cackling that sometimes she felt like she'd signed on to Downton Abbey when she became a sister.

"This is some twatting nonsense," she trilled in her poshest English accent.

"Just wait, it gets worse," Crina said, humor twinkling her dark eyes.

"I've been in New York slightly less than fifty years, and I'm pretty okay with never having gone to that boathouse. How can you make it worse?"

"Your wardrobe," Crina said, reaching down and hauling a vintage Chanel leather satchel onto Sara's coffee table. "I knew this was coming, so I took a quick walk down Broadway. I have gifts for you all."

Sara glanced at Teddie, not surprised to see no sign of humor on her face at Crina's transparent attempt to lighten the mood.

"Here." Crina handed Imani a t-shirt. Imani unfolded it and held it up. It said 'New York Is For Lovers.' She handed Teddie a navy shirt with a Mets logo, and Sara got a gray shirt with the I heart NY logo. "Accessorize however you wish, but remember, we need to be extra forgettable."

"I'm going to wear a wig," Sara declared, out of nowhere.

"Good idea," Crina was in full cheerleader mode. "Sunglasses for all, no makeup, and head coverings if possible."

At the end of last night, Sara had collapsed onto her bed, bone tired. Plus there was the issue of the young woman still sleeping off her opiates in the surrender room. Resting atop all of her worries was the almost-unfamiliar tug in her heart.

She missed Silas.

Pulling her phone out for the first time in hours, she saw a screen of texts and missed calls, all from him, and her heart swelled with a mixture of excitement and pressure.

In all of the relationships she'd had as a cursed woman, she always felt pressure. To perform, to conform, to compromise and to lie.

Those feelings were still there, but this time excitement was beating them down. It felt better than she remembered. Opening her phone, she read the texts in chronological order, a string of nice platitudes interrupted by an address on Washington St, with no explanation. She typed back.

> Hey! Sorry, it's been a disaster day at work, I have been in meetings non-stop til now. What's the address?

Immediately the little bubble with the ellipsis appeared. He was replying. First came a map, a blue dot on Washington in the West Village.

> That's my place. Now we are even. I realized last night we didn't set up a next date. Can we?

Sara sighed. The building was on lockdown. Her clients for the week had all been switched to Zooms. After the meeting with Marguerite, they'd all be pitching in with monitoring April Veronica. There was no way she would be able to see Silas.

> Work is pretty stressful at the moment. I might be able to see you later in the week. I want to. Can I get back to you?

> Yes.

And then no bubble, no ellipsis. Sara waited, staring at her screen long after it went black, drifting into reverie, and then, surprisingly into sleep. When she woke up confused, in the middle of the night, her lights on, she experienced the same discombobulation as she'd felt a morning earlier, in her new fake apartment. Silas hadn't written anything further.

Now, in the distance, obscured by newly-budding tree branches and zipping-by joggers, Sara saw Teddie, who was still ignoring her calls and texts, which made her feel sick to her stomach. Allowing Teddie to come to this meeting might not have been the smartest decision but Sara couldn't see an alternative that wouldn't hurt her feelings or alienate her further. The best she could hope for was that Teddie wouldn't make too much of a scene.

Teddie was in attention-deflecting mom jeans, the shapeless navy Mets hoodie with the hood up, and bland, comfy-looking dirty white Adidas. Sara watched as Teddie arrived at the Boathouse and disappeared inside, its ornate New England façade clean and inviting in the late morning sun, the neon green lake behind it looking like Godzilla was about to come stomping out of its nuclear depths at any second.

As Sara stepped up to the door, she felt her jaw clench ferociously. She breathed in twice, deeply, and pulled the door open.

"I'm here for the Villaseñor table," she told the maître d', using Desdemona's tempus name. Wordlessly, she was escorted to a six-top table away from the open windows over the lake. Teddie and Imani were already seated, their backs to Sara. As she approached, the three women from the Madrid all raised their faces, showing sunglasses, pale lips and in one instance, a burka.

"Lily Berger?" said one of them, her Castilian accent very thick. Sara nodded.

"Your table is over there," she said, unfurling an arm gracefully, pointing to a smaller table at a window, where Desdemona was seated, looking out over the green lake.

"Muchas gracias," Sara said, to both the sister and the maître d', making her own way between the tables. As Sara drew near, Desdemona sensed her, and stood in one smooth motion. Sara kept her face still as she took in Desdemona's outfit, head to toe black, the uniform of mourning across the Mediterranean. Somehow it made her look older, plainer. It also sent a message that was not lost on her.

"Lily, mi hermana," Desdemona said, her deep voice resonating in her chest. "It has been too long since I have seen you. May I hug you?"

Sara knew she had to follow tradition so she remained silent.

"I take that as a yes," Desdemona stepped to her and wrapped her strong arms around Sara's shoulders. Sara did not reciprocate, stepping back as soon as the other woman released her. Wordlessly they slipped into their seats, and Desdemona returned her gaze outward.

"You have done incalculable damage," Sara said, gazing at Desdemona's striking profile, her long straight nose, full lips, hair pulled back into a tight ponytail.

"What would you have done, Sara?" Desdemona turned her face very slowly, and Sara knew that behind her dark glasses, her flecked almond eyes were boring into her own.

"I would have done what was necessary."

Desdemona nodded slowly, enigmatically, before jerking a thumb in the direction of their other table.

"You only brought two sisters today?"

"No, there will be three."

"In Europe, punctuality is expected."

"In New York, punctuality is also expected, but when the city conspires against us, we make allowances."

"And that, in a nutshell, is why we acted as we did. We don't make allowances. We leave enough time to be punctual. We..." she paused. "We do our homework."

Sara drew in a lung full of air, trying to derail a surge of anger up her throat. Before she could speak, Desdemona reached across the table and took her hand.

"My friend, I did you a favor. You have created a wonderful, p
eaceable...environment. This kind of... enforcement... is not easy for
those who are new to it." She glanced at Teddie, who was now deep in
conversation with one of the women at her table.

"She would have done it."

"Theodora has taken a vow of peace. She has counseled many of my
sistren over the years, she is a great teacher."

"I still wish you had contacted me.""I did, Lily. I explained my
position."

"You did not share your plans."

"I called you many times, just this past Sunday."

"Do you have any idea how many unsolicited phone calls I get every
day? This is America. You don't cold call important news on a burner
phone."

"I called to tell you that," Desdemona's voice dropped, "my sisters
and I voted last week on a change to our... organization. We voided
all credits. Our late sister was informed that her credit was no longer
valid."

A fiery anger blazed across Sara's chest. Marguerite *had* had a credit.
She hadn't lied about it.

"This is unprecedented," she said tersely.

"And necessary." Desdemona lowered her glasses. "Our sister was
notified."

Sara put on her best poker face and thoughts swirled. She herself
had four credits; if Marguerite had come to her, would she have volunteered one of hers?

"But I was not," she said finally. "Your authority does not extend
this far. I possess the necessary credits. I would have helped her."

"This remains a Madrid matter."

Stalemate. Sara struggled to force her anger down to a manageable level.

"You set her up."

"Be very careful with your accusations." Desdemona's voice was steel.

"I don't need to be careful of anything," Sara spat. "What you have done is a declaration of war. There can no longer be cooperation between our Locks." Sara paused, enjoying Desdemona's shock. "If you can rewrite your rules to get your own way, so can I. Our relationship is based upon nothing but history. There is nothing that says we have to work together. What you have done has severed my sisters from yours."

Desdemona gave a short dry laugh. "You trusted our late sister," she whispered. "She made a fool of you. Ever since she left us, she has complained about you, and told us of the poorly run operation that you oversee."

Unsurprised, Sara leaned forward.

"Oh, I'm sorry, is gossip now punishable by death? I have one thing to say and then we are done here. My sisters and I no longer work within the federation. I shall contact all the relevant mothers today and inform them that as a result of your trespass, we've gone lone wolf. There's nothing to say that we can't, just the same as you were free to change your rules. We will cease all financial support to you and communication between our sisters will be forbidden. As for the other Locks, we will assess our ties on an individual basis."

"'I didn't get my way,'" Desdemona said, her voice dripping with sarcasm. "'I'm going to take my toys and go home.' You haven't changed a bit."

"And that," Sara leaned forward, her voice low, "is *your* fucking problem. It's you who hasn't changed, and the world has."

The narrowing of Desdemona's eyes told Sara she'd hit a nerve, which satisfied her.

"One of us is fighting to minimize our threat to the changes of the world," Desdemona said, her voice quiet and sharp. "You, as usual, are acting like the spoiled bitch who's been at La Sorbonne for three centuries. Who hasn't changed? Not fucking me."

"Are you still hurt that mommy didn't bring you to America? You could have transferred into this city at any time, Des. Enjoyed a little freedom, maybe even gotten laid."

"And live under your roof? Your rules? *Pinche cabrona*! I'd rather die."

"Right, because that would involve adapting to modern ways."

"No, it would mean kissing your ass and seeing your smug, shitty face every day. That's no life."

"Don't get me started on quality of life. You've run your house like a prison camp. Marguerite couldn't wait to get away from you."

"Then why was she on the phone to us, daily, weekly, complaining about your disaster of a house?"

"Let's ask her... oh wait. Too late now, huh?" Sara reached across the table and took Desdemona's hand, gripping it tightly before she could yank it away. With a cold smile, she continued. "By all means, dear sister, continue with your suicide march. Hell, if you're looking for someone to push the button on your surrender, I volunteer. Nothing would make me happier. But know this. If you come within a mile of my city, much less set foot anywhere in my house again, you're dead. I'll do it myself, and I'll fucking smile as I do it."

Twisting her hand inside Sara's, Desdemona dug a fingernail painfully into Sara's wrist.

"As if a weak, failing snowflake like you could kill a fly."

"Try me. I beg you."

Desdemona went to reply, but Sara squeezed harder, making her gasp.

"You are behaving like a *man!*" Sara whispered. Desdemona visibly flinched and the pressure of the fingernail stabbing her wrist lessened. "You *murdered* someone."

Things were getting too heated for a public setting. Releasing Desdemona's wrist, Sara jerked her own arm back, rubbing at the indentation in her wrist.

"If we had caught you on our premises, we could have tribunaled you."

"Except I was able to waltz in and out undetected. Another area of weakness under your watch."

"You abused the trust that is granted to all mothers. In the eyes of my... house... you have violated a law. You know what this means."

The bustle of the restaurant around them grew louder in Sara's ears as her jaws clenched in anger.

"Yeah, right, bitch," Desdemona said eventually. "Know this: The five houses on my side plan to vote to change the rules. We have the numbers. Enforced surrender is coming."

"Ooooh, you have numbers and you're all planning to surrender, which means that eventually, I will win this battle."

"I vow one thing, sister. You will surrender before me."

"Save it," Sara raised a palm. "Are we done here?"

The moment spun out as the other woman returned her gaze out over the stagnant green lake.

"Geraniums," Desdemona said finally, her voice flat as if nothing had occurred, a tactic she'd used on Sara for centuries. She loved to start an argument, and then pretend it didn't happen by switching the conversation entirely. Sara refused to be baited, watching as Desdemona gestured at the flowers in the window boxes with her chin. "Glorified weeds. Why put them in such a fancy place?"

"It's New York," Sara said. "Spring and summer are short and sharp and then everything dies. Geraniums are hardy, I find their scent calming. It's very earthy."

"You make excuses for this city every time I talk to you," Desdemona said, turning her face back to the table. "Don't you miss Europe? The forests, the coastlines, the mountains, the seasons?"

"I don't do nostalgia," Sara said, anger in her voice. "So, if we are done, I have to get back to cleaning up your mess... your brutal, selfish, illegal mess."

Desdemona stiffened, and briefly, Sara assumed she had actually scored a point against her.

"You brought Crina?" Glancing at the other table, Sara saw that their maker had arrived while they argued. Her head was thrown head back in laughter, and she was holding Teddie's hand.

"She can't sit at that table," Desdemona spat, standing suddenly and waving to Crina, who smiled in acknowledgement, then feigned confusion. "Go and get her!"

Sara remained motionless, then turned her gaze outward to the lake. She heard Desdemona sigh and then bark at a server in Spanish. A seat was squeezed in on the open side of the table, pressing into the side of her knee, and seconds later, she felt Crina squeeze her arm.

"Apparently I'm not allowed to sit at the kids' table," Crina said with a smile as she slid into the seat. "I ordered some appetizers, but they're going to bring them here."

"What a pleasant surprise," Desdemona said, before turning back to their server and speaking in Spanish again.

"I wish I could say the same," Crina said, her voice tightening. "This was not the return to the city I envisaged. I trust you have proven yourself."

"The opposite," Sara said coldly.

"Mother, did you know that Madrid voted to nullify all credits?"

Crina's head jerked up but her face remained still.

"When was this?"

"Last week," Desdemona said. Was it Sara's imagination or did she seem nervous?

Crina sat perfectly still, considering the information. Slowly she faced Desdemona.

"You do not have the power to strip a credit from anyone."

"A motion was taken up, voted on by all sisters, unanimously, that this would be adopted by us."

Leaning forward and dropping her voice to a whisper, Crina spoke. "A vote such as that only applies to a Lock's current members. What you have done is the most egregious thing a Lock has done since the Purge. My child, this is entrapment. It is also... I cannot say here, in public." She paused, shaking her head. "That poor woman."

"She was informed."

"She was right to refuse you," Crina said, anger in her voice. "You have no jurisdiction here. You informed her of your wishes, and when she ignored your wishes, you... did what you did."

A server carrying plates of food arrived, and Crina fell silent. Desdemona took the plates of food from his tray and set them on the table.

"She's acting like a man," Sara said, enjoying the disgusted shock that registered on Crina's face. Sara popped a crab cake onto her plate, breaking it apart with her fingers, mainly because she suspected it would bother Desdemona.

"And as usual, she's acting like an entitled spoiled bitch," Desdemona said to Crina.

"Have you always been this heartless?" Crina glared at Desdemona, who recoiled as if she'd been slapped. In silence, Crina took a crab cake and set it on her plate. "Desdemona, imagine the situation being reversed."

"I can't imagine ever presiding over such sloppy Lock," Desdemona said.

"That is not what I'm saying. I'm asking you to imagine if Sara came to your city and did something so awful, so brutal, and her explanation was simply that she had changed the rules. One of your great failings as a sister is your lack of empathy, always has been."

Sara couldn't take her eyes from Desdemona's face as the woman's chin trembled. Crina had never spoken to them like this.

"As for a sloppily-run house," Crina continued, her voice steady. "You and I both know that you have had more than your share of problems as a mother. I will respect your privacy, but please, do *not* force my hand."

Sara glanced from one woman to the other. Both were still as granite, commonplace among elder sistren. An argument could continue for an hour in silence. She knew that right now, both of them were mentally reviewing whatever Crina was talking about.

Sara was surprised by the level of support her maker was giving her. She glanced over at the other table. Teddie was speaking quietly, but emphatically. Imani was nodding in support. There was surprise on the faces of the three Spaniards facing them. Nobody was having a pleasant lunch.

Inside her hip pocket, Sara's phone buzzed. Normally, she would never have considered taking a look at her phone at such a tense meeting but... without looking at her companions, she fished her phone out.

> Hey Lily. Thinking of you on this gorgeous day. That's all. S.

A smile spread across her face as she replaced the device.

"Good news?" Crina asked with a smirk. Sara nodded.

"A phone at the table during a summit," Desdemona began. Anger flared in Sara's chest.

"Do not speak to me about respect," she said, fighting to keep her tone light. "Do. Not."

"She's right," Crina said. "I think it's best if we all go our separate ways."

Seizing the opportunity, Sara slid her chair back and stood.

"Thanks for lunch, *hermana*," she said, her voice dripping in sarcasm. Without looking back, she walked briskly to the other table, theatrically snapping her fingers twice. "Girls, we're out," she said as she passed, not stopping until she was outside and a hundred yards from the restaurant, the bright sunlight making her squint. As she began her walk north through the park, she pulled out her phone and texted Silas.

> Well, congratulations on being the only good thing in my day. More boring work crises. Gonna be another late night. I'm thinking of you too. Thanks for the smile.

"Nice storming out, love," Imani said, shockingly close to her. Sara jumped.

"I didn't even hear you approach," Sara said.

"It's my isotoners," Imani said. "Retro fashion and stalker appeal."

"What went wrong?" Teddie appeared beside Imani, Crina by her side.

"Oh, are you talking to me now?" Sara hated the childish notes in her voice, sensing Teddie's eye roll behind her glasses.

"Desdemona changed the rules," Sara went out. "She changed the motherfucking rules." Furious tears sprang into Sara's eyes. "They voided all Madrid credits. Marguerite knew and ignored it. She didn't tell me. Don't freeze. Keep walking. I'll fill you in completely at home. We should separate. Nakeah, would you be so kind as to come see me at two?"

Teddie nodded briefly before turning silently and striding off.

Crina jerked a thumb in Teddie's direction. "I'll walk with her and fill her in." And she was gone.

"Teddie is pissed," Imani said. Sara shrugged.

"No, I mean really pissed, you should have heard what she was saying to those poor Spanish bitches…" Imani trailed off into a dry chuckle.

"They deserved it," Sara said. "They need to hear it. This whole thing has been bullshit. I have credits, I could have given Marguerite a credit."

"But would you have?" Imani turned, her voice serious. "Not in hindsight. In the moment. Would you have been like, sure, girl, here you go?"

Sara shook her head. "Probably not," she admitted. "Probably not."

"Wait." Imani grabbed her arm. "Was Marguerite setting up a civil war?"

Sara shrugged again. "At this point anything is possible but I doubt it."

"That poor old bitch," Imani said. "But she should have known better than to call Desdemona's bluff."

"Is it breaking too many rules if we walk back together? I could use the company."

"No problem, guv'na," Imani said. "I hear you gots yo-self a man." Sara groaned.

"You'd think with eternity at our feet, we'd have better things to talk about than my personal life, or lack thereof?"

"Pish," Imani said, slugging her in the arm. "Is he cute?" Sara blushed.

"Oh shit," Imani spun to face her. "How bloody cute is he?"

"Okay fine." Sara almost didn't recognize her own voice. "He's really *bloody* cute, he's a gloomy bastard and we had a couple great dates, but you know, now there's this, so who knows when I can see him again?"

"But he's good-looking?"

"Don't be superficial."

"Why?" Imani linked arms with Sara and skipped her along the path. "Don't you ever get tired of every bloody thing being so serious? Bugger it, sister, let's be shallow."

And for the duration of their walk back uptown, that's what they did.

It wasn't until she got to her door and saw Heather's note pinned to it that her mood went back to the dark side.

My place, soon as you're back. Ta.

Chapter Twenty

The door to Heather's apartment wasn't locked. It rarely was, in a show of confidence in their building security. After what happened to Marguerite, Sara was a little surprised. She knocked lightly before letting herself in.

"In here, love," came Heather's trill from the bedroom. Sara gazed around the always-immaculately tidy living room, the neat turquoise couch, the geometric rug, the framed etchings on the wall that were at least a thousand years old. With very little decoration, the apartment screamed Heather, and Sara always felt an instant wash of calm whenever she stepped inside. She tiptoed to the bedroom door at the back of the living room and pressed it open slowly to reveal April Veronica propped up on pillows in Heather's bed, her eyes a painfully raw red from crying, an inconsolable sadness on her face. As Sara entered, April Veronica locked eyes with her, beseeching the newcomer to stop her pain. Sara's heart flipped in her chest like a dying frog. She bent and took one of April's hands in hers.

"My child," she began, before running out of words. The gravity, the hugeness, of the situation washed over her, like delayed shock, and she felt sick.

"It's okay, Sara," Heather said from her perch on an antique mustard chair on the other side of the bed. Sara glanced over, noticing redness around Heather's eyes too, which was jarring. Sara suddenly realized she'd never seen Heather cry.

"It's as okay as it can be, I guess."

"Did you meet with them?" April Veronica's voice was incongruously firm, considering she looked exactly like she should look, for someone who was pumped full of virus and smack just a day earlier.

Sara nodded.

"And are ye satisfied?" Heather said, her voice neutral. Sara angrily shook her head, evaluating how much to say in front of April Veronica.

"Dear girl, I'm not sure how much you're up for hearing. It's not good."

Consternation on her face, Heather came and sat on the bed.

"I'm always strong enough for the truth," April Veronica said, pushing herself upright." Let's have it."

Sara took a deep breath.

"Desdemona stripped all of the Madrid credits."

"She bloody can't," Heather said.

"Right. But she did. And she informed Marguerite, who, I guess, called her bluff."

"Well, that's something I'd never do," Heather said.

"So, they set her up and killed her?" the young woman asked, her voice breaking. "I thought you said that this was a peaceful society."

"This action of Desdemona's, it's unprecedented," Sara said. "It's an act of war, an opening shot."

Heather pulled her phone out of her pocket. "I'm texting Fran. We need our security as tight as a hummingbird's whatsit."

"What does this mean?" April Veronica said.

"I'm afraid I don't know exactly," Sara said. "Nothing like this has ever happened before." She squeezed April Veronica's hand. "I can only tell you this. You will be safe. I guess we will have to gather this evening to talk it over. Heather, while you're texting can you do a blast that nobody is to be off-campus for the foreseeable future? And please ask Fran to monitor immigration. We need to know that all four of those women leave this country."

Heather nodded and continued pecking at her phone. Sara thought about Silas. She wouldn't be able to see him for at least a week. She pushed the thought out of her mind and turned to April Veronica. "How are you feeling?"

"I feel like my heart is destroyed and alive for the first time, all at once," she replied, her voice wobbling. "When I woke up, in that weird room, I honestly felt like I must have had a nervous breakdown, and this was Bellevue. My veins are glass and my blood is surging smoothly along incredibly smooth tunnels. I can feel it. I can smell so many things at once. You smell like fried food and a forest. That kind of thing is weird, but then I think of her," she paused, and a fat tear dropped down her cheek, "then the pain washes over me. Was I the reason she was murdered?" She burst into tears.

Sara folded herself forward, wrapping her arms clumsily around the crying woman's shoulders. April Veronica threw her arms around Sara, unaware of her strength, nearly crushing Sara who realized just in time and steeled herself for the grip.

"No," Sara said firmly. "Marguerite was collateral damage to Desdemona's ulterior motives. But you, she loved. She nurtured. She believed in you, and I have inherited that belief."

"Really?" April Veronica pulled back, her eyes still streaming. "On top of the grief, I have this whole layer of me not being worth all of this trouble. Marguerite is dead and now a war has started and I'm just this person who walked into what? A disaster? And now everyone has to spend their time fixing me."

"I approved you, child. You were not an impulse buy." Sara gave a wan smile. "All of us see the potential in you, the light, the love. It sounds cheesy, but now, instead of one mentor, you'll have many. In the meantime, until we get your viral load under control, you probably can't be left alone too much. How do you feel about that?"

"Honestly, I don't want to be alone," April said plainly. "I... you weren't there... that feeling, when I found her, the horror, that passed quickly when I smelled the... you know... I was powerless, I found a puddle on the floor and I just wanted to smash my face through it, the power was horrible. I knew it was disgusting, I knew everything was falling apart, but all I wanted was that. And," she looked at both of them, slowly. "I just lay there, sucking at a puddle on the floor, then I blacked out. When I woke up, my mouth was on her neck. In my head, I wanted to throw up, to get the fuck out of there, but something else kept me there, wanting to be there, doing that. I never want to feel that again."

"Ye won't, pet." Heather took one of her hands. "Us oldies, me and her, we've been there. It wasn't always this easy, and sometimes, we had to, you know, help each other out to survive. We learned the hard way, sharing blood with a sister, you just increase your viral load. We didn't even know of such a thing, viral load, at the time. That's what happened to you yesterday. We can gradually get your viral load back down. But right now..." Heather got up and briskly went out to her kitchen, returning with a glass of water and four heems.

"Dinner time, lass," she said with a smile, handing April Veronica first the pills, then the water.

"What's the dosage?" Sara said, her voice light.

"Four an hour, for now, day and night," Heather said with a grimace. "Yukari says that there's no point making it any harder than it has to be. After this first week of maintenance, we can start to decrease, in line with lassie here's comfort levels."

"You're going to be exhausted," Sara told the girl. "But it's just for a week."

"It's okay," April Veronica said, closing her eyes. "It feels like I've had surgery or something. Naps are good. I feel like a burden. You guys don't even know me, and now it's like someone's dumped an orphan on your doorstep. For the second time in my life."

"I see you as a gift," Sara said, leaning forward. "And for a Lock, all of life is caretaking. It's not a burden, it's life. You'll get to repay all of us, many times over. You'll learn that keeping score of debt is pointless. This will pass, April Veronica, and you'll be involved in a life beyond your wildest dreams."

April Veronica squeezed her hand and her eyelids fluttered as the heems hit her bloodstream.

"I'm so tired, suddenly. Don't be offended," she said.

"Not at all." Sara stood, smoothing the bed, and Heather took the now-empty glass from her hand. "We'll let you sleep."

"See you in an hour, love," Heather said, ushering Sara out of the bedroom ahead of her and pulling the door almost shut.

"Do you think she's going to make it?" Sara asked.

Heather bustled into the kitchen without turning back and Sara could tell that she was agitated with her.

"Heather, spill it."

Heather stepped into her small kitchen and began fussing about, setting a kettle to boil and pulling down cups and saucers. She turned to face Sara, her expression no less serious.

"I've been expecting something like this for a long time," she whispered. "I've tried to talk to you. You have let deep divisions come into this house, and you're always asking me or Teddie to smooth them over, instead of you putting in the time with Liz or Rosa or any of them. And now, Desdemona. We all underestimated her, but Sara, you've known her most of your life. You're my dearest friend and you're my Lock mother, but it just feels like you've taken your eyes off the prize. Please don't be mad at me. I'm speaking to you plainly, because I love you. And I want to help. What can I do?"

"I think I'm bored," Sara said simply.

"News at eleven," Heather said, seating herself at the other end of the couch. "We all know you're bored. You've been holding this fort down for too long. We all love you. There hasn't been any turnover for decades. Nobody wants to leave. And everybody wants to help. We just need a roadmap, and that's where the only person who can guide us is you."

"And, unfortunately for all of us, I don't know what I want. I don't know the next steps. I don't want to go Scholar. I don't want the isolation. I love being around you, and Teddie. Imani is hilarious, Yukari is spectacular. I don't want to leave here. I built this, this whole compound, the way we function, this has been my life's work."

"There's nothing to say you have to leave. Just because Crina took off doesn't mean that you'd have to. I'd love it if you stayed here."

Heather added tea bags to the cups, and poured boiling water over them. In silence, she jiggled the tea bags, then lifted them out with a spoon and set them in the sink. After adding a splash of milk to each, she passed one to Sara.

"Thanks, friend," Sara said at last, blowing on the hot tea. There was nothing left but to be honest. "The crazy thing is, in all of this, I just want to be with Silas."

"Sara." Heather shook her head. "Right now, it's sisters before misters."

"I don't even know if it's him, exactly," Sara ruminated aloud, nodding to acknowledge the truth of Heather's words. "I just don't want to think about the Lock at all. I know the timing is terrible, but it is what it is. I want to be someone falling in love with someone else. I want to just have a job and an apartment and to be able to go through one day without subterfuge. Doesn't it ever drive you crazy that all we do is lie to the outside world? We can only be free inside our prison? We may have built it but it's a prison."

"It's a refuge, my dear, and it has served us well," Heather said matter-of-factly. "And—"

She was interrupted by a light rapping at the door, which swung open to reveal Teddie, in a loose jumpsuit, her hair wrapped in a towel, with Crina behind her.

"Oh, sorry, we're interrupting," she said.

"Not at all," Heather said, not moving. "Come in."

Sara stood, cautiously approaching her best friend. "Can I ... hug you?"

"Honey," Teddie said. "I just swung by the cleanup crew. I need a hug bad."

Relieved, Sara threw herself against her friend, and to her horror, burst into tears.

"Easy, girl, easy," Teddie said into her ear. "Whoa... Come on. It's fine, we past the worst of it."

"Fuck." Sara pulled away, wiping her face angrily on her sleeve. "You all already think I'm falling apart and then this happens."

Teddie rested a palm against Sara's cheek. "Girl, none of us gonna be fine when I tell you what they found."

"Well then, fuck this tea, we need some bloody wine." Heather bustled into her kitchen, with Crina close behind her.

"Is the cleanup done?" Sara said, fighting every instinct to ask what they found.

Teddie nodded. "Yeah," she said, exhaustion in her voice. "The apartment is spotless. The... cleanup... is complete. I gave Fran and Rosa some joints. As soon as we are done meeting, they'll get as high as humanly possible."

"That was sweet of you," Sara said, returning to her seat on the couch, patting the cushion next to hers. "Come sit. We don't have to talk about whatever you found. Right now."

"Oh, no honey, we gotta talk." Teddie elegantly slipped down to sit on the couch while accepting a very full glass of pinot noir from Heather. "I'm sorry I was so extra yesterday, Mom," she said, raising her glass. Heather settled on the far end of the couch and they cheered. Crina, a troubled look on her face, remained standing.

"Look at Sara sitting at the other end of the sofa pretending she's not dying to know what your news is." Heather chuckled, not unkindly.

"I'm not gonna torture you," Teddie said, sipping her wine. "Can we speak freely?"

Heather nodded. "She's out," she said, tipping her wine glass in the direction of the bedroom behind them.

"Marguerite left notes in her lockbox," Teddie said, referencing the box each sister filled with a will and any last wishes, just in case of the unexpected. "There was one for me, and one for April Veronica."

"Where are they?" Sara asked, looking at Teddie's pockets.

"I have April Veronica's in my pocket. I read mine and burned it, as is the law."

"You what?" Sara sat bolt upright, glancing at Crina, who nodded a terse affirmation.

"That's what we always do when a dead sister leaves a note, Sara. We read it and we burn it. So that's what I did."

Glancing around the ceiling, Sara tried to keep her emotions in check. The rule that Teddie was referencing usually referred to the notes left by a sister before she chose surrender, notes which were always burned alongside the body. She tried and failed to think of a way to say something that wouldn't further alienate Teddie.

Crina broke the silence.

"What's done is done," she said softly. "Just tell them what it said, Theodora."

"It was just bitter bile. You guys, it was horrible. She said that she hated it here, she hated the whole Lock, she told me to get the hell out while I still could."

Heather whistled. "What a piece of work."

Sara was still struggling. "Why do you think she left a note for you? You and she weren't close. And this wasn't a surrender note, this may have been evidence. You shouldn't have burned it."

"Listen, Mom, I watched a human body get fed into the furnace, then Rosa handed me the notes. I read mine, and I panicked. As soon as I was done, I tossed it into the furnace." Teddie sounded defensive, and Sara was leery of pressing her further. Technically, she had abided by Lock tradition.

"You said there was a letter to April Veronica?" Heather spoke quietly.

"Yeah." Teddie reached into her pocket and pulled out a lavender envelope.

"Oh, you didn't burn that one," Sara said, her voice sharper than she intended.

"It isn't addressed to me," Teddie said simply, handing it to Heather.

"Shall we wake her?" Heather asked.

"I think we have to," Sara said. She, Crina, and Teddie sat in silence, avoiding eye contact while Heather went into the bedroom to fetch April Veronica. They heard muffled conversation and then the young woman appeared in the doorway, rubbing her eyes like a child.

"What?" she asked groggily. "Oh, hey Crina, hey Teddie. What's happened now?"

Teddie stood up. "Marguerite left you a note."

"Oh no," April Veronica said, looking fearful. "What does it say?"

Teddie handed the small pale purple envelope to April Veronica, who turned it up to her face, looking at her name, written in Marguerite's hand.

"You guys, I don't think I can."

"If you could, lass, it might prove helpful."

April Veronica closed her eyes tightly as if steeling herself for a blow. When she opened them again, her eyes were clear.

"Sorry. That was overly dramatic. Okay, here goes." She tore the envelope along its top seam, withdrawing a single sheet of paper in matching lavender. She began to read aloud, her voice thickening.

"Dearest April Veronica,

If you are reading this, then Desdemona has lived up to the promise of her threats. And I am sorry beyond measure that once again, you no doubt feel abandoned.

May this little note serve as both benediction and farewell.

I am so invested in you. I have never met anyone so perfectly suited for Lock life. You will find the years rewarding. Your endless supply of love and curiosity will enrich any Lock that you spend time with.

By the time Desdemona made her threat, I was too far along in your future to step back. I know the risks, but I have no alternative. You are

*too important to me for me to let anything or anyone get in the way of
what I want for you."*

April Veronica choked back a sob.

*"I am not afraid of death. Honestly, I have been considering my
demise ever since I arrived in the Americas.*

*You could not have saved me. As it was, you kept me going for longer
than I expected, and you showed me that there is always something better
on the horizon.*

*Beware of Desdemona. Her recent actions have convinced me my fate
was sealed before I even came to this country.*

*I know you will be cared for. All I ask is that you love without aban-
don, never stop investigating, and may your heart and its kindness bless
this earth for many years to come.*

In love, death and life,

Marguerite"

Sara wrapped her arms around April Veronica, expecting tears that
didn't come.

"You okay?"

April Veronica nodded, slowly extricating herself from the hug.
"Yep, that actually helped," she said, looking around the room. "It's a
hell of a responsibility to dump on me, but I've already figured out that
I am just going to have to coast along for a while, not understanding
motivations fully."

"That's a good way to look at it, love," Crina said.

"You have to burn it now," Teddie said, reaching for the note. April
Veronica snatched it away and took two steps back.

"Not this time, Teddie," Sara said, rising from the couch. "There is
nothing forbidden in that note, and I think that Marguerite was very
careful to make it so."

"I'd like to keep it," April Veronica said.

Teddie glared at Sara, then looked to Crina for support.

"I don't see the harm in it," Crina said.

"Fine," Teddie said, pacing back and forth before settling on the opposite end of the couch to Sara. "But it's borderline at best. Sara, do you still need to see me at two?"

Sara shook her head.

"I just wanted to apologize for putting you through all this and to ask if there's anything I can do for you. I don't want us to fight."

"We ain't fighting," Teddie said. "You're not the only one who needs a day off. But hey, after talking to those poor Madrid bitches today, I really can't complain."

"How were they?" April Veronica asked. "Did you know any of them before?"

"Nope, they were all strangers to me," Teddie said, swigging her wine. "I went in there planning to sow some seeds of rebellion against Desdemona, but honey, she's got them trained like some cult leader or shit. I mean, I called her Desdemona and they flinched, and literally one of them crossed herself. They call her Holy Mother, and the way they talk about her, it's like she's a god to them. She's got some definite cult leader vibes happening. And she keeps them in line. Real tight. They all work, they all provide, and none of them have lives outside of the Lock. They literally think we are the worst thing in the world. It was hard to listen to."

Heather interrupted her by filling all their glasses almost to the rims before she sat back down. "Sorry to wake you, April. You can sit with us if you like, or you can go back and lie down again. But if you stay, you can't drink. Not yet."

"Yeah, thanks, I'll just—" April Veronica trailed off. She looked exhausted. She thumbed over her shoulder at the doorway, then turned and went in, closing the door behind her.

"We've all had a beast of a day," Heather said, before leaning in conspiratorially. "But wait, Crina, how did your grand entrance go over?"

The elder scuffed her foot on the rug, a surprisingly girlish move that made Heather smile.

"I feel bad laughing about it now," Crina said. "But yes, the look on Desdemona's face when she saw me sitting with her girls was worth everything. But," she cast a loving eye at Sara, "it was nothing compared to the look on her face when this one said Desdemona was acting like a man!"

Heather gasped aloud.

"What?" Sara said, her face serious. "It's true. This is the same kind of unreasonable power grab that we attribute to men."

"It's not without precedent," Crina said. "But now I do need to say my goodbyes. I want to get home and start talking. Some of the truly elder Scholars have done a lot of work on the role of gender in areas like this."

"I thought that was all hypothetical," Teddie said.

"Until now, yes," Crina said. "But the qualities and strengths we assign to females seem to be absent in Desdemona. She's not reasonable, and she's engaging in violence as part of her crusade. I sat at the table with those girls for like two minutes, and the way they talked about her has really got me freaked out. They exist to serve her. And somehow she's convincing other Locks to join her in whatever madness she's devising."

"She has five Locks on her side," Sara said. "This is all new ground. I need to get back to my flat and call the Lock mothers I can still trust before it gets too late."

"I want to help," Crina said. "I've got a car coming, but please, let me spend the long drive home figuring out where things are with the other five Locks before you call the other Mothers. We can't afford to alert any Locks that might be close to siding with her. We have to keep our cards very close to our chest."

"Smart," Sara said. "Will you call me tonight?"

Crina nodded, then moved around the room, kissing each woman on the forehead. "Farewell for now, my loves," she said, pausing at the door. "There are dark times ahead. Increased security and vigilance all around, please."

And she was gone.

After the door clicked shut behind Crina, the three women sat in silence.

"She really tore into Desdemona," Sara said eventually. "I don't think Crina ever expected this from her."

"Desdemona has broken so many rules," Teddie said.

"Desdemona has always found ways to bend the rules to her wishes," Sara said. "When she and I were young, in Barcelona, she showed signs of ambition, a need for power. I think that today, Crina realized that something should have been done a long time ago. I think she feels responsible."

"Speaking of responsible..." Teddie's voice was calm. "Can I offer to be April Veronica's new sponsor sister?"

"How lovely," Heather said, raising her glass.

"Are you sure, Ted?" Sara asked, swallowing a lump in her throat. "You're very busy at work, and April Veronica's detox is going to keep you nurses extra busy."

"I know, but I don't have any credits, and I would have made this girl. I like her. I like women that come from broken beginnings. I can relate."

Sara nodded gently, reached out and took Teddie's hand.

"Of course. She's all yours."

Chapter Twenty-One

Three days later, and the demands on the nursing staff and April Veronica's caretaking were fraying everyone's nerves. Alone in her apartment after a day of zoom sessions with her remaining patients, Sara took stock of the week so far. Desdemona and her sistren had flown out of La Guardia late on Monday on a flight bound for Edinburgh, which threw Heather into a funk. Rosa and, surprisingly, Fran had stepped up to assist Yukari in watching over April Veronica, but both of them also had work commitments, so Sara volunteered to step in and help whenever.

Which of course had just bitten her in the ass.

No sooner had she made plans with Silas for a phone date that evening that Teddie called to say that Yukari had just fainted and could she bring April Veronica to her apartment immediately while Yukari got some long-overdue sleep?

Angrily, Sara picked her phone up from where she'd thrown it, between the cushions of her couch. She'd had to say yes, of course. It wasn't Teddie's fault, nobody could have predicted that April Veronica's blood type – O negative – would lead to such problems, but then again, they'd never had to replace someone's blood before. Inhaling deeply, she called Silas. He answered on the first ring.

"Lily, hey, how are you?" Silas sounded so happy, Sara's heart ached.

"Hey Silas, I'm annoyed, I guess, is the best answer that I can give you."

"Uh oh," he said, still playful.

"Yeah, look, I am calling to cancel. Really, I shouldn't have even agreed to talk to you tonight, I'm sorry. I really am.""Oh…"

"Yeah, work is a shit show, obviously, I can't say what's up, but I just got offered as tribute. Someone threw my name into the ring for something, and I just can't dodge it. Believe me, I tried."

"I believe you," Silas said. "It's fine, you're just having a rough week."

"Thanks for understanding," Sara said, feeling a pang of something worse than guilt at the concern in his voice. "Yes, I am. We suddenly … lost a team member here and all of us are picking up her patients, and I've inherited some difficult transitions."

"I understand," he said. "Do you think your weekend will be any better?"

Sara pondered the question for a little too long, and Silas jumped back in.

"I'm sorry, forget I said that, this is definitely way too early for me to be applying pressure. Sorry, sorry."

"Silas, don't. I was just mentally going over my schedule, but it's the unknown stuff that makes me wary. What about if we agree to play it by ear, with me promising that I want to see you and that as soon as this passes, I'll see you?"

"That will do," he said, his voice neutral. She'd heard it before, in session. He didn't like the answer.

"Silas, I—"

"Yes?"

"Nothing. I feel like a flake, and that's not what I want to be, not now, not with you."

"Lily, you have a job, and right now, it's demanding. I understand, and I know you can pick up on my voice, so yeah, I'm disappointed, but I'll get over it. I'll go see a movie."

"Okay, enjoy the movie. Thanks for understanding."

"Bye, Lily."

Holding her phone so that the glass reflected the late afternoon gray of a cloudy spring day, she tilted it back and forth, as if it could cure her mood, the sour feeling of resentfulness that was clouding her heart.

Flicking her phone awake, she texted Yukari..

> How's the patient? Is it time for me to come get her?

> Yes please now is great.

Sara grabbed a long sweater from her closet, its loose gray knit reminding her of spiderwebs. She slipped on a pair of flat mules, grabbed her keys, and moved to the door. She paused for a second, then went back to the kitchen, retrieving a small carrot from a bag in her fridge for Sir Hopsalot, Yukari's house rabbit.

Yukari's door, two floors below hers, was locked, of course, and Sara hoped that April Veronica would never know just how tightly she was imprisoned in the building during her transition. She heard Yukari's light footsteps, and then the grinding of two deadbolts and one twist lock before the door opened.

"That was quick," Yukari said with a wan smile. She looked absolutely exhausted. Sara stepped inside and hugged her, scouring the floor for the bunny, spying him hiding between furniture legs below Yukari's record player.

"Yukari, are you okay?"

Yukari turned away from Sara, waving a hand dismissively. "You know what it's like. I had some really interesting breakthroughs in studying her blood, and before you know it, in between her transfusions and her medicine schedule, I forgot to eat, and worse, I forgot my heems."

"Must have been some interesting breakthroughs. But you won't be much help if you keep on fainting."

"Yes, boss," Yukari said with another half-smile. "As soon as you leave, I'm gonna go to sleep."

Nodding, Sara spotted Sir Hopsalot's twitching nose, now under the coffee table.

"Who's my favorite wabbit?" Sara knelt and revealed a carrot. The small gray rabbit, with gorgeous black around both eyes and on his ear tips, sniffed the air, his ears tilting forward with excitement. He hopped across the rug and took the carrot from Sara, then hopped back to his spot.

"He's hiding a lot today."

Sara laughed. "Me too, Yukari. Me too. How's the patient?"

"Better than me, it seems." Yukari said, raising her phone and sending a text. Sara's phone dinged immediately, and she looked at the screen.

> I stopped the opiates today. Watch closely tonight.

"Is she awake?" Sara asked, nodding to say that she had read the text.

"I sure am," came a voice from the bedroom at the end of a sort hall. "Come in."

"Go," Yukari said, sitting at her iMac by the window. "I have to log the last round of bloodwork and then I can sleep."

Sara blew her a kiss and walked down the hallway. Entering the room, Sara halted, surprised. The change in April Veronica in twenty-four hours was astonishing. Gone were the red eyes and hollow cheeks. Instead, she looked vibrantly happy and healthy.

"Wow," Sara said, honestly. "You look great."

"Yeah, I think this thing is working. Every time Yukari gives me cleaner blood, I feel a little bit less feral."

"Good," Sara said. "Do you feel like you could walk up to my flat? We can hang out, I'll order delivery, and we can catch up."

"Are you tired?"

Sara's brow furrowed. "No. Why?"

"It's gonna be a late night. I've been making mental lists of the things I don't know."

Sara reached across and squeezed her hand. "I'll do my best, kid. But nobody has all the answers."

The gray day turned into a gray night, and the half-eaten containers of pad Thai and drunken noodles and green chicken curry were sprawled across the coffee table. April Veronica, in jeans and a too-big t-shirt with a kitten on it, had eaten voraciously.

The small talk over dinner was easy and effortless, with Sara asking most of the questions, and she found herself understanding Marguerite's desire to bring April Veronica into the fold. She was delightfully curious, judiciously fair, and gifted with the kind of sense of humor you didn't find too often in America – self-deprecating, aware, and salty.

"Let me turn on some lights," Sara said now, gazing around the darkening room.

"No," April Veronica said, waving a hand. "Let's sit here, in the dark. It never gets truly dark in New York. I love nights like this, everything is silver, like a gelatin print. I only turn lights on when I'm reading, and even then, usually a headlamp will suffice."

"I think you're going to like this life," Sara said, relaxing cross-legged at the opposite end of the couch.

"Why's that?"

"If moonlight can make you happy, you're already fulfilling the most difficult facet of our... happiness. Other things are important for our survival but finding the beauty in every single day is the most essential."

"So what was the beauty in your day?"

Sara smiled. "I think it was maybe feeding a carrot to Sir Hopsalot."

"Oh my god, he's so cute, I never even considered that we can have pets."

"We can have pretty much anything we want, except children."

"Seriously, I got lost in thought, thinking what pet I would like."

"I have only had a few," Sara volunteered. "When Crina made me, pets weren't really a thing. We had farm animals, we kept guard dogs, and I loved them, but they were a service. When Teddie was younger, we had a parrot, it delighted her. Its name was Perry. I think that was technically the first being that I called a pet."

"Do you consider Teddie to be your daughter?"

"Good question. I can lose myself for hours pondering that one. She isn't my daughter. She had a mother, her mother sought refuge with us, she was very ill. There was no other family, so when her mother passed, we agreed to raise her here. Crina and I. But something about her eyes caught me."

"What was it?"

"Her heart. I see it every day. There's such depth there. It's beautiful. Anyway, to answer your question, once she reached adulthood, I was faced with the choice, to bring her with me forever, or not. And I chose that path for her, but not as a parent. You'll come to understand. There are many roles we can play other than parent, sibling, lover. There just aren't adequate words for what we become. Teddie is everything to me. And yet she is separate to me, and not of me, so 'daughter' doesn't really cut it, but it works for lack of a better word."

"Marguerite warned me you were evasive."

"That wasn't evasive," Sara said, smoothing her voice to hide annoyance. "Simple answers get longer as you age. I can't do sound bytes. I just can't. The longer you live, the more your brain will churn ahead of a sentence, and the longer that sentence will be."

April Veronica laughed. "I'm okay with that. I liked your answer. I think I just need to learn to be more patient when I listen to you. You speak in thought processes, which is interesting. Maybe Marguerite found it challenging since English wasn't her first language."

"It also wasn't mine, child."

"Touché."

"Eh, it's not a duel," Sara said, picking up her wine glass from the floor.

"You seem tired," April said. "Is that due to... me?"

Sara eyed the girl across the darkness of the couch, her elfin nose, her bow lips pursed expectantly, the silver rectangles of windows reflecting in her bright eyes.

"Only partially, to be honest," Sara said. "You're being asked to absorb fifty years of learning in two weeks. That's where we are at with you. And I plan to be completely honest and transparent with you, so I just want to give you a caveat. I'm not going anywhere, I'll always be available for you, so maybe just ask questions tonight that you can handle the answers to."

April Veronica nodded slowly. "You still didn't say why you're tired."

Sara gave the girl a rueful grin. "I wasn't trying to be evasive. You asked if my tiredness was due to you and I said partially. That's a full answer. But if you want to know why else, then sure. I started dating someone. Like literally a few weeks back, and I haven't dated in, well, since before you were born, and this guy looks like someone I could love. And then this awfulness with Marguerite happened, and I haven't been able to see him. I was supposed to talk to him tonight, but I was right to cancel. I'm in not currently fit for human consumption."

"Is that a vampire in-joke?"

"Yuck, that word," Sara said. "What I mean is I was wrong to put myself first during a period of indoctrination. I let myself get caught up in something romantic, and I lost my head a little."

"But that's always love, right?"

Sara nodded. "And that's where I struggle. I know Marguerite explained it to you, the whole relationships thing."

"Yeah, she told me about the four-year time limit, and I'll have no problem. I've never had a lover want to stay longer than six months, male or female." April Veronica laughed with only a tinge of bitterness.

"Yes, but eventually you will. And that's where it gets unpleasant. The first time you do it will probably be the most painful, but after that, it's just another routine to fall into. Most relationships lose their luster after four years as it is, so, you're really only just accelerating what's coming down the pipe anyway."

"I think you're absolutely right, but it's crazy to hear it expressed so proactively. It's actually exciting."

Sara chuckled. "But once again, I warn you, as you live and live and live, three years of something becomes a moment, and eventually that moment is not worth the pain and hassle of the breakup year. Also, your position now will not be your position in twenty years, or fifty years, or a hundred years from now."

"That's why you guys don't indulge in nostalgia?"

Sara nodded. "Nostalgia is toxic, in general. Subscribing to a fondness for that which is gone is particularly toxic when you're faced with the chore of finding hope in a longer future. It's so tempting to find solace in a memory, but that thing is as dead as a dodo, it's gone. You're clinging to an iceberg and asking it to heat you."

"Wow," April Veronica whispered. "Harsh."

"Accurate. You wouldn't believe the things that we've done, just to pass the time. Have you ever made lace?"

April Veronica screwed up her face so comically that Sara laughed.

"So that's a no. I probably spent three or four decades making lace. It's incredibly soothing."

"I've never even thought about lace being handmade," April Veronica said.

"It's crazy." Sara sat on her haunches. "You have a pillow, like a velvet pillow, and then you have pins, and then you have bobbins and thread and you just work methodically."

"Well, that was quite the word salad. Don't worry, I'll look it up on YouTube later. You've got me curious."

Sara set her wine on the coffee table and sprang upright, dashing into her bedroom, where she pulled a heavy, small safe from the back of her closet. Returning to the living room, she set the safe on the couch between them.

"I keep my finest bobbins in here," she said, turning the knob back and forth. "I want to show you."

Opening the safe, Sara gazed at the contents. It had been decades since she opened this safe, one of several stashed in her room. She had many more boxes of things stored in various apartments around the compound, but the things she treasured most she kept close by. Staring at the contents of the safe, she was overwhelmed by ancient, evocative scents and had to struggle to keep a reverie at bay.

"Those fabrics, they're so beautiful," April Veronica said, looking at the various velvets and tapestries wrapped around each of the safe's contents. After thinking for a moment, Sara pushed to the safe's second layer, pulling out a small parcel wrapped in embroidered russet velvet, unthreading the gold twine that held it closed and pulling the fabric open. Even in the dim light, the crystals threaded at the bottom of each wooden bobbin sparkled.

"These are the weights that you use to pull the thread evenly," Sara said, running a finger over them.

"May I hold them?"

With a nod, Sara passed the bundle to April Veronica, who inhaled their scent deeply before looking up.

"Would you teach me to make lace? I'll warn you, I was never able to master knitting."

Smiling, Sara shook her head.

"I would have to first teach myself, all over again," she said. "Our minds, unfortunately, are the same as any other humans. We forget. When our brain is full, we forget."

"I didn't expect that."

"Well, you can't have everything," Sara said with a laugh, her fingers tracing the various packages in the safe. "The best way of putting it is, after a period of time, you remember your past like a book you read a long time ago. The strokes get broader and broader until there's no visual to go along with the facts. I know my first century, I know the cold of the winters, the harshness of traveling, various things that happened, but it almost feels like someone else's life."

"I find that oddly reassuring," April Veronica said, handing the bobbins back to Sara, who folded them back up, neatly tied the knotted twine and set them back atop the contents of the safe.

"Hang on." Sara perked up, gently pushing things aside until she reached the bottom of the safe, revealing a small black box. "Oh yes. I thought these were in here."

In silence, Sara took the black box and set it beside her on the couch. Then she closed the safe and moved it to the floor, returning her attention to the box.

"I'm going to show you something. Don't tell anyone that I have this. It's not supposed to be here."

She opened the onyx box slowly, revealing first the blood-red velvet lining, and then, nestled within it, a silver crescent shape.

"I don't know what that is," April Veronica said.

Setting the box on the couch, Sara gingerly lifted the item out of its velvet nest, turning it over and setting it flat on her palm, a set of silver upper dentures with all the front teeth ending in sharp points.

"It looks like a grill," April Veronica said, then her eyes widened as the realization dawned on her. "Oh, shit, is this..."

"This, my dear, is Lama Lupului, the wolf blade. A horrifying, cruel weapon that the men of our kind used to kill." She extended her palm to April Veronica. "Very gently, touch the tip of a fang."

Obeying, April Veronica let out a small gasp as, before she realized she'd made contact with the metal, a drop of blood appeared.

"It pierced me before I even felt it," she marveled, pulling her hand back. She almost put her finger to her mouth, then thought better of it and just pressed it against her pants.

"The menfolk... they were despicable, they would wear these over their teeth and... you know what? Some memories don't fade. Forget what I said earlier. They... April, they would tie a woman up and feast. Biting ankles, wrists—"

"And necks. Oh hell, this is too much."

"I'm sorry, I probably shouldn't have shown you that." Sara turned her palm, dropping the metal fangs sharp side down into the velvet and closing the box.

"No, no, don't be sorry, it's more like, when something is that obvious, I feel like I should have seen it coming. Does everything have a basis in reality?"

"Most folklore does," Sara said, lifting the lid of the safe and putting the onyx box away. "Crina did not want me to keep them. Most of the sets were melted down. But I didn't want to forget. Whenever I tire of the rules that keep us safe, I like to get those things out. I hold them in my hands and try to imagine the kind of mind that came up with them, the type of person who wore them, and how easily it was for them to convince a room full of men like us that it was okay to... kill a woman, so brutally."

When Sara looked back from the safe, April Veronica's eyes were wide.

"Would it be all right if I had a small glass of wine?"

Sara smiled sympathetically. "I'd have to text Yukari."

"Could you, please?"

Sara picked up her phone to message Yukari, ignoring the ticker tape of notifications, from all the Lock members, and, she noticed heavily, not from Silas. She fired off a quick text to Yukari and set her phone down on the couch.

"You really don't have a poker face," April Veronica said. "What was the bad text?"

Sara glanced at the highly observant girl in her care. "Close, but not quite. That guy didn't text me."

"Oh, you got it bad."

"Maybe. At least, he's under my skin and I don't know if I like that or not."

"I think you like it," the young girl said as a text came in to Sara's phone, its weak glow on the screen throwing their faces into relief. Sara glanced down and read it.

"You're allowed to have no more than eight ounces," she said. "That's what I get for asking a biophysicist if a sick child can drink wine."

April Veronica laughed, a hearty, warm sound that made Sara relax a little as she stood and walked the few steps to the kitchen.

"I feel like I should serve you in a mixing cup. Would you like two servings of four ounces, or one big fuckoff eight ounce overserve?"

"Let's save you a trip to the kitchen," April said. "I'll take one heavy pour."

Sara pulled a mason jar down from the shelf beside the fridge and filled it with wine to just below the eight-ounce marker. She handed the glass to April Veronica, then retrieved hers and filled it similarly.

As she resumed her cross-legged position on the couch, her charge leveled another question.

"You've been Lock leader for over a century. Why haven't you gone scholar, or taken a break?"

"Girl, can an old woman enjoy a glass of wine without an interrogation?"

"Oh, I'm sorry, of course,"

"Nah, just fucking with you." Sara smiled. "Simple answer is, nobody wants the job. Plus, it has its benefits. I have more freedom with my days. I can study, I can work in any field I want to. I don't mind the peacekeeping. I always just assumed that one day, someone would say that they want this job, but so far, no go."

"I think I would like the job," April Veronica said. "Actually, now that I hear you describe it, I think I would really like to either work alongside you on it, or if you have like an apprenticeship going…" Sara went to speak, and April Veronica raised her hand.

"Please don't tell me I'm too young."

"I wasn't going to say that, at all. I actually think that it might be a good idea. I know that Fran wants some help on the cybersecurity front, and that's such an emerging role that I honestly don't know the shape of it yet."

"That's very appealing to me also."

"Well, let's try it. I do think we should wait at least a few seasons, just so you can find your feet before I haul you in to make peace between Heather and Rosa."

"Really? Wait, of all the women, they're the last two I would have picked as problems."

"They just kind of cover the same territory. Heather is in charge of most of the administrative, but Rosa is our real estate manager, and our investments adviser. Sometimes their territories overlap and then sparks fly."

"I can handle them," April Veronica said, tipping the wine jar up to her lips, draining it. "Eight ounces isn't much, huh? Who do you think I should be friends with?"

"Imani. Start with Imani," Sara said. "You'll feel like old mates five minutes into it."

"Cool, yeah, she was funny on Saturday night. Cracking jokes. What's her job?"

"She's our resident philosopher," Sara said. "She's gotten PhDs from every university in a hundred-mile radius. She laughs and jokes, but of all of us, she has the blackest hole inside her. She wants answers, she needs to understand the riddle of life."

"But what if the riddle of life is just that, a riddle, with no solution? Like an Escher stairway?"

"You may be very right, and ultimately, I don't think Imani would mind too much. She enjoys the journey. Ask her an existential question at your own risk. She'll still be talking the next day. You'll be tired but fascinated."

"I have one last question."

"Okay. Shoot."

"Do you think Marguerite planned to go out like this, in a blaze of glory?"

Sara nodded.

"She was always so fascinated by her art, by the output of her subconscious. She also had a weird taste for anarchy. In hindsight, I think that she orchestrated a lot of chaos. But the main thing, the only thing to concern yourself with, is that she chose you with a pure heart, and as we talk, I only become more certain of your place in this Lock."

April Veronica leaned over and took Sara's hand.

"The wine has hit my head," the young girl said. "I just get so tired, so fast. Would it be okay if I just curled up here for a bit? Before my next transfusion?"

Sara tightened her grip on April Veronica's hand and pulled her toward her, pausing to knock one of the couch pillows into her lap.

"Be my guest, child," she said, watching peacefully as the newest member of her family lay down and closed her eyes. Almost immediately, her breathing took on the sound of the sea, ebbing and flowing. Sara ran her hand through the hair of the girl asleep on her lap, the virus raging inside her veins, yet somehow so peaceful, so heartbreaking in her trust. Smiling, Sara turned her gaze to the silver sky, imagining the stars that she knew were there.

A sharp knocking on her door jarred her out of sleep, just as April Veronica groggily pushed herself up out of Sara's lap.

"Sara, are you in there?" Yukari yelled.

Sara heard Teddie's voice. "Where the fuck is my key?"

Then she heard lock tumblers grinding against each other and the door flew open, flooding the room in the queasy yellow light of the bulb in the hallway, and there were two more women in her apartment.

"I told you they fell asleep," Yukari said.

"We've been texting you for an hour," Teddie said accusingly to Sara before turning to April Veronica. "How do you feel, kid?"

April shrugged. "I'm good, I'm great, I mean, we had a nice night, talking."

"You gave her wine?" Teddie said flatly, facing Sara.

"Yukari said it was okay," Sara said, still groggy.

"I'm sure it's fine," Yukari said. "How do you feel?"

"Rested," April Veronica said. "I slept really soundly, not like before, there were no nightmares this time."

"That's actually a great sign," Yukari said. "But it's time for you to come downstairs for your next transfusion."

"I know," April Veronica said. "I can feel it in my bones when the virus starts to get into the new blood. It feels like when you're trying to quit smoking, like a hook in your throat."

Teddie and Yukari exchanged knowing glances.

"Right then." Teddie extended a hand to April. "Come on. Let's get you cleaned out so you can sleep again."

Last to leave, Teddie turned and gave Sara a wan smile.

"Thanks for watching her. Sounds like you gave her something she needed."

"I hope so," Sara said, and then they were gone.

Blinking away the cobwebs, she decided to try to move to the bed without thinking, so that she could just collapse fully clothed. She made it halfway before her mind sounded an alarm.

SILAS.

She'd promised to call him before bed. Darting back to the couch, she pulled her phone out from where it had wedged itself between cushions, and her heart sank. Two simple texts.

> Lily? You OK?

And then, just eleven minutes earlier, at 3:08am:

> Heading to bed. Text me you're okay, if you feel like it.

Her mind ran through a million excuses before deciding on the truth

> Silas. So sorry, I sat on my couch when I got home, and passed out. I just woke up. Sorry to worry you. I'll call you tomorrow.

She hit send, fell back onto her bed, and let consciousness leave her.

Chapter Twenty-Two

After dropping April Veronica back to Yukari's apartment for her transfusion, about halfway along the secret hallway that led back to her building, a wave of exhaustion washed over Sara.

What day was it?

Back in her apartment, she ran a bath, poured a small glass of rose, lit some candles, put Albert Ayler's New Grass on the turntable, shucked off her clothes, debated a bath bomb ("no" won, she was too tired to scrub a gaudy ring off the tub), and eventually lowered herself into the clear, warm water. Breathing deeply, she tried to relax.

Her babysitting gig with April Veronica had turned into a full-time job, as the nurses all worked sixteen-hour shifts to get the blood necessary to detox her. Heather, Rosa and Fran were battened down in Rosa's office, focused on updating the building's security. Yukari roped in Imani to help her log the research she was doing on April Veronica's blood. April Veronica now slept most nights on Sara's couch, or sometimes in her bed, talking long into the night, days passing in a blur. Sara was fascinated by the speed of the young girl's mind, matching the speed of the times effortlessly.

Swirling the bath water around herself, Sara thought about how much faster things could possibly get. As soon as she became accustomed to the speed of a generation, the next one was invariably faster.

She and Teddie used to joke about this, when radio came along, then television, then cable, but since the internet crashed into their lives in the nineties, the informational speed of life had gone into one long, relentless warp.

Which brought her to the warp of her own life. Two weeks ago, she was floating on a cloud after her date at the ice rink. She was about to oversee the conversion of a wonderful woman. Marguerite was alive. Desdemona was just a distant annoyance.

The light coming from the living room windows was curious, a deepening gray with a nauseating yellow tinge that usually meant a thunderstorm. She sighed and thought about Silas, like she had numerous times in recent days, usually at times when sending a text would be inappropriate. The messages between them had become brief. She sensed his disappointment but lacked the availability that would permit them to make plans. She ramped up the texting, hoping to fill the void, but he was down to one-word answers. April Veronica told her that he probably thought Sara was acting like a reverse fuck-boy.

She wondered if she'd blown it, and then immediately felt a twinge of guilt. Ugh. The bath was ruined. She wanted to dry off and text him, see if he wanted to ride out the storm at her Murray Hill apartment.

Just let him go.

That would be the fair, responsible thing to do. April Veronica was responding heroically well to her treatment, progressing much faster than Yukari predicted, but nothing was guaranteed. She had no business pretending that she was available to Silas. She just didn't know how to end it. Mainly because she did not want to.

Standing, she let the water run down her body, slowly, before bending and pulling the plug. She pressed a towel against the wet ends of her black hair, then slowly rubbed its threadbare scratchiness against her skin, flashing back to the new towels in the new apartment she didn't need any more. She felt relaxed and anxious at the same time, the tell-tale signs of tiredness. Stepping out of the tub, she tapped the surface of her phone, shocked to see that it was after four. She wasn't shocked to see that there were no texts from Silas. He'd gone quiet some time on Thursday.

Grimacing as she considered her options, she made her way to her bedroom, deciding en route that she needed a power nap, and after that she would call Silas and let him go. Flinging her wardrobe open, she pushed to the back row, skipping past her white fur coat to find a ridiculous adult romper, all electric blue fake fur, with footsies and a back flap. She hauled it onto her still damp body, and laid down on her bed, sleep taking her before she felt it close her eyes.

A crash of thunder startled her awake, sometime later. Sara sat up, confused at the color of her walls, before remembering the storm. The air was bristling with electricity. The sky was yellow and everything in her apartment looked like she was peering through a scrim that she couldn't blink away. Well, if it's still light, I didn't sleep too long, she thought as she stretched and reached for her phone on her nightstand. As she blinked her eyes to focus, she saw that Silas had texted her. As she read the text, her stomach dropped.

Lily. I'm writing to apologize. I shouldn't have ever pushed you to break the rules and go on a date with me. I realize now just how wrong this was. And I realize just how wrong I am for dating, at all, or really for anything much. No matter what happens to me, none of it is your fault. If anything, you showed me how things can be, even for people like me, and it was very nice indeed. Take care, Lily. Keep fighting the good fight.

Adrenalin leapt into Sara's body, so violently that her shoulders bent back. No. No. She needed to get to Silas. She pulled the text sideways to see the time sent, just a few minutes earlier. Her fingers shaking, she punched out an urgent text

> Silas, NO! I'm coming to see you. Wait. Let me talk to you. I'm at work at Columbia so I should be there in twenty? Thirty?

She pulled the onesie off so hard she severed one sleeve completely as she danced from foot to foot. Naked, she texted Heather and Teddie that an emergency had come up and she needed to run out. As she dressed, she did the rapid New Yorker transit math. Cab versus subway? She flicked back in his texts and saw his address, on Washington in the West Village. Too long a walk from either the 14th St or Houston stops. She opted for a cab, hauled on jeans, some hikers, a shirt and the stupid blue puffer she wore to work. Glancing at the window, still seeing no rain, she shoved a knit cap into her pocket, keys and phone into the other pocket and dashed out.

From the taxi, hurtling south on the West Side Highway, the Hudson looked like a choppy river of golden gray. She fired off constant messages to Silas, and texted briefly with Heather and Teddie, who both said she could take her time. Heather even volunteered to take April Veronica for the night. By the time she looked up, the driver was making a left up into the tight grid of the West Village. Sara's eyes scanned the streets ahead like a jaguar, wondering if she'd be quicker on foot.

The traffic gods were smiling upon her, and after several sharp turns, the driver announced that they'd arrived. Sara hurled three twenties through the opening in the glass and bolted for the door to Silas's building. It swung open. Maybe the security system was down. The light was fading as she ran to the darkening stairwell, a low rumbling thunder filling the air. The narrow building had just one apartment per floor, and Silas was number four. Sara vaulted up the stairs, three at a time, a keening litany coming from her throat. "Silas please wait Silas be okay" over and over until she was at the top of the staircase, in front of a dull brown door marked with an oxidized brass 4. She rapped her knuckles on the door, waited literally half a second then twisted the door handle.

To her surprise, it opened, stopping her briefly for a second. A lot of her patients talked about leaving their apartment unlocked "when they did it" – fear of rotting undiscovered trumped fear of death.

Pushing the door open, she quickly took in the landscape: an austere living room with couches in the center and a kitchen at the far end, three large windows looking out at high rise apartment faces, glimpses of the river in between. It was almost dark, and the apartment was not illuminated. There were only two doors leading out of the space, both of them closed. With trepidation building in her heart, she moved to the one closest to her, forcing her eyes closed as she opened it. Pitch-dark and claustrophobic, she sensed immediately that it was a bathroom, hurriedly smoothing her palm up and down the tiled wall by the door until she hit a light switch. Blinding lamplight filled the room. The single tub was empty. Turning hastily, she stepped from the bathroom to the other door, her mind racing with alternatives. In many, Silas was dead on his bed; in others, he wasn't home.

Steeling herself, she took the door handle in her shaking right hand, pushing it down and letting the door sail inward into an even darker room. Stepping inside gingerly, her hand failed to find a light switch by the door jamb. She pulled her phone out of her coat pocket and flicked on the flashlight, training it on an empty bed, a gray matelassé cover and tasteful pillows showing no signs of a human. She slumped back against the wall. He wasn't there. As her mind raced a million miles a minute to recall any clues that Silas may have given her, the phone in her hand sent a blurry spotlight around the room. Her heart stopped as the flashlight's beam jerkily illuminated a man standing upright in the corner, almost hidden inside the heavy gray drapes that blocked out a window.

A small scream burst from her lips, before she realized it was Silas, standing perfectly still, his eyes open, trained on her like a hawk.

"Sara," he said, and her eyes widened.

He knew her real name.

She tried to steady her light on the tall man in the corner, his face expressionless. Internally, she fought to control her body, to not panic, to not flood her system with adrenalin.

"Silas, are you all right?" Her voice sounded thin, like someone else's voice, someone she used to know.

"I am," he said, his voice low and steady. "Sara, I have one question for you: Did you come here to save me... or to feast on me?"

Sara froze. Her mind imploded with options, possibilities, fights, escapes. She wished she'd brought Slicer, or at least taken better stock of any potential weapons Silas had on his kitchen counter.

Distracted by a loud ratcheting sound coming from the living room, Sara focused all her discipline to keep her gaze trained on Silas. He stood unmoving, his face serious, his eyes twinkling.

"I came to *save* you," she said eventually.

"Interesting, but not surprising," the man said. "And I'll help you out here. That sound you just heard was the security system activating. You're locked in."

"What do you want, Silas?"

He parted his hands in front of him.

"To talk. I've been waiting a long time."

Sara felt like she had forgotten all of the training that she'd received, from Crina and others, about escaping, about dealing with it when someone figured out their secret. She was only forty feet above the sidewalk. She could smash a window and jump. There was a grizzled old tree out front; it would break her fall.

"If you're thinking about a window, please don't," Silas said. "They're reinforced and shatterproof."

"So I've walked into a trap," Sara said, her voice cold.

"No, Sara. I've waited a long time. A very long time. To have this… honesty with you."

"What is your goal here?"

"I don't have a goal. I want to talk to you."

"Was this whole thing a setup?"

"The dating? No." He laughed. "I've wanted to ask you out for centuries."

Now Sara felt fear with an intensity she'd never known. The apartment walls were moving away from her and a black vortex of panic was opening at her feet.

"I'm like you, Sara. I'm exactly like you."

"If that's true, then you know that I literally have to kill you, right now."

"So after letting your addiction skid off the rails, you suddenly care about rules?"

Sara batted away angry tears, her fingers opening and closing on air, her breathing shallow and erratic.

"Silas…" she began.

"To address the knowledge imbalance," he said with a smirk, "my real name, the name of my birth, is Atanase."

"You're from the old country?"

He nodded.

"I do not plan to hurt you," Silas said quietly. "Permit me to strike a deal with you. Spend tonight with me. Talk to me. Listen to me. And I swear to you, if, by morning's light you still wish to stick to your rules, you can alert your Lock to my existence, or, if you're feeling brave, you can kill me yourself."

Silas moved slowly, pulling a string that hung down from the ceiling. A light clicked on overhead and Sara gasped. On the dresser to Silas's right was a Slicer, the miniature executioner's blade with finger holes glinting silver in the lamplight.

"I'm confused, Silas. Atanase."

"You can still call me Silas. I deadnamed Atanase a long time ago," the man said affably, his calmness rattling Sara to the core. "Do we have a deal? Because I took the liberty of ordering sushi and I have some very fine bottles of red that are breathing on the kitchen counter. I swear to you, on all that I am, I will never hurt you. I don't think that doing this the dramatic way will be fun for either of us. Please. Just give me until morning."

Cautiously, he stepped toward Sara, his open palms face up, a half-smile playing across his lips. "Deal?"

"Don't touch me," Sara snapped, edging backward around the door and out into the living room area.

"Sara, if I wanted to hurt you you'd be hurt already," he said, following her slowly. "I'm sorry it had to be this way, but after you ghosted me, my options were... limited."

"This is bullshit," Sara spat. "This is entrapment."

"This is me playing my hand, Sara." He stepped close to her, raised his hand and cupped her cheek. She moved to pull away, then locked her eyes on his, drowning in his brown-orange cat eyes. "I'm one of you. I'm older than you. I survived, on my own, because I subscribe to the Lock rules. All of them. I've fought to avoid the fate of the other cursed men, and it's been a long, constant battle, but it has humbled me."

"Whatever your name is, how the hell do you think this is going to end?"

"However we want it to, Sara." Silas flicked a switch and a light came on under the kitchen cabinets. "Full disclosure, I wasn't planning to approach you for another year or two. But, and I don't know why, your blood stench went through the roof a while back. I didn't know if you were killing or what. It was..." he paused, starting deep into her eyes. "You scared me."

Sara held her head high. "That, the thing that happened, it was an accident," she said. "It's none of your business. I'm dealing with it."

"Are you, though?" Silas kept his voice warm, kind. "The blood stench isn't as strong, but your levels are still dangerously high."

Sara felt another surge of panic begin in her stomach. How did this man know so much about her? Her selfish double life had put her entire Lock in jeopardy. She glanced at the bathroom. If she could just lock herself in there, she could text Heather and the entire Lock would vanish safely overnight.

"Sara." He stepped closer to her, and she stepped back. "You're stronger than I am. You can take me. But that's not what this is about. You were headed for scholarship or Surrender, and I think we both know which one was looking more likely. Now, please, take a seat, I'll pour the wine, and we can actually, finally, talk."

Chapter
Twenty-Three

Circling Silas like a lioness circling a wolf, Sara kept her distance, sizing him up. He moved with infuriating calm, even turning his back to her briefly while he poured two glasses of wine.

"Are we going to square off all night, or would you find a seat more comfortable?"

Silas gestured at the couch, a wide wave indicating 'sit anywhere,' then seated himself in a rocking chair, his eyes never leaving hers as she snatched the wine from his hand and sat directly across from him, in the center of the wide leather couch.

"Good. We're sitting, we're sitting. I realize this is a lot. Do you need me to be quiet for a period, so that you can let your adrenalin settle?"

Sara nodded, sipping at her wine, inhaling to slow her pulse, distracted by the very force of her blood in her veins. Whatever the virus did to their bloodstream, it was most apparent in fight-or-flee adrenalin dumps. The blood did something, the cells jostling faster, whatever, all Sara knew was that when it happened, it felt like there was neon in her veins, and each beat of her heart pushed pure light through slick arteries, and her whole body drew power from it.

Staring at Silas still, she let her focus soften as she brought her breathing under control. Simultaneously she evaluated her situation. This supposedly run-down building was clearly retrofitted to the hilt, and if this strange man was indeed who and what he said he was, he'd had plenty of time to turn this place into a personal fortress, much like the complex she lived in. She would only be leaving with Silas's blessing. She wondered briefly if she could bluff him into letting her go.

"I don't understand," she spoke eventually, and Silas tilted his head, nodding for her to continue. "This is a setup. I just need you to tell me what your actual goal was in setting me up. Am I prey?"

Silas shook his head, smiling at her.

"I am doing this to save you," he said. "I will never harm you."

"So you said," Sara said, waving her empty wine glass at him. "How about you refill my glass, and then, tell me what's going on."

With a genial shrug, Silas stood, crossed to the counter, and gathered the wine, bending to pour it into her glass. When he was done, Sara noted, the bottle was moved back to the counter, out of her reach. Potential weapon...

"I was alive during the purge," Silas said as he sank into the rocking chair. "My mother was groomed by an ageless, as we called them back then. She would visit my mother every spring, during the harvest, and spend several months living in the village. My mother knew that remaining childless was one of the conditions of joining with the ageless one, and she wanted to join her, receive the gift of life. Until one season, the woman did not appear. That year, many crops failed and there was a spate of illnesses. A lot of people died. For survival, my mother coupled with a man, and became pregnant very quickly. With me. After three more seasons, the ageless one returned, but my mother had already set up a cover, offering silver coins to a nearby village woman to take care of me for as long as her mentor stayed in the village. The ageless told my mother of the great purge, the killing of all the male ageless. That bloody business was what kept her away for so long, traveling as she did across Eastern Europe. My mother joined the ranks of the ageless several years later, her maker never knowing that she had a son. And then, when I reached the age of twenty-nine, she changed me, and so, I began a very strange life."

"Who was your mother?"

"That's not information for tonight. That would be an over-give," Silas said. "All that you need to know is that she is no longer with us."

Sara watched as this strange man moved, every movement so smooth. He didn't appear to be nervous at all.

"I'm not being cagey, but that information, in the wrong hands, could still cause trouble for several of the old Locks, since my mother moved us around, and used her time at each Lock to create financial support for me, to the point where I am now as self-sufficient as any Lock. I built this building, over the site of a farmer's cottage, a hundred and some years ago."

"When did you come to America?"

"Pretty early on," Silas said, annoyingly like some sort of fireside raconteur. "It was... necessary. Things were getting tighter in London, and I heard from friends about the lawlessness of New Amsterdam, and as you know well, wealth and corruption go a long way. I was able to sail with a private doctor, whom I had convinced of a blood illness, so that he would remove my own blood, and then, I would consume it. Works in a pinch. I'm sure you must have used that tactic as a failsafe?"

Sara shook her head. "I have no desire to strengthen my addiction," she said bitterly. "This is why men are dangerous. Self-feeding is like doing steroids or something. You're just creating a hungrier monster to feed."

"You can scale it back down, with discipline," Silas said. "And I did." He fixed her with a raised eyebrow. "You might want to think about detoxing a little bit, Sara. The amount you've been ingesting has created a dependence in you."

"Can I just say one thing?" Sara's anger was bristly and fresh, and she was glad to welcome it. "It's not the best feeling to find out you have a stalker, who's been watching you for a long time. How long, Silas? How long have you been watching me?"

"I showed you my habit of walking around, eavesdropping on the city. That is what I've done to all of the Locks in the world. You see, as much as I am separate from the Locks, my fate is tied to theirs. To yours. I was drawn to your Lock, and then to you, by your progressive approach to life. This city, this self-contained island, and what you did on it, was a masterclass in how to adapt a Lock to modern life. Around the time of my arrival in New York, I familiarized myself with the Lock, such as it was at the time. Crina and you, some actual nuns scatting around, it was crazy to see what worked in Europe working even better here. And then, it just kept on adapting, in fascinating ways."

The room started spinning again. A whirl of conflicting explanations short-circuited Sara's brain.

"How many are you? How many men are in your Lock?"

Silas shook his head, smiling.

"Lone wolf at your service," he said. "As far as I know, I'm the only living male with the virus and it's been that way for centuries."

"And you've existed all on your own?"

He nodded. "It hasn't been that hard, actually. I lost count of how many times I've sat for my EMT license, how many hospitals I've worked in."

"Always in New York?"

"Hell no, that's too risky. All over the northeast. Detroit. Chicago. Hartford. Ugh, never visit Hartford. Boston. D.C. I do it like a circuit. I intersperse time in Europe to break it up, see what those Locks are up to. I move around."

"And you're never lonely?"

"I never once said that. I am accustomed to being alone. But there have been times when the isolation has been... counterproductive. I first met you in 1964. I was your patient. We talked, and your therapy was actually helpful. It was probably then that I felt a connection with you, on a deeper level." Sara rolled her eyes as she remembered exactly who this Silas was talking about. A beatnik caught in an existential crisis, she'd enjoyed having him as a patient. Wait, what was his name.

He read her mind.

"Do you want me to tell you that name?"

She shook her head, sifting through her mind for the information.

"You were Bill someone?"

Silas nodded.

"Bill Bornstein."

"With all that black clothing and those stupid sunglasses you always wore. And your stupid Beatles haircut."

"Don't hate the player, it was appropriate."

"Silas... Atanase, Bill, whatever the fuck your real name is, this is not ideal for me. Five hundred years of training has taught me that you need to be erased, quickly. You're a man. You're not worthy of my trust, and you'll use your strength to overpower me."

"I find it slightly hypocritical that someone with your illicit viral load is reading the rules to me, who has never broken any of the writings."

"Why are you doing this?"

"To save you, like I said." Silas's eyes widened. "Okay. Here goes. Last time we met, we connected but you weren't ready. You were a card-carrying rule-obeying Lock mother. I put out some bait, you ignored it. I left New York for decades after that, I was maybe freaked out or something. I swung by over the years, but your camouflage is great. It's not like I can stand outside your building and watch. You guys have a better setup than any other city's Lock. So, when the internet told me you were back at the old psychiatry thing, I figured I'd jump in, and in talking, I felt a kindred spirit."

"You were *acting*, in our sessions, that was all fake, so spare me this kindred spirit bullshit."

"I wasn't actually." Silas leaned back in the plastic rocker. "You're not the only one who is tired, living under a suffocating bunch of rules while a virus gives us infinite time and strength. I share the commitment of all sisters, I want to understand. I want to know the why and how of life, and like you, I'm coming up short. Real short. So, much the same way as you've gambled with your life, this is me, gambling with mine."

"Do you think that we are going to continue dating?" Sara bit out.

"Wouldn't that be a thing? A grand, unprecedented thing?"

"An impossible thing."

"Not if you're serious about leaving your Lock." Sara remained silent while her mind raced. In every iteration of the path that led away from Laura's apartment, and her embrace of addiction, the end was similar, a variation on being executed by her sistren. But that was an immature folly, she saw now, a coward's response to death, handing responsibility away the same way Marguerite had done.

"You didn't really want to die," Silas said. "You want change. You don't want to go Scholar. The push and pull of Lock life gives you purpose, but the meaning is starting to wear thin."

Sara was getting tired of being told what she was and wasn't.

"So, I finally meet a cursed male, and all he wants to do is mansplain?"

"I was waiting for that." Silas laughed. "All of this is me, guessing. If you'd like to do some talking, please, believe me, I'm all ears."

Sara shook her head.

"I don't want to talk. I want to leave."

"You're free to go." Silas removed his iPhone from his pants pocket and stabbed at the screen with a finger. The locking mechanism on the main door made an unwinding sound. "Door's open."

Sara stood, setting her wine glass on the floor. She glanced at Silas, who remained motionless, then moved to the door. She turned the knob, surprised that the door actually opened under her touch. She paused, considering her options. If she left, she had to tell her sisters about Silas, and they would kill him. And yet he was not doing anything to stop her.

"I meant it, Sara. Give me tonight. In the morning, if you wish, you may surrender me. Or, if that's too violent, you can go and tell your winged monkeys, let them tear me apart."

"You really don't care if you live or die?" She turned to face him.

"Yes, actually. I really care. But the living I want to do is part of something else. I want to see the world with someone. I want to share my life with someone, but not in the four years max that you prescribe. This is what I'm gambling on."

"You do realize that we've been on four dates, and now you're talking like super vampire marriage."

"I'm not, at all. I'm talking about taking a chance on something that might work. And if it works, it will make us happier than we've ever been. There are millions of options beyond us being a couple."

Pushing the door closed, Sara leaned back against it.

"I'm a little intrigued," she began, "that you are so set on this all or nothing scenario."

"It does feel a tad last-ditch, huh?" Silas smiled. "Sara, come sit on the couch. Help yourself to some wine. This has been like a bad job interview."

Sara bowed her head, walking past the couch, swooping up her glass en route to refilling it in the kitchen. Once it was full with the last of the bottle, she turned, and pulled her butt up onto the counter.

"Please, Silas, tell me how you thought this evening would go. You've used blackmail leverage over me, and you've informed me that you've been stalking me for centuries. And I'm supposed to like it?"

"Or," Silas shifted the rocking chair to face her, "I stepped in when I felt that flameout might not be your only option. I had come to admire you, Sara. You're strong and compassionate, but nobody is taking care of you. Your disappearance worried me. I'm not blaming you, not at all, but this whole stunt, this bullshit revelation, that's due to you."

"That's actually blaming."

"Circumstances is what they is," Silas said with a small shrug.

"When you ghosted with a work emergency, I called your office, they told me you were out sick, so I knew you were having a Lock problem. From the state of you, I'd guess it was severe. I needed to drag you out of that place before something bad happened to you."

"The shit storm didn't directly endanger me, stalker."

"Still, you had more pressure dumped on you, didn't you?"

"You have no idea what's going on inside my head."

"Have I been wrong so far?"

Sara jumped down from the counter and walked to him. "You're guessing a lot, like I'm some kind of vampire mad-lib and you're getting the sentences but not the nouns. Silas, nobody was going to find out about my... transgressions. If you think that sisters don't have secrets, you're so wrong."

"I never said that. Of course you all have secrets. Humans are secretive by nature."

Silas stood, unfolding from the rocker in one feline movement. "Sara, please believe me. I never lied to you. In therapy, those issues are my issues. My lack of forward motion in life is real. I'm the person you talked to, the person you... kissed."

"This is literally the worst booty call I've ever heard of."

He laughed, his face turning down as a blush ran up his throat.

"Oh. My. God." Sara said loudly. "This is why you didn't want to take things any further at my apartment."

Silas nodded. "Yep. Guilty as charged. As exciting as it might have been if you had figured this out while we were mid-bone, I didn't want to risk it if things went awry. We can... well, the virus can tell. My mother taught me of the blood attraction, how it was the most powerful thing she ever felt."

The elders had described sleeping with a cursed man as the "most dangerous thing" ever done. It was legendary among them, that the pheromones of a cursed man could sow doubt in the strongest mind. She felt fear, remembering how her last taste of human blood had made her so horny she'd invited this man, a former patient, to Central Park, wishing for nothing more than a solid fucking.

"I've heard the tales, and you're actually doing the seductive thing that they warn about. And I'm not going to find out the hard way. We are not sleeping together."

"That's fine," he said. "There is a spectrum of futures for us, not all of them include sex."

"You keep talking about a shared future, Silas. That's already very presumptuous."

"This is all protection speak," he said, softly. "I have just one thing to sell you, and that's my company."

"Sure, it's that easy."

"It'll take time. Go Scholar. When was the last time you visited a Scholar at her place? They get left to their own devices, eventually."

"You're right," she conceded. "I actually have literally no clue what those women get up to."

"Do you all really think they just sit out there, reading books and ruminating? No, Sara. They're pushing envelope after envelope, they're doing what you're doing right now, seeing where your limits are, how much you can give, how much you can take."

"Oh, well if it's that much fun, maybe it is time for me to go Scholar. Get a nice house in the country, bang a bunch of locals, have zero fucks to give. Nobody told me it was so much fun."

Silas smiled. "I stood up so that I could go to the bathroom," he said. "There's more wine in the wine fridge to your left. Help yourself."

She noted that the bathroom door clicked closed but he did not lock it. Was this a test to see if she would run? Did he expect to come out of the bathroom and find her holding Slicer? It was all too much. She separated her thoughts into three strands, a learning technique she'd picked up in the seventies: Plus, minus, interesting. She grouped her thoughts into three simple piles. The pluses, she hated to admit, were, she was attracted to him, despite the lies. She understood the why of the lies. Lies born of necessity, not intended to hurt, were a part of life. She wasn't bothered. He was smart, kind and apparently, fair and honest. The minus was obvious. He was the enemy, the one thing she'd been trained to fight her entire life. The interesting things were, that this was, as far as she knew, a first. They would be the first heterosexual cursed couple in five centuries.

It would kill them both.

So what? She forced her focus into the equation. Was her tortoise life better than the utopia he was describing? Her darkest heart said no. Nope. Did she need another hundred years of babysitting grown women and mending hurt feelings? No. Did she want to go Scholar, replacing New York City with some small-town nonsense? Not much. Her options were limited.

Her resolve picked up, and that same devil on her shoulder, the voice she called her fuck-it friend, told her to go with it. Just for tonight. Slowly, she moved to the bedroom, lying down on the rich coverlet, still in her shoes and puffer. She heard the bathroom door open.

"In here, stalker," she called out, and Silas appeared in the doorway, a half-smile on his lips.

"Sara, I can't hardly keep up with you."

"Here's the deal. We are talking. Clothes are staying on. I'm just tired of this feeling like some dramatic argument."

"So, where do you want me?"

Nodding at the other side of the bed, Sara raised a hand and carefully pressed a crease along the bed, making a line. "This line is lava."

Still smiling, Silas gently lowered himself onto the bed, twisting so that he was facing her, the light from the light that he'd illuminated earlier shining directly into his eyes.

"I prefer a comfortable inquisition," he joked.

Sara got up and pulled the cord on the ceiling light, and darkness fell in the room. As her eyes adjusted to the low light from the living room, she watched him intently as she moved back to the bed and laid opposite him. About to speak, she was derailed, and startled, by a brutally bright and violent lash of lightning that threw everything into sharp white blue light, and then, a reversed out negative print.

The thunder was almost instantaneous, and the building creaked as the boom rolled out.

"This storm feels staged," she said when silence returned. Silas didn't reply, instead he raised a finger cautioning her to wait. A few seconds later, she heard first one, then many, fat raindrops hit the windows in the apartment, and another electric flash lit them up.

"You knew it was going to rain?" she asked.

"I hoped it was. It's hard to have the discussion of a lifetime when the air is so charged with ions."

"You think it's gonna get easier now that it's raining?"

Silas shrugged. "Dunno. Hope so."

Then he was silent again. His eyes, still locked on hers, were mild. Not accusatory, not forcing anything.

"Wait," she said suddenly. "Are you content?"

He nodded. "Yeah, actually I was just thinking that. As crazy as it is, with everything going on right now, I'm kind of content. I suddenly have nothing to say."

Sara winced. She felt the same way. Not threatened. Comfortable. As she said in therapy to her patients, she felt contained.

"So we're gonna sit here in silence?" she asked eventually.

He shrugged again. "If you want to."

"You're going to think I'm crazy," she said. "But all I want to do is kiss."

He turned to face her, an eyebrow raised.

"We can do that too," he said, not moving.

Slowly, Sara leaned forward.

"Watch out for the lava," he said. Using one hand, Sara obliterated the line in the comforter.

"There, I swept it away."

"Phew."Since Silas was not moving, she leaned across him, and brushed her lips across his, inhaling his breath, noticing that he had more stubble than he'd had last Sunday.

He pushed ever so gently against her, his full lips nibbling at hers. She slid her face along his, wrapped a palm behind his head and pulled him to her. They kept it chaste. No tongues, no wandering hands, until she broke for air.

"Are we kissing because we don't know what to talk about?" she asked.

"Or…" he smiled. "When two people have eternity at their fingertips, they don't have to solve everything in five minutes."

She rolled that around in her head for a moment, the possibility of all the time, all the times, she would have with him, if she accepted his offer. It was too much to grasp.

She pushed away from him, onto her back, looking up at the ceiling, then reached out and took his hand.

"I think we're going to have to take this slow," she whispered, suddenly exhausted as the adrenalin finally drained out of her system and the long, unbearable week settled in upon her once more. "Are you really not going to kill me?"

His face registered such shock at the idea that it soothed her immediately.

"Sara, I would protect you with my life."

She felt his arms encircle her, one around her shoulders, one across her stomach, then he pulled her to him.

"Sleep, Sara. I'll hold you. We can talk when you wake up."

"You've really fucked me up, whatever your name is."

He kissed her gently on the top of her head.

"Dormi bine, dragă Sara. Voi avea grijă de tine."

Chapter Twenty-Four

Sensing morning light behind the curtain, Sara slipped out of a dream in which she was a caterpillar, cocooned inside a dry, raspy shell, static electricity coursing across the skin on her arms. Attempting to roll over, she was blocked, by something hard and soft at the same time. She enjoyed not knowing where she was or what was real for a moment, before the memories of last night flooded her and she realized the cocoon was her puffer, and the restraints were the arms of the man who fried her circuits with revelations. Nuzzling into the comforter between them, Sara decided not to open her eyes, not wanting to break the spell.

Her mind was a roiling sea of questions, and she wasn't sure that was how she wanted to start her day. She already knew she wasn't going to kill Silas herself, and even that acknowledgment sent her off into a pit of existential despair. Centuries of peaceful life had robbed her of the ability to be a murderer.

She flashed back to Teddie's trepidation over April Veronica's indoctrination, how abjectly terrified she'd been of possibly having to kill the young woman. She'd pitied her at the time, but now realized that she too would have struggled with dispatching the new girl if things had gone awry.

She ran through a lurid scenario in her head in which she bade Silas farewell and rushed back uptown, calling an urgent all-hands meeting as soon as she was within the walls of her fortress. She pictured the hand-wringing, the horror and the commotion in the meeting room, but then what? Who would volunteer to actually attempt to murder this interloper? Heather had supervised many Surrender ceremonies, and even though she rarely talked about her early years, Sara knew she'd seen violence in England before her transition. Rosa had seen some violence in her native Mexico, but she was so committed to peace that she was forever fishing bees out of puddles of water. Eleanor had served in the Israeli military, but refused to talk about it, saying only that the brutality she witnessed made her conversion into a life of peace the most compelling decision she ever made.

As usual in this Lock, Sara knew that the responsibility would fall to her. If she told them that Silas had presented her with a Slicer, and that instead of using it, she'd chosen to fall asleep in his arms after a bout of gentle kissing, shit would get weird.

It was uncharted territory. No Lock had dealt with the discovery of a cursed male in over four hundred years. Jesus, she'd had to take Yukari's last bunny to be put down because a centuries-old biophysicist simply couldn't do it, and that night, the whole room full of women had wept inconsolably. She knew the discussion was moot. By the time they returned, Silas would be long gone.

As Lock mother, she'd raised a bunch of pussies.

The thought pushed a chuckle out of her lips, and she tensed.

"The jig is up," Silas said, his deep, slightly rough voice tickling her ear, his breath sliding across her throat. "You're doing fake mimis. Cucuy can tell."

"Fake what now?" Sara wrestled herself around to face him.

"I hid out in Mexico for a long time, last century. It's something that grandmas tell kids. Don't fake sleeping or a demon will get you."

"So you're the demon?"

"Are you always so literal?" Silas bowed his head and kissed her slowly on the forehead.

"I do find it most efficient to only speak literally." Sara was aware of how dorky the sentence was as she said it.

"Well, it's morning," he said, moving a flop of black hair away from his brown, almond eyes, his impossibly thick and long eyelashes fluttering. "Have you made a decision?" Sara shrugged.

"Your plan is actually watertight," she said. "Either I kill you right here and now, or you escape. If I leave to get the Lock, you'll vanish."

"Huh. I hoped you'd forgotten about the killing. My plan was actually that you'd throw caution to the wind and see what this can be."

"Oh." Sara wished she could make a cute, funny face, but she wasn't that kind of girl. Never had been. Teddie always laughed at her attempts to make sexyface. It looked like a crazy person in accusatory mode. She tried anyway.

"Is something wrong?" Silas asked.

Sara rolled her eyes. "No. I was trying to look friendly, but it always makes me look like a psycho."

"You look your best when you're not self-conscious," Silas said, running the back of a knuckle along her cheek. "Sometimes, when you don't know it, you look so beautiful, when you're relaxed. Most times you look like the weight of the world is on your shoulders."

Sara screwed up her face.

"Penny for your thoughts..."

"Oh, nothing really." Sara smiled, craning her neck so that she could partially see Silas's face, above and behind her own. "I've never been one of those women who can pull off coquettish. If I tried to seduce you right now, you'd die laughing and then maybe ask if I'm stroking out. That happened to me. Not once."

Beneath her, Silas's belly heaved as he laughed at her joke, shaking her from side to side.

"So, Sara," Silas said when his laughter subsided, "what's the plan for today? We've decided against execution, and-" he paused, glancing out the bedroom window, "-the weather has improved substantially."

"You want to hang out?"

He nodded. "I do. If you do, that would mean we have a yes vote."

"Can I have five minutes?" Sara patted the pockets of her coat, searching for her phone, finally locating it in an inside pocket and retrieving it. Predictably, her home screen was a litany of texts and missed calls. She groaned, and Silas wiggled out from under her.

"Sounds like someone needs strong coffee and a heem or three," he said as he sprang from the bed. The sheer normalcy of the situation struck Sara like a pang in her heart. A man who knew her needs, shared them, and could help provide solutions. It had been so long since anyone truly took care of her. She felt an overwhelming wave of something, an undefined emotion somewhere between gratitude and affection, which was ludicrous.

"I'd house a heem," she said, making non-freaky eye contact before diving into her texts. She knew she'd pay a price for not checking in with at least Heather and Teddie last night before she fell asleep, so she quickly replied to both of them that she'd fallen asleep but was fine, then asked if all was well.

Immediately, her phone pinged.

Teddie and April demanded to know if she was "still with fuckboy?" and Heather told her to take the rest of the day for herself.

"Good news," she called out. "I'm free today." Silas appeared in the doorway, a glass of water in one hand, two heem pills in the other. He handed both to Sara, who dutifully necked both pills and handed the glass back to him.

"So…." he began. "This is the last overly forward thing I promise I'll do for at least the immediate future, but in the unlikely event that we made it to this part of the morning alive and tolerating each other, I prepared a picnic for us. Would you like to go for a picnic?"

Sara threw her head back and groaned.

"You're moving too fast, Silas."

"There's no right speed for this," he smiled, sitting on the edge of the bed opposite her. "I just tried to prepare for all eventualities. Slicer if things went bad, a delightful picnic basket from Dean and Deluca in case we arrived here, at this moment."

At the mention of D&D, Sara's stomach growled, but she felt strongly that she couldn't be such a pushover.

"Won't the ground be too soggy? Where?"

"It's early, anywhere will have tables empty. Riverside Park?"

"God no, too close to home."

"McCarren Park? We can take the L and walk around after."

"Do you have spare sunblock?"

Silas extended one pale, muscled forearm. "How else do you think I maintain this pallor on olive skin?"

"Can I shower before? I feel crusty."

"You most certainly can."

"Do you have a camera in your bathroom?"

Silas nodded. "But I already covered it."

"And you're not going to try to shower with me?"

He laughed, showing his bone-white teeth, shaking his head.

"No, because I'm starving, and I have a feeling that a shower would lead to us not eating at all."

The morning was brisk and bright with that preternatural clean that New York enjoyed, only briefly, after heavy rain. As they emerged from the subway at Bedford and began the schlep to the park, the sharp bright colors of signs and exercise clothing on joggers hurt Sara's eyes and she cursed her lack of sunglasses. As if he read her mind, without saying anything, Silas darted inside a boutique. Confused, Sara spun around on the sidewalk, taking in the industrial loft buildings that topped every main street in contemporary Brooklyn, inhaling the scents of passing joggers, the exhaust of cars, all hovering above the fertile, clean smell of New York after rain. It was a beautiful morning, and she realized she was getting swept up into something, but whatever it was, she needed to keep her feet on the ground.

"Do you still call it reverie?" Silas was back at her side.

"That obvious, huh? Yeah, That's what we call it. One of my sisters used to call it 'oldtimers' but it was insensitive to dementia patients, so we nixed it."

"Reverie has such an unsullied ring." Silas handed her a small brown paper bag with string handles. "I love that word for it. What's the longest you've ever spent in uninterrupted reverie?"

Halfway into peering into the paper bag, Sara's head shot up at his careless mentions of processes central to Lock life. None of her sistren would ever speak this openly outside of their home base, and Silas was way outside the rules. "Shhhh," she whispered. "No. No talking about things."

"Lock! Vampire nun! Slicer!" Silas said, loudly. Nobody turned around. "See? Nothing."

Ignoring him, Sara withdrew a leather glasses case from the bag, opening it to reveal vintage Chanel sunglasses, with black Bakelite frames, dark green lenses, and a single diamond at each temple, the diamonds twinkling as she tilted them. They were identical to a pair she'd owned a long time ago.

"Silas, these are gorgeous...thank you. But also, I'm pretty good with a pair of street shades. These weren't cheap."

"They weren't but that's immaterial to... uh... independently wealthy folk like us."

Well...true. She slid them onto her face, delighting immediately in the dark, cool green hue over everything.

Tentatively, Silas took her hand and they resumed walking along Wythe Street.

"Now you look like you did when I first met you," he said after a block in silence.

Sara very nearly skipped a step as she recalled that she did own Chanel glasses either the same as or very similar to these, and she would have been wearing them in the mid-sixties, the last time Silas visited her practice.

"You need to stop with this stuff," she said, not bothering to keep the edge out of her voice. "This still plays like a stalker situation. You've had how long to get used to this? Your whole life? I feel like a fraying rope today, so many loose ends and every time I try to organize them, they fray anew. I have more loose ends than I had an hour ago. And every time you remind me of the not-so-uncreepy stalking that has gone on for longer than I know, it makes me want to run screaming into the arms of the only thing I know."

"I'm sorry." Silas squeezed her hand. "I'll back off. I promise. It's not an excuse, but just for an exercise, replace all the confusion you feel with relief, and that's what I'm feeling today."

Sara nodded, not saying anything. She had not considered Silas's life in any real way since his announcement, and if he was telling the truth, he had lived a very lonely life.

"Why did you bother?" she asked suddenly. "Why did you do all this, create this network, of life, alone?"

"That's a story for the picnic," he said. "When we have privacy."

"I'm intrigued." After a moment, she smiled, quickening her pace. "Let's get this picnic started."

Silas's picnic set-up was next level. After producing a lightweight tarp from his backpack, then topping it with a lemon-yellow linen blanket, he opened the Dean and DeLuca box, setting the center of the blanket as carefully as one would set a formal table. It was not yet eleven, and they had plenty of space around them. When he was finished with the set up, he turned and extended a hand.

"If m'lady would be so kind as to take a seat."

Sara took his hand and settled onto the blanket, careful to keep her shoes off the edge. With an enigmatic smile, Silas sat beside her.

"Is it too early for wine?" he asked.

"It's almost too late for wine," she replied, causing him to belly laugh before grabbing a bottle from his backpack.

"I only have plastic cups," he said apologetically, producing two from a side pocket on the pack. He filled them both almost to the brim, handed one back to her, cheersed her, then started talking.

"I bothered with all of this because, quite simply, I love being alive," he said, his chocolate eyes boring into hers. "There are no bad days. Every day has something great in it. Some days, that's just five minutes – a sunset, a nice interaction with a dog, watching a bird build a nest. Some days, it's twenty-four hours of nonstop magic, but those days are rare, and believing in them, needing them, is self-destructive. But just knowing that *we* have so much time, knowing that I can spend time learning, appreciating and doing, that makes all the strangeness a very reasonable price to pay."

Sara nodded and sipped. She noticed that he used a lot of modern vernacular, which was one of the Lock's rules. It made her curious.

"Do you know the rules that we live by? I mean, like all of them?"

He nodded. "Yes, Sara, I was aware of them as they were being drawn up. In those days, I had still hoped that there would be some sort of clemency, leniency, where my existence could be..."

"Tolerated?"

"Ouch, but sure, that works. I was going for something more positive. Endorsed? Included?"

"Sorry, that was harsh."

"I'm used to it," he said, sipping his wine. "But back to your question, yeah, I like the Lock rules. I like a lot of the good rules of life. I like the Ten Commandments, I like the precepts of Buddhism and the familial aspect of Judaism. Smart rules."

"But weren't you lonely? You're probably the only human being who has survived for this long, five centuries, with no love, no companion for any significant period of time."

"I'm staring at another one right now."

Sara felt indignant protest welling in her chest, but alongside that rose another emotion. Agreement. He was right.

"Sorry, that was harsh."

"Touché." Sara laughed a little bitterly.

"I'm not scoring points. Our lives have been devoted to compromise, but outside of that, there is plenty of opportunity for magic. You do know that as much as you believe in your Lock, it's a jumble of disparate souls locked into a shared mission, nobody telling the truth to anyone else."

"You keep on saying that, but all it does is make me wonder how much of your time has been spent spying on—" Sara glanced around for eavesdroppers. "—people like me."

"Not much, to be honest. I know it probably feels like I've done nothing else, but I have my own stuff to take care of. I study, I spend half of most years off the grid, camping, hiking, exploring. I spent the seventies in Europe. America was becoming too conservative, and I needed to get away."

"I'm sorry, I do realize I've been non-stop accusatory over this whole stalkery thing and I haven't asked questions."

"I expected questions, actually, but I'm pretty sure we will get around to them. What's the first question that comes to your mind right now?"

Sara looked up to the right, pondering.

"What was your favorite period to be alive?"

Silas smiled, reached for a container of plump black olives, offered it to her.

"I wonder," he said. "I'm annoyingly drawn to the silver lining, so my initial response is to say all of them, but that isn't true. Life during wartime is rarely fun, but then I saw Piaf sing during a war, and that made a memory I replay often. The Trump presidency was a hard time to be in America, it's still not great. But I think that I've loved eras. I loved Paris in the 1870s, I loved Detroit in the forties. The earlier years weren't as defined. I feel like I miss the slower times, the lack of news, the lack of a metronome telling me days, weeks or years had slipped by. I like the New York of now, but I loved the New York of then. You do realize that we would never have been able to make this life of lies happen at any other time?"

Sara shrugged. "There's always a way, technology be damned," she said, demurely popping an olive pit into her fingers. "We have invested heavily in technology and one of us is a stellar hacker. If you just lean into the tech side of it, you can achieve as much as we did with handwritten birth certificates and poorly managed public records."

Silas lifted his cup to her in salute, acknowledging the truth of what she said.

"When were you last happy?"

Sara fixed him with a stare.

"At the ice rink with you. That felt like a dream."

Silas's warm, smooth hand cupped her cheek and he drew himself to her, dusting a kiss along her bottom lip. A swell of urgency grabbed her and she pressed her lips against his, enjoying the tingle of his stubble, electricity in his touch. The kiss spun out, and she allowed her hands to rest on his knees, pulling herself closer to him.

"Get a room, breeders!"

They broke their kiss to see a nonbinary teenager with dirty green hair flipping them off. Silas blew them a kiss. "Happy Sunday," he called out to the teenager's back as they walked away.

"I've never dated someone who gets heckled so much," he said. "Times of flux are always weird."

"Whatever." Sara laid down on the picnic blanket and reached for the collar of Silas's jacket. "I have one last question before we kiss again. Are we gonna do this?"

Silas smiled broadly. "I would like nothing more."

Sara shielded her face from the spring sunshine and watched as this weird interloper knelt beside her, the light breeze blowing back his wavy black hair, his eyes focused on hers. She reached an arm out to pull him closer when a familiar voice spoke, just behind her.

"Before you get started," said the voice, unmistakably Teddie, "I just wanted to say hi."

Athletically, Silas stopped mid-descent, pushing through down dog to standing, bouncing to his feet and taking a few steps back from Teddie, a wide smile spreading across his face.

"Help an old lady up?" Sara calmed her pounding heart and lifted a hand to Teddie, who gripped it and pretended to struggle to lift her to her feet. Once Sara was upright, Teddie wrapped her in a hug, and whispered in her ear.

"He's looking pretty fit for a depressed fuck-up."

In the corner of her eye, Sara saw Silas step forward, hand extended.

"I'm Silas!" he said. "We met at Boobies! Nakeah, right?"

"Hey, Silas who's manhandling my friend. That's right. Nice to see you again."

Smiling wanly, Sara pushed her away.

"I don't believe we were formally introduced." Silas's hand was still out, and Teddie finally shook it.

"Nice to meet you, Nakeah."

"You too." Teddie smiled. "I was walkin' over there and I thought I saw you."

"Yep, it's me," Sara said. "Good to see you, what brings you out this early?"

"Reverse walk of shame," she said. "I'm on my way to get some. Anyway, I'm sorry, I'm totally interrupting. Good to see you, Lily. Give me a call, yeah?"

Sara nodded, noticing that Silas was fidgeting. "I'll call, we can go get a drink."

Teddie nodded. "Yep. Okay. Sorry for making this weird, I'll just be on my way."

They both waved, watching until Teddie was almost to the other side of the park. Sara leaned back against Silas, feeling his chest against her shoulders. He nestled his face into her hair and kissed the nape of her neck.

He wrapped his arms around Sara, then let his hands slide down her sides and he pulled her to him, and she felt him hardening against her lower back.

"You're not going to tease me again, are you," she said, surprised by the dryness in her voice. One of Silas's hands released her hip and fished in his pocket.

"What are you doing now?" she sighed.

"Calling a fucking Uber."

The drive back across the Brooklyn Bridge was spent in palpable silence, an almost tactile warmth extending between them. At one point, just as they were reentering Manhattan, Silas laid an open palm on the seat between them, his eyes boring into hers. She laid her hand inside his, and he gripped it, not too hard, and for the rest of the ride, they both stared out their respective windows, watching the energy on the streets.

Sara always made sure to go for a walk the morning after bad weather, the brief period when the city seemed almost naïve and carefree, a million people seeing sun as if for the first time, playing with a child's guileless enthusiasm. Same as the first day after a snowstorm; she always wanted to drink in the brief period of pristine wonder, before the day turned the snow into industrial waste. As their driver began to wend his way north through the West Village, Sara was consumed by waves of something that felt a little bit like lust, but it was more akin to a light burning in her chest, a feeling of urgency and wanting that was intoxicating and unfamiliar.

She tried to analyze her feelings and was shocked at her answer.

She was excited to do something she had never done before.

The rush up the stairs to Silas's apartment was a blur of footsteps and urgency. When he was midway through punching the security code into the door, Sara grasped his shoulder and flipped him back to the door and pressed herself against him, her lips finding his, every touch sparking an overwhelming pulse that ran from head to foot, a fountain of blood. He kissed her, tentative at first, intertwined within seconds, hands roaming, hair pulling. Their breathing became shared, their bodies seared together, the clothes between them just another layer of touch. Hands fumbled at belts and rivets and button flies, neither of them sure whose hands were loosening what. Motion caught Sara's eye and she glanced to see her coat sliding down the stairs like a plastic snake, the sight blocked by her shirt being hoisted up over her face. Momentarily blinded, she raised her arms for the shirt to sail up, groaning when she felt the heat of Silas's palm against her side, before it slid around to her back and began to fumble with her bra. She doubled down on his shirt, not wanting to stop his hands, so she just pulled the front of the t-shirt up over his face, pushing it back over his hair before moving down to his jeans, unbuttoned and not offering up much of a fight as she pushed them down, hooking her thumbs into his white boxers on the way down.

They parted momentarily, prizing shoes off feet then shucking pants onto the staircase before coming together rapidly, as if the break in their touch was unbearable to both of them. Sara felt Silas's large hand grip the back of her head, guiding her back to him to kiss, deeply, with an urgent growl coming from his chest. Somehow he twisted her around, and the steel door was jarring, icy against her back as he lifted her up and brought her down onto him, effortlessly, and she drew him in, as if they could never be close enough, her arms and legs welded to his skin, behind his back.

As they became one, a darkness clouded the edges of Sara's consciousness, a growing nothingness that felt familiar. She felt herself slipping into it, until, with a shock that made her whole body jerk, she flashed back to the same sensation, milliseconds before she blacked out in Laura's bathroom. Jerking her hands into fists, she brought them between her body and his. "Sara, it's okay." Silas's voice, in her ear, was soft. "We won't hurt each other." Then his lips were on hers, and she felt her hands relaxing, fists unclenching, and then her arms were around him again, and the blackness consumed, her, but, unlike at Laura's, she was fully conscious, and she felt herself melting into Silas, as he became a part of her, and together, their atoms sparked and glowed.

Breathing became a singular sigh, their kissing ebbing and flowing in a whirlpool with their bodies, eyes closed, bellies heaving against each other. Sara felt him consuming her, physically, but something else, somewhere else, she felt him in her heart, her lungs, inside every breath, nerve endings all over her skin exploding hungrily as they moved together.

There was nothing inside Sara's mind except sensation, pleasure, proximity and heat. They stayed, locked, moving, endlessly for an age, until the first of a series of releases built and burst through Sara, exploding her into shards of white light, the opposite of unconscious, her grip on Silas intensifying as he kept her there, on the brink, before pushing her over the edge again and again until she wasn't sure of herself any more, and she felt him tighten somehow, changing his movement, moving faster and faster, with a long growl that threatened to break their kiss but never did.

As his hips slowed, and his breathing began to even out, she felt their hearts pounding, separated only by layers of skin and bone. In time, she clung to him, as if closeness was the only thing that mattered, and he held her steady and still, the door now warm against her back. The darkness cleared like clouds in fast motion, her eyes opening onto a vista of his sweaty neck and strong jawline. Breathing heavily, she raised her face and he kissed her, hungrily.

As she returned to her body, Sara broke the kiss.

"You don't have neighbors, right?" Her voice was hoarse.

Silas half-smiled, shaking his head.

"Good, because I'm pretty happy here."

"Stay as long as you like," he said, before planting another warm, rolling kiss on her lips.

Chapter Twenty-Five

"He heard you." Sara laughed, before chugging her glass of wine.

"Oh girl, I wanted him to hear me!" Teddie winked at April Veronica. "You hadn't gotten laid in so long, it was time. I mean, look at you. Girl, you glowin'."

"She's right," April Veronica said. "You definitely have the look of someone who got a good dicking."

"Is that really what they're calling it these days?" Yukari looked up from her phone. "But yeah, you look like the bunny who got the carrot."

They all laughed, and Teddie rose from the couch to retrieve more wine from the kitchen. Sara's smile was annoyingly persistent, as she sat and looked around Teddie's apartment, cluttered as it was with mementoes from their shared life. Her heart always broke a little when she saw the glass ink bottle that sat proudly on the mantel. The bottle once contained the ink that Teddie had used to write the first words she'd learned. The air bubbles trapped in the greenish glass hadn't moved or floated to the surface in over two hundred years. When Teddie was newly converted and adjusting to her new future, she used to say she'd live long enough to see the bottle melt, since "glass is a liquid." So far, the bottle held its shape and was now nested next to a framed ticket from a Nina Simone show at the Vanguard, and a bowl containing faded ribbons that had tied bunches of flowers, a long time ago.

Sara liked being in Teddie's apartment, it was sentimental and evocative. It was lovely to visit, but if she spent too long here, she'd be bullied into a reverie she'd likely never emerge from.

"Don't go drifting off, mama," Teddie said, jolting her back to the now. "We want to hear about your weekend of sin."

Smiling as she took the fresh glass of rose being proffered to her, Sara shook her head, suddenly bashful.

"It wasn't a weekend of sin," she said, prepping for the big lie. "You know me. I basically went there to break up with him, we argued, I nearly left, he convinced me to stay over, and we talked, fell asleep and woke up and he planned a picnic. How could I say no to that?"

"Who says no to a picnic?" Yukari said, a twinkle of humor in her eyes.

"Exactly." Sara smiled. "So, then along comes old Nakeah here, just as we are about to get down to some kissing in the park."

"Cockblock," said April Veronica.

"Not my intention," Teddie said, reclining in her beloved Saarinen chair. "I mean, you guys, if you saw a unicorn running around Brooklyn, wouldn't you want a closer look? This is the first guy she's shown any interest in since legwarmers were a thing."

"Legwarmers?" April Veronica's raised eyebrow made all three of them laugh.

"You'll learn, young padawan," Sara said. "Dating loses its thrill after the first hundred failures."

"I feel that way now," April Veronica said.

"Speaking of which..." Yukari leaned forward. "Your viral load has plummeted. The transfusions have really cleaned it out. It's fascinating, I've learned so much this week. Oops. I'm sorry, you're not a guinea pig. How are you feeling?"

The young woman shrugged, her expression changing to forlorn.

"I'm afloat," she said eventually. "Healthwise, I feel calm, and that awful jagged craving is almost gone." She paused. "I'm grieving Marguerite, you guys, I know she was a bitch to you all, but for me, she was the closest thing to a mother I ever had. I'm trying to understand why she did what she did, and I can't help but feel responsible."

"Responsibility for something you didn't create is pointless," Yukari said. "Her love for you was genuine, she just didn't know how to accommodate it."

"You'll make me cry," April Veronica said, her voice breaking.

"I'm sorry," Yukari squeezed her arm. "You'll get used to it. I've been speaking English for so long, but my foundations are still Japanese. Sometimes I talk formally, sometimes I'm blunt."

"It's okay. I'm also guilty because, I'm just so damned excited about my future and... this is fucking lame. It's corny. I feel alive. Like I didn't feel before this happened."

"Even though you feel like you have it under control, you know you're still not out of the woods?" Sara asked intuitively, and the girl nodded.

"She's already down to levels only slightly higher than ours," Yukari said, patting her arm. "In a few days, she will be on par with us, good with heems and the occasional vintage." She smiled at Teddie.

Eager to deflect any further discussion of her night and afternoon with Silas, Sara jumped in.

"So, I thought of something that might be fun," she said. "How's about we play that game that you young'uns like? The Ask Me Anything game."

April Veronica looked at her quizzically. "Like on Reddit?"

Sara shrugged. "Sure, I guess."

"It's not a game. It's just a format for interaction."

"Call it what you want. Fire away. You must have questions."

April Veronica leaned back on the couch, her eyes closing slowly.

"I fall asleep every night wondering things. I really should write them down."

"This ain't your only shot, kid," Teddie said, roughing the girl's newly-dyed blue-green hair. "You can always ask us anything. Mama over there is just eager for us to stop asking about her new boyfriend."

"He's your boyfriend?" Yukari sat upright. Sara indulged in a very dramatic eye roll.

"Like I said, ask me anything!"

"I just did," Yukari giggled.

"No, he's not my boyfriend." Sara's voice was mock serious.

"You seeing him again?" Teddie was staring out the window, twirling her head scarf in her fingers. Sara waited for her to turn to face her, but that didn't happen, so she answered.

"You call a one-hitter a boyfriend?"

Teddie stopped twirling her hair but didn't turn her face.

"You know I don't play like that," she said, slightly irritated. "Quit deflectin'. I don't do boyfriends, I do fuckin', but you, honey, the last time you engaged with a man at all, I think it was at Studio 54."

April Veronica managed to stop her guffaw when it was only halfway out of her mouth. "I'm sorry," she said quickly. "But you guys are so funny. I didn't expect funny."

"Yeah, cuz Marguerite told y'all we was bitches, huh?"

"Sorry, again," the younger girl said. "But gimme a break. Ten days ago, she was just Karla, a nice artist who helped me out from time to time. But yeah, the night after I got made, she wasn't very flattering about all of you."

"Even me?" Sara made a comically horrified face. "I was nice to her!"

"Because you had to be," said all three of them at once.

"Kinda," Sara said. "But come on, you guys. Too soon."

"I need to stop bringing her up," April Veronica said. "I can tell it makes you all uneasy and I'm just going to trust that if you learn anything about why she did this, you'll share it with me."

Sara nodded. "I promise," she said. "Now is that the best you bitches can do for an ask me anything?"

"Oh, no, I have a question," April Veronica said. "When I was detoxing this week, I did a lot of thinking."

"Get used to that," said Yukari, laughing.

"Right, and I wondered. How do you sustain interest in life? I mean, the last decade has been the most emotionally exhausting in human history. I got swept up thinking, what if this is the future? What if every year is this intense and stressful?"

"Very good question, new girl." Teddie finally turned her attention back to the room. Sara watched her intently; the two of them had rarely been at odds over the centuries, and right now, Sara sensed that something was off, and it troubled her. "Shall I take it, ladies?"

Yukari nodded, Sara shrugged.

"The secret to all of this is, feel lightly. We exist too long to let ourselves feel everything as intensely as one might, if one knew that they were only going to live for sixty or eighty years. When you have centuries ahead of you, you become very selective about the causes that can tear your heart out, and even then, it's best for us to avoid such deep, intense involvement."

"I'm confused," April Veronica said. "I thought that experiencing life was the core of sisterhood?"

"It is." Sara rested a hand on the girl's arm. "But indulging in intense emotion isn't the only thing that life is. We don't avoid, completely. It's just that deep engagement only leads to crippling heartache. Our nature always remains human, and regret is a very toxic thing to carry for hundreds of years. We just work in broad strokes instead of granular relationships."

"What does that even mean?"

"Okay." Teddie leaned forward. "Let's talk about social justice. You're saying that the last decade was the most fraught in history? Nope. No way. No how. I mean, it wasn't pleasant, but when you've lived through slavery, the civil war, the Spanish flu, prohibition, presidential assassinations, AIDS and that's not even talking personal loss, you have to realize that you can observe, and you can help, but taking each step to your heart, deeply, is too taxing. So, saying that we feel lightly doesn't mean we don't feel. It means we maintain a healthy distance from things that will crush us, and we work outside the system to improve it."

"But you never let it get to you?"

"It's unavoidable," Yukari said. "I love my rabbits, and when each one dies, I am distraught. I do it to remind myself of the pain of loss. Also, because the little babies are damn cute and they're great apartment companions. So every ten years or so, I have a heartbreak that proves that I'm still human, still alive. But I don't extend that openness to society. When something is wrong, in New York or out in the world, you'll see, we will meet, and we will direct funding to wherever we think the most difference can be made. Then, in the longer span of attention that we have, we get to see the change that we effect. It's just a different approach, managing the depth of your involvement."

"Is this why you all seemed to so quickly move past what happened to Karla... Marguerite?"

"Oooh snap," Teddie said. "Naw, I think that a lot of us are still in shock and we are waiting for some peace time so that we can indulge a long reverie over what went down. This one has shaken us. I've chosen to focus my feelings on you, because you deserve to be smothered in kindness and care, and you've kept me very busy, with your weirdo blood." She leaned over and tousled April Veronica's sea green curls. "I honestly haven't dealt with my feelings about Marguerite at all. Some days I forget she's gone, and then I keep on tripping over it. It's not healthy, but I have to compartmentalize it for now."

"I've thrown myself at a man to avoid thinking about it," Sara said openly, feeling a small twinge of success at the surprised look on Teddie's face. "Being Lock Mother isn't a magical job that turns you into something other than human. It's like how children think that their parents have all the answers. Parents are just unqualified people thrown into a job that's hard and unrewarding, but kids are like, oh mom doesn't mind doing laundry, dad likes mowing the lawn. That's what happens when you're a Lock Mother. I absolutely did not want to go meet Desdemona, I didn't want to play politics with a murderer. I wanted to punch her right in her stupid face."

Yukari laughed loudly.

"I did," Sara's voice rose. "We are the most peaceable Lock in the world. I resent what she did, so absolutely that I cannot permit myself to feel it any more deeply. This is the kind of anger that can turn a person rotten, and that's why I need to let it go. Lock Mother isn't the worst job, but I'm not going to lie to you. Ushering you through your confirmation, when the entire Lock was refusing it just because they didn't like Marguerite, that was parenting. And it sucked. So of course, a handsome man comes along, and he's gloomy and intellectual and he snags my attention and suddenly, I want to feel deeply again."

"Is it weird to ask sisters for their origin story?" April Veronica said abruptly.

"Depends on the sister," Yukari said, trying to buy time for the other two. "Mine's good, but it's more of a history lesson. I'll tell you sometime."

"Tell her now," Teddie said. Yukari shook her head. "It's not my story she wants, honestly, and also, I haven't heard your story for many a moon."

"My story with Theodora is not that dissimilar to your story with Marguerite." Sara spoke very directly. "I first met her as a very young child."

"My mom and I were trying to make it to Canada. She got sick. Nobody would take us in, and we heard about a convent that helped Black folks, back when the convent was downtown. Crina and Sara helped us, and after my mom died, I stayed." Teddie's voice had an edge. "And to your earlier question about feeling deeply, here you go. The years have done nothing to dull those memories, and I wish every day that soon, in the future, I'll feel it less deeply. But so far, nope."

"I am so, so, sorry," April Veronica said. "I'm sorry, I didn't mean to make you cry."

"I ain't cryin', my eyes always well up. Truth is, I can barely remember my momma. I know she existed, but her face has faded. I remember her love."

"I do too," Sara said. "She loved you so much. We couldn't figure out what was wrong with her at the time, but I think it was a faulty heart valve. I remember watching you on the nights when she was too weak to leave the bed. You were so brave, and so smart. And I remember after we lost her, you and I went for a walk along the river and you caught a beetle. It was sitting on a tall blade of grass, and you asked me if God made all the colors in the world. You showed me the beetle and you ran a fingertip over its metallic green back, and you said that was your favorite color in the whole world. And I asked what you wanted to do when you grew up, and you said you wanted to see all of God's colors in the world, and my heart just broke. I knew then that I wanted to help you. Crina didn't bat an eyelid when I told her."

"Do you remember when I was a teenage nun, scatting around with you two?"

"I love to remember that time," Sara said. "As horrible as the world was at that time, or at any time, actually, I had the feeling of being a mother, I cared for you more than anything in my life. Still do, actually."

"You guys, this is amazing," Yukari said.

"This is the origin story I needed this week," April Veronica said. "And these stories, they're never written, it's always just oral tradition?"

Teddie nodded forcefully. "'Never may it be written' doesn't just refer to the virus. We can't leave markers of any period of our lives, of any persona, nothing. And I know what you're feeling, that this is a shame, a waste, all these women living significant lives without any record, and you know what? That's fine. Nobody is truly remembered. Houses get demolished, gravestones weather their letters away until they're just stones above bones."

"Dark," Yukari said.

"Accurate," Teddie shot back.

"Deciding to bring you in was not an easy decision." Sara looked Teddie dead in the eyes as she spoke. "Crina encouraged me, and the deciding factor was that there was not a good alternate life for you available at that time."

"How old were you when you got made?" April Veronica asked.

"I was only twenty-six," Teddie said. "A terrible flu came that year and people were dying. It was kind of a shock, and at the same time, it wasn't. I'd heard the two of them talking for twenty years. I knew something was up. You grow up how I grew up, you don't sleep. You listen. So, I heard stuff that didn't make sense, and as I got older, I knew there was something special about them. Didn't you feel that as you got closer to Marguerite?"

April Veronica nodded. "Yeah, but even after growing up on *Underworld* and *Twilight*, I was thinking more along the lines of *The Eternals*."

"Not bad!" Teddie laughed. "Do you remember, mum? I asked if you two were magic, if you were angels?"

"You always had a lot of questions." Sara smiled warmly. "And when we explained the virus to you, the first thing you said was, yes, I want to be like you, I want to help kids like me, and maybe the moms of kids like me."

"Still do," Teddie said.

"And that's phenomenal," April Veronica said. "You guys, I want to thank you, this little chat has given me more peace than I've felt all week."

"And here I was, thinking you guys just wanted to hear about my sex life, now that I have one."

"Oh sister, we ain't done with that!" Teddie laughed again. "How many times did you go?"

"I had to stop after four," Sara said, feeling heat creep up her neck. "I think both of us were making up for lost time."

"You go, girl," Yukari urged. "Welcome back to the club."

"How long until I can date?" April Veronica said with a cheeky smile.

Sara shrugged. "That's a discussion between you and your Lock mommy."

"And mommy says you'll need to be sixteen before you start bringing the boys around," Teddie said, stretching in the bean bag chair before standing elegantly then presenting a flat palm at April Veronica.

"And if you talk back, it'll be eighteen. Who needs a refill?"

Three wine glasses were raised into the air. Teddie gathered them all in her hands and headed to the small kitchen. In unison, all three seated women pulled out their phones and got lost in notifications.

Sara smiled to see some texts from Silas on her screen, ignoring texts from Heather, Eleanor and Liz to get to them. He missed her, he hoped she was okay and the last one was the best one: Would she like to get away from the city for a few days?

Sara's head swam, a woozy mix of infatuation and excitement. Since Lock sisters weren't really able to be seen together out in the world, travel wasn't something that they often did. No amount of sunblock made beach shares doable, and winters on the east coast were ugly and grim. She tried to remember her last trip, recalling a jumble of fun weekends away with lovers long dead, but not the year of the most recent.

"Teddie?" she called out. "He wants me to go away for a weekend."

"Of course he does," she said, emerging from the kitchen. "You're moving fast, mom. If the shoe was on the other foot, you'd be urging caution."

"If the shoe was on the other foot, you wouldn't be telling me anything." Sara laughed.

"That's because I take care of my shit. I don't catch feelings and I don't do whatever this is that you're doing."

"Where are you going?" Yukari was always supportive, and Sara loved her for it.

"Oh hell, I didn't even ask." Sara quickly fired off a text. He responded immediately.

"I've always wanted to go to the Finger Lakes," Sara said thoughtfully.

"Not badly enough to actually go, apparently." Teddie slipped a very full wine glass into Sara's hand "They've been here longer than we have."

"Well, now I have an opportunity," Sara said. "Thanks for the wine. Also, after a century of low-key Lock leader grooming, it's time for me to step down. Want the job?"

Teddie froze, a glass of wine in her hand on its way to April Veronica, who reached up and took it.

"You serious, Sara?"

"I am. It's time for fresh eyes, and also, what you said about the divisions within this Lock...I think it's going to take a new Mother to help heal them."

"Are you going to go Scholar?" Yukari couldn't hide the disappointment in her voice.

"Not right away," Sara said. "I'll just step back and be a pain in Teddie's ass for a while."

"Whatever works for you, mom." Teddie sat on the couch next to her. "Are you sure? Are you okay? I'm sorry I rode you so hard. I just don't want you to get hurt."

"It feels weird," Sara said. "I had my blinkers on, that's one part. But the other part is, Teddie, I wanted your childhood to go on forever. I knew deep down that someday you'd be the Lock Mother, but every time I saw you out having fun, I just wanted that to continue."

They exchanged warm looks. "Do you want to think about it, Theodora?"

"I do," Teddie said. "I need to spend some time with the idea, and right now, with this new addition and her need for fancy blood."

"She won't need it for much longer," Yukari said. "Pretty soon she'll be good with heems and the same fresh that we get at meetings."

"Oh, that's great news," Teddie said. "Still," she looked from Yukari to Sara and back again, "Y'all know I like to take my time."

Chapter Twenty-Six

After letting herself back into her apartment, Sara did a little happy dance, two full laps around the sofa. She'd never done one before, but she'd seen it on enough TV shows to know that her happy dance was a bit sad. She didn't care. She shuffled her feet and waved her arms around giddily, her eyes closed. She breathed in the scents of her home, a home she'd have to leave once she stepped down. In the near future, she would just box all her stuff up and put it in one of the storage apartments and live full-time at Murray Hill.

She fell back onto the sofa. She inhaled again, candles, fabric softener, and New York Must, that weird smell that originated in the heaters, and gathered in the dark corners of every apartment, waiting for the right conditions at the end of winter. Elusively, floating above all of it, was a faint scent of Silas on her skin.

Smiling, she glanced at the ugly puffer she'd worn to his house, the one they'd had sex on. It needed to go on a date with a dry cleaner, but first... she reached across the couch and slowly lifted the coat, pressing it to her face, inhaling his various scents: his breath and saliva around the collar, his armpits atop the shoulders. She was immediately beneath him on the stairs in his building, and her breathing faltered at the intensity of the memory.

Ignoring the stream of texts on her phone, she sank into the couch, feeling weirdly young and vulnerable, like a schoolgirl with a secret.

Man, did she have a secret.

And Teddie as Lock Mother would be formidable. Teddie would be new to the job, with all the fresh energy and vision that came with new responsibility. She'd likely be much better at running the Lock than Sara had been for a long time. And she'd be really hard to sneak things past.

There was no time for regret. She thought about her decisions with Silas, how refusing to kill him was another rule broken. She put a half-life on herself with that decision. No matter how it progressed, the end result was that they would be discovered, and they would be killed.

She knew that other Locks joked about the pacifist nature of their sisters in New York. The London Lock called the New York Lock a "no-kill shelter." But this, the simple reality of Silas, would put that reputation to the test.

Would Teddie kill him? Sara shuddered to consider it. Teddie fastidiously stuck to the rules. All rules. In her personal life, she was decidedly rebellious, but only socially, never against Lock rules. She proudly boasted that there wasn't a man alive who could interest her for four years, she was contentedly atheist, and she loved being a "shadow activist" as she called it. She didn't ever cleave tightly with any other members, and Sara had sometimes wondered why Teddie and Crina didn't have the bond that Sara had with her maker. For even though Sara stepped into the mother role during Teddie's pre-change years, Crina had been there too; although Crina was prone to long journeys on her own.

Having a child to care for gave Sara an excuse to really figure out their shared future in New York, creating the fifth Lock to which she had belonged. Romania, Madrid, Paris, London, New York. Teddie only ever knew one city, this city. She marveled over every step of New York's evolution, digging deep into every nascent scene, first as a novelty—a Black student from a nunnery—and in the last century, as a participant.

From the moment that Sara agreed to accept Marguerite, a legendary enfant terrible who'd caused stinging flareups in Milan and Madrid, Teddie was against it. Marguerite was the closest thing to a threat that the New York lock ever tolerated; and each time there was a burst of animosity, Teddie reacted with almost military precision, not even waiting for Sara's intervention, always confronting Marguerite with hard facts and the brick wall of Teddie's own commitment to the rules of the Lock.

Sara shivered, then the shiver gave way to a pit of hollowness in her chest that she couldn't identify, a sweeping emotion of gray and muted blues that pulled at her like guilt mixed with something deeper.

For a moment, she considered Crina. Surely she or some of the other Scholars were out there breaking rules. There was no way to really find out.

This was all a drag. The boredom that led her to working as a therapist, the repetitive need to connect with people, to understand their life, was a problem she always kept at arm's length, its roots too deep and tangled inside her for any workable answer to ever be possible. If she was indeed tired of living, she had nothing to lose by gambling on... she couldn't even let her mind end the sentence with *love*. She was gambling on excitement. Cheap, schoolgirl excitement.

You need to grow up.

Standing angrily, she went to the turntable, lifted the lid and was happy to see Muriel Grossman's Reverence sitting there, a black disc scattershot with moonlit circles, containing soothing, challenging

rhythms that she needed. She dropped the needle, then powered up
her amp, smiling as the first round of drums filled the air of her dark
apartment.

She wanted to call Silas, but she also knew that ahead of that, she
needed to do some hard thinking.

"Hard thinking calls for hard drinking," she said to nobody, moving stiffly to the kitchen and pulling the cork off a half-done bottle of
Hudson Valley cab sav, filling a single wine glass almost to the rim. She
pulled her phone out of her pocket, habitually. But she should have
known better.

A text from Heather.

> You up? A bunch of shit that can't really wait
> 'til tomorrow.

She wanted to pretend that she didn't see the text, to call Silas,
to sleep peacefully. But Heather knew her routine and if she didn't
answer, Sara knew that a knock on her door would be happening in a
few minutes.

> Just getting in shower, give me twenty min-
> utes and bring wine.

Heather sent a smiley face and a rose emoji.

Sara called Silas. He answered before a single ring.

"There you are," he said, his deep voice fluffy with sleep.

"Oh, I woke you..."

"I'm on the couch. Been here since you left. I need to move to the
bed, so thank you for the motivation. How are you?"

"Well, I've survived the trial by fire. I faced my gossipy friends, and
Heather will be here with some urgent matter in twenty minutes, and
I have to shower before then."

"So I have you for ten minutes? I'll take it."

Sara smiled.

"Thank you, Silas, and I guess…I just want to let you know that I'm getting closer to okay with what happened, with what I learned."

"Good, good," he said, and she could hear the sound of his couch as he moved to sitting upright. "Sara, for a while this will seem weird, even stalkery."

"It will always feel weird," she began, "but, it's in the past, I don't have any control over it, and you were kind of driven to it by necessity. The only weird thing is that you know so much about me, and you know how much I know about you, which isn't much."

"That's why I want us to have some time. I want you to have an even playing field."

"I wish I was there now, but Teddie's hackles are already up. I have to play this open-handed and cool, for now."

"We have time." Silas's voice was almost a whisper.

"You sound tired."

"I am. I didn't sleep last night, I was convinced that you would freak out, leave, whatever."

"I just wanted to hear your voice. Go to sleep, I'll call you tomor-row."

"And Sara?"

Another shiver as the weirdness of hearing her real name spoken by a man.

"Yes?"

"Can I book our trip away? Can you do a three-day weekend?"

"I can, and yes, let's. Thank you."

"Leave it to me."

"Thank you, Silas. Now get some sleep."

"Aye aye cap'n," he said with a laugh. "Sleep well, *draga mea*."

And he was gone, the Romanian echoing in her head as she leapt across the couch, shucking her clothes and starting the water, knowing it took forever to get hot.

Shutting off the hairdryer created a sonic boom of quietness in the apartment, the steam from the shower already vanquished by the rattly ceiling fan. Sara inhaled deeply: a mixture of shampoo and face cream smells, half old lady, half random flowers, all traces of Silas gone.

Muttering to herself, she stepped through to the bedroom, pulling a Sherpa-lined adult onesie out of the closet, stepping inside it fully naked, luxuriating in the feel of the faux sheep wool against her skin. The human obsession with comfort knew no bounds, she chuckled to herself, thinking of the fabrics of her youth, the rough wools that few could afford, the stiff leathers that always retained the smell of rotten meat and lye. She had considered them comfortable at the time; and now this—a strange child's outfit in adult size, purchased at the Walgreen's on Broadway for seventeen dollars—was the height of comfort in her closet.

As usual, Heather's brisk rat-a-tat knocking brought her back to herself, and she opened the door.

"Bloody hell, you look like a Care Bear!" Heather said, pushing past her, using the bottle of wine in her hand as a divining rod to the kitchen.

"Looks like you've started without me," she muttered to herself while futzing with the screw top on the bottle she'd brought.

"I was just finishing a bottle, there wasn't enough for two glasses." Sara plonked down on the sofa, her still-full glass of wine perfectly level on its journey. "I'll be right with you."

"Yes, m'dear, you will," Heather said, her voice full of foreboding that Sara had learned to register but not react to. Heather saw drama and consequence in everything, and while she was right, it was usually possible to head off the worst of it. "Oh shit, what's wrong now?" Sara took a sip that wiped out half the wine in her glass.

"I have been doing my favorite thing!" Heather said, leaning against the wall beside the fridge.

"Digging?"

Heather nodded from her vantage point. By now she would normally be seated across from Sara, and Sara finally began to worry. She forced her face to remain still and her voice to remain even.

"You seem a bit shaken…"

Heather nodded, then took a sip of her wine without speaking.

"You're freaking me out."

"It's not good," Heather said. "Simply put, Desdemona and her winged monkeys were here a lot longer than we knew. They were in the city for almost a week before they… before the thing with Marguerite."

Sara sat bolt upright.

"Where did they stay?"

"I don't know," Heather said, her voice bubbly. "But Sara, I am certain that Marguerite knew."

Sara jerked so violently that she spilled wine on her romper.

"Dammit!" She leapt to her feet and into the kitchen, mopping at her front with a dish towel. "Heather, what if Marguerite was on her way to meet them the night I met her out on the street?"

Heather froze.

"I'd say it was bloody likely!"

"What a snake that woman was," Sara downed the remainder of her glass and refilled it from Heather's bottle without rinsing it. "She was probably never friendlier to me than she was that night. We went sprinting in Riverside Park, but then she went weird and left. I thought nothing of it, but motherfucking goddamn, what if she went and met with Desdemona?"

She returned to her seat and gazed into her friend's eyes. Heather took a deep breath.

"Well, we'll never know," she said. "I've been scouring immigration records, and I've been having some of my better contacts try to get in touch with them. They ain't home yet. Then I called the Boathouse, pretended to be checking up on credit card fraud. Got the card they paid with. It hasn't been used again since."

"Do you know where they went?"

Heather shook her head and finally joined Sara on the couch. "After Edinburgh, they vanished. It's Europe, it's harder to trace. But nobody's talking. It'll come out soon enough," she said. "In the meantime, I've been busy overhauling our security system. We have fingerprint locks on all doors now. I wanted to ask you for permission to finally upgrade the emergency basement tunnel with new steel doors."

"Aren't they steel now?"

"They're steel from nineteen seventy-two. They're just heavy. I want to install state of the art glass, hidden cameras and motion sensors, plus I really want to replace all the individual apartment doors. It's also time to move us all around."

Sara had refused to move the last two times Heather had insisted on a residential shakeup, because she loved her apartment. This time she didn't mind. "Where am I going?"

"Take one of the top floor ones by Rosa. They look straight downtown, no neighbors at your level."

Sara shrugged. "I've actually never lived in any of those," she said, trying to sound agreeable.

"Yeah, I don't know why you haven't, I'm quite partial to them. They're quieter than this, believe it or not, and way more private."

"Heather, you don't need to sell me on it. Um, I may be mainly down in Murray Hill anyway."

"Well, I'm just going to give you a spoiler here. It gets worse. I've been reviewing the security footage, at least the stuff that's left after Marguerite meddled with my shit."

"She deleted footage?"

Heather nodded tersely. "Not just that. I had to wait until the blood scent was gone from her apartment, and honey, that took a lot of incense and sage. I even had to go and buy a gallon of Fabuloso from the bodega and just spray it directly onto everything."

"And?"

"And..." Heather stopped to take a deep breath. Heather was not usually quite this dramatic, and Sara fought to retain her composure. "Her sent messages on Signal were still there. She was corresponding with the Madrid Lock... about you."

Sara was genuinely perplexed. What could Marguerite have known about her? Or said.

"And?"

"Is that all you can say?"

"Lil bit."

Heather chuckled. "Nothing terrible, it's just that she didn't like how she was treated here, she was asking to return, it's hard to figure out exactly but I think that they'd told her no previously and she was trying to gain favor with them."

"How?"

Heather sighed loudly. "By reporting on you."

"I figured. Anything specific?"

"She must have been deleting their replies, or they weren't replying via Signal. I don't know. It's a one-sided conversation. Basically, she said you are running a loose ship and that your Lock was in freefall."

Sara winced, mainly at the truth in the sentence but also in anticipation of worse. When Heather remained silent, Sara looked her in the eye.

"Anything else?"

Heather shook her head. "Not yet. Not until I crack her laptop."

"Did she use the word 'Lock' or any other forbidden words in her communications?"

"Oh no, of course not. She said 'sisterhood.' All of her terminology was in approved lexicon. But she definitely indicated that things in our Lock were chaotic."

"Do you think they are?"

Heather smiled gently.

"No, my friend. I do not. I think that we are no more or less dysfunctional than any of the Locks, and we are definitely the most progressive. We are also the most tech-savvy *and* the most innovative. The inroads that Yukari and Eleanor have made in modern virology will help all of us in the long run, and we are entirely self-sufficient. We provide assistance to more causes than anyone else.

Sara was thinking deeply. "Have you talked to Crina about this?"

Heather nodded. "Yes, but only as part of my investigation, boss. She doesn't know everything. Yet."

"You can tell her. She may have some insight."

"Well, I know, but I wanted to get your permission. This is potentially a huge issue."

Sara nodded. "Yes, it is. And I might be about to complicate it."

Heather stopped mid-sip. "Oh?"

"Heather, I'm tired. The Marguerite thing was really my last straw, in a lot of ways. And she was right, I *have* gotten sloppy. I think it's inevitable when someone is in a job for too long. We have a finely oiled machine, but I am not tending to it with the eagle eye that I had when Crina first went Scholar."

"Sara, that was a hundred and forty years ago. You're one of the longest reigning Mothers, of course you got tired." Heather paused. "I am sorry, I should have seen this coming, I should have been more of a buffer for you."

"Bitch please." Sara laughed. "You are the brains and the backbone to this whole operation. I'm just a figurehead and I know it."

"I'm just grateful I don't have to wipe all those runny noses."

"And that, my friend, is what I'm burning out on," Sara said. "If I get my phone, there will be a screen full of new texts. Liz will be angry at Yukari. Eleanor and Fran will be at odds over something that they could certainly resolve without my input. Nobody wants to be the bitch, so they all ask me to be the bitch for them."

"I wish you'd ask for help. I love an excuse to be a bitch." Heather laughed

"You all think that I peaced out on dating, on private things. I didn't. I just fell into the parent role and typically, the kids don't think that the mom needs anything for herself."

"Gets a boyfriend one day, rethinks entire existence."

"Don't even try it." Sara raised her wine glass as defense. "I was burned out before Silas came along. Honestly, I probably fast-tracked April Veronica to spite Desdemona. We got lucky that she's a great convert. But, with the ZPG thing and also the increased surveillance tech, we need new eyes on the job."

Heather nodded slowly. "I trust you've been preparing for this for some time?"

"Ish," Sara said thoughtfully. "I've been trying to give Teddie as long a life without responsibility as I can, but it seems that's now come to an end."

"Have you even asked her if she wants the job?"

Sara nodded her head. "She's thinking it over, but she wants it. She's a stickler for rules and she needs to learn that the rules all bend. I was much more militant when I started being the Mother."

"You're not exactly easygoing now," Heather said with a smile.

"I'm literally as easygoing as a Lock Mother can be! I care more about peace than I care about protection, and that's not necessarily ideal. Teddie's time as a nurse must be coming to an end. Do you know exactly how long she's been in her current job?"

Heather nodded. "Three years and nine months. She told me she wants to continue as a provider nurse, so I've already found her new identity and set her up with the necessary degrees."

"Sorry to waste your time," Sara said glumly.

"She can keep on working as a nurse if she becomes Mother."

"Indeed she can. But it's not sustainable for long. Nurse provider is a full-time j-o-b and getting home from a nursing shift with a bag of stolen blood in your purse and facing four million texts from a bunch of adult babies will wear her out in no time."

"Are we really that bad?"

"Don't lump yourself in with them, Heather. You're literally the person best suited for this lifestyle. You have mastered so many secrets to a long, interesting life, and you still find joy in every day."

"I make it look easier than it is."

"Of course you do. But still, you always date, you always smile, and you always find something to love."

"I take no credit for that, boss. That's New York City in a nutshell. She makes it easy for me."

"I love you, Heather."

"I know." She smiled. "Is your mind made up?"

"Yeah, it is, as of ... this moment. May change by morning, but can you start my exit strategy from being Doctor Lillian Berger? I want to close my practice. I'll keep the name for..."

"Another four years?" Heather smiled knowingly.

"Yep, another four years." Sara felt a slight twinge at lying to Heather. She changed the subject.

"And Heather, yes, you have my permission to completely overhaul our security. No other Lock in the world is to have our codes. They don't deserve it, not after Desdemona's... visit. Actually, you know what? If you see something that needs improving, do it. Let's make this fortress safe for ourselves. And Heather? Let's just keep it between ourselves that no outsider can have the codes. Just until we are sure we're not in any danger."

"Music to my ears, boss," Heather said, raising her glass.

"I love you, Heather," Sara repeated, making Heather's eyes widen in surprise. "I don't think I tell you often enough. I'm just so lucky to have you."

"Daw," Heather said. "No need for mush, it'll just make me uncomfortable."

Chapter Twenty-Seven

The following night, Sara sat with her phone, flipping it from one palm to the other, rock paper scissoring herself over and over to divine whether she should call Silas. An unshakeable strange feeling, like a black stone in her heart, was stopping her from calling.

"What? I can't like a guy?" she asked the four walls of her living room, the living room she would be vacating soon. The way the room deadened sound appealed to her, but now it felt like her words vanished before the soundwaves could even be absorbed by the walls.

She felt lonely.

"Damn you to hell," she said with a bitter laugh, cursing her loneliness, another byproduct of her recent spate of fast-paced changes. For a second she considered canceling her weekend away, just to get some breathing room. Nah, she was already making mental notes of questions to ask him. His entire existence didn't make sense. How had he survived centuries, feeding his habit while maintaining his anonymity? What if he *wasn't* the only male? Was this a trojan horse situation?

There was no way to know the truth.

Flip. Flop. Flip. Flop. Her phone kept a primitive beat against the palms of her hands. Was she willing him to call? To sense her need and reply? Kinda sorta. Frustrated, she tossed her phone onto the couch cushion, immediately regretting the loss of something to do with her hands.

Footsteps on the landing outside her apartment froze her in place. A tentative shuffling that sounded closer, and then further away.

She inhaled deeply, silently, for any scent of the Spaniards, but nothing unfamiliar came to her. The footsteps fell silent, followed soon after by a soft knocking at her door. None of the sistren would approach in this way.

Rising slowly, Sara glided into her bedroom, reaching beneath her bed for the engraved Slicer she kept there. She slipped four fingers through the custom-made holes in the flat metal, the low light from the window bringing the engravings to life, the impossibly sharp blade managing a glint in the darkness.

Swallowing before she spoke, she called out, her voice strong.

"Hello, is there somebody there?"

Some shuffling, then silence.

Fuck. What if it was Desdemona? She fell back into a combat crouch, Slicer by her hip, her other hand ready to unlock the deadbolt and swing the door in. She listened, her ears feeling like they grew to capture more sound but found none. 3-2-1 she counted down, then rapidly flipped the deadbolt, unlatched the lock on the knob and heaved the steel door open, her back pressed against the wall, her left arm humming with tension, prepared to launch the silver blade at her intruder.

The yellow light that spilled in from the hallway made her blink, and years of training made her left arm come up forcefully, against an intruder she still couldn't see.

"Sara!" yelled a familiar voice. "Sara, no, stop it's me, it's April Veronica!"

And indeed it was. The young woman was now halfway down the first flight of stairs, an expression of horror on her face.

Sara inhaled deeply, enjoying the thrum of adrenalin in her veins.

"April Veronica, why didn't you say something?"

"It's late, I've been trying to get to see you, I... I... come up here most nights and then I chicken out."

"You could have had Teddie ask..."

"I ask her to do so much already, I figured this was something I could do by myself. I apologize, it's late, I'll go back to my place."

"No, no, I'm wide awake, please come inside," Sara spoke, her eyes still closed.

"You look pissed," April Veronica said, not moving from the safety of her step. "I can come back."

Melting as the adrenalin rush subsided, a clammy chill running over her arms and throat, Sara tried to hide Slicer behind her, cautious of the blade.

"It's okay, I can see you're armed. Don't hide it from me." April Veronica stepped up one step.

"Well, fine, but get your ass in here if you want to visit. This door is fucking steel, I can't just hold it open all night, and I would like to sheath my weapon."

Smiling, the young woman bounded up the steps and came inside the apartment.

"Wait on the couch," Sara said, ducking into her bedroom and carefully sliding the blade back into its cured leather sheath screwed to the bottom of her bed. When she returned to the living room, she saw that had April Veronica a brown paper bag clutched in one hand hanging limply by her side. The young woman's brown eyes were open wide, her loose curled blue green hair framing them in such a way that Sara hadn't noticed her delicate beauty before. She wore blue jeans and an orange Princeton sweater.

"You can sit down, you know," Sara said, brushing past her, indicating the couch with her hand. "Can I get you a glass of wine?"

Pausing halfway to sitting down, April Veronica made a stink face. "If I tell you something can you promise not to laugh?"

Sara smiled. "No."

Shrugging, April Veronica continued. "This wine thing. It's kind of old lady, and you guys all try to like be modern right? I don't like wine. Nobody my age likes wine. Wine is gross."

Sara laughed. "Are you going to sit or stand, kid? Because watching you hunched over like that is even funnier than you not liking wine."

April Veronica plonked down noisily onto the couch, bouncing like a child. "What? Why are you still laughing?"

"Is that what you came sneaking around my apartment late at night to tell me? That wine is passé?"

"Well, no, not just that, I wanted to ask you some things and Teddie said that you are easy to talk to, and she also said that the best time to catch you is between midnight and two."

Sara smiled. "I'm really happy to see you two getting along so well."

"Oh god, she's amazing, like literally." April Veronica's eyes lit up. "She's been so kind to me. I think I'm back to normal, after... after what happened, and she said it should have taken longer but she's been really diligent with my dosing and my comedown."

"You don't have to convince me, kid. There isn't anyone in this world I love more than her."

"She says you're like her mom."

Sara rolled her eyes, feeling slightly at a loss since she wanted a wine herself but now felt too self-conscious to get one.

"Oh wait." April Veronica thrust out her arm. "I come bringing a modern alternative to wine."

"Do I need to prepare it?" Sara reached for the crumpled bag, which April Veronica pulled back at the last second.

"No, I just didn't know what you'd like or what you'd be into so I kind of brought everything."

Sara seated herself on the other end of the couch, smiling expectantly, politely. It was going to be weed. She knew it.

"I don't smoke," she began.

"God, who does?" Tearing the paper bag open, April Veronica held up a small brown glass jar. "These are fast-acting edibles, ten milligram." She set that down, then held up a small pen-like object. "This is my vape, but it'll kick your ass. But the best thing is this." She proffered a mason jar filled with an orange liquid. "I make this myself. It's a distillation, and the only problem with it is, I make it too delicious. Do you have shot glasses?"

Curious, Sara nodded, stood and retrieved two dusty shot glasses from the top shelf above the sink, rinsing them quickly under the tap.

"Wait, do you use weed?"

"April, I wasn't always this boring. I lived through prohibition, the jazz era and the sixties. And the seventies and the eighties."

"I just don't know the protocol to ask if anyone in this Lock wants to share my weed?" April Veronica said plaintively. "There's a trillion things I have to learn, and I keep on stumbling over stupid shit like this."

Sara held out the two shot glasses as April Veronica twisted the top off the mason jar and carefully filled each one. When she was done, Sara sat down, closer to her this time. There was something about her energy that was definitely bewitching. Casting her mind back,

Sara tried to remember the last time she'd talked to an actual younger person. It had been at least a decade. Or two.

"Cheers," she said, holding her shot glass aloft, handing the other to the kid.

"Cheers, but don't shoot it," April Veronica corrected her gently. "Treat it like a liqueur."

Raising an eyebrow, Sara brought her glass to her lips. She tasted a bouquet that had notes of orange, rose and sandalwood, all floating above the normally pungent funk of the weed. The liquid was a deep orange, opaque and swirling like oil.

"This *is* delicious, dangerously so," she said after a sip. "You make this?"

April Veronica nodded. "I will have to get the still from my old apartment at some point," she said. "I think that Eleanor is going to clear my stuff out in the next week or two. Until then, this is all we have."

"I do like it, very much. How long until I will feel the effects?"

"I say twenty minutes as a guide. You could finish this and wait twenty minutes, then decide if you want any more."

"Well, thank you for sharing, I'll definitely be partaking in the spoils from your still once you have it set up. Now, young grasshopper, is there something that you wanted to ask, before I get, wait, how do you say it? I know this." Sara made a cheeky grin. "Before I get turnt."

They both laughed and April Veronica nodded.

"I do have a question, I just don't know how to say it."

"I find blurting works best. Blurt it out and we can walk it back from there, or take it forward. Let it rip."

April Veronica set her shot glass on the coffee table and inhaled deeply, her back oddly formal and straight. "Okay. Here goes, and if you don't like it, I'm sorry. I just need to know..."

"It's fine, go on."

"I just need to know if you agreed for Marguerite to convert me because you believed in me, or were you just so tired of fighting her that you gave in?"

Boom. The words knocked the air out of Sara. The question wasn't as hard as the answer, and she struggled to come up with a starting point.

April Veronica spoke first. "I think that you've actually answered it."

Sara shook her head. "No, that's a great question, one that I've been asking myself ever since Marguerite's... murder. There's no simple answer. The short answer is both. At first, I was just exhausted, then Desdemona tried to force me into her crusade, so I got defiant. This isn't the usual process for approving a new sister."

The whole time that Sara spoke, April Veronica's face remained motionless, but her eyes revealed fear, and then disappointment. It tugged at Sara's heart.

"Don't try to make sense of this in a day, a week, or even a decade," Sara spoke softly. "Once you take the end date off life, you'll find that your mind will expand to accommodate your new timetable."

"Marguerite spoke of that the night before she... you know. And I'm excited to think of spending decades investigating the things that fascinate me."

Sara nodded. "It's cute that you're still thinking in decades."

They both laughed.

"How many instruments have you learned?"

Sara laughed again. "Do you mean how many instruments have I forgotten how to play? I've lost count. I was a decent lutenist for a while, but I've forgotten all of it."

"I don't even know what a lutenist plays," April Veronica said with a small giggle. "I don't even know if that's a real word."

Sara felt that separation of consciousness that told her the weed was working in her system. She finished her shot of orange nectar and said, in her poshest British accent. "M'dear. A lutenist plays the lute."

"Does a flutinist play the flute?"

They both burst out laughing.

"I think you're making it up," April Veronica said, wiping tears from her eyes.

"I'm not, it was a thing! They're really awful. Imagine if a harp and a guitar had a baby, and you're on the right track."

"I'll look on the internet tomorrow, I trust you."

"To get back to your question…You'll always remember some things, but other things require constant exposure. And memory is a terrible thing, a shapeshifting ghost that we try to force into a uniform shape. Our brains still only hold a finite amount of information. We retain our narrative but a lot of contemporary thought stays in its own era, discarded when it's useless."

"That was another question I had, or concept, I dunno."

"Shoot." Sara was aware that the weed was relaxing her. Arching her back, she pushed herself down into the softness of her couch.

"Well, it seems almost counterproductive: if your memory fades like a normal memory, but you can't write anything down."

"It's what you kids call mindfulness."

"Touché, but I don't think anyone could be mindful if she was simultaneously aware that the things that were important to her now would be forgotten."

"Your memory replaces things with memories of equal importance. It's a fair trade."

"But the things you've forgotten are historic!"

"Why, thank you." Sara smiled. "I recall all facts of my life. I don't have any lost time. And we *can* write things down. We can write and publish academic papers, under our temp names, and clearly we text each other, we do write. It's more of a 'leave no trace in a way that would reveal our truth to the world.'"

"So you've never kept a diary?"

The innocent question hit Sara's fuzzy brain like a mallet. She flashed back to the night months before when she did write, too much.

"Um. I keep a dayplanner. I write in it when I do normal things like go to a movie or a concert. That kind of thing is excellent for jogging the memory. But at the end of an identity, I have to burn them. I read them all, as if I'm fanning the flames of memory, trying to keep that person alive as I transition into the next identity, but it's not as important to me as it once was. I have to fight myself to keep from saying 'you'll see' all the time, but at the same time, you will see."

"And have you ever dated a sister?"

"You do have a lot of questions bottled up. Did Teddie answer that one??"

"I haven't bothered her with most of my questions."

"Oh, no wonder you're so bottled up. No. I have not dated a sister. Things go awry in all relationships. Who wants to spend eternity with an ex? Some of our sisters transferred in after relationships ended at other Locks. You're free to do it, but you should see it as I see it: A half-life applied to your time here."

April Veronica nodded. "I figured as much. I have one more. Can a trans woman be a Lock member?"

Sara nodded. "I would consider all women equally in relation to their conversion, cis or trans," she said carefully. "But I do not know if that is the position of other Locks. Some of the older Locks are much more parochial and they would insist that the tendencies that are born with cis men do not erase with hormones."

"Do you like men?"

"Did you come here to get me high and pick my brain?"

The young woman replied by nodding vigorously and rubbing her palms together like a villain.

"I do like men. I quite like the one I'm dating. This is a weird thing to even say aloud."

"So do you think every guy is inherently evil?"

"Evil's a weird word, and I don't tend to use it. I think men are men and that is one discussion. Desdemona's current crusade, and what she did to Marguerite, this is a first for us. Still, no sister has ever gone on a blood rampage, inventing torture devices and playing human suffering like a game. That's something you need to understand. It was so truly bad, what men did. That's the stakes of this discussion. It's too costly to experiment."

"Have you ever worried about what would happen if we got discovered, or if the virus was discovered?"

Sara winced at the question.

"This is the predicament we are in," she began slowly. "The earth already can't feed its entire population. Now imagine someone finds out about a virus that can extend life. Everyone would want it. It would be a disaster, and people would definitely kill for it. This is the main reason why Locks are talking about, like, ending this whole thing. We've been selfish, we've stayed alive, supporting a virus that could end modern civilization."

"Whoa," April Veronica whispered. "I didn't even think of that."

"Right, and why would you at this early stage? But for me, for us, this is where things stand. Our continued existence is a threat. I do think we need a foundational shakeup, and I think it's going to take new minds to figure it out, us elders are too entrenched in the past. There are definitely options beyond ZPG."

Sara paused, and April Veronica watched her carefully. When Sara remained silent, she stepped in.

"Do you think that would ever happen?"

"I think it will come close to happening, but there's no guarantee everyone would follow through. I don't trust Madrid. Those women behaved like the men of the old days when they came and did what they did. No discussion, no remorse."

"What about in the wild? Do you think the virus exists in nature?"

"The eastern European locks have searched for it for so long, and they've never found it. There was a rumor it came from bats, and after Covid, we've seen what that can do. So, yes; we live in fear that the virus is hanging out in a remote bat cave, or it's frozen in some permafrost in Greenland that's about to melt."

"Holy shit."

"Indeed, but you know what? We can't predict the future. We can only handle our gift with care and caution. That's really the biggest responsibility that we have. To keep the entire world safe."

"That's huge," April Veronica said. "And you sure talk good when you're high."

"It's easy to put thoughts into words when you've worried over them as long as I have. This is why we don't fux wit our rules. Is that the right use of that term?"

April Veronica laughed and nodded.

"Teddie was right, you do have a way of making sense of this life."

"She said that?"

The young woman nodded.

"Thank you for talking to me tonight, I feel much better. And Sara?"

"Yes?"

"I want to also thank you, for seeing the potential in me. I'm really excited to learn and grown with you as my Lock Mother."

"Well, enjoy it while you can"

"But you'll still be around?"

Sara paused, looking deep into this neophyte's sweet eyes.

"They're moving me to a back apartment." She laughed. "Maybe it's time for me to pick up the old lute again."

April Veronica twisted the top back off the mason jar, deftly filling the two shot glasses.

"A toast to new beginnings." She paused. "And this time, let's shoot it."

The orange liquid warmed Sara's throat as it worked its way over her tongue, floral and citrus and a flavor like a candle flame.

"This reminds me of absinthe," she said as she set her shotglass on the coffee table.

"Oh yes!" April Veronica clapped her hands. "We absolutely should get an absinthe serving set and do this properly."

"I had a gorgeous one," Sara said, "I wonder, Teddie may have kept it. It was inlaid with real gold, exquisite green glass. It might be in the crazy storage apartment. You need to have Teddie or Heather take you there."

"Teddie liked absinthe?"

Sara nodded, realizing that the newcomer had slotted Teddie into a parental role, and couldn't envisage her having fun.

"You think she's straight-edge or something?"

April Veronica shrugged. "She likes talking about the rules."

Sara nodded. "Because at your stage, the rules are very important."

"I accept that, but she has also really not liked my questions, so she seems less... fun than you? Don't tell her I said that."

"She's a lot of fun, when she's not suddenly dealing with a foster parent situation. The week before you got made she and I had a big night out in Greenpoint."

"She says it's hard to get you to go out."

"She's right." Sara inhaled deeply as the weed relaxed her further. "It's not something I currently enjoy. I'm sure I'll enjoy it again at some point. We all have cycles of being public-facing followed by a time of withdrawal. The cycles are funny and unpredictable, and they work in our favor. If one of us is a student at in-person study, or working in close proximity to other people, it's best to follow that with a period where you rarely leave this compound, or you travel to another Lock."

"What? The other Locks are like our AirBNBs?"

"It's not that easy, and the hidden charges are appalling." Sara laughed. "Like most things in this life, it's available to you, but not necessarily recommended."

"I have so much to learn."

"Yes, and the best teacher is experience. That's why we ask you to stay in for a period of years. You'll avoid the uncomfortable run-ins with people you knew, and you'll also get to learn via the oral history of each of us. You will find yourself gravitating from one of us to the next, whether it's friendship or work. Your company and something about you has engaged me more than I thought I was still capable of. This has been a very nice thing to share, so I want to thank you."

"Do you mean that or are you just really stoned?"

"I mean it, and I think I'm probably two more shots away from being really stoned. I'm at the chatty conceptual phase of marijuana intoxication. I like it here. Let's stay."

"I think you just gave me a compliment, but I'm not sure."

"I gave you a fact, kid. Wait 'til you're a couple hundred years old and a sweater in the bottom of your wardrobe reminds you of a kitten you rescued, a century earlier. And the memory arrives just like that kitten, unannounced but needing your immediate attention. You'll be tempted to then see what else you remember of that kitten or the cat that it became, and the memory will have tendrils to other things that were happening at that time. It's intoxicating, but it's important to always make new memories, to continue to dig deep and stay involved at almost a visceral level. I do think I've moved away from feeling so deeply, for maybe the last forty years. I told myself I was busy with this. Why do you think elderly people rarely seek a partner? It's just exhausting, we need a fallow time after a fertile one."

"Wow, I listen to you talk and I just get butterflies in the pit of my stomach." April Veronica smiled, stretched her arms overhead and then pulled her legs up, folding them beneath her on the couch. "But is it normal for a newcomer like myself to struggle with the rules?"

Sara shrugged. "Yes and no. It's normal for you, alarming for us. This is the hardest stretch of our existence."

"I feel like you're more open to even discussing this stuff than Teddie, and Marguerite was even worse. I heard so much man-hate from both of them, but it just sounds so sexist. I was so relieved that you said you'd admit a trans woman. It means you are doing what you all say you're doing, which is staying open minded and listening."

"I wish we could bring a reform to the rules, I really do," Sara said as an image of Silas flew across the front of her mind, his wide smile and the way his eyes crinkled. "I've talked about it, with most of the Lock, individually at some time. As we learn more and more about gender and the absolute weirdness of assigning behaviors and expectations based on a baby's genitalia, I see that we may have aged out of the legitimacy of our gender bias."

"Whoa." April Veronica crossed her eyes. "You talk like a millennial."

Chuckling as she shook her head, Sara reached over and rubbed her palm along the girls' forearm. "Kid, I've been a therapist for the past decade. I'm about to phase out of that job, but I'll return to it. I can talk the talk, but I'm not changing it for you. It's true. I was talking about intersectionality a long time ago, I tried to expand upon it last time I did psychiatry, fifty years ago.

"I've watched the evolution of women, socially, and I do not believe all men are bad. I don't believe that men born in 2030 will have the same propensity for careless violence and selfishness that men had when I was a child. I was born in brutal times. We learned only that which our parents shared, or other children. Knowledge makes people soft, and I think that we've moved past the issue of men being stronger than us. If we made a man now, all of us would be stronger than him, we could take him. But that's not the issue. Power has changed. Today, vanity is power. I've seen it wreck more women than any other scourge I can remember."

Sara paused, filling her lungs. She forgot how much she enjoyed weed, even though it made her verbose.

"Even when I was a child, seeing your reflection, accurately, was a challenge. You had to look at a still pond, or a highly polished piece of silver, and even then, I saw the bewitchery that occurred. The last twenty years have terrified me. High-definition cameras on phones, and computer applications that encourage vanity...I've never seen such a rapid decline in the human condition. Until you came along, I didn't think we'd be getting any new members until a significant social change occurs."

"I fucking hate social media," April Veronica said bitterly. "It's all lies and, you're right, vanity and hollow claims and everyone just dying to be heard. It's like a tunnel of wind and light with no substance, it's exhausting."

"And that's why you're here."

"I'm so glad I came to your door tonight."

"You tried to sneak away."

"You're formidable!"

"Still?" Sara twisted a cable of her thick dark hair in her fingertips.

"It shifted. Not in a scary way anymore, now you're just formidable in the way you kind of internalize and handle this weird life."

Sara raised her eyebrows. She looked at this elfin wanderer, a tumbleweed blown in by Marguerite's carelessness, her wide eyes constantly betraying her feelings.

"Thanks, I guess?," she said, after a long silence. "Tonight has been good for me too, I forgot that I could just shoot the shit like this. Normally, someone needs me to do something, or I have to referee an argument. It's not fun. Tonight has been fun."

"Well, that's fucking awesome!" April Veronica reached for the mason jar, and Sara raised her arm, blocking her.

"I'm high enough, kid. And I do need to get to sleep soon."

"I have one more question..."

"Shoot."

"Are you staying Lily Berger for the new guy?"

Sara glanced at the woman sitting at the opposite end of the couch. If Teddie hadn't put her up to this question, she was sharper than Sara anticipated.

"I mean, if he wasn't in the picture, I could just slip into a new persona, so yeah, because of him, I'll stay Lily Berger for a bit longer."

"So you like him?"

The blush that came blooming up her spine colored her face before she knew it. There was no point to lying.

"Yeah, I do. It's nice. It hasn't felt like this for…" Ever? Her mind asked. "…a long while."

"I'm happy for you, and on that note," the younger woman uncurled her legs and leapt to her feet in a feline motion. "I'm not as nocturnal as you, and unless you want me to sleep on your couch again, I need to get back to my own bed."

"I could fall asleep very quickly right now," Sara said, standing and walking to the door. "April Veronica, thank you for such an unexpected pleasure. I look forward to many more visits. I want to hear about you. I'm afraid I did all the talking tonight, and that just ain't right."

"Au contraire." The young woman wrapped Sara in a hug. "I asked all the questions, and you were very honest."

"How long does it take you to make that demon nectar?"

April Veronica chuckled. "I have to get the still out of my old apartment. It takes about a week, but tonight's brew was a special one, it took a long time. I'll get it started for you."

The young woman screwed the cap onto the mason jar and held it out to Sara.

"Keep the rest, Sara," she said earnestly. "I'm good with my edibles 'til I can make some more."

Sara took the jar almost solemnly, enjoying the feel of it in her palms.

"I can't wait 'til you tell Heather that wine is an old lady's drink."

"Oh god, please don't tell her then, let it be our secret."

Sara extended her little finger. "Pinky swear."

April wrapped her finger around Sara's. "Pinky swear. Okay boss, it's good night from me."

She bowed, stepped backward out the door and pulled it closed with her.

Sara shucked her clothes as she passed the couch, leaving them where they fell. She climbed into her bed, her huge, comfy, springy, decadent bed, gathering up the down comforter around her like a cloud, and lay there in the gossamer New York darkness, an unfamiliar optimism raising the corners of her mouth, even as she drifted into slumber.

Chapter Twenty-Eight

"Good morning, beautiful!"

The male voice in Sara's ear was almost as surprising as the fact that her phone was already smooshed between the pillow and her face.

"Muh... uh..."

"Sara, are you okay?"

Silas! Clutching her phone to her ear, Sara struggled to sit up in bed, her lower half caught in a wild tumble of bedding.

"Hey, I was sleeping, good morning to you too," she managed, her voice dusty.

"How did you call me if you were asleep?"

Now she was awake.

"I called you? I just woke up with you talking into my ear."

Silas's rusty gate chuckle sounded dirty and amused at the same time.

"Well, that explains the missed calls. I figured you were out jogging and butt-dialing me."

"Jogging, lol." Sara's brow was furrowed. "Look, I have a confession."

"Uh oh."

"I got wasted on some newfangled weed drink with the new girl, and I slept like a stone."

"Good, you needed it," Silas said. "But also, bad, your phone is a liability. I'm gonna text you an app so we can talk securely?"

"Signal?"

"Uh, yeah. Why?"

"We use it, but I'm only supposed to use it for talking about, you know, stuff."

"But you never used it with me."

"Not yet. I prefer to talk vaguely than securely."

"Call me back on Signal, Sara. No need for any additional risks."

He made a noise that may have been a blown kiss and was gone. Scrolling through screens of apps that she vowed to organize every time she did this, she found the button to launch, and called him right back. He answered before it rang.

"That's better. Now let's talk about being secret vampires in lust."

"In lust, huh?" Sara tossed the sheets off and stood, gazing at herself in the mirror by the door, her hair a tangled nest, dark circles under her eyes ."If you could see me now, you'd find me a very effective cold spoon."

"Tell me more," Silas whispered. "What did you wear to bed?"

"Nothin'," Sara laughed. "At least I didn't sleep on the couch. I feel decidedly twentysomething."

"I wish I was there to see it."

"Be grateful for small mercies."

"Sara, I can't wait to wake up next to you."

"I can't wait to throw down on a real bed." She laughed. "We still leaving Friday?"

"Why yes we are," he said, excitement rising in his voice. "What time would work for you in terms of a pickup?"

"You'll have to get me from the Murray Hill apartment. I'm gonna be busy with lots of loose ends to tie up. I'm stepping down as Mother, which is good. Just involves lots of heavy lifting."

"You're a fast worker."

"Or, I should have done this fifty years ago. I'm a little nervous, and Silas, it's so significant. I've been the captain of this tiny little ship for over a hundred years. It's a lot of weird. But I had such a great time with April Veronica last night. She made me feel both optimistic and hopelessly out of touch."

"It really is hard being a five-hundred-year-old millennial."

"Ha ha," Sara said drily. "I wish you could meet her. She's just the freshest mind I've been around. If Teddie turns me down, I'm tempted to offer the leadership role to her, really shake shit up."

"Teddie would flip."

"They'd all flip. They are all in such ruts, with routines that they love and never want to break."

"And you need a break. We are going to a farmhouse by a lake. No people for at least a mile. I'll bring massage oils and all the things that we will need. All you have to bring is clothes for the drive there and back."

"What about when we are there?"

"You won't need clothes."

She smiled at his relentless flirtatiousness. It felt comfortable and warm, not gross or abrasive.

"Okay, Captain Hornypants, I'm going to hurl myself into a scalding shower and put my big girl pants on and get shit done so I can pack and get down to the apartment. I'll text you when I get there."

"From this app?"

"Yes, narc. From this app."

"Oh, and Sara, before you go?"

"Yes?" She grinned, expecting more double entendre. "

"Can you see if you can get some of that hipster weed drank? It sounds like fun."

"I kept the dregs." She laughed and hung up, holding the phone in her hand, weighing whether to look now or after she showered. A glance at the clock above the stove made her gasp. It was after ten. She rarely slept past seven. Demon weed indeed. She had to look at her messages.

Get into the habit of silence.

Heather texted at 5am. Sara groaned. This meant that outsider contractors were coming on premises to do work, probably on security stuff, and the sistren all had to wear nun outfits and remain silent in public areas.

There were a few texts from Eleanor, Yukari and Fran, plus a happy meme that she didn't understand from Liz. They were pleasant, friendly texts, which usually meant they'd be asking for something by lunchtime. There weren't any texts from Teddie, which was slightly unusual, and Sara chided herself for not actually knowing if Teddie had work today or not. Turning the water on in the shower with her left hand, she punched out a quick text to Teddie with her right.

Wanna take our nasty habits out for lunch?

She darted to her kitchen, shaking six heems onto her palm, pausing, then shaking two more from the bottle. Before the incident with Laura, she often went days without taking a single pill, and now she was taking at least twenty daily, just to stay normal. She promised herself that in the coming weeks she would actively detox, once these crises passed.

Spoken like a true addict.

Swallowing the pills down angrily, she moved to the bathroom. As she waited for the water to heat up, she heard replies come in as she stepped under water that really was a little too hot for her skin. She relished it. Of all the things that she'd come to love about progress, nothing could beat hot water coming out of the wall in your home. Oh, and flush toilets. Better than electricity, any day. Forcing her head beneath the faucet, she let the water run over her hair, feeling little zings when the jets hit her scalp directly, her thick black hair writhing snakes down her back. Oh god, she was still high. Was she? Could she be? She decided *not* to ask April Veronica; she already felt square enough.

Tipping her head back so she could see, she quickly lathered herself from head to toe without stepping out of the shower's warm deluge. She felt ironically exuberant, given the fact that she was about to dress in a scratchy old nun's habit for the day.

Stepping out of the tub, she flicked the screen of her phone. Good news, Teddie was available for "Sister Act 2: The Brunch" and would be at her door in around an hour. Sara busied herself with hair drying and very light makeup application, then moved to her computer, in its nook under the spiral stairs. She hit the on button, then made herself a Nespresso while she waited for it to boot. She couldn't remember the last time she had even turned it on.

Oh.

She inhaled sharply. She hadn't touched it since the night she stupidly word-vomited and broke every rule in the book.

"Calm down, sister," she said, blowing on the top of her espresso shot, thinking she should pour it over ice, anything to get it into her system faster. First, she needed to delete that file. Tucking a strand of hair behind her ear, she settled in at the screen, clicking around with her mouse until she found the file, hidden away where she hid all her files. She dragged it to the trash without opening it, shaking her head at how juvenile she had been that night, just months earlier.

Her relationship with Silas was something that she could never have predicted that night. She would need to mask up for her lunch with Teddie, downplaying everything about it except the thrill of sex. Teddie had wanted her to get laid. She could hardly complain now that was happening.

The little red bubble on her mail program icon told her that she had five hundred and sixty-eight unopened emails. A quick glance over the inbox titles told her that it was all clinic related, mostly about whether she was ever coming back. She quickly wrote an email detailing a serious family illness that would require her to leave New York City for an extended period. With a pang of guilt, she messaged her remaining patients, explaining the situation and offering referrals. Every time she had ended an identity, she went through this and it never got easier. Suddenly, she knew with conviction that this would be her last incarnation as a psychiatrist, and that came with another sharp realization. Once again, she'd been selfish. Was that endemic to the lifestyle of a sister? The old ways really were no longer applicable. Maybe she could work with Teddie on some long-overdue improvements to the way the Lock operated.

She wrote to the building manager, giving notice on her office space. After answering the essential questions from sundry other business acquaintances, she paused to sip her coffee, now cooled and delicious.

A quick call to Heather revealed that the workmen coming on premises were indeed focusing on a new security system. They would be clambering all over the central building, the one with the entrance on West End. The one she currently lived in.

Moving to her bedroom, she retrieved the nun habit from the hanger in her wardrobe. Once it was on, she decided to complement it with gray, threadbare socks and the ugliest black nursing shoes she owned. Fewer people approached a nun that looked down and out. Tucking her hair carefully in her wimple, she clipped on the face covering that was a trademark of their silent order, leaving only her eyes uncovered. She'd wear some cheap old readers that she'd had since the eighties, with automatic darkening lenses. She called in a pickup order to Absolute Bagel – Rueben for Teddie, salmon for her, two waters, one pickle – then decided to use the remaining free time to pack a bag for the weekend.

Huge mistake.

Two decades of not dating had rendered her wardrobe a patchwork fashion quilt slash literal disaster area.

After lunch, she'd relocate to the Murray Hill apartment and do some shopping in SoHo. She needed a haircut, so she texted Liz to see if she had time to do it since hair salons were off limits—beauticians paid too much attention to faces. Liz replied immediately, saying that tomorrow morning was peachy. Sara continued to take inventory. All of her makeup needed replacing, and all twenty of her nails needed help.

A mani-pedi was an absolute necessity before the weekend, but the rule of thumb for such things was that it had to happen "off-island" – she usually took the train out to Hoboken or Jersey City. Getting ready for a weekend away was going to be a full-time job.

Annoyed at the stresses of dating, she felt increasingly unsettled. Moving to her record player, she flicked the power on, thumbing quickly through the favorite LPs she kept on her shelf top, pausing when she came to Roland Kirk's Rip Rig And Panic, ring wear on the cover, its spine split wide open. If anything could kick her into the here and now, it was that. She slid the vinyl out of its worn sleeve, carefully dropping the needle onto the surface and smiling broadly as the first atonal skronks of saxophone filled the room.

Seventy something years ago, Teddie took her to see Kirk at the Village Vanguard, both of them in wigs and dark sunglasses, a memory that never faded with age. They spent the night laughing like children, in between sets of jazz so intoxicating she had chased the high ever since, haunting the clubs of the Village, and then the Bowery. Music was her life, from early on, playing the dulcimer, to opera in the great houses of Europe, then to America, where she fell in with gospel clubs in Harlem, the bluesmen in speakeasies, and the happenings of the sixties. They all felt like they existed at once, at her fingertips. The first time she loaded music from all of her life onto one gadget, an iPod, she wept at having so much magic readily available to her. The music from the speakers swelled, filling the air with soul and life.

Just sit down, she told herself, somewhat officiously, so she did. A few minutes of box breathing, five in, hold five, five out, hold five, and she was clear, lost in the music and not thinking about the women she took care of, and only thinking of Silas briefly, banishing each reappearance like a gauzy cloud on the shore. Now breathing deeply and evenly, she felt peace in her heart, her limbs feeling heavy, her body getting heavier against her ancient couch. A knock at the door, Teddie, didn't surprise her. She could have set an alarm for it. She didn't get up. Teddie had a key, which she heard sliding into the lock.

"Girl, you breakin' out the Roland Kirk?"

Opening her eyes slowly, she saw Teddie's shining eyes and broad smile headed her way in a sea of black and white.

"Wait – did you go glam nun or Payless shoes nun?" Sara craned her neck over the back of the sofa. Teddie was wearing black Chanel buckle flats and opaque tights that Sara knew were pure silk.

"I can't with those things." She nodded at Sara's shoes. "Nobody's gonna notice."

"If those shoes lure in some crazy rich lady seeking benediction, it's on you. I don't feel like blessing anyone today."

"Where are we headed?"

"It's so beautiful out," Sara said. "We have an order for pickup at Absolute Bagel, then I figure we can go sit up by the Cloisters." Teddie's face lit up.

"My favorite things all at once."

"The Cloisters is closed today..." Sara laughed, raising the cross around her neck. "But I know a guy."

Sunlight spilled across the courtyard of the venerable art museum. Bumble bees bounced from flower to flower, their legs dripping pollen, and the scent of sage filled the air. Settling onto a stone bench, Sara opened the paper carryout bag, setting Teddie's wrapped bagel on the bench beside her.

"Thanks, mom." Teddie smiled. She looked around. "This place is such a headfuck. It's like a time machine to the way things were."

Sara nodded, knowing exactly what her friend meant.

"It must be worse for you," Teddie continued. "You lived through all this, for real." With a shrug, Sara unwrapped her bagel. "Buildings don't trigger me much anymore. It's just a pile of stones. It's been what? How many years since I was in London or Rome or Paris. If anything it just smells of sand and earth. If I push it, sure, it could be the London abbey."

"Interesting," Teddie said. "Everything still triggers me."

Sara reached out and took her hand. "You've had a rough couple centuries."

"Me less so than others like me," Teddie said, squeezing her hand once and letting go.

"April Veronica was delightful last night," Sara said. "I'm still getting over it."

"She fucked you up good, huh?"

"I'm a lightweight."

"Drinks weed once, craves jazz and bagels."

"Guilty."

"She's amazing, isn't she?"

"She is," Sara paused between bites of her bagel, reflecting. "I haven't interacted deeply with her generation at all and to be fair, I think I was developing dismissive opinions around them. That's stupid - the only person that it damages is me."

"The young are always a key to their times," Teddie said. "I believe a wise woman once told me that when I felt like I couldn't connect with the young folks of the... what was it? The 1920s?"

"In hindsight, they *were* a fluffy-headed lot, you may have been right." Sara chuckled, happy to see a smile reach Teddie's eyes. Her dearest friend shrugged and ate her food in silence.

"I brought you here for a reason," Sara began.

"You want to know if I want the j-o-b?"

"In a nutshell," Sara said, unsurprised by Teddie's insight.

"Sure," she said. "I'm sorry I acted ungrateful."

"You didn't. If someone *didn't* hesitate before accepting the role of Lock Mother, I'd be worried."

"I've wanted to offer to take it over from you for so long, but – and I'm guilty about this – every time I've gotten close, something in me has rebelled against the adulting. Every decade brings a new distraction."

"And they always will," Sara said, taking a bite of her bagel.

"True dat." Teddie smiled. "But I can't put off adulting forever."

"And as a parent, that's all I've ever wanted for you."

Teddie set her bagel down on its paper wrap and took Sara's hand.

"You've been too good to me. It's time I repaid you. And it's time you had a century or two to yourself."

"I won't go anywhere. I want to stick around and help you. This job can really wear you down."

"If you let it, mom. I think the women will have a rough time adjusting to me. The word no is a full sentence. You rarely use it. It's gonna be my first response."

"In my defense, Theodora, I have tried. I have tried repeatedly, and as you'll see, no turns into a snowball that rolls unchecked, and before you know it, you have a messy situation and bruised egos and usually a feud that can last a generation, or result in another tiresome Lock switcheroo. All of those things are usually more work than saying yes to the original request."

"You're not stepping down because of the man, are you?"

Something in Teddie's tone struck a note of alarm in Sara's gut. Quickly quashing it, she pitched her voice as innocently as she could muster at short notice.

"Not because of the man, no." She paused, picking at a leaf on her habit. "But the man was definitely a catalyst to shining a light onto just how deep the toxic codependency between me and the Lock had become."

"Interesting. How so?"

"I was just really tunnel vision on being Lock Mother. Truthfully it's a job that I complain about but have loved. And then, against all odds, a stranger got under my skin. I thought I had all the edges tamped down, that nobody could invade me. And somehow, he did. And then, and this is new for me, I wanted to toss all my responsibility in the air and be a free spirit."

"So, you think this guy will last the full four years?" Teddie held the last bite of her bagel in front of her face, something she'd done all her life when she wanted to hide the serious set of her face.

Sara shrugged. "Who knows? I know the tidal wave of emotions that come after a long period of abstinence from talking to new people."

"And fuckin' them."

Sara nodded. "Amen sister."

"Oh he good." Teddie smiled, the tension vanishing from her voice.

"He is good," Sara said, "At sex, if that's what you're asking. But he's also nice to talk to."

"Oh, she loves a talker," Teddie said with a laugh. "Do you remember that weirdo you dated in the forties? These days, we would have realized he was probably Asperger's or on the spectrum in some way. That one time we all went to a supper club and he talked the whole night? I wanted to stab him in the throat to shut him up."

"I found him charming! He was a scientist at NYU."

"He was a crushing bore. Is this one a bore? He looked like a hipster."

"I don't like broad strokes," Sara said, finding it harder to keep her tone light, knowing it was becoming more important with every question. "He's kind of a depressed nerd. He's not a hipster. He doesn't have beehives on his roof, he doesn't use artisanal beard wax and he hasn't forced me to listen to Radiohead."

"Well, bullet dodged then." Teddie's tone softened. "Look, mum. I'm happy to step in and run this shizz, and I'm happy to do it forever, or as long as I want, and I'm also okay with doing it while you're off playing happy families. I mean, you can have the job back at the end of this relationship."

"No, Teddie. That's not rules. The rules are, I step down, someone else steps up, and after they're tired, someone new steps in. It's healthy for the Lock, and it's aspirational. You've been like my sous-chef this whole time. You'll be a great Lock mother."

"Thanks, mom." Teddie finished her bagel. "Wanna walk around the gardens? I love it here when it's deserted."

"Sure." Sara stood, brushing crumbs from the front of her ridiculous habit. "I hate this thing, have I ever told you?"

"You may have mentioned it once or twice."

"It's like wearing a heat-attracting tent. I'm schvitzing so badly and it's only spring."

"Did you consider giving the job to anyone else?"

Sara was accustomed to Teddie's quick-switch interrogations and she saw this one coming. She also knew the only way to handle it was with blunt honesty.

"Of course, Ted. And let's face it. In some ways, Heather is the backbone of the whole Lock."

"She loves what she does."

"She is happy in her lane. I've kind of playfully bounced the idea at her, and she's playfully bounced it right back."

"So who else?"

"Fran could do it if she could just toughen up a little, but we need her where she is. Clearly our security needs to stay up to speed with modern technology. She loves that stuff, so it's best for all of us if she stays where she is, for now. And last night, for five glorious minutes, I entertained the absurd notion of asking April Veronica."

Teddie stopped in her tracks in front of an azalea folding under the weight of its cascade of scarlet blossoms.

"You are fucking kidding me."

"Girl, I was high and she was saying something that I can't even recall that made me think, just for a minute, that maybe this whole thing needs a shot of new blood."

"Bitch, you were so tripping."

"Maybe, but don't be so quick to count her out."

"Sara, she is so new to this. Of course she's full of new ideas and vision for the future. She hasn't lived a constrained life. She will see ways around all the rules, she will probably also want to open the doors to men. She hasn't seen the wreckage that men create, centuries of it."

"She's seen thirty years of it," Sara said brusquely. Turning slowly, she placed her palms on Teddie's shoulders. "You asked who I considered, and the full answer included everyone that crossed my mind."

Teddie pulled a face like a child.

"There's funny and then there's bullshit, Sara. Another thing I was wondering is, why isn't there a rule for like the length of time a person must live this life before they can run a Lock?"

"We have enough rules. The rest of our reality is governed by logic and learning."

"Well, I wouldn't have let you nominate April Veronica."

Sara cocked her head.

"Not to pull rank, Ted, but if I decide that it's for the best, then my decision would stand. And also, your quick anger right now is something that you'll need to work on ahead of taking the job."

Teddie blinked angrily and breathed deeply. "I'm sorry. I know."

"Staying even-keeled is the hardest part of the job. Not holding grudges. Listening to boring problems. Not reacting from your own needs, but trying to see many needs, many sets of feelings, and remain separate. It's draining beyond imagining. It's also selfless, by design. I hadn't ever reflected on it but clearly, I transitioned into a selfless life because in the walls of our home, that's what I had to be. I wasn't good at separating my work and my life, and here we are."

"I'm sorry I cracked your ass."

"I didn't even notice. When we get home, I expect the same from at least half the sisters. Nobody is happy at the moment."

"When do you plan to announce your retirement?"

"Everybody already knows. You know the way they talk. I can send a text. Do you want a ceremony, or do you just wanna get on with business?"

"It's too soon after Marguerite for a party. I know I'd feel weird. Just send the text, I guess."

Sara pulled out her phone, fished around for Signal then sent a very brief text.

Just to confirm the gossip that you've all been spreading, Theodora is now Lock Mother. I'm off to my retirement village in Boca.

Teddie laughed as she read the text on her own phone.

"You're such a dork."

"Never said I wasn't." They both slipped their phones back into the pockets of their habits.

"Will you move to the Murray Hill apartment?"

"Yes, and I doubt anyone has ever been so excited about Murray Hill."

Now it was Teddie's turn to freeze.

"Wait a goddamned minute," she said. "You're going Scholar?"

Sara's patience was surprisingly thin all of a sudden.

"Theodora, your tone! And yes, it's looking likely."

Sensing she'd gone too far, Teddie resumed walking in silence.

"This is why I kept on telling you to have meaningless sex."

"I've forgotten more meaningless sex than you have ever had, kid. You forget I had my wild times in Europe. You told me to take a lover. Don't guilt me for taking him."

"I'm just not good with change. I did the kid thing. I expected you to be a parental unit, not a human being. I'm sorry. I really am."

"Can we please stop the serious shit and go get a gelato and walk all the way home along the river?"

Teddie threw her arms around Sara and hugged her, as hard as she could.

"I love you, mom," she said. "Thanks, for everything ever, and for believing in me right now. And I'd like nothing more."

Chapter Twenty-Nine

A warm breeze rich in earth and jasmine fluttered the white gauze curtain, its motion startling Sara, snapping her back from a reverie so broad and potent she couldn't remember its origin. Shaking her head gently, she gazed out the window, over a still expanse of lake ringed with trees in the distance, irises blooming at their feet. She was in a farmhouse, as promised, rustic on the outside, renovated to within an inch of its life on the inside. She could hear Silas puttering about somewhere in the house below her, and felt torn about joining him or indulging herself with more solo time.

During the long drive upstate, she'd been transfixed by verdant fields, rivers, flowers by the roadside. She regretted the hundred or so springtimes that she'd missed, huddled inside the compound. She also felt naked and far from her security blanket, realizing she'd become borderline agoraphobic without even noticing it, the rhythms and tumult of the City meshing deeply within her, giving her a sense of comfort and place.

Since arriving at the farmhouse, the tension building inside her had only increased. Silas, thoughtfully and gently, showed her around, and then, sensing her rising unease, suggested that she set up in the upstairs bedroom and have some alone time while he put everything away.

The root of her discomfort was a persistent train of thought that always ended the same way, with Silas uncovered and her Lock in rebellion against her. No matter the variables, that equation always ended with both of them dead. Then came the guilt about putting Teddie directly in Desdemona's line of fire. Then came the general worry about her future, or lack thereof.

Breaking off the reverie before she had a panic attack, she lay back on the cloud-like bed, rolling herself in the soft white comforter until she felt calmer, restrained, and tried to breathe in a pattern, hoping for sleep.

Which didn't come.

Angrily, she wriggled out of her tangled bedding and opened her small suitcase, gazing sadly at its contents. Instead of shopping for her getaway, she'd spent the past days in meetings with Teddie and Heather, as well as physically closing down her shrink space, taking all her books and plants in cab after cab to the Murray Hill flat. Her life had gone from zero to sixty and the road was icy.

Blinking away dark thoughts, she lifted up a black silk Alaïa slip dress that Teddie had given her as a gift many years ago. She'd worn it maybe twice, never in public, enthralled at the way it caressed her body. Tossing it onto the bed, she sought out matching black lingerie, eyeing the gift box from Agent Provocateur that Heather gave her that morning..

"In for a penny," she said aloud, the wooden house echoing her voice. She missed the silence of the heavy brick building she'd lived in for so long.

Stepping out of her jeans, then pulling her t-shirt over her head, she stood naked in front of the window, feeling the breeze across her whole body, closing her eyes, fighting off rapid flash memories of Romania, France and Spain, different times of her life when she did this kind of thing much more often.

"Get it together, Sara," she whispered, opening the box of lingerie and unwrapped the tissue paper. She smiled at the tasteful black bra and panties, satin with small embroidered bluebells at the hips and between the breasts. She stepped into the panties, but decided to save the bra for another time, pulling the dress over her head, feeling it slide down over her goosebumps. A shiver started at her feet, then rustled all the way to her scalp.

Moving to the bathroom in the hallway, she stared at herself, dark hair tousled from the attempts at sleep, her face pale, dominated by dark lashes and full lips still perfectly done in a dusky rose. The smell of whatever Silas was cooking drifted to her nose and her stomach groaned in response; she was starving. Quickly pinching each cheek for color, she turned for the staircase.

"Hello, beautiful." Silas's voice floated up from across the room, causing her to pause. In a lifetime dedicated to being unremarkable, compliments were infrequent at best, and this one hit the mark.

Consciously softening her voice, she replied.

"Something smells amazing, what is it?"

"Come over and see," he said, coming into view as she reached the bottom of the staircase. He was shirtless, behind a kitchen counter, a mountain of chopped vegetables on a cutting board in front of him, something bubbling in a cast iron pan on the stove behind him. As she crossed the living room, her feet padding across the heavy oak floorboards, she felt his eyes on her and again that weird disparate sensation of discomfort and lust, overtaken by a now-familiar burst of irresponsibility.

"You're struggling," Silas said, setting his knife onto the cutting board and coming around the counter. "Anything I can do to help?"

She stopped walking maybe five feet from him, her head down, shrugging.

"This is overwhelming. Lovely, perfect and overwhelming," she said, still unable to meet his eyes.

"I know, and I'm really grateful you're here," he said, his voice quiet. "Can I show you something?"

She nodded, and he took her hand, gently leading her to the living room doors, a double glass arrangement that led onto an enclosed covered deck that extended out over the shore of the lake. Swallows dipped and trailed their wings along the water's surface, the tiny ripples shattering the mirrored reflection of the sky.

Silas bent and snatched a folded towel from a basket, then led her out, down some stairs and along a stone path that ended at a wooden jetty extending out into the lake. The old wood was smooth and worn beneath her feet and she gazed from side to side, drinking in the beauty of her surroundings, the blue of the sky, the pond weed and little fish in the clear water.

At the end of the jetty, Silas refolded the towel, placing it at her feet. Holding her hand as she sat, he waited until she was sorted before he sat beside her, releasing her hand and, she noticed, not taking it again once he was seated.

"I feel so overdressed," she said.

"How does one dress for Mother Nature?"

"Good point." Sara chuckled. "Hey Mother Nature, this is vintage Alaïa!"

In the distance, a loon called out.

"She approves," said Silas. "So, do you want to talk about how you are feeling? Or would it help to be silent? Whatever you need, I'm here for it."

"Thank you," Sara said, reaching for his hand, happy when he squeezed hers in return. "I've never had an honest relationship with a man. And I'm putting you in danger."

"I pursued you, and you feel like it's your fault?"

"Ding ding ding."

"Don't be worried about me," he said. "Seriously. I've gotten myself out of situations a lot riskier than this."

"Well, I haven't." Sara turned to face him. "I care about you, and I know that you are risking more than I know, just for this. And..." Her voice faltered. "Every scenario that I run though in my mind ends the same way."

Opening her hand with his, he traced a finger on her palm.

"What if there are other options?" Silas cleared his throat. "Sara, when I can tell you everything, I will. And because you don't have all the information, sure, you only see one ending to this story. In my mind, our story has multiple endings and a large number of them are happy."

"I'm not good at blind faith."

"Who is?" Silas smiled.

"I forget that we are still a young relationship."

He nodded. "We are getting to know one another."

"Essentially," she said, her voice raspy. "With an almost unbearable weight above us."

"Yes, and no," he said. "I admit we are at a disadvantage, given my..."

"Stalking?"

He didn't chuckle, and she wondered if she had gone too far.

"I like to call it caretaking," he said. "Watching, maybe, but only in the sense that I watched over you. I watched over many of the Locks in the world, in between periods of doing... I dunno, other stuff."

"What do you mean, other stuff? And how did you find the Locks?"

"First the other stuff. I did what you did. I studied. I learned. I traveled, and yes, I had a lot more freedom than you, physically at least. Once I discovered that all Locks are based in nunneries, it's not too hard to figure out which one is chock full of vampires."

She laughed. "You realize that Lock Mothers around the world would die of shock, knowing that they'd been spied on by a cursed male."

"I do."

"And you've never been caught?"

She felt his fingertip pause on her palm.

"I do have something to tell you," he said, pausing as their dark eyes locked. "I did almost get found out. I'm... uh... I'm the guy that caused the dissolution of the San Francisco Lock."

"No!"

"I had to do it, Sara." Silas's eyes narrowed. "One of the women was dating someone, and I trailed him."

"Is that what you did? You stalked Lock members and their men?"

"Don't ask me to justify how I used my time," he said softly. "I have lived a solitary life for five centuries. So I basically did wellness checks on Lock security. And if I see a guy hanging around the nunnery a few days after I see him on a date with a sister, of course, I do a deeper watch, and that's what happened."

Sara relaxed, and Silas went on.

"At first, I thought that the guy might have been like me, another survivor of the purge."

"Have you ever met another male survivor?"

Silas nodded, looking out over the lake.

"After the purge, there were a few of us, but we hid from one another. Sara...the sisters tortured the men they caught, before they killed them."

"Those men built lives on torture and killing. It's hard to feel compassion."

"Never have I killed."

"I know. I wouldn't be here if I didn't believe that one."

"You also would feel differently about your women-only rule if you saw how well those women adjusted to torturing a living human."

"They were just wrapping up loose ends," Sara said defensively.

"Sara, they enjoyed it."

She shuddered, struggling to unpack the information. Silas waited for her to speak, then gave up, resuming his answer.

"Back then, I followed some of the men, as they tried to start new lives. One by one, they returned to preying on humans. So I left clues, incriminations, for the avenging sisters to find. And as far as I know, they were all wiped out."

"So you're like some sort of stealth vampire avenger?"

"The one fault of the Lock structure is that it's inward-facing, by nature. Insular, self-absorbed, and take this the right way, a little cocky. Just by looking frumpy, dowdy, not wearing makeup, being unmemorable...it's not enough. It works fine, most of the time, but that's ending. Surveillance cameras and the fact that nothing dies on the internet is a perfect storm for all the Locks of the world."

"Do you think we aren't aware?"

"Not at all, but you can't deny there's a level of complacency. The San Francisco thing was forty years ago. They were sloppy, and they almost got caught. Your Lock sisters are the same as sisters the world over. You all cheat a little bit. It's human nature."

"Silas, this is why I'm uncomfortable here. You clearly have an agenda, and also, it feels like I'm getting in trouble."

"I do have an agenda, Sara. I want to talk to you, I want us to be open and to communicate and I want to just once feel like I'm sharing my truth with someone. I hedged my bets on this for longer than you know. And the way you were going, you'd get found out, and they'd push you into Surrender. I don't need your confession, that's your business. But I'm sure you've broken other rules, before the not-killing-me one. Do you think they'd ask you for a Ted talk on it?"

Sara gulped. Visualizing the tribunal that would befall her always froze her blood, mainly because it was ugly and violent, and she died at the end. Just hearing the words spoken aloud, by a man, in public, sent a spike of panic through her.

"You're so comfortable talking like this," was all she could manage.

"There's nobody within miles of us; this entire lake is on private property. I'll stop if it makes you upset."

"It just makes me feel sloppier."

"Please, Sara, you've been a literal masterclass of Lock stewardship. There's not a Lock on earth that has managed to bend with the times like the New York one. You have doubled down on tech, science, and security."

"How do you know?"

"Because I've also doubled down on tech, science and security. That's why I'm being so open with you. Sooner or later, all the traditional Locks will all be threatened."

Sara gazed out over the lake. It was getting harder to remain neutral with what Silas was saying; these were conversations she would have to have with Heather, with Fran, maybe even with Eleanor.

"You and I are being honest with each other, but I am being deeply dishonest about this relationship, mainly to Teddie," she said.

"More dishonest than you've been about your blood consumption?"

As soon as the words were out of his mouth, hanging in the air like something dead and rotten, Silas saw he'd said the wrong thing. Sara jumped to her feet and took off back along the deck, her feet leaping from stone to stone on the path, tall grass whipping her bare legs as she sped past. She listened for his footsteps following her, but all she heard was the flat puff of the soles of her own feet on the smooth river stones.

Passing the farmhouse, she kept going, following the path along the curve of the lake's bank until she reached a gnarled old tree, its trunk split in two by lightning, a thick branch extending out over the water. She leaped up onto the branch effortlessly and walked along its curved surface. It didn't bend or move under her weight. Glancing back, she saw the house was lost behind a curtain of tumbled greens. She willed her breathing to slow, centering herself, focusing on the beauty around her.

"What the hell is wrong with you?" she whispered, feeling suddenly foolish and flighty. If Silas was right, the entire Lock system was vulnerable, and the time was indeed coming where Locks could no longer exist. This whole existence was in its end stages, she realized, disappointed in herself that she had been too smug to see it clearly.

A noise from along the path turned into Silas's black hair, and then all of him, emerging from the emerald thicket.

"Hey," he said, his voice deep but gentle. "I overstepped. I shouldn't have said that. Would you like me to give you some space?"

"It wasn't even that,' Sara began. She paused. "No, wait, it was that. I'm super aware of the dishonesty in my life, and it's always been hard to lie, to Teddie, to Heather, to any of them. It was frankly just a lot to hear it from someone else's mouth..."

"Especially a man?"

"Especially a man. Still, it wasn't a trigger so much as a final straw. You just casually dropped one hell of a truth bomb, that the old ways are about to die. And I look at you, you've somehow managed to live as long as I have, without a support network, and for some reason you're risking it all for me? Silas, I'm not worth it."

Taking just one step forward, Silas stopped, his arms hanging limply.

"Two things. I get to decide what's worth it, for myself. And even if this is stupidly doomed, it's worth it, so worth it, for..." he paused, changing direction. "And, what you're going through is a lot more common than you realize. I would guarantee that at least half of your Lock gets plasma on the side."

A breeze off the lake rippled across the sweat on Sara's chest and she shivered.

"Silas..." she spoke through chattering teeth. "That's a huge thing, if it's true. These things you say, so casually, they rip away a veil over my entire existence, and they make me feel stupid for not seeing them all along. That is and was my job, to oversee a group of women, keep them fed and safe and working for a peaceful existence."

"And you excelled at it. The rest of it is forest and trees. No way you could have known."

Tears shocked Sara, flooding over her lower lids and rolling down her face.

"What the fuck? I'm not crying, what is this?"

Silas took another step forward.

"You're exhausted," he said quietly. Sara blinked and looked away, wishing that the flood would stop. "Would you like me to give you a moment?"

She shrugged again.

"No, not really, this is a conversation I need to have, and you… you're literally the only person I can have it with."

"I have an idea." Silas stepped beside her. "No more observations from me. I've been rushing the info at you, but I'm trying to make you feel better. And clearly, that's not how it's working."

Sara's fingers fumbled forwards, taking Silas's hands in hers.

"I don't know what I'm doing," she said, her voice breaking.

"Spoiler, no one does," he said, kissing the top of her head, then wrapping his arms around her shoulders, warming her instantly.

"Do you do reassurance?"

"Not when it involves lying."

She raised her face to his.

"Maybe we can work on that?"

He nodded. "Sure. But first, dinner?"

Chapter Thirty

The face in the mirror was almost what Sara and her makeup kit had envisioned when she set out to do her face. Neither Teddie nor Imani responded to her texts for advice, and YouTube tutorials made the difficult look easy without improving the results. Still, her deep plum lipstick was in the right place, and while her attempt at a smoky eye looked a lot more like seventies punk she didn't hate it.

As usual, her thick raven hair had its own agenda, so she tied it back with a ribbon in a low, loose ponytail. Glancing in the mirror, she made a gagging sound. She looked like a goth schoolteacher. Angrily she snatched the ribbon from around her hair, which instantly ballooned out into an angular fright wig. Why had she not packed a hair dryer? Wait – did Airbnbs come with hair dryers?

Bouncing off the bed in her new bra and panties, she skipped into the hallway bathroom, and there inside the vanity drawer was a brand-new hair diffuser, still in its box. Powering it on, she ran her fingers through her hair, gently pulling on the ends then flattening it with her palm, to no use. The hair at her temples always stuck out, like Bozo the Clown. Suddenly she heard Heather's calming burr in her head, telling her to do "the braid trick."

Smiling, she quickly did two braids, one at each temple, then tied them together behind her head, under the rest of her hair.

Another glance in the mirror: at least she didn't flinch this time. Silas hadn't given a time for dinner, just space to get ready and an amorphous promise that it would be ready when she was. She stepped into her Chanel black dress, the same one she'd worn to their second date, buttoning it slowly, enjoying the vintage glamor as it settled over her seductively.

Again, she felt alive, every tiny hair on her surface was comfortably on end. It was horny adjacent, but deeper. Now, the results in the mirror were better. Her dress was doing its duty, perfectly fitted and flattering; she looked taller, even in bare feet, the wide collar showing just a hint of cleavage. She brought strands of hair forward, letting them curl over her exposed chest.

"Enough," she said absently. Vanity had never sat well with her in the same way that makeup had never entranced her. She reached into her suitcase and unrolled a pair of black ballet flats, sliding them onto her feet. Teddie's parting gift, a pair of brand-new black Jimmy Choo wedges, felt too ostentatious and also, given the uneven flooring, unnecessarily dangerous.

Having already decided to leave her phone upstairs, she checked her texts one last time. It was crazy how quickly the incoming texts dropped off once she abdicated. The texts she received now were friendlier, more supportive. She fired off quick yes no answers to Liz, Yukari and Fran, a cute GIF of a high fiving kitten to April Veronica, and a miss you to Teddie.

Stop. Procrastinating.

Her emotions around Silas were complex, occasionally rising up in waves and swamping her. As much as she wanted this to just be a weekend away with a lover, that charade was above her talents as an actress. She stalked across the wooden floor, her mind roiling like an ocean storm. In a moment of clarity it occurred to her that it wasn't Silas she was avoiding. It was the weight of the situation.

With a loud exhale, she turned and opened the bedroom door, stepping out into darkness.

"Silas?"

"Come to the patio," his mellow voice sailed from the darkness.

Treading the uneven stairs cautiously, she padded across the darkened living space. Through the double glass doors, she saw Silas seated at a dining table at the end of the enclosed deck. Fairy lights hung outside the mesh windows, framing the entire tableau. Candles flickered on the table, points of white and orange light danced across the silverware and Silas's face, staring out over the lake. He looked careless and happy, and once again, she felt herself falling a little further.

Silas turned, his face crumpling into a gorgeous smile.

"Good evening, Sara." He stood, formally. Walking to her seat, Sara was grateful she'd bailed on the heels, certain she would have tripped and spoiled the moment. As she slipped past him, she was both aware and disappointed that he didn't try to kiss her.

"I thought outdoor dining was ambitious for folks like us."

"Have Deet will travel!" Silas laughed, pointing at a spray bottle of bug repellent on the table. "We can't be too careful."

He pulled her bench away from the table until she sat, then gently, easily pushed it forward, returning to his seat across from her.

"Shall we spray now eat later?"

Sara nodded, taking the unscented bugspray and coating her arms, legs and hair with it. She offered the bottle to Silas.

"I'm already sufficiently doused in it," he said affably. "Wine?"

Sara nodded, sorting out the skirt on her dress, looking anywhere except at Silas. The fairy lights created a shimmering haze around them, blocking out the world.

"This feels nice," she said, her voice very small.

"Good," Silas said. "I was hoping you'd like it here."

"I do," Sara said, watching as he poured two glasses of wine, to the appropriate level, something she couldn't recall doing in forever. Setting the bottle down, he handed her glass to her, and she raised it to her nose.

"Spanish tempranillo?"

Silas nodded, light in his eyes.

"You remember everything."

"No, just the important stuff, like the wine you like, random stuff like that. I forget so much, and also, I try to not access good memories too often. I don't want to degrade them."

"That's lovely," she said. "Oh, wait, did I tell you that April Veronica said wine is for old ladies?"

Silas made a surprised face, then burst out laughing.

"She's lucky she made it out alive."

"Well, she drugged me, is how she survived."

"Sounds like an astute move." Silas laughed.

Sara held her glass up. "To astute moves," she said. "And the end of wine."

He pushed his glass against hers. "Well, we have several bottles to get rid of, old lady."

She took a sip.

"Silas, there's something I should tell you, in the spirit of honesty..."

He nodded, his smile not faltering.

"I'm... I'm getting more used to this."

"To this?"

"To you."

"In a good way?"

"Yeah, it's all right, yeah," she said with a half-smile. "Sorry about my freakout at the lake. I just can't drag you down with me. It's hard to talk this stuff through."

"Don't need to explain," he said gently. "I've gone years without speaking to anyone other than like a barber or a delivery guy. It's definitely an uphill battle."

Sara squared herself against the table.

"So, have you ever wondered why people even bother talking to each other?"

Silas laughed aloud, nodding. "Yep. That's usually what precedes a year or two of not bothering with small talk, or conversation at all."

"It's funny, and crazy and it's also reassuring to hear this!"

"Vampires have commonality of experience?"

"You use that word?"

"Only when I'm joking... with you..."

"I feel special."

"I mean it, Sara, you said you find it weird to talk to a guy openly. And you've had women around you your whole life, you've been able to speak of things in your life. I haven't. So this is all... I dunno, don't be annoyed, but it's exciting to me." He paused and locked eyes with her. "Right now, I can't imagine ever getting bored of talking to you. If I'm lucky enough to be in your life for any period of time, Sara, I don't think I'd ever wonder why people talked to each other."

"Silas, I did realize that, how limited your communications must have been for all these years. I'm sorry, I really am, I feel it deeply, that even though the women who've passed through my Lock have been annoying at times, I've always had at least four or five people around me that I could talk and laugh with."

The appearance of a tear in each of Silas's eyes stopped her cold.

"You *weren't* faking the depression in my office, were you?"

He shook his head slowly. "Never said I was."

"True," she said slowly, humbled into silence as she considered the depth of his existence. Hundreds of years of solitude. He was doing shockingly well, considering.

"Do *you* still wonder why people talk to each other?" he asked, his wine glass in front of his face as if he was dreading her response.

"Yes, still, all the time," she said, lightly. "It makes no sense, the sharing of, frankly, boring information with a chosen circle of friends. I think that fundamentally, that was what drove me to my first stint as a therapist. I'd done several PhD dissertations on the role of shared language and information, and I wanted to experience that level of controlled communication, where the therapist is involved in a conversation only passively, hearing and reacting along a set of prescribed guidelines. I still don't really have an answer."

"I think communication is love." Silas lowered his glass. "Unless it's meant as a threat, all communication is a shared experience, and it sustains us. There's a charge we get from talking, and as someone who has gone years without talking to strangers, I've noticed the things that I've become deficient in. It's probably parallel to depression, but it's easier to lift."

"How so?"

"Well, now, when I feel the dark tendrils of too much solitude, I can literally go sit in a bar and talk to someone. Might not click right away, but usually, a good bar-side chat that engages me will shine some light in my darkness."

"Silas, I..."

"Shit," he cut her off. "Dinner. There's a dinner, and it's in the oven, and it should not still be in the oven."

She laughed at his clumsiness as he stood abruptly and vanished into the darkness of the house. Soon, the familiar noises of meal preparation echoed out to her. Oven door creaks, drawers sliding, cutlery on china, all mixing with the rising hum of bugs and the occasional nightbird song. Familiar sounds, the tiny lights sending their energy off into forever, the mesh walls inhaling and exhaling around her like a protective lung. Peace descended over Sara, a sensation so unfamiliar that she almost rejected it before breathing deeply and letting it be.

The sounds from inside stopped, and she turned her head to see Silas standing at the table, a plate in each hand. She smelled lamb, and rosemary and something clean, fresh.

"This looks wonderful, Silas," she said. "How long exactly was I upstairs, because this wasn't five minutes' work?"

"It was a decent reverie." He smiled as he sat down. "It's just a lamb rack, marinated, plus some potatoes baked with rosemary, and fiddlehead ferns."

"Are you trying to lure me in with some ancient cooking?"

Silas shrugged. "When in doubt, I find that comfort food does wonders."

"We could have eaten this together even before we got changed."

"Indeed we could. It's harder to find the ferns these days but this kind of meal helps to ground me."

"That ground is long gone. Have your travels taken you back to Romania?" She bit her lip, unsure if he'd answer.

He nodded. "I went several times. Only recently, though. After hemoglobin pills became easier to get. I went in the sixties, it was shocking compared to America. Parts of it were very depressingly similar to when we lived there, just unchanged, for better or worse. I went again in the eighties. I had some time to kill before I could come back to the United States."

Sara raised an eyebrow.

"Long story," he said. "Not terribly interesting."

"I never went back," Sara volunteered. "It was somewhere I had to flee, and I'm someone who likes to move forward. Once I got to England, I learned English, so that opened me up to the possibilities of the new world."

"But once you got here you never left?"

"The years flew by. And once I made Teddie, I felt grounded. New York was the easiest place I'd ever settled. All those zealots were so respectful of our Silent Order. We interacted a lot more then, because life expectancy was so short, the people that helped us all died before they could notice how little we aged. And then, it was just living in such a vital, alive city. It wasn't possible to get bored. I imagine London is the same, just so much academia and art and a high turnover of fads and interests."

"I do love London," Silas said. "It's somewhere that I could live."

He paused, cutting into his lamb, taking a bite.

"Sara, eat," he said. "It's getting cold."

She cut into the meat on her plate, smiling at the amount of blood pooling around it, enjoying the taste of the rare muscle on her palate, mindful to chew quietly. Teddie always scolded her that she chewed like a hungry dog, another side effect of living alone. The truth was, she enjoyed the animal aspect of eating, and had ever since the advent of the Victorian dining manners. She avoided dinner parties still. They ate quietly for a few minutes.

"So?"

"It's very good, Silas, thank you for..." she paused. "Well, thank you for this meal, and also, thank you for bringing me up here. I needed a getaway more than I realized."

Silas stopped eating, set his cutlery down, and took her hand.

"Is this okay?"

Sara nodded.

"Good, because I really needed to touch your skin."

His warm hands engulfed hers.

"We're never going to finish this dinner." Sara smiled.

"It'll reheat marvelously," he said with a grin.

"I have a mason jar of April Veronica's delightful weed elixir up-stairs."

"What if I'm a five-hundred-year-old clean teen?"

"Oh, pish," Sara said, using a word she often wished hadn't gone out of fashion.

"I kinda am," Silas said. "I think of drugs the same way as I view Facebook or whatnot. It's all perfectly good for wasting time, but it just gets sadder and sadder when you are alone and that's what you do."

"Fair point. We don't have to try it."

"Nah, I want to try it and be silly with you. Now, being silly, that's something I can't get enough of."

"Right, because when are we silly?"

"Is that a challenge? I'll bus the table, you get the drugs?"

"You sound like a horny teenager."

"Guilty as charged." Silas raised his eyebrows and smiled, and she felt her heart flip and a blush bloomed on her chest. While Silas cleared the table, Sara sprinted up the stairs to her room. It was lit only by the moon, and she saw the mason jar sitting on a chest of drawers, glowing orange like a talisman.

Snatching up the jar, she descended into the living room, surprised to see Silas already back out at the table. The ringing of frog song filled the air, and as she approached, he turned and gave her another heart-shaking smile. Sara noticed that he too had a small jar between his hands on the table. She set the mason jar in front of him and sat down.

"I realize that the good time I had with April Veronica doesn't mean I'll have the same good time with you. I'm not chasing the dragon, and this might be a bad idea, so... we don't have to do it."

"Thank you," Silas said. "But I'm curious. I just wonder, you know, what happens to people like us when they relax?"

"Well, if recent events are any indicator, I'll just talk too much."

Silas nodded at the jar. "Well, get pouring then."

"Before I do that, what's in your jar there?"

"Ha, I was wondering how long you'd wait to ask. It's something that I distilled for you, for us. It's...well, it's good old vampire moonshine."

Sara gave a start. It was blood liquor.

"Silas, you... uh... I guess the rules don't apply to you, but all of the Locks voted in unison to forbid its production."

"Yes, as soon as refrigeration became possible. I know that. But I don't have an army of winged monkeys stealing me fresh blood on the reg. I don't have to follow the laws of a group who would kill me on sight."

Sara froze. He was right. She was naïve to assume that he followed the Lock laws as blindly as she did.

"What did I say? You jumped like a scalded cat."

"The rules, Silas. They're the foundation of my entire life."

"You've been bending them."

"Bendin' ain't breakin', son."

He stood up and walked around to her side of the table, standing behind her. He kissed the top of her head, his voice whispering in her ear.

"My name is Atanase, and never have I killed. This blood liquor is cruelty free."

"I haven't seen that stuff in so long," she said quietly. "You're quite a mystery."

Placing his hand beneath her chin, he tilted her face up to his.

"Sara, I am an open book for you. Here. I will clear up a dishonesty that has bothered me. This house isn't an AirBNB. It's mine. It has been mine for many years, and I also own the land around the lake. This is my safe house. Well, one of them at least. This is my sanity and my fortress. And now, you can do what you want with that information. That makes me vulnerable, but also, I hated my lack of transparency."

"You own this lake?"

"Yes, and so, I wanted to say to you, there is another house on the far side, and it is always at your disposal. If you wish to go Scholar in privacy, I will not bother you, but it is there, and you have it as an option."

"Heather has to set up my Scholar life."

"Sure, but it's not like they check up on you, right?"

Sara shook her head, wondering how many Scholars he had spied on.

"It's weird, how you know so much," she said. "It's somewhere between alarming and disarming."

Leaning down, he kissed her warmly, softly, slowly. She inhaled his breath and her head went blurry. She pushed to her feet, and his lips found hers as she rose. Her hands flew to his hair, pulling against him. They stayed like this, wrestling as one until he broke it off, pushing her away with a hand to the chest.

"Stop, I haven't had a heem, I'm..." he paused. "I split your lip, a little. I could taste your blood, and I was starting to feel that fucking burn in my throat."

"I'll get you one." She turned to leave but his hand gripped her wrist.

"No need." He lifted the jar of blood liquor with his other hand. "We have this."

"Silas, that's against the rules."

"Technically, it's not. Bendin' ain't breakin'."

Sara smirked.

"Hook a sister up then."

Silas reached around her, opening the jar. The smell hit her nostrils immediately, transporting her back to the ship she and Crina took from England to New York—the creaking wood, the waves of stench below decks and salt air.

He raised the jar to her lips, and she sipped. The bouquet was iron, salt, roses, unlike anything she'd tasted.

"Silas, this is exquisite," she said, her top lip stained with blood.

"I've had a long time to perfect my recipe." He smiled. "Just pretend I'm a Brooklyn hipster and this is my home brew."

"Does it come in an IPA?" she said, taking another sip.

"As a matter of fact, it does." He raised the glass to his lips. When he was done, a small drop of blood liquor ran from his bottom lip to his chin, and she stepped onto her toes to kiss it away, the flavor of it and the scent of his breath combining to make her swoon.

"Shall we take this to the bedroom?" she asked.

"Yours or mine?" he asked as a wolfish grin spread across his face.

"Shut up or it's gonna happen right here," Sara said, her voice hoarse.

Silas gripped her hips and lifted her easily onto the table.

"That's what I hoped you'd say."

Chapter Thirty-One

A burning feeling spread across her bare ankle and woke Sara, groggily, in a pile of blankets and quilts beneath the patio table. Without opening her eyes, she knew it was the sun. Reaching for some stray bedding she could cover her legs with, she encountered Silas's furry stomach, and as tempted as she was to run her hand a bit lower, she propped herself on her other elbow, secured a heavy quilt and yanked it over both of them.

"Are we waking up?" Silas mumbled, his face pressed into a jumble of pillows.

"No, I just saved your life is all. The sun's up."

"I have sunblock in the cupboard in the kitchen," the mumbling continued.

"Can't we just hang out in your pillow fort all day?"

He rolled over, his face puffy with sleep, his eyes barely open, the pupils entirely obscured by his thick lashes.

"Any negotiation must begin with a kiss." He pulled her closer to him and nibbled on her bottom lip. She kissed him back, but as he went deeper, she pulled back.

"Silas, I can't go back to New York with third degree burns."

"I would never let that happen to you." He smiled.

"I can't see the view."

"Wait there," he said, booping her nose with a finger before exiting the cover of the comforter. Not wanting to miss the sight of his ass, Sara pushed her head out too.

"I saw your butt," she yelled as he went inside.

"Drinks blood liquor once, becomes a five-hundred-year-old teenager," his voice came from inside the house.

That's right, she drank blood liquor, and then she had sex on it. Six times. Each time, when her consciousness slipped into blackness, she went with it, losing herself in wild oblivion. After, they sipped April Veronica's elixir and fell asleep in each other's arms.

She ran a palm over her stomach, remembering their night. Her skin was alive from the intoxication, electricity running over her entire body. The previous evening played like a set of random stills, all lit by candles. Strong arms, holding and lifting and squeezing her. His lower stomach framed by her legs. His thick neck, veins bulging, his head thrown back. The fade to black, the unison that followed. Memories that she didn't want to degrade. Memories of something she had never felt before, too precious to fade. Her body temperature rose, deciding that they would be throwing down again before any breakfast.

"You lost in thought?" came his voice from in the house.

"Just remembering the good parts of last night," she said, just in time for him to step out of the house, sunblock in one hand, a bottle of water in the other, and in between, his boner.

"Me too." He smiled. "Obviously."

"I was thinking we might use this pillow fort one more time before we do any hiking or fly fishing or whatever the hell people do around here."

"As m'lady wishes," he said, slipping beneath the netting with catlike agility. "It's nearly nine. We are lucky we didn't burn already."

He handed her the water, waiting patiently while she sipped from the bottle.

"Roll over," he said, and Sara obeyed, unwillingly, sighing as she turned.

"Your skin is so flawless," Silas whispered. She heard a spray noise, and a sheer film of cold sunblock coated her back, and his warm hands began to spread the sunscreen languidly across her skin.

"What SPF is that? It feels like you're covering me in honey."

"It's 100, I import it from Australia. I apologize in advance, you'll need a Silkwood shower to get it off. But being able to be outdoors under the noonday sun is a luxury I'll always be grateful for."

"Damn straight." Sara chuckled. "I think I better do my front, or sunblock residue will be the least of your problems."

Laughing, Silas flopped down beside her. "Do my back, yeah? Then we can do our own fronts, to avoid any danger."

After she was done, they stood naked on the deck, spraying their legs and torso, then Sara watched as he ran palmfuls of sunblock up over his face and into his thick curly hair.

"You look like a prehistoric mud man," she said, laughing, grabbing the sunblock. "My hair will be set like this for weeks."

When they were done, they slipped out of the enclosed patio, walking quietly to the edge of the deck. Sara looked down, seeing a clear sand bottom shimmering through layers of cool green water. She inhaled deeply, smelling only sunscreen when she wanted the clean air around them, and took his hand.

"It's so peaceful here," she said quietly, her voice blending with the hum of insects and the breeze in the reeds.

"It's easy to forget there's a world outside the banks of this lake," Silas said, leading her to the end of the deck where their blanket was still folded from the day before. Sitting on it, he swung his legs over the water, then held Sara's hand as she sat beside him.

"So where's this other house?" she asked.

"Pretty much directly in front of us," he said, raising an arm, finger pointed. "Between those two trees.""Is there a path?"

Silas nodded. "If you'd kept going yesterday, you'd have come to it eventually."

"I was thinking we could maybe check it out?" Sara ventured, a little unsure. She smiled when Silas nodded. "I'd love to show it to you."

"I was thinking…" Sara leaned her head on his shoulder. "If I go Scholar, I could tell Heather I want to live somewhere in the area. That could be my cover, and I could spend my days here on this lake. I think that I would like it very much."

"Like I said, you're not obliged to see me. If you want solitude, there's really no better place. I've lost years on this lake. Once I could get internet and heem deliveries, the world was my oyster."

"Is this where you learned to ice skate?"

"It's where I perfected my craft." Silas chuckled.

"I have a question," Sara said, lifting her head.

"Fire away."

"How do you get your identities?" Sara paused, trying to detect whether the question made him tense up.

"The old-fashioned way. Used to be black market, now is dark web. Sounds very James Bond, is rather pedestrian in reality."

"Answered like a true spy."

"It's really not that hard. Most times I live in the States as a foreign national. It's easier for me to get passports and visas overseas, then live here until it's time to retire. Then I head back out, start all over again. The only difference between us is, I didn't hang onto my birth name. I didn't need it."

"I'm afraid you'll always be Silas to me."

"I'm okay with that."

"What was the worst name you ever had?"

Chuckling, Silas rolled his head back, sunlight bathing his face as he thought.

"Once, and really, I got what I paid for, I was Petros Tripolitsiotis. Which is what happens when you take advantage of the sloppy bureaucracy in Athens in the seventies."

"What did people call you?"

Silas looked into her eyes, smiling. "Pete. I was Pete. Nobody in America could pronounce it. When it came time to change it, I vowed to wait until I could find something with less syllables. What about you? What was your weirdest temp name?"

Sara kicked her legs in space, looking into the deep. Clear water beneath her feet. "Hmmmmm. Let me think..." Sara smiled. "I really hated being Birdie Bickerstathe."

"Lemme guess. Eighteen thirties?"

"You're good. I became Birdie in 1817. I think I kept her a really long time or maybe it just felt like it."

"It's not so bad..."

"You're right, it's not. I'm sure I'm spacing on something worse. Right now, old Birdie is what sticks out."

"Do you pay much attention to your alter egos?"

Sara shrugged. "Not really. I literally had to cram before our first date. I hadn't had to talk about Lily's history in any depth."

"Do you have a binder?"

"Yes, Heather makes them. When we get renamed, we burn the old binder."

"You women love symbolic gestures."

"Give me a break," Sara said, socking him gently in the ribs. "All of human nature is rituals. As if you're above it, Mister Let's Have Ice Skating As A Tradition."

Silas shifted closer to her on the folded sheet, their hips touching. Taking her chin in his palm he turned her to face him, kissing her lips quickly.

"Rituals with you? Sign me up."

She kissed him back, sliding an arm around his naked waist. Sitting here, on a private lake, speaking honestly, she felt calm and she felt content. She was happy.

"I think they'll happen naturally," she said, her lips brushing his.

"Does this mean we can get a Christmas tree?"

She nodded, laughing.

"What?" Silas's brown and gold eyes narrowed.

"I already looked to see when Harlem Meer rink reopens in the fall. Ice skating can be one of our things."

"And we can practice here next winter. When this lake freezes, it looks like a postcard."

"You should be a realtor." Sara smiled, kissing him again.

The noon sun filtered through the trees, dappling the deck in moving shadows. The wreckage of brunch spread out before them. Sara gazed across the table at Silas, shirtless but wearing shorts, his eyes closed. He'd sprung another perfect meal on her. Crusty bread, a sharp sheep cheese, English pickle spread, and the leftover lamb from the night before. A plowman's lunch, he'd called it.

As if he sensed that she was watching him, he slowly opened one eye.

"Wanna go see the other house?"

Sara nodded and he yawned, stretching an arm above his head. "Well good, but let's go now before I need a nap."

Standing slowly, Sara straightened her Alaïa slip dress and slid her feet into her ballet flats.

Silas joined her, taking her hand and leading her down along the path she'd fled along twenty-four hours earlier, marveling at how much calmer she felt now.

They continued in silence, each lost in the beauty that surrounded them. It occurred to Sara that Silas had likely either built this path, or was responsible for keeping it clear, and the thought that she too might have the chance to nurture this land the way she'd tended to her Lock filled her with happy excitement.

Eventually, they came to a clearing at the side of the lake, a small natural sand beach with bulrushes at each end; behind it, a grassy knoll dotted with small white wildflowers. The path continued ahead, but there was a smaller trail heading off to the left.

"We're nearly there," Silas said, leading her along the smaller path. When Sara began to walk more carefully, he paused.

"What's wrong?"

"I'm terrified of poison oak," she said.

"You won't see any on my land, young lady. I am the sworn enemy of that evil shrub."

"Reassuring," she said, picking up the pace until the trail opened up into a wide space in the trees, a perfectly round hill rising up in front of them across a bubbling stream that emptied into the lake to their right. There was a wooden bridge spanning across the stream, and halfway across, Sara paused, her eyes following the stream to a water wheel spinning slowly in time with the tide.

"Welcome to your potential new home," Silas said, waving an arm like a model on the price is right.

"You want me to camp here?"

Touching a finger to her lips, Silas led Sara around to the front of the hill, and she gasped. A row of slanted ceiling-to-floor windows flanked a glass door with a metal handle: a home built into a hillside, visible only from the lake. Turning the doorknob silently, Silas pushed the door open and stepped inside. Sara followed, eyes wide. During the walk she hadn't noticed that it was getting hot, but stepping inside, the temperature dropped instantly, comfortable and dry.

Turning slowly, she took in the room, heavy wooden beams holding up the ceiling, thick floorboards beneath her feet. A stone fireplace at the far end. A long peacock blue couch against the rear wall. Three doors along the back wall, all closed.

"Silas, this place, how... "

"I built it," he said without any trace of pride. "In the seventies. It's so insulated, and a few years ago I took it entirely off grid. The stream powers backup batteries. I'm the only person who knows this is here."

"It's beautiful," Sara said, turning to take in the lake vista from the windows, surprised that she couldn't see the other house.

"Come, see the rest." Silas took her hand, opening the first door with the other, revealing a dark room. Flicking a light switch illuminated a bedroom substantially larger than the one she had in New York, the far walls curved and sloping, mirroring the hill behind it. The only furniture was a queen bed, its bare mattress, and an ancient dark wood armoire against the wall by the door.

"This room is amazing to sleep in," Silas said. "Pitch dark and silent."

"It's very crypty." Sara laughed. "You're leaning into legend here."

"If you don't like it we can put in a skylight," he said.

"Stop being so... accommodating!" She whirled to him, kissing him on the lips. "The living room has so much light. This is perfect."

"There's not much more to it," Silas said, heading back to the living room. He turned and opened both of the other doors, hitting wall switches that lit both of them. The central room was a shockingly modern kitchen, silver and white appliances, a concrete countertop and halogen bulbs in the ceiling. Stacked in the corner was a combination washer-dryer.

"I really do feel like you're my dream realtor right now," she whispered, lost in imagining actually living in this beautiful house.

"Well, Doctor Lily Berger, please step into this newly renovated full bath." Silas stepped aside as Sara moved from the kitchen into the bathroom, stopping dead at what she saw.

At the far end of the room, where the ceiling sloped down, there was a full sunken bathtub; above it, a raindrop shower head. Beside the door, a sink and toilet completed the picture.

"Silas, this whole place is..." Her voice trailed off and tears sprang into her eyes.

"Sara, I..."

She waved her hands in the air, trying to derail the flood of tears, only partially successful.

"This is so generous," she said finally.

"I'm glad you like it," he said as Sara walked back out to the living room, sitting heavily on the couch. Silas sat next to her, placing his arm around her shoulders, and they sat in silence, watching dragonflies dart across the sparkling expanse of the lake.

"I love it..." she began, pausing again.

"But?"

"There's only one door. Silas, I haven't lived in a house with no escape hatch in eons."

"There's a trapdoor under the bed. Leads to a crawlspace that exits near the water wheel."

"Of course there is," she said, scolding herself for forgetting that Silas's survival all these years had been much trickier than even her own.

"I planted a lot of the trees around here," he continued. "Now, I have a forest. I built this house very slowly. I never wanted it to feel like a chore."

"Why did you build it?"

"Insurance," he said. "In case I needed to hide out."

"Oh, so not as a love nest?"

Silas rolled his eyes. "Ladies and gentlemen, we have a jealous one."

Sara elbowed him. "Listen buddy, I just wanted to figure out if you're offering me the chance to live in your private sex palace."

"Well, maybe it'll be a sex palace if you move in, but as of right now, you're the first woman I've ever brought onto this land for... romantic purposes."

"I'm honored."

"This is my forest, my private postage stamp on the world. To be serious for a minute, this is the answer to when you asked how I stayed sane, how I fought off the loneliness. To plant a forest and see it become a reality, that's the gift of our virus."

Sara felt her heart swell, empathizing with this strange man and his curious, lonely past.

"Yes..." was all she could say.

"Yes?"

"Yes, to what you're saying," she said, her voice cracking. A rushing sound inside her ears, inside her head, caused her cheeks to flush hot. "I want to do this. With you. This—" she glanced at the lake around them. "I want it. I want to... what did you call it? Date you. I want to date you. Whatever that means, I want to see what this is and what it can be, and hopefully, you get to keep your lake."

His hand gripped the back of her head, pulling her to him and in the split second before they kissed, she saw tears in his eyes. They kissed hard and simple, lips mashed together, but something deeper at play. They stayed locked as time stretched, the kiss staying exactly the same, the intensity swirling around them. Eventually, Sara broke the kiss and rested her forehead on his shoulder.

"Thank you," she said quietly.

"No, the thanks are all for you," he said into her ear, his breath tickling her. "This is going to be a wonderful next chapter for us both."

Sara stood and walked slowly to the windows, taking in the ridiculously peaceful vista, the diametric opposite of the city she lived in for so long. An impulse gripped her. She wanted a photo of this view, a souvenir that she could look at, a beacon for her future. She slipped her phone from the pocket in dress and flicked the screen on, her stomach dropping when she saw a stack of text notifications on her home screen, mostly from Heather and Teddie, the top one saying only:

> Lily where the hell are you? Code red. Come home now.

Chapter Thirty-Two

Insisting that Silas drop her at the corner of 110th and Broadway, and promising to call him as soon as she knew what was wrong, Sara strode purposefully along Broadway. The day was darkening into twilight. She passed people and stores without noticing, her pulse so loud in her ears that it blocked out the sounds of a new York Sunday evening.

Teddie's text replies since the first texts remained infuriatingly vague, and she'd had no luck getting any information from anyone else. Most of the women simply didn't respond, and a phone call to Heather only slightly assuaged her panic.

"Teddie's asked us to wait until we can all talk about it together," Heather said, her voice tight. "Between you and me, she's taken this Lock Mother roll altogether too seriously. Be prepared for some drama, but don't worry. Hurry home, pet. And I mean it, do not worry."

As she carried her bag up the stairs, her footsteps echoing upward, a shiver ran up her spine. A lot of these apartments were always empty, but right now, she felt strangely alone. Dropping her overnight bag at her door, she slid her key into the lock.

Heaving her bag from the floor, she put her shoulder into the door and shoved it open. She came eye to eye with Teddie, standing just feet in front of her, hands behind her back, tears staining her face.

"Teddie, what the—" Sara exclaimed, dropping her bag. "What the hell is going on?"

Teddie didn't move at all, except for her bottom lip, trembling, and her chest, heaving. A fat tear fell from one eye, sliding into the stream that was already there. Sara forced herself to breathe, holding her door open with one foot out of habit.

"Teddie, my love, I asked what the fuck is going on?"

"I... uh...I uh need you to come with me," Teddie said, speaking as if every word was a struggle, her voice hoarse in a way that told Sara she had been crying. A lot.

"Teddie..." Sara stepped forward, one step, not releasing the door. Teddie stepped back the same amount, then slowly brought one of her arms forward. She was holding a Slicer.

Sara's eyes widened and she struggled to piece together what was happening, in her own home, with the person she loved more than anyone in the world.

"I need you," Teddie said, her breath uneven, "to come to the basement."

"Theodora, Teddie, please, just tell me what's going on, we can sort this out."

"Sara, shut up!" Teddie barked, her voice steel.

A noise in the hallway, a shuffling, caused Sara to turn. Rosa, Eleanor and Liz were standing there. Unintelligible thoughts tumbled through Sara's mind, too quick to read, but one thing started to emerge, and her chest tightened.

Silas. They knew about Silas.

"Sara, please hand me your phone," Liz said, her voice completely flat, her blue eyes downcast.

In response, Sara slid her foot out from the edge of the door, and it swung closed, blocking the interlopers outside on the landing. Turning her attention back to Teddie, she reached out a hand, and Teddie brought her other hand out from behind her back, fingers tightly wrapped through a second Slicer. She brought her arms in tight by her sides, the blades at forty-five degrees, ready to deflect any contact. As Sara struggled to take in the scene unfolding around her, she heard a key slide into her lock, and felt the air displace around her as the door opened again.

"Sara, hand me your phone now, please." This time, Liz's voice was non-negotiable, her normally dreamy wide blue eyes were cold, gray. Sara reached into her jeans pocket and pulled her phone out, passing it backward without looking, holding onto it slightly harder than Liz expected, forcing her to tug it free.

"Go," Teddie commanded. "Now."

Turning, Sara briefly made eye contact with Eleanor above her burka before she too gazed at the floor.

"Rosa, Eleanor, you walk in front of her, Liz, hang back and walk behind me," Teddie said.

"Is this a coup? What the hell?" Sara said carefully, her words designed to take Teddie out at the knees.

"I never expected you to..." Teddie bit back, then stopped herself. "Never mind. Turn around. Follow the girls. Don't try anything. And Sara?" Their eyes locked. "Don't underestimate me."

"I never have," Sara said, locking eyes with her closest human, raising her chin defiantly before she turned, and walked out of her apartment, maybe for the last time ever. She watched as Liz opened the wall in the corner by the spiral staircase, and Sara's heart began to hurt.

The basement meant tribunal.

Eleanor pushed past her, and she and Rosa led the way into the dark catacombs that linked the compound. Without waiting for instruction from Teddie, Sara stepped in after them, not looking at Teddie or Liz as she walked past. Slowly, all five of them began to make their way along and down, along and down. She knew these passages so entirely she could have made the walk in pitch dark.

Struggling to calm her mind was a losing battle. The whole drive back to the city she had downplayed the seriousness of what was going on, but Silas was nothing if not a survivor. If she didn't answer his calls tonight, he would figure out that something bad had happened to her and he would vanish. A wave of relief washed over her when she recalled that they'd moved all their chats to Signal, grateful that Silas had added a two-factor authentication to it before the drive, and that she'd deleted all of his messages on the drive back. Fran would be able to crack it, but at least he would have a head start.

As the walk continued, the silence grew more and more oppressive. Teddie sniffed occasionally, and each time, Sara almost expected to feel the dull pressure of Slicer piercing her spine, sending her paralyzed to the floor. The way things were going, that might be the better outcome, and surprisingly, she felt resigned to it.

Finally, she saw light spilling from the doorway to the meeting room, the big one. The one with the surrender room attached to it. Normally, ahead of a meeting, chatter would be bubbling out into the hallway. Tonight, silence met her approach. She decided to go down calmly. She remembered her conversation with Silas, about facing a nuclear blast. She said she'd stand and face the oncoming wave of obliteration. Squaring her shoulders, she stepped into the room.

The remainder of the Lock sat in their chairs. Yukari was sobbing, silently, in Imani's arms. Imani looked up, her eyes red, offering Sara a wan smile. Fran inspected her hands, not looking up. Heather, her face pale and drawn, was attempting her usual stoic appearance, but as Sara passed her, she noticed that her chin shook. April Veronica sat by herself, in Marguerite's old chair, which had been hauled almost to the back corner of the room. Her face was frozen, except her eyes. They were full of terror.

"Step up onto the dais," came Teddie's voice from behind her. Sara obeyed, stepping up and standing beside her beloved chair, likely to be donated anonymously to a museum in the coming days.

"Cuff her, Heather," Teddie said. Sara watched as Heather's eyes dropped to the floor. She stepped up onto the dais beside Sara.

"I'm sorry, matey," Heather said quietly. "Just let me do this and we can get on with it."

Obediently, Sara crossed her arms behind herself, feeling one metal cuff rasp closed on her left, then the weight of the chain dragged her arm down before her right wrist was cuffed.

"Everybody, take your seats," Teddie said, and Sara finally raised her head as she turned and sat in her chair, her arms twisted uncomfortably behind her.

Teddie sat facing them in her chair, now on the dais in the Mother position. Sara cast her eyes across the downturned faces of women she had guarded like a wolf, singularly and proudly, for over a century, some of them for much longer. Fran and April Veronica looked back at her, and April Veronica offered a thin, pained smile. Nobody else moved and the room was silent except for breathing.

"My name is Theodora and *never...*" she paused, looking at Sara. "*Never* have I killed."

Teddie turned slowly, her eyes boring holes into Sara. "Sara, I always looked up to you, for fairness and what I thought was your unfailing ability to see and do the right thing, at all times."

Sara turned to face her, her face set to stun.

"And?"

"Please be serious, Sara," Teddie said, her voice softening almost imperceptibly. "I don't want to do this anymore than you want it to happen, but I... Sara, what the fuck have you been doing?"

"Honestly, I don't know what's going on," Sara said, surprised her voice sounded like she was telling the truth.

Reaching down beside her chair, Teddie pulled out a sheet of paper with a photo printed on it. It was of her and Silas at their picnic in Brooklyn, just a week ago.

"You took a phone photo of me?" Sara said, anger in her voice. "That's a violation. Maybe you should be the one sitting here."

"Don't play me, Sara." Teddie was getting testy. "I lied to you. About Marguerite's note. Sara, she told me that I should watch you. That the blood stench was rich on you. You were so gone, you didn't even think it was a coincidence that I would be in McCarren Park so early in the morning. Bitch, I put AirTags all over you. Your puffer. Your bag. And I'm glad I did. After literally a hundred years of smooth sailing, you meet a man and fall apart."

"Yes, please, trust Marguerite over me, Theodora."

Teddie nodded at Liz, who stood, shaking, a piece of paper in her hand.

"Show her," Teddie instructed, and the slender blonde stood shakily, taking each step separately as she approached the dais. When her toes kicked against the wooden riser, she held the photograph angrily in front of Sara's face. It was Silas.

Sara shrugged.

"Okay?" she said.

"I told you, quit playin'" Teddie said, anger and desperation in her voice. Inside, Sara was freaking out.

"This photo was taken in 1981," Liz said tersely, her blue eyes boring into Sara's. "Nineteen eighty goddamned one. And do you know who it is?"

Sara shook her head.

"This is the guy, this is the fucking guy that caused us to shut down the whole Lock. This is the guy who tripped my alarms and totally fucking ruined my life."

The Silas in the photo had longer hair, and it was lighter, artificially.

"I guess they just look alike," she began.

"Don't," Teddie said. "For the last time, Sara, we know. We know everything."

"Then why don't you tell me?"

"Sara, this man, this man that you just went away with, did the same thing to one of the San Francisco girls, and now he turns up here, looking exactly the same. So I'll put it bluntly. Sara. Is this man, who calls himself Silas Oppenheimer, is he," Teddie swallowed. "Is he like us?"

"Silas Oppenheimer was my patient... I don't know. I'm processing this-"

"Just tell her!" Liz yelled, spittle hitting Sara in the face.

"Sara, I went into your computer this weekend, after Liz told me." Teddie reached down and held up another piece of paper, a simple printout. From her computer. "This was in your trash. Do you need me to read this to you? Or do you remember what you wrote?"

Sara took a moment to decide whether to fight or fold. She chose fight.

"Theodora, I have never broken any of the rules."

"You wrote it. It is written. You do realize that that alone is enough for me to insist on your Surrender."

"Oh for fuck's sake." Fran shot to her feet, surprising Sara. "We have all broken the rules. We all lie. We all skirt everything. We are all addicts, you guys. *Addicts*! Nobody can follow rules for hundreds of years. Most people can't do it for five minutes."

Teddie turned to face her.

"Good to know, Fran. Good to know. But I can look you in the eye and swear that never, not once, have I broken a rule. The rules keep us safe, and they keep the whole damn world safe. Sara, you taught me that. You taught me iron clad. You instilled this in me. And you've done something, I don't know what, but you've broken the fundamental rules. Whether you choose to tell us the truth, or continue lying, we have enough proof to insist upon..." her voice broke and she delivered the final word in a whisper. "...surrender.

"Can I speak?" April Veronica stood up. Teddie nodded. "Devil's advocate. We are a progressive Lock, from what I understand. Why can't we look at the rules here? Sara isn't the problem, the rules are. Why isn't there a gray area where we can find a solution that works out?"

"A bent rule is a broken rule," Teddie said, glancing at Sara, the woman who had used this adage on her daily for her entire childhood.

"And a society that doesn't bend will break." April Veronica stood up straighter. "Look. I don't know if I'm too young to be taken seriously in this... mob... but you guys made me and you're stuck with me, and come on, this is *bad* and we need to look at the whole picture here. Is there some sort of honesty policy that nobody told me about? Or are we independent women governed by a handful of rules that were written hastily after a particularly dark period featuring men who, by modern standards, were clearly mentally ill, most likely psychopaths? Haven't you ever tried to adapt any of this stuff to the changing times?

I mean, the Catholic Church is more flexible than you, and that's not a solid recommendation for a survivalist sexist vampire cult."

"We are getting sidetracked." Teddie waved a dismissive hand at April Veronica, who scowled back at her. She held up Liz's photo again. "Sara, what do you know about this person?"

Inhaling deeply, Sara gazed around the room.

"You need to believe me when I tell you that he is harmless."

"He wasn't harmless to me," Liz wailed. "As soon as Teddie showed me that photo, I totally died. Sara, I never forget a face."

"What if he was trying to save you, Liz? What if *you* were the one endangering your Lock, out drinking and partying every night, getting drunk and letting your guard down? What if you were the one whose behavior destroyed that Lock?"

Sara had never seen Liz so angry. Her skin reddened from the chest up to her eyes, which were clear and full of hate.

"He is gaslighting you," Liz whispered. "You betrayed us all."

The room erupted in chatter, with Heather snapping at Liz, Fran starting something with April Veronica and everyone else yelling their opinions. Sara watched as Teddie oversaw the mayhem, her head turning left and right, her mouth a rictus of pain.

"Everybody," she barked. "Silence. The issue of Silas Oppenheimer is something that we will be dealing with long after tonight. For now, we must convene formally to discuss the infractions committed by our sister, Sara. Your letter, an infraction in itself, says that you have tasted human blood."

"Nomine Sara," she said forcefully. "Never have I killed."

"You're lying," Teddie hissed.

"No." Sara shook her head, her voice gentle. She told the truth. "There was an accident. One of my patients. The one who killed herself. She sliced her vein, and it sprayed me, in the face—"

Again the room erupted, in either horror or disbelief.

"I blacked out, and when I came to, her wrist was in my mouth." Sara stood taller. "It was not something I did of my own volition. I moved without control. I speak the truth to you, the whole of the truth."

"Liar," spat Eleanor, her eyes narrow.

"Ironic..." Sara faced her. "Eleanor, do you remember the problems you had last year, the nightmares? Should I break your confidence now?"

Eleanor pulled back as if she'd been slapped. Sara returned her attention to Teddie.

"Theodora, I can guarantee you, every woman in this room, with the possible exception of yourself, has transgressed, has tasted blood that wasn't harvested medically."

"Well, I will add that to my to-do list after we are done dealing with you," Teddie said, her guard up so impossibly high that Sara felt her internal fear turn into acceptance. There was no way for her to win this.

The ancient cushion beneath her felt scratchy and she could not get comfortable on it. The heavy weight of the chains on her wrists dragged her down into it. If she tried to run, she would feel the cold pressure of a Slicer entering her spine. She had lost. She'd envisioned this end for herself, many times over the last half century. But nothing in her imagination prepared her for the ugliness of the women around her, nor the depth of her hollow indifference.

"I deserve this," she said, coldly, and a palpable silence fell over the room.

"I'm not taking anyone down with me," she continued, her voice now full of empathy and kindness. "I know more of your secrets than any one of you can imagine. I can only ask for an exemption, a similar forgiveness. I watched over this Lock for longer than any Lock Mother in history, before I knew how badly the pressure was affecting me, and clouding my judgment. But I kept watch, and I saw. I let all of you explore the world, because living under stringent rules is not easy. But that's your job now, Teddie."

Across the dais, Teddie was staring at the floor, her chest heaving.

"I accept Surrender," Sara said, her voice even. Teddie didn't move. "And I will tell you one thing. I'm braver than Marguerite. I will face my end alone, and I will face it full of excitement."

"Sara, no, please!" April Veronica yelled, her voice breaking. "There has to be another way. I... I can't lose someone else." She crumpled into the ornate throne, sobs wracking her body.

"It's the only way, pet," said Heather, walking to her side and placing a hand on the girl's shoulder. "I don't like it any more than you do."

"Then fucking *do* something about it!" April Veronica leaped to her feet, eyes wild. In front of her, Liz and Eleanor stood, carefully unclipping tasers from their belts.

"What? They can't slaughter all of us!" the young woman demanded. "Imani, Yukari, we can't let this happen!"

"I am still hoping for a different outcome," Yukari said quietly. "Theodora, is there an alternative to Surrender? Something that can buy us some time? Surrender is a death sentence, not a slap on the wrist."

"We had something like this in Hamburg, back in the 1920s," Heather said. " We let the woman go Scholar, and she came back in a decade, asking for Surrender. I feel like that might be worth considering."

"Are you all forgetting that she's been sleeping with the guy who shut down my old Lock?" Liz was never afraid of being dramatic.

"Liz, if Silas is cursed like us, then isn't it accurate to say that *you* let a cursed man live? Maybe it's you who should be facing this tribunal, alongside me," Sara said coolly.

"No." Teddie stood and faced her. "It's a reason for me to insist that you choose it. You've written, probably more than we were able to find. You've tasted human blood from a living host."

"No, I have *not*," Sara yelled at her.

"The contents of this letter, found on your hard drive, are, by themselves, enough to ensure the end of your life. Coupled with your involvement with a male accursed? And your feasting? How am I supposed to react, as a new Lock Mother, with the eyes of our sistren around the world watching me?"

Now Sara felt worse, a sickening pit forming in her stomach as she realized that deep down, she had thought she could talk her way out of this, and she had been wrong. Very, very wrong.

"I told Desdemona everything last night." Rosa stood up, glaring at Teddie. "The letter, the mystery man. I thought you'd let her get away with it, Teddie."

In the silence that fell, Sara watched as Teddie swallowed twice, thinking.

"There was no need for you to break the confidence of our Lock," she said. "Breaking one law is enough to invoke Surrender. Sara has broken three. I am perfectly capable of handling this, Rosa. And if you're so unhappy here, why don't you just transfer to Madrid?"

"As a matter of fact, that's what I plan to do. Desdemona is on her way here now. She will take me with her when she's done."

A shot of adrenalin ran through Sara at the thought of Desdemona coming into the room. Suddenly even her peaceful Surrender seemed like an impossibility. Desdemona would relish the opportunity to use a Slicer on her.

Forcing herself to focus, Sara watched the effects of Rosa's news ripple around the room. She almost sighed with relief as she watched Heather slyly pull her phone out and quickly tap tap tap at the screen. Sara instinctively knew that Heather was overriding all of the building security. If Desdemona wasn't inside already, she wouldn't be getting in.

"I'm going too," said Eleanor with childlike pride. "I'm not going to stay here and risk everything with a newbie like you, Teddie. No offense."

"I have trained for this role for centuries," Teddie said, her voice commanding. "I am more than capable."

"Sure you are," Eleanor said sarcastically. "Mommy's little helper got the big job just like that. We didn't even vote for you."

Sara watched the tell-tale signs of panic wash over Teddie, her fingers twitching, her eyes blinking rapidly, her teeth chewing her bottom lip. More than anything, Sara wanted to hug her.

"Sisters," Teddie said, her voice wobbly but strong. "We can discuss all of this at some future time. Right now, we have the most pressing emergency in front of us, the greatest threat to this Lock since its inception."

"This Lock is a danger to the world, it needs to be shut down," Liz yelled. Disappointment washed over Sara as she watched Rosa and Eleanor rally around Liz, applauding her.

Without warning, Fran leaped to her feet and slapped Liz across the face, sending her wheeling back against the wall. Before she could get up, Heather jumped up and squared off at Fran.

"No more violence," she yelled, but the sound of her voice had the opposite effect and the room erupted into chaos.

Rosa and April Veronica were face-to-face arguing. Yukari pleaded with Eleanor, who physically pushed her away from the dais, and

Fran and Imani approached Teddie, both speaking at once. Over the din, Sara locked eyes with Heather and shrugged. A tear spilled from Heather's left eye and her chin quivered again, and that was what broke Sara. She saw that in all of this, she'd become blind to simple friendship, and in turn, she'd jeopardized more than just her own life. She'd destroyed the utopia that she'd painstakingly built. She suddenly wished that she could have one more year with Heather, or Teddie. Her heart spasmed painfully in her chest, and her breathing became sobs.

The strident arguing reached a fever pitch, and clumsily, the chains at her wrists pulling at her balance, she stood.

"Nomine Sara," she projected her voice powerfully, and the hub-bub died down instantly. "After a full and magical life, it is time for my next adventure. I choose tonight for my Surrender. I love you all, deeply and in different ways, and have admired you all for as long as I have known you." She turned to Teddie.

"I request privacy at my Surrender. I do not require a companion, nor do I wish for a witness. I realize this will leave you with yet another mess to clean up, but it is my right, and it is my wish."

Without looking at her maker, her oldest friend, Teddie gestured to Liz and Eleanor that they were to flank Sara. They moved to positions at either side of her.

"Nope," Heather said. "Not those two. I will accompany my friend tonight."

Teddie nodded at Liz and Eleanor, signaling them to stand down.

"The rest of you may leave," Teddie said. "This is..." her voice broke. "Impossibly hard. For all of us. Please return to your apartments. We will reconvene in the morning, and we will address the..." she paused, glancing at Liz. "...outstanding issues."

"This is murder," said Imani. "This is what we are united against."

"Imani, please," Sara said quietly, "go, this isn't murder, it's just life. I'm sorry that it got so messy."

With that, Sara bowed her head and waited as Heather unlocked the chain that snaked around her throne, but not the cuffs around her wrists. Once she was free of the shackles, she blindly stepped down, walking between the chairs and out into the hallway for the last time.

Turning left, she could sense that the antechamber's door to the surrender room was open, and, knowing the layout of this entire building better than she knew her own mind, she closed her tear-filled eyes and walked to it. As she stepped inside its cold interior, she opened her eyes, blinking. She drank in one of the last things she'd ever see. The room where Heather would push the button if she couldn't do it herself, lighting the fire that would rob her of oxygen, then consciousness, then life.

Raising her head, she saw, directly in front of her, the heavy steel door to the surrender room already open, the dim yellow glow of vintage incandescent lightbulbs pulsing out from it. Turning slightly, she glimpsed Teddie, her face twisted in agony, tears pouring down her cheeks, standing wordlessly in the doorway.

"Go, child," Sara said. "Please. Now."

Teddie went to speak, then bit down on her words. Without a sound, she turned and vanished into the dim light of the hallway. Heather closed the door behind her, holding the key to her wrist restraints.

"Don't worry about Desdemona," Heather said quietly. "Sara, I'm sorry."

"Don't be," Sara said. "We've had a lot of time together, old friend. To want any more is just me, being greedy."

"I... uh..." Heather's voice broke.

"Shhhh, it's okay." Sara turned, pushing her wrists back, feeling the key grate into each cuff, then the freedom and lightness as the heavy metal fell from her arms.

Without a word, Sara crossed the small antechamber and stood stock still on the threshold of the inner room, her arms folded in front of her. "Heather, this is impossibly hard, for both of us. I can take it from here. No funny business. I promise."

Gingerly, she stepped further into the surrender room, her heart aching for Heather and the task that lay ahead of her, so much so that she could not bring herself to look back. She stepped into the room. Behind her, the heavy door closed, followed by the grinding clank of the bolts on the outside sliding home.

She was alone.

It was time to die.

Chapter Thirty-Three

The room had been readied for her. A bunch of heavy pink peonies heaved out of a stone vase atop a small, old teak table. Next to the vase sat a simple white writing pad, a pencil, several pens, some White Out and an eraser. She smiled at the White Out.

I didn't know they made that anymore.

And next to that, a box of matches.

Across from the table was the fireplace, sooty and impermeable in the rear, stacked with tinder beneath several larger logs, freshly split, lending the room the aroma of pine. Above the fireplace was a wooden mantle that had once been part of a sailing ship, its underside charred black from the fires that robbed previous sisters of their oxygen, a battered metal cleat barely discernable in the darkness. Atop the mantle sat the small speaker from her apartment, and beside that, her old iPod, a 40gigabyte dinosaur that Teddie had proudly gifted her, probably around 2004.

"You can always take your music with you now," she'd said happily as she pressed the still-wrapped gift into Sara's hands. Now wasn't the time to get sentimental. Or wistful.

It was time to die.

The thought became a mantra that held panic at bay. She couldn't help Silas. She could only hope that he was faster than her Lock. He had survived a lot, but his cover was blown, and all of the world's Locks would unite against him. He had gambled everything on her, and this was the cost. She felt suddenly numb, like all of the pain, the loss, the hurt, was happening to someone else. It was too late for her to change anything, but the weight of lost love was growing inside her.

It was time to die. Dying would be easier than living with the mess she had made.

Facing the fireplace was her throne, the one from the rooftop suite. She remembered purchasing it, from a furniture artisan in Paris whose workshop stank of wormwood and tobacco and sweat, a paunchy balding man who swore that the wood came from the Black Forest in Romania. She visited his workshop often, marveling as he soaked hand-tooled beams of wood in pure water, and then slowly bent them into identical curves for the arms. The filigree was of her own design, a seemingly random pattern carved into wood, but looking at it now, for the last time, she rejoiced to see her initials hiding in plain sight on both arms, and the name of her mother, Marie, spelled in a vine that trailed among roses carved into the top of each arm. Nobody had ever noticed.

Because they never looked.

Turning slowly, she folded down onto the chair, sinking into its worn seat, anticipating every creak as it adjusted to her weight. Images of Silas flickered through her mind, his smile, his eyes, the way he held her, the lightness that he had brought into her life, however briefly.

"I hope they never find you," she said aloud, part benediction, part promise. Her voice didn't echo, as if the dead air at the back of the fireplace was a black hole. The silence became oppressive and she stood, stiffly, and took the few steps to the mantle. Heather had even brought the little cord that connected her iPod and the speaker.

Sara thought about Teddie, trapped between the rules and love. She knew with certainty that in time, Teddie would regret her actions. She hoped that someday Teddie would find peace.

I'll never know.

Many times, Sara had lain awake at night and passed the time by planning the perfect funeral playlist. She knew there were even several of them, under modest pseudonyms, on this iPod. "Last Party' and "Goodbye Mix" and "This Will Make Them Cry." She briefly considered each of them, but they were not designed to ease her out of this world; they were one hundred percent designed to wreck those she left behind.

She felt slightly childish and capricious, but those playlists weren't what she wanted to hear. She considered Nina Simone, Bill Evans, Huddie Ledbetter, and Patti Smith before landing where she knew she'd always land. Mazzy Star. She picked up the iPod and clicked its little wheel around, enjoying the analog feel while obtaining digital music. Arriving at their discography, she pondered her choice. Was she looking for something to listen to as she wrote her final letter, or something to listen to when she lit the fire? For now, she chose her writing music. *Among My Swan.* The most deliberately quiet album she'd ever heard, a masterpiece of subtle emotions. She clicked the iPod and as the slow ring of guitars and wind chimes filled the room, she hauled the chair closer to the table and took a seat.

When previous sisters chose Surrender, Sara had accompanied them to the door, and even bolted it herself a few times. After that, she would go and pace her apartment of the time, different homes inside this same building, walking back and forth, her mind unsettled, wrestling with the power of goodbye and the weight of decision.

And now it was her turn.

There's nothing to gain by stretching this out. What is an additional few minutes after so many centuries?

She knew that some of the sistren would be waiting on the roof, or huddled together in each other's apartments, waiting for Heather to let them know it was done. Her heart ached for Heather, and she hoped that her old friend would take April Veronica under her wing, because her outburst in the tribunal room had made her some enemies for sure.

In Sara's time as Mother, the women who'd chosen Surrender were all Scholars, removed from daily Lock life for decades. Her Surrender would be different, leaving a hole in the daily lives of all, and there'd be a shadow to it. Her letter, by ritual, would be read aloud by Teddie, and then burned, its contents existing afterward only in the memories of those present at the time.

I wonder if Crina will come in for the reading?

She knew that the woman who made her would be angry and disappointed, but the time for that consideration was past. She closed her eyes, the soothing music wrapping around her like a shroud. Blinking her eyes twice to clear them, she took up the pencil, flipped the notepad cover back and under the pad and began to write.

Theodora, my child, my one true love

This letter is for you. Read it alone if you wish, or if you feel like it's your duty to read it to everyone, then you can. Actually, I'm sure you will. Rules are rules.

I don't want to talk about myself. Our secrets are our own and the way of life we choose pushes us to be forgotten. I'm happy for my memories to die with me, as magical as they are.

But you, Theodora, I want you to protect yourself. I don't want you to stay Mother for a hundred years, just because nobody else wants the job. That's what I did. I don't regret it. Watching the last fifty or sixty years through your eyes has been one of my life's greatest gifts. If I had stepped down even fifty years ago, you would have missed out on the thrilling times you've had, the lovers, the marches, the art, the music, the revelations and the liberations. This was the childhood you never had but always deserved. You worked hard for it, and you made me happy, and proud.

Time is a funny thing. I've had so much of it, and now that I can see the end of my own piece of it, I realize that perhaps we are greedy, that living endlessly under rules that rob us of parts of our humanity is not the answer. Love is greater than our choices. Find ways to honor love. Don't keep it at arm's length. Embrace it, and let it embrace you in return. As you would say, catch some feelings.

Do not see April Veronica as a challenge or a threat. See her as a lifeline to our future, and treat her with patience and kindness, and an open ear. Much like I did, the first time you took me to see Hendrix at that college upstate.

There's no way to romanticize what I'm about to do. I'm about to turn off the light switch. It'll go black, and I'll be gone.

And that's okay.

As I pass, I will think about love. It was the greatest part of whatever I am, or was, or will be.

With nothing but love,

Sara

PS: Of course you get my credits. Check with Heather. I have four. xo

Setting the pencil down, Sara noticed that the music had stopped playing. She debated another full album but realized that her resolve might falter as time passed. She wondered if unconsciousness would take her easily, or if she'd feel something when she died; would she feel herself, her soul, separate from her body? Then, with slight panic, she wondered if staying inside a body for so long might have messed with a natural order she didn't know about yet. Too late now, she told herself, mainly to avoid a panic attack.

She needed to move before this became more traumatic than it needed to be. She cracked open the pill bottle on the table and tipped it up, spilling four fat, round pills onto her palm, in a line, along her lifeline. She chuckled at the irony, then slipped them into her mouth, washing them down with the cool water in the glass by the vase.

Returning to the fireplace, she again took down the iPod. This time her choice was simple. Terry Callier. She wanted to hear his mournful tones as she slipped out of this world.

She was being dramatic for her own enjoyment, and she loved it.

As rustic guitar filled the room, she picked up the match box from the table, and without pause she lit three matches, placing them in the tinder at the base of the wood piled in the fireplace. It caught instantly.

Returning to her chair, she settled comfortably into it. Her mind offered a jumble of competing images: Silas, kissing her at the lake just that morning, a memory that already felt ancient, faded. Theodora as a child, in a lightly brocaded dress, showing her etchings of rhinoceroses in an encyclopedia. She hoped the opiates she just took would prevent her from thrashing about in death when the virus overloaded her adrenal system and her muscles spasmodically fought against themselves. She didn't want to leave a mess for Heather to clean up.

Before her, the fire began to swell and spread, its heat reaching her cheeks.

She focused on it, letting her mind drift along with the guttering, febrile motion of the flames flickering along each piece of wood, tasting the oils, looking for purchase as they consumed the oxygen that kept her alive.

She vowed to keep her eyes open as long as she could, suddenly wanting nothing more than to see flame as her final vision, the mystery of it, the heat and the energy and the color, indigo pearls below orange soaring wings. Maybe her soul, if she had one, would join it.

Lightheadedness washed over her. Her eyes fluttered, and a final image of Silas came to her. Shirtless and smiling kindly, that morning in the pillow fort. Suddenly, Sara wished she'd had more time, to truly be in love.

Five hundred years and I still didn't get it all done.

Part of her wanted to fight, and part of her was just getting cloudy and tired, and she leaned to that part, pushing aside the feelings of want that coursed through her heart.

This wasn't surrender, this was regret.

Was this what every sister went through at this point? A realization of unlived potential?

We never get long enough in life.

Focus on the fire, she told herself. A numb lightheadedness clouded her thoughts, and she was unsure if it was the opioids or if the oxygen was thinning. Either way, she was grateful that she felt sleepy and unafraid.

Her whole world was orange, and warm. The blue pearls at the heart of the fire fuzzed and vanished as a blanket of rich, moving orange became all she could process. Terry Callier's voice sang mournfully of being buried by strangers, and she felt it like a sting in her heart as the edges of her vision started to go dark, like black fur creeping inward.

This is it, she thought, and her eyes fell closed.

Over the music, she heard something outside of that: a grinding of metal, and the pressure thwomp of a vacuum being broken.

And then everything went black.

Chapter Thirty-Four

"Oh no oh no, c'mon lassie"

"O"h no oh no, c'mon lassie" Sara felt steel hooks slip under her armpits and haul her from the chair. Her brain warped dizzily, confusion clouding her peace and release. Her equilibrium spiraled on a new axis and she felt herself falling for a millisecond that spun out indefinitely until her skull connected with something hard. She hadn't expected dying to be so eventful, she thought absently as the hooks dragged her along the floor.

"Breathe, lassie!" came the voice again, Heather's voice floating in darkness, like she was inside her skull, but the breathing thing made sense so she did it; suddenly there was less pain in her lungs and a deep breath felt like someone reconnected the power to her eyes. She opened them, and there, above her, was Heather, concerned like always, ruddier than usual.

"What the...?"

"Not now, girlie," her friend said. "We don't have time for chatting. Suck down some more air. I'll be needing you to stand up here short-ly."

Sara's head was full of pudding and the pivot that she had just made left her dizzy and unsure.

"No, Heather, put me back..." she gasped finally. "They'll kill you too."

Blinking to restore focus to her eyes, Sara watched as Heather re-bolted the door to the surrender room, then stepped over her supine body and leaned against the wall at the end of the antechamber. Carefully, she reached into her shirt and pulled out a key on a chain, slipping it into a dark spot in the mortar between the old bricks, and silently, the wall fell back, a doorway to what? Where?

Heather stepped into the darkness, then returned, hauling a heavy burlap sack. Confused, Sara watched as Heather went the furnace door on the far side of the antechamber, yanked it open with a rusty drag, then dumped the bulging sack down the chute and pushed the door closed. Dusting her hands together as she stood, Heather pressed the button to ignite the furnace, then looked her in the eye.

"Can ye stand, Sara? I don't think I can get you to the street without your help."

Pressing one palm and then the other against the worn carpet on the hallway floor, Sara lifted herself onto her knees, and then, with Heather's help, she made it to upright, but overbalanced and fell, her back hitting the door to the room she'd just attempted suicide in.

"Quick, lassie, get in."

"What is this place?" Sara muttered as they slipped into the darkness of a dark, cold room, and Heather paused, pushing the brick wall back to its place and locking it with the key around her neck.

"What the hades do you think it is? It's a secret passageway."

"Heather, I built this place, there's no secret passageway."

"It's always been here, Sara," she said hurriedly, gripping her arm and leading her straight ahead in the darkness. Sara tried to estimate where they were in the building, guessing that they were behind the back wall of the tribunal room.

"Heather, they'll kill you if they catch us."

"They'll never know, if we're lucky. I just tossed an old skeleton and some hams into the furnace, and I'll be blind drunk in me gaff by the time they come looking. Nobody ever suspects old Heather, if they think about her at all."

"I don't have anything on me, I don't know what you're expecting me to do."

"Sara, Sara, Sara," Heather scolded as she quickened her pace and they turned a right-angle corner. "As if I'd send you on without a plan."

"Heather!" Sara stopped cold, forcing Heather to stop with her. "When the fuck did you build this tunnel?"

"Nineteen thirty-eight. This is the old coal store. You built it. I fixed it. I turned the old coal slide into stairs, they'll be coming up on your right. The walls are still sooty, sorry. Your clothes will be pretty dirty after this and mine will need burning. Now come on."

After a few steps, she felt Heather's hand on her shoulder, pausing her in place. A light clicked on, Heather's phone, and Sara saw the staircase leading up.

"I'll go first, lassie," Heather said, bounding past her, the light from her phone bouncing erratically on the blackened brick walls. Sara heard a key go into another lock, and the opening of a door that let in a small amount of light and a gust of feisty New York air, exhaust, cigarette smoke, and mainly, ripe garbage.

"Okay, girlie, just follow me," Heather paused at the ancient metal door, through which coal was delivered to the building many years ago. After tapping at her phone for a few seconds, Heather turned to her. "I've just restarted the security system, the cameras will be down for less than a minute, we have to hurry."

In the dim light, she watched as Heather fell to all fours and began to crawl through the tiny steel opening, then she followed, sighing as she felt the change from inside to outside on her face. It was nighttime. They were in a pass through between buildings, trash cans lining the narrow space.

"Squeeze through here," Heather said, reaching for her hand. When they were both standing upright, Heather pushed Sara between two dumpsters and darted to the street, Sara leaning forward to watch as Heather waved her arm, then stepped back into the shadows.

"What did you just do? Hail a fucking cab?" Sara said. Heather only laughed in response. A shadow moved into the end of the hallway, blocking the light, a silhouette she recognized. Her heart soared.

"Sara, it's me," Silas's deep voice echoed across the trash cans. "Come on, we gotta go."

Sara glanced at Silas, tears in her eyes, then she grabbed Heather in her arms, hugging her as tight as she could. "I love you, Heather, I love you and I need to know you'll be okay."

"Lass, when it's safe you'll hear from me. Now, please, you gotta go."

Heather broke from the hug and fairly pushed Sara out of the alley into Silas's arms. They wrapped around her and she felt an overload of emotions and wondered for a moment if she was about to faint, or if she was actually dead and this was what happened in the afterlife.

"Well, we're both going to need to get changed at some point," Silas said into her hair. "I'm sorry, this is the best plan we could come up with. Now, get in the car, fast."

Sara turned to say goodbye to Heather, but she was gone.

"Don't worry about her, Heather will be fine," Silas said, directing Sara to his car, double-parked at a hydrant on 103rd street. He opened the passenger door and half lifted her inside, then locked the door before he closed it. In seconds, he was seated beside her.

"Silas..."

"Rest, and keep down," he said. "We aren't out of the woods yet."

He buckled up and inched the car forward to the green light on Broadway, a clean getaway. As they drew near, the lights changed to orange and a surge of pedestrians blocked the road. Silas swore as he slowed the car, glancing nervously in the side and rear mirrors. Sara sat quietly, blinking her eyes and wishing they'd focus better. When they refused to obey she slammed them shut, squeezing them until she saw negative space patterns form on her eyelids, then she opened them slowly, and there, in the last of the pedestrians crossing the street, was April Veronica, crying hysterically, a backpack over one shoulder. She must have escaped when Heather restarted the security system.

"Silas, that's April Veronica, the new girl."

"We can't, Sara. This is all arranged."

She gave him a curious glance and then opened her window.

"April," she called out. "April Veronica."

The young woman spun, fear in her eyes turning to wonder, then incomprehension.

"Sara, I mean, Lily, I mean, fuck, what the fuck is going on?"

"I'm leaving."

"Sara, the light in changing, we need to go."

"Take me with you," April Veronica said, her eyes wide. "Please. I can't go back to that place."

"Silas?" Sara said.

"Fine. Tell her to get in."

Sara heard the doors unlock and she waved April to the back seat. As soon as she was in, Silas peeled out onto Broadway, driving aggressively in silence until 110th where he made a screeching left and floored it until they were on the West Side Highway.

Nobody talked. The enormity of their shared situation needed to be processed separately. Sara, her mind clearing, wondered if the pills she took weren't even oxycodone. Feeling decidedly paranoid, she wondered just how far Heather's subterfuge extended. It felt like she had fallen into a game that she didn't know anything about, and the rules changed by the minute.

In the back seat, April Veronica sobbed softly.

"Thank you," she said eventually. "Thank you both. I'm sorry I crashed your ride. You can drop me off anywhere, I'm going to do my own thing, I'm just gonna—"

"Don't be silly, April," Silas said, surprising the women with his light tone. "I'm glad to have you aboard, it's just going to take a little while to sort out the extra details. We need to get Sara out of her sooty clothes. Me too, apparently." He glanced down at the black smudges scattered down the front of his white t-shirt. "There are heems in the glove compartment, why don't you two take a couple while we drive."

"Where are we going?" April asked. Silas glanced in the rear-view mirror and saw the young woman pull an iPhone out of her backpack.

"Oh shit," he said quietly. "You have a phone on you. Slight change of plans."

April rolled down her window and pulled the phone back to toss it.

"NO!" Silas yelled. "Keep it with us. I have a plan."

"Oh right, they're tracking us, you're sharp," April said, her face lighting up when Silas smiled.

"They put AirTags in my clothing, my bag, everything," Sara said, remembering.

"Good to know," Silas said, his brow knitting as he plotted and drove.

"By the way. April Veronica, I'm Silas. I'm like you. I have your virus. I'm older than Sara here. And never have I killed."

"Mind. Blown." April laughed, digesting the revelation easily. "See, Sara? I told you gender was a construct."

"You guys, half an hour ago, I was busily committing suicide. Can we kind of just unpack in silence?"

"Sure, you want to put something on the radio?" Silas pressed a button on the dash and the console lit up.

"I hate the radio," Sara said. "I hate listening to music that I didn't choose."

"Just pair your phone?"

"They took it," Sara said.

"Well, what's that in your pocket?" Silas asked

Sara reached down and felt a familiar rectangular shape in her jeans pocket. Thicker than an iPhone. Her fingers couldn't believe what they felt. It was her first generation iPod, and its little cord. Fucking Heather!

The tears came suddenly, hot and urgent, and her breath failed her. She felt April's hands reach from the back of the car, rubbing her shoulders, and then the weight of Silas's hand on her thigh.

"I... I.. I don't know how you pulled this off, but Silas, please, tell me what's going on?"

"Heather got my number out of your work planner, in your office somewhere. She just told me to be waiting where I was. She tried to get to me earlier, but you were already in your apartment. Sara, I've been a fucking mess. Is this the wrong time to tell you I love you?"

A brutal sob echoed out of Sara's chest.

"Am I dead? Is this what happens?"

"He fucking loves you, Sara. This is amazing!"

Blinking tears away, Sara looked across the front seat, to where Silas drove their escape vehicle, the billion lights of cars and New Jersey and glints on the Hudson refracting in her tears, her heart swelling.

"I love you too, you weirdo. Now where the hell are we going?"

After a stop at a Target in Clifton for clothes and food for all of them, they headed for a UPS store where Silas sent April Veronica's phone via road to a homeless shelter in Miami and her backpack to a woman's shelter in Charlotte. Sara gave up on asking where they were headed, at times not sure Silas knew himself. They took the parkway, and then they took various Jersey routes, north, south, east and west.

"Silas, I ran that Lock, I can tell you we don't have like a secret service that's following us."

"Desdemona is in New York," April Veronica said.

"Heather told me," he said quietly. "I need you to just trust me for now, in case something goes wrong. Let's just get there, then I'll tell you everything."

"They found out that you caused the San Francisco lock to fall apart," April Veronica said.

"That Liz is one fucked up person," he said quietly. "She brought that on herself."

"You guys, this is so juicy. What happened?"

Silas smiled. "Later. But not now."

Close to midnight they pulled into Hartford, Connecticut.

"I thought you said never to come here," Sara said.

"It's not much to visit, but it's a great hiding place," Silas said.

They drove in silence through a neighborhood of large, well-manicured homes, stopping at a simple, bland two-story Cape Cod. Silas clicked the remote that was hanging from his sun visor and a gate swung open. Pressing another button, the garage door opened, and he parked inside. While April Veronica helped Sara to her feet, they heard a series of keypads being punched and large bolts sliding.

"Come inside," Silas said with a tired smile.

They stepped into a small mudroom, waiting while Silas dealt with more locks and another door. They followed him into a pink and gray kitchen straight out of the fifties, all Formica and vinyl, metallic flecks in the floor reflecting the moonlight.

"Okay, we are safe here," he said, gazing at Sara, who was by now shaking, unable to speak. "Let's keep the lights off if we can. April, can you get Sara showered and into bed? I have to go back out. I'll return as soon as I can."

Sara started to protest, and Silas wrapped his arms around her.

"It's okay. I need to set up some protections for our new friend."

In the silence of his departure, April told Sara about the aftermath in the tribunal room. There had been screaming and crying and bitter recriminations. Teddie angrily instructed everyone to reassemble on the roof for the "witness of the smoke of Surrender."

April was horrified to see the women become excited at the command, as if it were a party, particularly Liz and Eleanor. "It was like they felt powerful, it was exactly what we say women can't be capable of." April Veronica paused, batting away tears. "It was the opposite of what Marguerite told me it was like, and yet, it was also exactly like she warned me."

In a tiled bathroom, with April Veronica by her side, Sara shrugged off the clothes she'd been wearing all day, the longest day she could remember and somehow still not finished. She stepped into the shower, wobbling a bit, and was happy that April Veronica was there to hold her up. As the water ran down her body, it created a black puddle around her feet, as centuries-old soot began its latest journey. Sara watched it as it swirled around the drain, free after a century lining the walls of her compound, feeling an affinity with its journey.

Once she was clean, April Veronica dried her with a towel, then wrapped her in another one, leading her to the living room. "This place is a hipster's wet dream," the young woman said as she led Sara across a white rug. Everything in the house was clean lines, mid-century. Sara guessed that Silas had bought it in the fifties and hadn't given a single thought to updating the interior ever since. Except for the large flat TV on the wall. That was new.

A long, sleek couch beneath the windows beckoned her, and she fell onto it a bit harder than she intended to, panicking April Veronica.

"Let me help you, Sara."

Like an invalid, Sara let the young woman fuss over her, moving her shoulders back against the couch. As the shock faded from her system, Sara began to feel antsy. She watched April Veronica relax into the new settings with the ease of a kitten in a new home, and she wished she felt the same. Eventually April broke the silence.

"Do you mind if we put the TV on?" she asked. Sara nodded her consent, and watched as April Veronica effortlessly corralled the remotes. Within a minute, *The Office* was playing, and they were sprawled on the scratchy wool couch, chuckling along until Silas's key in the lock nearly gave them both heart attacks.

"I'm sorry, I guess a real super spy would have a secret knock," he said when he saw their faces. "Anyway, Santa is here," he went on, kicking four large Wal-Mart bags through the door. Picking one up, he tossed brand new flip phones to each of them. "We only have each other's number," he said, "and that's only in case of emergency. No calls unless we get separated."

He then handed them the rest of the stuff he'd bought. Puffer jackets. Sweaters.

"Silas, it's almost summer, and I fucking hate puffers." Sara said, starting to wish he'd trust her with their destination, certain that he wouldn't.

"We will have new passports for you both tomorrow morning," he said. "We will wait here until they arrive."

"But how?" Sara began.

"You and I both know the answer," he said. "You weren't kidding when you told me that Heather runs that Lock. She knew this was coming and

Sara's mind flooded with questions, but she already knew that Silas was telling her as much as he could ... or would. It was infuriating.

"With that, we are prepared," he said, reaching into the last bag and pulling out two bottles of pinot noir.

"Now, can we celebrate?"

"I'm afraid I can't really go for a walk while you throw down," April said sardonically, "like, I would, but I don't think superspy here would agree."

"After the day I had, "throwing down" is not gonna happen," Silas said.

"The day *you* had?" Sara slugged him in the arm.

"Hey, at least you're still alive!"

When Sara awoke, it was almost eleven. She could smell food, bacon, toast, coffee, and her stomach growled. She hadn't eaten since lunch the day before. Her throat was raw from the suffocation. Wandering to the kitchen, she smiled to find Silas and April Veronica deep in conversation.

"Anything you'd like to share with the group?" she said from the doorway, and Silas rose, wrapping her in a hug.

"Sorry about the deep state stuff, but you'll understand soon enough," he said into her hair. "Now let's eat, and then it's time for us to hit the road. A messenger dropped off the passports a few minutes ago."

While Sara ate, Silas went to the garage, returning with some plain black suitcases. He removed the price tags from everything he'd bought at Target and Wal-Mart and packed a suitcase for each of them.

Once they were all dressed, they got in the car and drove. Sara struggled to remain quiet. Every time she looked in the rear-view mirror, she'd catch a glimpse of April Veronica, a half-smile on her lips as she watched the world pass by. Soon enough the road signs revealed that they were entering Boston. Silas remained tight-lipped as they exited the freeway, wending their way through a run-down part of town. At the end of an alley behind a bodega, he parked the car.

"Get your bags and just wait over there," he said. The women obeyed, watching as he removed the license plates from the car, stuffing them into his satchel

Together, they walked back to the bodega, where he called a taxi from the payphone in the doorway. Sara's confusion was becoming unbearable by the time they arrived at Boston Logan airport.

As Silas handled paying the taxi driver, Sara and April stood on the curb, nervously glancing from side to side.

"We are really in no danger," Sara said, wishing her voice sounded more certain. "There's no way they could trail us here."

"I know what you're trying to do," April said with a smile. "It's okay. They're looking for us, but at this point, we're a needle in one hell of a haystack, and your boyfriend seems to know his way around not getting caught."

"He's not my boyfriend," Sara said. April raised a single eyebrow and rolled her eyes, combining her two habits that Sara found most annoying. "What?"

"Who's judging? He's hot. I don't blame you. Give it a shot!"

"I'm fine with that," Sara relented. "He and I are giving it a shot."

"Yep. No pressure at all," April laughed, causing Silas to turn.

"What did I miss?" He grinned mischievously as he walked to them.

"Are you going to tell us where we are going?"

He shook his head, still smiling.

"Not long now," he said. "We have to go check in, you'll find out. It will all make sense, I just don't want Teddie jumping out from behind a bush and… there's more at risk than you know. Give me your passports, I'll check us in."

Both women rustled into their backpacks, producing their passports and handing them over.

"Thanks, I'll be right back."

And he was gone.

"Do you feel safe standing out here in public?" April asked while looking side to side, not sure what she expected to see.

"You're making me jumpy," Sara said. "Your annoyingly reasonable questions are freaking me out."

Nervously, Sara reached behind her head, twisting her long dark hair into a solitary cable that she then twisted into a knot.

"April, can you reach into my backpack and pull out the knit cap please?"

She waited patiently while April rummaged for the cap, then took it with her left hand, slipping it over her hair. "Thanks." She reached into her backpack and took out a surgical mask and put it over her face. "There. Now I feel safer standing here."

"Genius," April said, following suit.

"I almost didn't recognize you," said Silas, suddenly behind them, making them both jump.

"Let's go. We're all set."

"You didn't need us to check in?" Sara asked, one eyebrow arched.

"You can do anything when you're flying first class." Silas laughed.

They remained largely silent as they cleared security, with Silas striding out into the terminal ahead of them. "Come on, you guys, it's free sushi time!"

"He's like a big kid," April said. Sara was now running on fumes and was no closer to being comfortable letting someone else have all the power than she'd ever been. They caught up to him at the desk to an American Express flight lounge. A uniformed attendant walked them behind the matte black walls, with Silas close to her, talking low. She eventually led them to a table that was tucked away from the rest of the lounge and faced out of ceiling height windows over the hubbub of the Boston airport runway system.

"Settle in, you two. We have about two hours to kill before we get going."

"I want free sushi," April said perkily. Silas nodded in the direction of the food stations.

"Off you go."

And off she went.

"We're safe, Sara," he said, reaching across and unhooking the mask from Sara's ears. "I know this is a lot—"

"Do you?" Sara said, her voice tight. "Do you know this is my first time in an airport this century? My first time in an airport ever without stupid nun robes on? And also, just a little thing, almost a side note for you, this is the first time I've been out of control in my entire life. So, please do forgive me if I seem a little, I dunno, edgy as fucking fuck!"

Silas took a deep breath, his eyes closing.

"I'm truly sorry. Sara, I'm not doing a single thing unnecessarily here. As soon as I can tell you everything, I will tell you anything you wish to know, and I'll give you the keys to the kingdom. Queendom. Whatever keys you want. The thing is, until then, it's too risky. And I know you're out of your element and it might even seem like I'm playing the man card, but I'm not. I will very happily cede control of all things to you once we land."

"Now you're talking," she said with a half-smile. "And I know you understand. I've lived like a fucking land tortoise for hundreds of years. Some decades, nothing special happened, and I've forgotten them entirely. But in the last two days, I've had amazing sex, believed in happiness or something close to it, lost my closest friend, who then tried to make me commit suicide, and now here I am, a common-law wife to an outlaw with a newly adopted daughter? I hated being a tortoise, but now that looks like a damn good life."

He reached over and took her hand.

"Thank you, for trusting me, and thank you for indulging me. Now, can we get some sushi? I'm starving."

After eating, April Veronica fell asleep on the lounge chair in the corner.

"She's fun," Silas said. "I'm cautiously optimistic about how things have worked out."

"That's great, I guess," Sara said. "Silas, wherever we are going, will you and I have time to, I dunno, be alone? Talk?"

He nodded. "Yes, Sara, we will have time to grow and learn, together and apart. I don't know how we will work out, you and I, but I feel good about it and I know that whether our thing works out or not, you'll be happier than you've been in a long time."

"So... is this something you've been working on for a long time?"

He nodded. "Yes, but save the questions for the flight. I checked the manifest and there should be some vacant seats by us in first class."

"I haven't flown first class since the seventies," Sara said. "Thank you."

"I meant what I said. I do love you. Getting close to you was the last piece in the puzzle. I knew you were strong and fair and loyal, and smart and deep and resilient. But getting to talk to you, without borders or falsehoods, has shown me that our connection is real. And we don't have to start right away. We have years to think about it, act upon it, and make decisions."

"Fuck that." Sara laughed, pointing at his crotch. "If you're not going to join the mile high club with me, we better be going somewhere where I can get more of that D quick."

"Got it," Silas noted. "No more serious statements." He kissed her.

Later, they walked past boarding gate after boarding gate. Each time, Sara checked out the destination at the gate – London, Mexico City, San Juan, Newfoundland, Quebec – and her heart would race a little at the possibility, but they would just keep on walking.

Finally, as they approached a gate, Silas whipped their passports and boarding passes from a pocket inside his jacket, handing them to a gate attendant in the middle of the crowd, and they were spirited onto the jetway. Things happened so quickly that Sara had to step back to look at the screen at the side of the door. It said KEF.

They were going to Iceland.

Chapter Thirty-Five

S ara stared out of the window of the plane. Boston faded behind wispy clouds, then thicker clouds, until all she saw was bright blinding sun atop an endless white, bumpy expanse. She stared until the glare became too much and she turned to Silas, casually reading the in-flight magazine in the seat beside her. April was seated in front of her, in the very first row of the plane, but Sara couldn't see her, which made her slightly uncomfortable.

"You holding up?" Silas said, cautiously placing a hand atop hers on the table between them.

"Honestly, I was feeling nervous because I can't see April Veronica."

"I can see her leg," Silas said. "We're all safe." He gave her hand a squeeze.

"So, Iceland, huh?"

He nodded happily. "Say goodbye to sunblock."

"Fucking hell," she said, her voice slightly loud. "If you'd told me that six months ago, we could have cut out a whole lot of bullshit."

"Hindsight is twenty twenty," he said, flipping her hand over and running a finger on her palm. "So, we're as safe as we are ever going to be. Our getaway has been a success."

"What will we do when we land?"

"You don't have to do anything. I have built up the center of my operations there. It's a very smart location for people like us."

"It's been considered off and on for centuries, for a Lock, I mean, but the Icelandic people are closed and proud and suspicious of outsiders. It always seemed like it was too small, too personable for what we need."

"That's only true for the traditional Lock structure. Setting down roots as a fake catholic order of silence in a country that values technology and progressive thinking is not a good idea. However, setting up vast data mining farms atop geothermal energy and employing a lot of sharp local teenagers and paying them super well is a great idea. Additionally, it's a great smokescreen for a small society of us."

"Wait. There are more sisters there?" Sara was shook. Deeply.

"You never considered it?"

"Silas, you position yourself as a lone wolf entirely."

"And I am. And I have been, but you're not the only person who tired of Lock life. Don't worry, we won't be having a party to welcome you. Most of us are scattered around a small area."

"How many?"

"We were six. Now, we are eight."

"Do they know I'm coming?"

He nodded. "I was able to alert them from Boston. We mostly avoid communicating via any tech," he said. "None is safe. We learn so much from the hacker kids that we hire. Maybe one day we will have a reliable encryption and we will be able to talk, but for now, that's the one tradition that has survived. We write nothing. We're a small in-person gang."

"Silas..." Sara didn't know here to begin. "Are there other men?"

"Not yet," he answered casually, and her stomach twisted. "It's still too much of a gamble, but it's not expressly forbidden. I expect that at some point, it will be considered, and I'm hoping to have a new viewpoint, from April Veronica. The old ways aren't working any more."

"Is it wrong that I'd love a drink?" Sara said, not wanting any more information for a short while.

Silas smiled, pressing the flight attendant button. The woman arrived within seconds, and he ordered them Icelandic gin tonics, which arrived in delightful little bottles.

"Watch this," he said, twisting the cap off one and pouring it over the ice in Sara's glass. The liquid turned purple as it hit the ice, then melted to blue when he added the tonic. He filled his glass, and cheersed her.

"Cheers, and let me ask you one thing,"

He groaned. "Go ahead."

"Did you sleep with Liz? Are we eskimo cousins.?"

Silas downed his drink. "Nope. I told her I was gay. It's the best way to get a woman to tell you everything."

"Manipulative," she said.

"Sara, I've stayed alive for so long, it's a basic survival skill."

"I'm sorry, you're right, it's just hard for me to let this shit slide. Liz literally thought a vampire hunter had discovered the Lock. It was crazy. We all nearly voted for immediate surrender. You kept us all on our toes for many years."

"I know, and I'm sorry. Liz wasn't militant. She was so approachable. She spoke about her life vaguely, how hard it was, how she was tired of the rules she had to live by. As the months went on, she became more and more comfortable with me, I don't know why. And eventually, I had to play my cards. I wanted to see if she would take the bait, leave and come with me, but of course, as soon as she sensed that I knew more than I was saying, she ghosted. She played that part well, she pretended she needed to pee and never came back. And the next day, the huge building on the mountain was entirely empty. I hung around for several weeks until a For Sale sign appeared on the front wall of the compound."

"You should have heard her, when she got to New York, how a vampire hunter tricked her, that someone was onto all of us, it was almost impossible to integrate her into the Lock. She was on the verge of hysteria for years. You cost us very dearly, in terms of upgrading our security."

"You could afford it. In hindsight, I'm so glad Liz didn't take my bait," Silas said, signaling the attendant for more cocktails. "She was probably a bad pick in the first place, and looking back, I think I only went as far as I did with her because my loneliness clouded my judgement."

"So you returned to Iceland empty-handed?"

"No, I went back to New York, upstate. I stayed by the lake. I came into the city occasionally, annually, and I'd make sure you were as okay as you could be. And then I'd take off again. In twenty or thirty years, if you like, we can go back to America. I have good setups in some nice places. Detroit, New Orleans—"

"Cliché!" Sara laughed, taking her drink from the attendant. "Could you be any more predictable?"

"Kansas City, Dayton..."

"Ohio?"

He nodded. "America is beautiful. Cursed, but beautiful. Anyway—"

The gin was working in her system and lifting her mood. She reached over and placed a finger on his lips.

"I've heard enough for now," she said, downing her second drink in a single gulp. "Can we just hold hands?"

"We should try to sleep," he said. "It's a short flight and we get there early in the morning."

Sara glanced in the direction of the airplane bathrooms and nudged Silas in the ribs.

"You're impossible," he said. "No. Not this time."

She leaned across the little table and kissed him on the lips.

"Thank you," she said, breaking the kiss. "I don't know where I'm going, but I think I'm okay with it. I'm glad you took the chance. I'm feeling pretty excited, and that's weird enough to be good enough for me."

Silas reached across Sara and pulled the shades down on the two windows by her seat, then loosened his seatbelt and turned to face her.

"Get some sleep. I'll watch over you," he said, and with that, she fell asleep.

After clearing customs at Keflavik airport, they stepped outside into the pre-dawn gray, an icy wind whipping through their coats.

"The air smells different," April Veronica said.

"She's still getting used to the improvements," Sara explained.

"Our car is waiting just over there," Silas said, pushing the luggage cart in the direction of a chunky SUV with blinking hazard lights. As they neared it, the driver's side door opened, and a very tall woman stepped out. When she finally raised her smooth, elfin face, a grin spread from ear to ear.

"Silas, darling, it's so good to have you home," she said, her voice soft and deep like velvet, her accent thickly Icelandic. Without a word, Silas threw his arms around her. Confused, Sara hung back, April Veronica at her side. This new woman dwarfed Silas. Her eyes were closed and visible above the top of his head.

Breaking the hug, Silas stepped back and waved Sara and April forward.

"Sara, April Veronica, please meet Embla, Embla, this is—"

The woman cut him off, striding up to Sara and engulfing her in a hug.

"Sara, the pleasure is all mine. Welcome to Iceland, my home and also, the best place on the planet. You will be safe here."

Sara froze. This woman was using her real name. In public. Stepping back, she glanced at Silas, who just smiled as he opened the trunk of the car and began loading their suitcases inside as a bitterly cold wind blew snow flurries around their feet.

Sara moved aside and Embla leaned down to hug April Veronica.

"I'm so glad you joined them," Embla whispered. "I'm not the baby any longer."

Sara's eyes widened in shock before she could catch herself. Embla noticed, smiling warmly at her.

"Get in the car, I see you have questions."

With a wink, the tall woman returned to the driver's seat. Silas held the front passenger seat open for April Veronica, motioning Sara into the back seat, where he joined her, immediately clasping her hand.

"So, how was the flight?" Embla asked as she pulled out onto the flat, nearly empty road.

"Tight," April Veronica answered. "I watched some movies, slept a ton. I don't *think* the lovebirds joined the mile high club, but I could be mistaken."

Embla laughed, waiting for a response from the back seat. When none came, she continued speaking.

"We've been monitoring the situation in New York. It seems that Heather has successfully faked your death, Sara. Desdemona is there now."

Sara gasped.

"If anything, it's a blessing," Embla said, her voice calm. "With her and Teddie fighting over leadership, it took the spotlight off Heather. And right now," she paused, patting April Veronica on the leg. "Their focus is entirely on finding you. It was genius to send your backpack off. As we speak, Liz is traveling to one of the Carolinas, I forget which, in hot pursuit."

Sara heart leaped at the news of Teddie squaring off with Desdemona. Silas squeezed Sara's hand as April Veronica shrugged off the news that she was being hunted.

"She deserves North Carolina," Sara said. "So, wait. Embla, you're a new... what's the word? Recruit? Convert?"

"Compared to you, yes. It has been now nineteen years since I became... like you."

Sara's mind raced, wondering if Silas had made her, another violation. As if he sensed her tension, Silas squeezed her hand.

"I didn't make Embla," he said quietly.

"I bet he wishes he did," Embla crowed. "It's better to rip off the band-aid, so I will tell you that I'm not a cis-woman."

April Veronica inhaled sharply and clapped her hands together. "Amazing," she said.

Sara was more surprised at her own lack of reaction than she was at the news. Out of the corner of her eye she saw Silas staring at her, gauging her reaction.

"So..." she began quietly, "the old rules, they don't apply here?"

"Only the good ones," Embla said enthusiastically. "We're all about science and equality and you know, fun stuff."

"How do you feed?" The question fell out of Sara's mouth without warning, its tone harsh.

"Heems, synthetics," Embla answered, unrattled. "Blood liquor for birthdays and equinoxes. But I'm vegan, so I abstain."

"I'm sorry, I sounded like a bitch," Sara said, making the other occupants of the car laugh.

"Are you the only... the first... I dunno," April Veronica faltered. "I don't want to offend you."

"You'd have to try a lot harder, newbie," Embla pulled out onto a larger highway, and they picked up speed. "As far as I know, I'm the world's first trans vampire millennial vegan."

"This excites me so much," April Veronica said, her hands now clasped at her chest.

"Me too," said Sara sincerely. "Silas, what the hell kind of utopia do you have here?"

"You'll see soon enough," he said. "I'm fairly certain nobody has followed us, but it will be safer to show you the set-up once we get there. It's about an hour drive. Sleep if you can, it's going to be a good day."

And they drove, Embla and April Veronica chattering in the front seat, Sara quietly attempting to focus in the rear. Occasionally, Silas leaned over and ran a finger along her cheek. Sara was grateful that he didn't push her to talk. Her mind was racing and she had to remind herself over and over that she trusted him, that this would be all right.

Focusing out her window, Sara's attention darted from familiar things, like gas stations, to the strange language on signs outside restaurants and small patches of shops. She was tired. It felt like they had been running for weeks, but it had only been days. For some reason she had expected Iceland to be unfamiliar, alien, but the wide open, rugged landscape felt at once welcoming and familiar.

Eventually the road widened and there were more houses and schools and familiar things. It looked western, reminding her of her last trip to Scotland some fifty years earlier. Silas remained fairly silent, only speaking when one of them asked him something. April had also gone silent, gazing out her own window. Embla turned the car stereo on and Sara recognized the music immediately. Bill Evans at the Village Vanguard. She glanced at Silas, who nodded and smiled.

"I may have curated the playlist."

Sara felt a strange pressure, but she couldn't place it. She figured it was just the fear of the unknown. Two days ago, she'd been ready to die, so whatever happened next, this undisclosed adventure was just gravy, gift with purchase. It didn't matter if she lived another five hundred years or just five hundred days. This was either a coda or a new beginning, thrilling either way.

The humming of the car lulled her into sleep again, and she started when Silas's arm touched her shoulder.

"Sorry, Sara, I didn't mean to scare you. I just wanted you to see our home, and how hidden we are."

"Yes," she said groggily. "Show me."

It was daylight, the sky was the richest blue, but the sun's light was different, golden. The road they were on was surrounded by so much open space that it looked like it had been photoshopped. There were no other cars in either direction, and in the distance, a stream sparkled as it flowed between emerald meadows. Her eyes landed on endless fields of yellow and green, with small patches of ice or snow hanging on in shadowy depressions. Far ahead, she could see a long, low building, modern yet boxy, the golden sunlight reflecting off a wall of windows.

"Is that our house?"

"No, that's our smokescreen," Embla said.

They drove for several minutes until Embla turned right onto the road that led to the building, driving into the parking lot, then around and behind the structure where the ground rose up into a hill that seemed to go forever, gently sloping upward.

Guiding the car to a basic cinderblock building with symbols for danger and heat and electricity on it, Embla clicked a remote and a garage door at the end of the building rolled upward silently. She drove the car inside, parking it alongside two other, much larger cars already parked there.

The roller door came down behind them, and bright blue-white LED lighting illuminated overhead.

"Here we are," Silas said, and Sara noticed that his voice was strained. Was he nervous?

April Veronica unlatched her door and jumped out of the car, and Sara followed suit, confused. They lived in a bunker?

"I'll come back for the bags," Embla said, exiting on her side.

"Come with me," Silas said, walking to the rear of the garage. He entered a lengthy code into a panel on the wall. Sara heard heavy machinery moving inside the cinderblock wall, and Silas pushed on the simple gray door ahead of him. It opened. He stood aside and ushered them into a long, brightly lit hallway that echoed with the sound of running water, though Sara couldn't tell where it came from.

"Come on!" he said lightly.

The three women stepped past him, Sara in the lead.

"Let's go right to the end," he said. "There's a side entrance but I want you to see your new digs from her good side, first impressions and all that."

They walked, passing a door that had a similar keypad to the one in the garage. "That leads to the mud room and the rear of the house," he said.

"Actually, I need to pee," Embla said with a laugh as she began to punch in the key code. The rest of them kept walking. Silas hung back slightly.

"When you get to the end, just let yourself out, it's not locked."

Sara glanced back, shooting Silas a confused glance. He was behaving like they were arriving at some weird Airbnb, not her home for the foreseeable future. When she reached the door, she pressed down on the heavy metal handle, surprised at how easily and quietly it clicked open. The door opened out onto a vast outdoor space, a flat expanse of land at the foot of a mountain—green fields dotted with small flowers. She had to shield her eyes from the morning sun to look up in order to find the place where the mountain ended. The sides of the mountain came down like arms, enveloping the land behind the tunnel in a small valley.

"Sara, look," A cry from April made her turn away from the mountain, to her left, where, built into the side of the hill, a curved wall of gold-tinted windows hinted at a house beneath the mountain, built directly into it, completely hidden from view of anyone except people atop the mountains behind it. It was a massive version of the hill house at Silas's lake property.

"This is your place?" was all she could say. Silas pulled the door closed behind him and walked over to her, wrapping his arms around her.

"This is *our* place, for now," he said. "Shall we go inside?

A third of the way along the long wall of windows was a door, ten feet high and six feet across. Silas nodded at it, then gave Sara a gentle shove. "Go open it, it's unlocked."

"I'm so not ready for the unlocked door life," Sara managed to joke.

"I opened it via remote, silly."

Slowly Sara walked to the door, trying not to pay attention to her reflection in the golden windows as she approached. Again, the door looked so heavy, yet it glided open at the faintest touch, revealing an open living space, with deep brown leather couches facing the windows. In the rear, behind an island with stools, a woman was in the kitchen. As Sara stepped into the room, the woman turned to face her, a smile wide on her face.

It was Crina.

Sara's heart melted at the sight of her maker.

"Sara, my child." Crina stepped around the kitchen island and walked faster and faster toward her. Sara, tears springing into her eyes, could not move. She stood frozen as Crina reached her, wrapping her arms around her and pulling her in tight. Huge sobs burst from Sara's chest, and suddenly she felt safe, safer than she could remember feeling. She couldn't decide what to do; she wanted to hug Crina, she wanted to slap Silas for not telling her, and also, she suddenly understood so many things. How long had this been planned? Why couldn't Crina have told her?

"April Veronica, I'm so happy to welcome you to Iceland!" Crina said into Sara's hair.

"Don't worry about me," April Veronica said with a grin. "Crina, it's really great to see you again." And with that, she flopped onto one of the couches. Embla appeared from a darkened hallway, taking a seat beside April Veronica.

"I'm so happy to have you all together," Crina said. "I am glad you finally met Embla, Sara. I see the same potential in her that I saw in you."

Sara glanced at Embla, smiling widely on the couch beside April Veronica, and a new flood of tears began. She hugged Crina close to her.

"Don't cry, child, this is where you were always meant to be," Crina said. "I'm only sorry it got as bad as it did, at the end. But you don't have to worry about them anymore. You can thank your dear friend Heather for it."

"Heather knows about this?"

"Heather knows about everything," Crina said. "And Heather will join us, in time."

Sara squeezed Crina so hard that Crina had to flex her arms apart to be able to breathe.

"My darling, I've made us coffee and there's some bread that's due out of the oven any minute now. Just wait 'til you try Icelandic sheep cheese, it's going to remind you of how we ate when we first met, so long ago."

"I think my head is going to explode," Sara said as she finally released the other woman.

Crina walked to the kitchen island and tapped on one of the stools. "Best you come sit down then."

Sara did what she was told, inhaling the aromas of coffee and baking bread and something else, a cleanliness to the air that she never smelled in New York. A noise behind her startled her and she turned, but it was just Silas with their suitcases.

"You did it, Silas," Crina said, turning back form the coffee maker to look at him. "You made my dreams come true; you brought my Sara to live with us."

"I told you we'd do it," he said, walking toward them both, a strange, almost apprehensive expression on his face.

"What?" Sara said, alarm in her voice. "What now?"

"You didn't tell her yet?" Crina's voice was playful.

Silas shook his head. "No, Mom. I figured I'd leave that up to you."

Sara's eyes widened and her jaw dropped.

"Aw shit," came April Veronica's voice from the couch. "Aw hell nah. You guys, even I didn't see that one coming."

To be continued...

Acknowledgements

With gratitude...

Firstly, I'd like to thank you for reading this book. I hope it entertained you. It really became clear to me while I was writing this book that the time of reading, or even having time to read, is perilously endangered. Every day is a battle between a million distractions, and it's really hard to prioritize setting aside time to lose yourself in a book. The fact that you did this really increases my gratitude a million-fold. Thank you, truly.

I first had the ideas for this book a decade ago, but circumstances dictated that I write a few other books first. On the day my second novel was published, my mother was admitted to hospital. She died three weeks later, and I was not able to write for a time thereafter. Gradually, I lost myself in thoughts of Sara, a five-hundred-year-old vampire, and the challenges she faced, both practical and philosophical.

The first person I shared Sara's story with was my husband, George Castro, and it was really his enthusiastic reaction that finally compelled me to get back to writing. His patience and generosity of spirit as he listened to this story unfold really showed me I was on the right path. He was my first editor and consistent cheerleader throughout the writing of this book, and I'm forever grateful for literally everything he has brought into my life. Here, specifically, I want to thank him for standing at my side as I brought this book into existence. Also, he deserves props for recognizing the vacant-eyed writer's-block burnout look on my face, and knowing to immediately drive me to Los Angeles Zoo, where I can sit for an hour, watching the Amazonian otters swim around and let my brain sort out what needs to happen next.

The second person who shaped Sara's story was my wonderful editor, Laura Arnold Bernier, whose incredibly astute and sharp eye whipped this book into shape and then some. I would never have seen the issues that she uncovered, and this book is much better for her input. A world of thank yous to her.

Also by my side during the entire process of this book was my sister-cousin Skye Pyman, a lifelong best-friend, phenomenal sounding board and a very effective cheerleader on days when that's exactly what you need, even though you don't know it. Skye, I love you more.

This book was written entirely during the process of grieving my mother, Veronica Grace Dickson. This is my first novel that was not worked on at her kitchen table in North Avoca, a few hours north of Sydney, Australia. Her absence in my life was something I could never imagine, and the reality of it was worse than I could have anticipated. I was incredibly lucky to have friends who took care of me when I needed it most – Heather Taylor, Christine Linardon and Christine Beidel. I would never have survived 2018 without them, and their love and support permeates this book.

I'm also super blessed to count author Lindsey Kelk as one of my best friends. Whether it's drunken Vegas getaways or writer's block commiserations, or a million other things, I'm a lucky guy to have her a few miles away. Lindsey, I'm just sorry they knocked down our sushi restaurant. We will find another. Thank you for always helping me with the burden of writing, and, you know, other stuff.

I drew a lot of inspiration for the women in this book from the astonishing group of powerful women that surround me in my day to day life. In no particular order, I deeply love and am wildly indebted to Heather Long, Emily Thompson, Amanda Bigford, Toni Smith, Sara T. Russell, Courtney Kerzner, Patricia Stone, Rosa Castro, Priscilla Wardlow, Liz Tooley, Lynne Watkins, Joan Oexmann, Kim Kahl, Yukari Fujimoto, Denée Segall, Adriane Boat, Tammy Germani, Nichole Fifield, Barbara Binstein, Robyn Hardy and last but never least, Giselle Knight.

Believe it or not, a few men helped me too. Thank you, Paul Amirault, for your astute advice and friendship (and ghostbusting). Danke schön, Felix Schliebitz, for your enthusiasm when I acted out this story during the pandemic and plying me with liquor during writing blocks. To my dear friend Nicholas Harding, who always knew when I needed inspiration and sent it along under the guise of friendship. Larry Hardy, an endless font of music, horror movies, dogs and friendship, gave me encouragement on this book when global events made it very difficult to go on. And lastly, my friend and right hand for too long to mention, Steve Gidlow, thanks, and then more thanks.

The artwork for the cover of this book was created by André Trindade, and I'm grateful for both his talent and his patience. Find him online @cvspe

I listened to music while every word of this book was written, and often times I found it reflected in the moods on the pages. To that end, I must thank these women, many of whom remain vastly underappreciated: Siouxsie Sioux, Kim & Kelley Deal, Hope Sandoval, Su Tissue, Florence Shaw, Alice Coltrane, Meg White, Muriel Grossmann, Patti Smith, Lorena Quintanilla, Björk Gudmundsdottir and Neneh Cherry. I listened to all of you daily as I wrote this novel.
-KJD

About the author

Kevin Dickson is an Australian-American author who lives in Los Angeles with his husband George, three spectacular dogs, Miss Tuna, Graciela and Olivia, and an irascible parrot named Chapulin. After working as an entertainment journalist in Australia, Dickson relocated to Los Angeles in the late 90s, and found himself in the epicenter of the reality TV explosion. Bouncing between LA and New York for the next twenty years, he had a ringside seat for some of the most scandalous media events in recent history. Dickson exorcised his demons from that time in the thinly veiled tell-all bestseller Blind Item and its sequel, Guilty Pleasure before quitting the business forever. After a brief stint in a punk rock band that toured and recorded a well-received album, Dickson once again turned his attention to the written word, and the Vampire State series was born. These days, Dickson divides his time between writing, hiking, traveling and devouring films, books and music, and running a screen printing business with his husband.

The author does not endorse or enjoy social media.
Any official accounts will be poorly and sporadically managed at best.
To contact the author please email vampirestatebooks@gmail.com

Also by Kevin Dickson

From Him To Eternity: Vampire State Book One

Seasons Of Blood: Vampire State Book Two

...

Blind Item

Guilty Pleasure

(co-author)